PRAISE FOR HEATHER BURCH

"Heather Burch has proven herself to have such an exceptional storytelling range that one might be tempted to call her 'the Mariah Carey of romance fiction.' *One Lavender Ribbon* blew my expectations out of the water and then swept me away on a wave of sweet romance. Don't miss this one."

—Serena Chase, contributor to *USA Today's Happy Ever After* blog and author of *The Seahorse Legacy*

"Burch's latest combines a sweet, nostalgic, poignant tale of a true love of the past with the discovery of true love in the present . . . Burch's lyrical, contemporary storytelling, down-to-earth characters, and intricate plot make this one story that will delight the heart."

—*RT Book Reviews* on *One Lavender Ribbon*, 4.5 Stars

"Heather Burch draws you into the story from page one and captures your attention, your emotions, and your heartstrings until the very end. She reaches into your very soul with a story that is so real that it stays with you for weeks after the last page is turned, the last sigh has floated away, the last giggle has played out, and the last tear is shed."

—Carolyn Brown, *New York Times* and *USA Today* bestselling author on *Along the Broken Road*

in the light of the garden

ALSO BY HEATHER BURCH

Adult Fiction
One Lavender Ribbon

The Roads to River Rock
Along the Broken Road
Down the Hidden Path

Young Adult Fiction
Summer by Summer

Halflings
Halflings
Guardian
Avenger

in the light of the garden

A Novel

Heather Burch

LAKE UNION
PUBLISHING

Text copyright © 2017 by Heather Burch
All rights reserved.

Published by Lake Union Publishing, Seattle

www.apub.com

Amazon, the Amazon logo, and Lake Union Publishing are trademarks of Amazon.com, Inc., or its affiliates.

ISBN-13: 9781503941144
ISBN-10: 1503941140

Cover design by Laura Klynstra

Printed in the United States of America

For Isaac, my favorite artist, my parkour hero, and my son. All your talents amaze me. I'm honored to be your mom.

CHAPTER 1

Baxter House

When Charity Baxter was little, she believed in fairies and pixies and the kind of magic that made unicorns and cotton candy. To her, Gaslamp Island itself was as magical a place as any in this world, except maybe for the one Alice found while chasing a white rabbit. Charity's island was perfect, mainly because of Grandpa George and Grandma Marilyn and the big mansion of a house they lived in. It had towering arches and comfy rooms, cozy beds and warm tomato soup, and, best of all, Gramps's potter's wheel.

Charity witnessed the magic each year while traveling to Gaslamp Island on Florida's Gulf coast. Every summer she and her mother would board a water taxi. Fluttery excitement would fill her belly, and she would stand at the front of the long, flat boat—a marvel in itself, really, hauling people and cargo and even a few cars. She always counted down the days to the end of school, packing and repacking her suitcase. Marking each sunset on a secret calendar she hid beneath her bed.

This year was no different. Except, of course, now she was eleven and that was practically grown up. She'd matured over the long months since seeing her grandma and gramps. They'd be amazed at how grown-up she'd become.

"Charity Monroe Baxter!" Her mother's sharp voice shot through Charity's heart. It always did. And she hated that. One day she'd grow up enough that the shrill sound wouldn't cause her hands to shake and her teeth to clamp. "Step back from the railing, young lady. You're scuffing up the new shoes I bought you."

They're not new, Charity wanted to say. *And you didn't buy them. Your boyfriend, Kendrick, found them,* or at least that was the story Charity and her mother had gotten. It was after her mom had complained about having to make that *awful* trip to that *horrible* little island. Momma never stayed with Gram and Gramps. Sometimes she'd stay for dinner, but that was all, checking and rechecking her wristwatch so as not to miss the last ferry. Never overnight. And never seeing the miracle that was the island. Some people couldn't see magic, Charity supposed, but she saw it everywhere.

Not wanting to disappoint her momma, Charity slid her feet a few inches from the railing and glanced up for her approval. She received the quick flash of a half smile, and her momma turned on her heel, mumbling about the ghastly wind and her hairdo.

Charity chewed her lip. She supposed she was a disappointment to her mother, and now that she was practically grown up, she was beginning to understand such things. Momma was what Gramps liked to call a free spirit. Gram said her daughter needed to grow up, stop acting like a teenager and act like a woman. A mother. That's why Momma never spent the night on the island with Charity. It always ended in an argument with Charity's heart at the center.

Sometimes at home she'd hear her momma and Kendrick talking, and Momma would say the island was too small for her. She had big dreams, and an insignificant place like Gaslamp couldn't contain them, and maybe they'd float right off her and disappear in the waves or be carried off by the coastal breeze.

Charity tightened her fingers on the railing. What did the waves and the breeze want with her momma's dreams and plans? Nothing. That's what she'd decided a while back while watching soap operas and eating Pop-Tarts. Sometimes she wondered whether her momma thought she was *living* a soap opera. Gram said Momma's flair for the dramatic had always gotten her into trouble. Charity didn't know. And she didn't mind helping her momma with things like dinner and housework because it all seemed to stress her out so much. Housework was something Charity was good at. There weren't many other things. She was an OK student. She wasn't pretty or popular. Or a sports girl. She liked to read but often got lost after the first few chapters of a book and sometimes never picked it back up again.

But she could cook spaghetti and hamburgers, pancakes and dip eggs, where the yolk was runny but the white part cooked. She liked to use Windex and wipe down the windows until a rainbow of colors appeared and disappeared in the sun's rays. She always did the windows when it was sunny, and, sometimes, she'd curl up like a cat in the warm pool of light on the carpeted floor. There were strange shapes from the windowpanes, and she'd drag her knees to her chest and pretend it was a box of sunlight. A safe, perfect box where no one and nothing could hurt her.

The first time Momma saw her curled up like that, she'd made fun of her. But that was OK. She wouldn't expect her to understand. After all, what did her momma have to hide from? She was beautiful and popular with all the gentlemen who lived in their apartment complex. Kendrick, the upstairs neighbor, had practically moved in. Charity didn't like him much because he laughed when her momma made fun of her. And he always left a mess for Charity to clean up. She liked Rover Gentree. He lived across the hall and taught at the college nearby. With his wool coats, round glasses, and kind green eyes, Charity thought he was almost perfect. Then, one day, he'd seen her getting frustrated while reading a book, and he'd stopped to help her. But Charity's momma never even gave him a glance, even though he looked at her with moonbeam eyes—just like the men on the soap operas. Rover steered clear after Kendrick moved in.

Charity sighed and shook off the soap opera drama of her momma's life. Besides, she'd be gone for the whole summer. No Kendrick. No cleaning, except her room and making her own bed. No Momma. It made her sad that she didn't miss Momma more when she was away. She closed off the thought and concentrated on the sea spray peppering her cheeks. It was full of salt, and by tonight, her legs and arms would taste salty from splashing in the spray. She'd fall asleep touching the tip of her tongue to her arm . . . just to make certain she was really at the island.

Her heart quickened as the island came into view. Charity's head jutted forward, her hair flying behind her. Sun rays of pure silver danced on the water, so bright she had to squint to look at the rolling sea. Suddenly, something rose from the water, some tiny flicker, and when her gaze traveled to the spot, it was already gone. A pixie, no doubt. Rising from the water and teasing her with its shimmery wings. Off to the right, another one appeared and disappeared, and Charity's heart beat faster. Her smile grew. Her knees weakened with excitement. On this went until they neared the sandy beach and the long pier that poked out into the water. Waves rose and fell, sneaking onto the beach, then retreating and dragging shells and seaweed along. The motion made the island appear as if it were breathing, deep intakes of air as the sandy shoreline expanded, slow exhales as the water rose and engulfed the long, narrow beach. To Charity, the island was alive.

By the time the boat landed, Charity had wiggled from her new used sandals. Her feet hit the wooden deck, and even though her momma was yelling her name, she ran toward the end of the pier. Charity was never disobedient. Except on the island. She ignored her mother's pleas that had grown tighter with frustration. "Charity Monroe Baxter!"

But Charity let the wind and waves and even the smell of boat fuel carry her mother's orders away. She ached to feel the water, the sand against her feet, the pulse of the ocean. When she reached the part of the beach where the water would hit her knees, she leaped off the pier and into the warm, moving liquid. Instantly her feet sank deeper, and she knew there'd be a slurping sensation when she went to take a step. She opened her eyes and saw her mom, so she turned and faced the island. Overhead, palm trees swayed, their giant leaves like curved ceiling fan blades. She spotted a cluster of green coconuts near the top of one and wondered if she'd ever learn the trick to climbing the slick trunks of palm trees. Every year, she tried . . . to her gramps's delight. He'd laugh, head tossed back, fists on his hips. Sometimes he'd give her a boost, but she never made it more than a few feet before tiring out.

Charity breathed in the scent of sea air and fish. The tide was out, so the smell was stronger. Smelly or not, this was always one of her favorite moments . . . when she was finally here. As if she'd been on fire and burning for the last several months, and now her charred skin was getting the chance to heal.

She spotted her gramps at the edge of the beach. Her eyes darted, looking for her grandma, but she didn't see her anywhere. Gramps waved, his Florida-tanned hand high over his head. She ran toward him, splashing enough water to draw sharks. By the time she got to the shore, her shorts were soaked, and her shirttail sported sand confetti where her feet had kicked up a mess.

Her momma gave her a disapproving look, so she ran full speed toward Gramps for support. He grabbed her up, catching her with one strong arm and tossing her headfirst over his shoulder, saying, "Come here, you sack of potatoes. I'll take you home to Gram, and we'll drop you—peeling and all—into the hot iron skillet."

Her stomach rolled with delight, and a laugh escaped her mouth. She was too old for this kind of silliness, but she loved her gramps, so she'd play along. Small fists pounded his lower back. "I'm not a sack of potatoes."

"What?" He tossed her forward, examined her from head to torso. "Well, of course, you're not. Let me get a better grip on you, you sack of onions."

"Gramps!" She giggled and squeezed her eyes shut tight as she hugged him hard. He smelled like the coal oil he used to keep lamps burning in the pottery studio. There was a hint of cinnamon around his mouth and the very faint smell of tobacco. He'd been trying to quit for years.

Charity felt her gramps's muscles stiffen as her mother neared.

"Dad," Momma said, and Charity already knew she was planning to take the water taxi back to the mainland.

"Ellen." Gramps's tone was short. "Doing OK?"

Charity watched the thoughts flicker in her mother's eyes. "I suppose."

He chucked Charity in his arms. "She feels thin."

Momma's eyes turned to ice. "Good for her."

He looked at Charity. "You been eating? Plenty of food in the house?"

Before she could answer, her momma spoke up. "Rent went up. It's tough, you know. Making ends meet."

"Won't give you money, Ellen Marie. I'd be happy to send boxes of food for Lil' Bit."

Momma's gaze went from cold to fiery hot. "We don't need your charity. We're fine. She eats plenty. She grew taller is all."

Charity hugged his neck. "I eat whenever I want to, Gramps. Really, I do."

Momma looked past him. "Where's Mom? Didn't even care to come see me?"

"She's down with a flu bug. Maybe you'd like to come back to the house for the night. It'd do her good to lay eyes on you."

Momma scoffed. "And risk taking the flu home with me? Really, Dad. I have a *job*. I can't just take off whenever I get sick. I'm not retired. Or rich." There was such a bite to her momma's tone.

"Well, guess this'll be good-bye, then."

Charity hated the crackly tension in the air between her momma and Gramps. It was even worse with Gram. Maybe she hated it because it was her fault. She was the topic of all the heated discussions. She'd ruined her mom's life by being born when Momma had big plans to be her generation's Marilyn Monroe. No woman had captivated like Marilyn for fifty years, and Momma was ripe for the task. So she said. Gram and Gramps called her a fool and told her that Charity was the one thing that mattered, and she was ruining that too . . . just like she'd ruined so many things.

Gramps took the suitcase and kept Charity tight in his arms, as if Momma might change her mind and force Charity to return home with her. The thought shot like fire into Charity's stomach, and she tightened her own grip around her gramps's neck.

"I'll be back at the end of August to pick her up." Momma adjusted the new handbag on her arm. Charity didn't know where it had come from, but Momma was proud of it.

"I love you, Momma."

She flashed a smile, patted Charity's cheek. "Be a good girl."

"I will."

Gramps huffed. He didn't like it that Momma didn't tell Charity she loved her. Charity didn't mind. It hurt on the inside, but Momma had once explained that it was a difficult thing to say, and even though she felt it, she had a hard time saying it. She constantly told Kendrick she loved him, but Charity supposed that was different. It certainly *sounded* different on the other side of the thin wall that separated Charity's bedroom from her momma's.

Gramps walked the length of the sand-and-shell parking lot to his pickup truck. Most of the folks on the island had cars, *sedans*, Gramps called them. He waved to a fisherman and put the suitcase in the back of the truck as Charity's momma disappeared on the retreating water taxi.

"Hey, George!" The man held up a stringer. "Got dinner?"

"You get into a school of amberjack?" Gramps closed the truck door and Charity propped her arms on the frame and watched her gramps and the man meet in the middle of the parking lot. They were discussing "fisherly" things. By the time they were done, the man was dropping two large fish into Gramps's cooler beside Charity's suitcase.

"Much obliged. You sure I can't pay you?"

"Nah, let me borrow the pickup next week so I can haul those boat parts."

The men shook hands. "You know it's always there for you."

When Gramps first bought the big house on the beach, the neighbors didn't want his beat-up old pickup sitting in the driveway. There were rules, they claimed. But Gramps said that was silly because there were lots of work trucks, and they were frequently in driveways. In the end, Gramps won over the people on the island, and now every neighbor around borrowed the truck on occasion. Gramps didn't hold anything against them. He called them "old money."

"We're new money," he'd say.

He'd been poor most of his life, but when his little hardware store grew and doubled and tripled in size and more stores came along, all of a sudden, he was a self-made wealthy man. When the doctors told him he had too much stress and not enough relaxation, he'd left the business in capable hands and discovered a love of pottery.

Gram and Gramps had left Atlanta and drove until they ran out of road. Then they boarded a boat and found the island. The only house for sale was a giant home built at the turn of the century by William Baxter, the famous circus man. And wasn't it a strange coincidence that his last name was the same? Gramps claimed the place, Baxter House, was too much money, too much house, and too perfect to pass up.

Serendipity, Gram called it. The fact that the house already had their name attached to it.

Charity's momma tried to get them to let her and Charity live in the Atlanta home, but in the first week, Momma had filled every room with traveling actors from the play she'd hoped to audition for. Gramps threw them all out, including Momma. He rented her and Charity a little apartment that didn't have room for visitors. It was nice, though. And Charity had her own space and a canopy bed and gossamer curtains on the window, a perfect place for pixies and fairies to pause and catch their breath after swirling across the night street below her room.

"Is Gram OK?"

"Fine, Lil' Bit. Just conserving her energy so we can walk the beach this evening." But the lines around his eyes seemed to deepen, and his fingers flexed and then tightened on the steering wheel. His nails were dirty, most likely from a morning at the potter's wheel. The moment of sadness—or concern, or whatever that was—passed, and Gramps was right back to his regular self, whistling as they drove with the windows down and the salty air flying into the truck. Stretches of beach with sand as white as powdered sugar rested on both sides of the long, narrow road. The sand danced across the path as if it were alive, drifting and flowing to a tune only it could hear. Seabirds appeared in the window, pacing the truck, and Gramps would point them out as if Charity had never seen one before.

Far off the beach, a sailboat kissed the horizon, and all of Charity's excitement lulled into a sort of satisfied restfulness. The island was the best place in the world, and Charity would love it forever. How could anyone come here and not believe in magic?

That was the year her grandmother died.

That was the year magic ended for Charity Monroe Baxter.

CHAPTER 2

Cobwebs

Present day

They'd had a hard time finding a good vein. George Baxter fingered the IV needle and the dark-purple skin around it. Nurses came and went, and in the last three days, he'd watched their demeanor change. A favorite patient, he'd been. Always quick with a joke, a smile, a kind word. He'd told them they could call him Gramps. Their faces lit up each time they entered his room where they'd hover over his hospital bed, fretting as if he was their own child taken sick, not an old man readying to leave this world. A few of them had bitten back their emotions—no one saying what he already knew. He'd asked pointed questions, and they'd fluff his pillow and consult charts without making eye contact, all the while telling him to not worry. All of them but one had done this. Sunshine was her name.

He'd been frank with her on a long night when his lungs had filled with more fluid than his body could remove. Sunshine had sat with him for hours in the Intensive Care Unit, which he now called home. He'd been frank by telling her that husband of hers wasn't going to change. George and Sunshine had an understanding about honesty, so when he asked, "How much time you reckon I've got?" she'd squeezed his hand and said, "None, George. Your time's run out." And then she'd cried silent tears that left her eyes and landed on the back of his aged hand. He'd wanted to comfort her. And thinking back on that moment less than an hour ago, he'd decided that hearing the truth about one's mortality and wishing you could comfort another soul was . . . well, it was OK with him. The mark of the kind of life he'd want to leave. The legacy he'd choose if all the things men held in regard were splayed before him.

Sunshine bent and kissed his cheek in the quiet, sterile room. "Would you let me call your daughter? Or your granddaughter?"

His eyes trailed to the window, where he searched for comfort from the Florida sun, but the building next door always blocked it. "Charity would want to be here." He shook his head, squeezed Sunshine's hand. "But no. Just—"

Sunshine tilted forward, ready to fulfill any request. "Yes, George?" She didn't try to hide the hope in her voice. She'd not been the first nurse to urge him to call family. But he didn't want Charity to see him like this. He wanted her last memories of him to be when he was healthy.

"I'd—" His craggy voice broke. He cleared a throat filled with gravel. "I'd rather not be alone when . . . when."

Her other hand reached out, squeezing his thin fingers harder than she should have, a feeble attempt to hang on to a finite soul in the infinite domain of creation. "You won't be." Her pink, painted lips pressed into a hard line. "I swear. My shift ended an hour ago. I'm staying right here."

George closed his eyes. Somehow, the sun slipped between the tall buildings and found its way into his room, searching out his face and warming the skin that had begun to feel cold from the inside out. In a far corner of his mind he heard a soft, rustling sound.

Will you come, sit with me

He knew if he opened his eyes it would disappear, so with eyes tightly shut, he searched the darkness around him for the source.

We'll tell our troubles 'neath the tree

The rustling intensified, and he recognized its soothing tone.

The tears we shed will surely be
Water for the weeping tree.

It was the weeping tree. There, at the edge of his consciousness, it stood, a brilliant light shining, illuminating each leaf as if a blade of sunshine had been stolen and tacked above the swaying branches.

And in its shade our woes will fall
Pain and suffering, sorrow and all
They'll fall like glistening diamond drops
You see, the tree, our pain, it stops.

The weeping tree called to him, beckoning him to come. Its melodic tune was as clear as the sound of his own laughter, as pure as water from the deepest well.

And at 11:09 a.m., George Baxter answered the call.

∽

One month later

Charity Baxter loved everything about Baxter House. The European design of the ten-bedroom mansion, the glassed-in sleeping porch, the library. She loved the tall, round posts that anchored the porch and the long strip of Gulf coast beyond the grounds perfectly framed by a lush garden.

She loved everything except the eyesore in the right corner of the backyard. Now thirty-one years old, she'd have thought that the eerie mystery surrounding the tree would no longer bother her. But just thinking about it sent a shiver down her spine. It didn't matter that she was a grown woman. There were things in the world that defied explanation. And sometimes a lack of knowledge was as debilitating as facts.

"Miss Baxter?"

Charity blinked, tried to find her focus. Emily Rudd, the executor of Gramps's estate stood at the foot of the steps leading to the large front door. Emily smiled and held her clipboard against her tailored suit jacket. She was shorter than Charity, with tall, spiky heels that seemed to make it difficult to stand without the faintest hint of a wobble with each step. Charity herself preferred flats or even tennis shoes. Sandals were good, strappy ones with—

Ugh, she was doing it again. Tuning out. Changing her focus to reflect anything and everything except the reason she was here. Because what she was here for was the one thing she'd never wanted to face.

Certainly not alone. Not without Gramps at her side.

Get a grip. You're a grown woman, not a child. She clamped a hand on the banister and gazed up up up at the towering house. Hers now. Hers alone. The air was tempered here at the foot of the wide stairs, where she stood in the shadow of the mansion. As a child, she'd sat on the porch swing with wind from the Gulf blowing right through the house as if the entire first floor was one giant wind tunnel. She'd swim in the Gulf, her feet sinking deep into the sandy, muddy ground, and then she'd lie on the porch swing and let that wind dry her skin and hair. Gramps would make sun tea, and he'd catch her tipping up the entire jug for a drink. He didn't mind, though. Gramps had easily forgiven all her transgressions. At least those he'd known about.

Emily Rudd stepped away from her and searched her handbag for the keys to the front door. She'd given Charity a few moments to ready for the task at hand after they'd both exited their cars.

Charity unintentionally compared herself to the spotless, tailored Rudd. The spikes of Emily's deep-red hair matched those of her red-soled shoes, letting everyone know she was both a dangerous package and one that could stab you in a courtroom and still look like a million bucks while doing it.

Charity's T-shirt had a stain along the belly, compliments of clay. Dark and dirty and a marking that decorated most all her day shirts. Her clothing was collateral damage of her profession.

"Ah, here they are." Emily rattled the keys, a wide smile on her perfectly lined lips as she approached Charity. She was nice. And Charity understood why her grandfather had chosen the spitfire attorney to be his executor. She wasn't pushy, didn't pry . . . at least not yet. But they'd only just arrived. There was plenty of time for a third degree.

Emily remained beside her, and Charity was thankful that she wasn't taking this first trek back into the house alone. The comfort of another human alongside her made her both appreciative and achy. Achy because she spent too much time alone, if the way she was sucking up the human contact was any indication.

"We can take as long as you need." Emily adjusted her bag on her shoulder and dropped the key into Charity's hand.

Charity drew a breath and with it, the strength to unlatch the front door. The key, now warming between her fingers, was the old-fashioned kind with a round loop at one end and what looked like a tiny flag on a flagpole on the other. She lifted it slowly to her nose and closed her eyes while she inhaled the scent of the key. Iron, rust, oiled perfume from human hands—Emily's lotion or maybe even an expensive, scented hand sanitizer. As Charity breathed in the aromas, others entered her nose. Coal oil. Cinnamon. Tobacco. Her eyes flew open, and her breath caught. Those smells were as common to her nose as was the scent of her own shampoo, the toothpaste she used every morning, the expensive bags of Ethiopian coffee she purchased. Though older, the coal oil and tobacco were just as familiar; they were aromas from her childhood. And that could only mean one thing. Gramps was here. Right here with her. She wasn't doing this alone, after all.

"Are you all right, Miss Baxter?" Emily's words were so soft, they barely made it to her.

"I'm fine." She tried a smile, but Emily was blurry in Charity's vision until a single tear abandoned its post in her left eye. One in her right eye followed. With the hand that held the key, she swiped both cheeks, trying to remember when she'd last shed a tear.

When she'd gotten word of her grandfather's death, she hadn't cried. She'd stood up from the wheel, where she'd been working on a vase, and went to her apartment window, where the lights of New York City ever flashed beneath her. There she'd stood from dusk until the sun poked her in the eyes as it bounced off the fifty-seven-story building next to her.

Emily shifted beside her. "I've cleared my entire afternoon. As I said, we can take all the time you need."

Quite suddenly, it was important to Charity to know what Emily knew of her relationship with her gramps. "Did my grandfather confide in you a lot, Emily?"

The professional smile disappeared, replaced by a fondness that looked too spontaneous to have been phony. "Yes, he did."

"Did he tell you I hadn't been back here for years?"

Emily moved to the porch swing and sat down where she could see the driveway, the narrow sandy road, and a few other large houses that dotted this section of coastline. She rested her fingertips on her handbag—the expensive sort—the kind Charity often found hanging off white plastic arms in tall store windows in the city. She'd never understood the attraction until now. She watched Emily's hands rest upon it as if the dyed leather and shining buckle held all the power a woman needed to survive any and all questions. A spark of envy skated over Charity. She was going to go right out and purchase one of those shields. Maybe a sword to match. Emily spoke. "Your grandfather was—and still is—my client."

Embarrassment rushed over Charity's shoulders. Didn't she know by now to mind her own business? "I'm sorry. I didn't mean to push."

Emily patted the seat beside her, so Charity sat down while the wind worked hard to get to them. But up there, on the safety of the long, covered porch, the wind was kept at bay. It would have to be content with rustling the brush at the edge of the porch. Later, perhaps in a day or two, Charity would open all the windows and let it have its way. But not yet.

Emily glanced over. "Your grandfather told me you might have a lot of questions as we go along. He's given me strict instructions to tell you anything and everything you ask."

Gooseflesh spread across Charity's neck. "You speak of him as if he's still alive."

Emily's perfect, red mouth tipped into a sad shape. "He's here." Color-coordinated fingernails tapped her heart. "He's right here, and I'm thankful I was the one he came to. Knowing him made me a better person."

As if she needed more sorrow, Charity quickly realized all she'd missed by being too busy to come visit. "I wish . . . I wish . . ." But her voice cracked, and what could she say? She wished she'd been a better granddaughter? She wished she hadn't wasted the last years. All that was true, but what good did it do now? Off in the distance, a seagull screeched. Charity lifted her gaze and caught sight of it, tilted wings spread wide and catching the wind as it prepared to dive for food. "There's a seagull." She pointed it out to Emily just like her grandfather used to do for her. Charity used to watch the seagulls for hours. From the glassed doorway on the sleeping porch, she'd rest on one of Gram's quilts while Gramps would prepare pottery for the kiln. He had a room inside the house where the potter's wheel waited to be turned and used. She hoped it was still there. Maybe he'd given up pottery. The thought rushed her like a sudden flu, but Charity forced the intruder aside. No. No. Even when she was small, her gramps had promised to pass the wheel to her. One day.

Her nose tingled. One day had come.

As if recognizing the tiny thread of courage that had gently wound itself around Charity, Emily stood. "Would you like to go inside?"

Charity brushed sweaty palms over her thighs and followed Emily, her heart lurching and then settling in her throat. After a few slow steps, she held the key out toward the door, but some invisible magnetic force stopped her cold. "Would . . . would you?"

One of Emily's brows rose. Moments ticked past, and Charity felt like the kid on the playground who possessed the ball, but suddenly no one wanted to play. "I mean. Could you open it?"

Emily swallowed. Charity watched what felt like a barrage of emotion cross Emily's face. Red-tipped fingers gently landed on Charity's sleeve. "As I said, your grandfather left me instructions." A tiny smile, a light squeeze, and Emily took a full step aside as if moving out of the way of a falling vase.

Heat snaked up Charity's cheeks. Anger scraped at her consciousness. After all, wasn't Emily supposed to be there to help? Supposed to be the hand Charity could hold on to? Wasn't that why her grandfather paid her?

After a surrendering sigh—complete with key still dangling in the air—Charity gathered her sanity. Emily hadn't been sent to be the shoulder she could lean on. Like everything, Charity had to do this on her own.

She forced the key in the lock and gripped the door with enough force to loosen the salt-water erosion. Sea air worked on everything, chewing away at the patina and leaving sandpaper in its stead. She had to jiggle the doorknob a few times to get the right angle. WD-40 would help. She'd purchase some later in the day. After a short skirmish, the lock clicked, and the doorknob turned. Charity swung the door open, its groan of hello greeting her first.

Windows off the back of the house filled the space with light. Sixteen-foot ceilings, cracked with age; two wide, circular banisters in half-curlicue shapes led to the second floor, making the marble entryway resemble a pool at the bottom of a mermaid's castle.

Charity stepped inside, surprised that the old place still looked the same. A bit more run-down, a bit more faded and aged. But still, the home she'd known. There was comfort in that. On the left, beyond the arched double doorway, stood the library's tall bookshelves. Opposite the library, the giant fireplace anchored one wall inside the parlor. The entryway alone was as big as her entire apartment in the city. Even so, it felt comforting and cozy to Charity.

"Some updates have been made over the last several years. Your grandfather kept all the warranties and lists of workmen in a drawer in the kitchen."

Charity moved to the wall and rested her hand on the plaster. "I know that drawer," she said and realized she was smiling. She'd feared she'd feel like an intruder here, an outsider, an interloper. Someone who'd once belonged but no longer did. Someone who'd turned her back on the place so in exchange, the place would turn its back on her.

But that wasn't how she felt. The plastered wall was cool to the touch, and her hand made a soft, scraping sound as it moved across the surface. Her index finger rested over a crack. There'd always been cracks in the plaster. Maybe this one was new. Maybe old. What did it matter? They were hers now. The cracks, the space between the walls, the floors to the ceilings. And quite suddenly, she wished she had a mop in her hands. Windex and paper towels and a bucket for the floors. Charity had a rushing need to clean and scrub and *tend* the house. Make it proud. Make it shine.

She must have mumbled something to that effect because Emily answered her. "There are supplies for tidying up in the kitchen. Your grandfather—"

Charity spun to meet her eye to eye, bold with her new objective. "What did you call him?"

Emily blinked. Perhaps not understanding the question, perhaps surprised that the mousy woman was finally finding her voice. "Excuse me?"

"My grandfather. Did you call him Mr. Baxter? Or—"

Emily cocked her head in a way that suggested fondness. "George. He insisted I call him by his first name."

Charity nodded. "OK. Call him George. You don't have to say 'your grandfather' anymore. It makes him seem too far away."

Emily's mouth quirked. "*George* made sure there were cleaning supplies, even had Mrs. Cready pick up a few groceries for you. Mrs. Cready helped George over the last few years. George's arthritis made it difficult for him to do every task. Louise Cready was a big help and a good friend. She'll be back in a couple of months. She's gone to visit her sister in Nebraska."

And just like that, all the good feelings about the house and the windows and the seagulls all disappeared in a swirling cesspool of Gramps's rheumatoid arthritis. Though she hadn't seen her gramps in the last few years, she knew what rheumatoid arthritis did to the body, to the joints. Thinking of him like that . . . "I wish I'd known." Did she wish she'd known? Would it have changed things?

"How long had it been since you two saw each other?"

Charity swallowed the cotton in her throat. "Three years, Christmas. I'd sent him a plane ticket, and he visited me in New York. He hid his pain." She thought back to decorated storefront windows and snow and Christmas lights. How Gramps would rub his hands together as they walked, curl them carefully around a mug of hot cocoa or steaming coffee. Now she knew the joints in his hands must have been throbbing. Back then she'd assumed it was just a habit.

"He was very fond of you."

Charity's gaze landed on Emily. *I was fond of him, too.*

Their steps and voices echoed as they crossed from one room to the next. Parlor, library, crisscrossing the entryway again and again. Just beyond the entry was one of her favorite spaces in the house. The large, open dining room anchored by massive white columns. Back in the day of turn-of-the-century parties, it had been filled on one side with a long dining table and the rest of the space open for dancing. Charity and her gramps had found a picture of a group of people enjoying the space in the 1920s, the men in smooth, dark suits and the women in waist-length pearls over flapper dresses. It had looked magical, and when Charity told Gramps she'd like to step inside the photo, Gramps and her great-uncle Harold—he often visited in the summers—had hauled the massive table so that it fit into the same spot as in the photo. Then he told Gram to turn up the music, and, right there, they became a 1995 copy of that picture. Gram wrapped tablecloths with tassels around Charity's shoulders and waist and piled on pearls from her jewelry drawer. From that day on, the dining table remained there.

Charity rubbed her foot back and forth over the smooth marble floor. "Gramps used to say we'd wear out the flooring."

Emily came to a stop beside her and stared down. "What?"

"He loved to dance." She tipped her head. "I bet you didn't know that about him, did you?"

Emily grinned. "No. I'm certain he never offered to take me dancing."

Charity hugged herself and swayed ever so slightly from side to side while the echoes of the decades of old music played softly in her memory. "We'd dance here." She moved to the center of the room. "Right here."

Emily's gaze flittered around the room. "So that's why the long dining table is off to the side. I'd always wondered."

Charity nodded, glad she knew some things about her gramps that Emily didn't know. She was thankful for Emily's knowledge, but Charity was his granddaughter, and it seemed wrong that there was nothing secret, nothing private about their family. That every detail had been spread out for a stranger.

They continued around the house, and Emily filled her in on various details that Charity would need to know. *A window in the parlor wouldn't open. Did Charity want her to contact the handyman George preferred?*

"No, thank you," she'd said. Really, there were plenty of other windows, and she wasn't ready to share the space with anyone else. Her gramps was still here, in spirit, and what if someone came in and stole him away? That was silly, she knew, but she didn't have the energy to fight silliness right now. Instead, she'd humor it and choose carefully who came and went for a while. Emily was OK. She made Gramps feel as though he was even closer, more tangible.

He needed to be here with her because this was a huge, massive, giant, towering house. Too big to be in all alone.

Just as she stepped through a doorway and into the kitchen, a new level of calm descended. The kitchen smelled like her gram's gingersnaps and bread and old wood. Her gaze drifted up to the candelabra where tiny cobwebs connected the wrought iron arms. Back in the day, it had held real candles over the table for illumination, but for the sake of modern convenience, it had been wired years ago.

"Looks like we have a cob infestation," Charity uttered.

Emily's sharp gaze shot upward. "A . . . a what?"

A knowing smile crossed Charity's mouth. It was an inside joke. "Cobs." She pointed to the candelabra.

Emily stepped away from her to examine the fixture, but Charity was already learning the woman's tells. How she turned subtly away when uncertain what to say or how to react. Probably no poker face. That was unfortunate for an attorney. Emily spun back around with a winning smile on her face. "I assume Mrs. Cready has given up climbing on chairs to remove cobwebs."

"It's no problem. I'm sure I can combat them. There's undoubtedly a pot in the cupboard big enough to fit over my head and a spatula for a weapon. Plus, knowing Gramps, he's always got a good supply of honey and cinnamon for bait." Why the ever serious Charity had launched into the disparaging topic of how to best divest cobs, she wasn't sure. But here, in the kitchen of her gram and gramps's house, she felt young again, childlike, if only for a few moments.

Emily's wide-eyed stare brought her right back to earth. Her face said it all. *Cobwebs are made by spiders. Not cobs. There's no such thing as cobs.*

Maybe Charity'd sailed into the topic simply because it was clear that Emily liked her. And she liked Emily, and Charity was so very good at pushing potential friends away. She could explain about the cobs. It would be easy. *You see, my grandmother made a game of taking care of the cobwebs. She'd sport a pot on her head and a broom handle in her hand and would come find me, and we'd try ever so quietly to sneak up on the cobs. They're hard to see, you know. Fast little things. I'd shine a flashlight on them, and she'd swipe the broom across the ceiling. Sometimes she'd go into a fit of jumping about, saying, "One's on me. One's on me." And I'd laugh until my belly hurt.*

Instead, Charity remained quiet and let the awkward silence saturate the room.

"Charity, after you've had a bit of time to settle in, could you come by my office? Or I could meet you here. There are a few other matters regarding George's estate that we will need to discuss."

"By other matters, I'm assuming you mean my mother."

Emily's hand landed on her sleeve again, just near the elbow. "I understand the difficulties that could arise, but George was very clear about his wishes."

"He didn't cut her out of his will, right?" That would cause her mother to go into a fit.

"No. That could easily be contested. She is the only child. Actually, he left her a small house in Atlanta."

"The house Gramps grew up in?" It was old, worn down by the decades, but a fine little house with a white picket fence. And it had family history, though Charity doubted her mother would appreciate that.

"Yes. You understand, I'm only discussing this with you per his wishes."

Charity nodded.

"She was also left a trust."

Charity frowned. "That means she will have some access to a certain amount of money, but not actually be in control of all the funds, right? Kind of like an allowance for grown-ups?" It didn't matter. Charity's mom had everything she wanted. She hadn't become the generation's answer to Marilyn Monroe, but she'd landed—her words, not Charity's—a fine, rich New York doctor who loved nothing more than doting on her. She was living her dream in the big city, where she attended private parties and fancy affairs and helped raise her husband's nearly grown daughters. "My mother has all the money she needs. I don't think any of this will be an issue for her. She hated this house."

When Emily pulled a chair at the kitchen table and sat down, Charity followed. "The estate became sizable when George sold the hardware stores a couple years back. All left to you. It's not just the house, Charity."

"He called me two years ago when he sold and wanted to know if I needed money."

Emily smiled. "Yes, he wanted me to keep an eye on your pottery business once it was open in case you needed anything."

"Always taking care of me," Charity mumbled.

"As I said, the estate is sizable."

Charity chewed her thumbnail. It tasted like dirt. "Sizable?"

Emily smiled. "That's an understatement."

Charity's gaze left Emily and flittered around the room. Well, there'd be need for money. What if she had to replace the terracotta roof on this place . . . or rewire the thing, or redo the plumbing? She remembered a friend back in New York who kept having tiny drops of water appear on her carpet and blaming her kids when really, the water pipes had rusted through. Charity must have muttered something about that because Emily was addressing the issue.

She chuckled. "There'll be more than enough to reroof or rewire."

Charity nodded because everyone knew *that* equaled understanding. One second she was scraping to make ends meet; the next, she was wealthy enough to rewire a mansion.

Emily rested her fancy bag on the table. "Would you like to discuss numbers?"

Charity flew up out of the chair with enough force that it toppled backward. "That's not necessary." Her voice was a high squeak. "Not now, anyway."

Was she insane not to be curious about the money? Well, yeah. To the passerby, it would seem ridiculous. But money was a strange thing. Having great power and yet none. It could buy you the world but not happiness. It could purchase perfection but not make you feel any more whole. At least, that's what she'd assumed . . . having never had an abundance of it but watching her mother always needing more, more, more.

Emily closed the purse. "There's plenty of time. Don't worry, Charity. Your grandfather's legacy is in capable hands. When you're ready, we can talk about amounts. OK?"

"Can I make us some tea?" Charity asked because the money thought niggled at her, and right now she just wanted to move on. She took the teapot from its designated spot on the back burner of the stove and headed to the sink. Her gramps had only been gone a few weeks, so she knew there was tea in the cupboard without having to look. Twining's Earl Grey. The kitchen overlooked the backyard and the ocean beyond. She glanced at it as she filled the teapot. The sleeping porch was off to the right, and until she sloshed water from the overfilled pot, she hadn't noticed the haunting mass of green in the far right corner of the property. When her gaze trailed there, drawn by a seabird that had angled across the colorful ribbons of clouds, Charity's heart stopped. Cold flashed from her head down, leaving her nerve endings raw and exposed. The teapot shook in her trembling hand. It was the weeping tree. The one black spot on the perfect property. Growing up, she'd hated the tree and all the legends surrounding it, especially the legend about trimming the branches. *If the willow's branches aren't trimmed, and one touches the ground, someone you love will die.*

Why she had assumed the tree would be gone, she couldn't say. Even when she'd entertained the thought that the tree might still be there, she'd brushed the idea aside. She was a grown woman now. Trees were plants. Rooted in the ground and nothing more. But as her eyes sailed over the long, swooping branches and the narrow, green leaves, she knew. The weeping willow was so much more. Once, a long time ago, it had devastated her life. The sour taste of hate rose like bile in her throat. She'd dig it out of the ground by the roots. She'd hire a man tomorrow and fell the tree.

A voice behind her brought her lethal thoughts to a stop. "It's beautiful, isn't it? George once told me his favorite thing on the planet was to watch the occasional beachgoer sit beneath that tree." Emily was just behind her. "One of his main requests is that you tend the tree. Everything around it has become so overgrown. I suppose it was too much for George in the last few years. But you'll get to bring it back to its former glory. Now you'll tend the tree."

Those words brought Charity's world to a sudden and complete halt. Tend the tree? She'd have it chopped, not tended. She'd have a crane come in and drag it from the ground. She'd have her final revenge on the green monster. After all, her grandmother's death was because of the tree. *Not just the tree* . . . her mind added, but she refused to listen.

"Emily," she said, forcing the despair from her voice as best she could. "Could we do tea another day? I'm feeling tired, and I still need to unload my things."

"Of course." A perfect smile. An attorney's way of shifting gears without ever giving away the thoughts rummaging through her head. "The landline is still on, and I have your cell. Shall I give you a call tomorrow?"

"Mm hmm." Charity had just agreed to something. What was it?

"Fabulous. I'll call tomorrow." Emily headed out of the kitchen.

Oh. That's what she'd agreed to. She didn't have to answer the phone tomorrow if she didn't want to. She could decide when the phone rang. Talk. No talk. It was up to her.

Emily reached the front door and spread her spiked shoes. She grabbed the knob and jerked. That made Charity smile. The woman really had been here a lot to know the secret of the door. To know one must throw one's whole weight into opening it. With the Florida sun shining in on them, Emily straightened her spine. "Great to have you here, Charity. I hope we'll get the opportunity to become friends." Red smile again. White teeth. Genuine niceness.

It all made Charity wish she was better at friends. Maybe she could be. Maybe here she would be. But then she thought of the tree. She wasn't even sure she could stay with it out there. And that just wasn't something she could explain to Emily Rudd, potential friend, attorney, wearer of dangerous heels and purchaser of handbag shields. The woman—sweet as she was—had been ready to cut and run when Charity had started talking cob talk. Cobs. Maybe Charity's head was full of cobs. Maybe that's what was wrong with her. They were hard to see. And practically impossible to get rid of.

Maybe cobs were why she was a thirtysomething with no real friends, no real relationship, and a business that failed practically before it even began. Cobs. That was her problem.

⟡

Dalton Reynolds was tiring of the inquisition. Especially when he knew there were snook to catch just beyond his window on Gaslamp Island. "Did Mom write down these questions, or are you working from memory?"

His brother, Warren, huffed and then stood up from the little wooden table that held two fresh cups of coffee, a smattering of various cans labeled STAIN, PAINT, and THINNER, a bouquet of paintbrushes, and, finally, cinnamon rolls. "Look Dalton, we're all suffering from the loss, OK?"

It was strange to Dalton that anyone in his family could assume their loss compared to his. He had an empty house in Jacksonville that would never again hear the laughter of his family.

Outside the kitchen window there were multiple tasks that needed his attention, so whether or not his brother was visiting, fishing would have to wait. Early spring on Gaslamp Island had brought coastal winds ripe with fresh waves of heat. He'd need to get whatever spring plants he wanted in the ground before the summer heat came and singed their delicate roots.

"Dalt, listen to me. I can understand why you needed a little time away. But it's been long enough." Warren had aged over the last year. They both had. But his brother was more than capable of handling the landscaping business back in Jacksonville, so Dalton wouldn't allow himself to be guilted into returning home before he was ready. He'd tried that once. It was an epic fail. He'd only been on Gaslamp for three months, fixing up a tiny cottage for an elderly couple who planned to sell it next spring. And it had become the first time in the last year when he'd actually been able to take inventory of his life. Or what was left of it.

Dalton sat back down at the table, leaving the sunshine through the window on his back.

Warren stood. "I told Mom I'd bring you home."

"Really?" Dalton knew his brother didn't understand. He himself didn't even understand, but it didn't matter. This was where he was, and this was where he was staying . . . for as long as it took to begin to heal from the loss of his wife and child. He'd known he was coming here the second he'd seen the small ad stuck to a bulletin board in a gas station on the mainland. He'd driven aimlessly for hours, but as soon as the handwritten ad was in his hands, he'd had purpose.

**COTTAGE REMODEL NEEDED. ROOM AND BOARD PROVIDED.
AT LEAST SIX MONTHS OF WORK.**

It was a perfect fit.

Warren, tall as Dalton's own six feet, stared down at his brother, a cloud blotting the sun and darkening the sky. A sky already filled with gray. "You can't hide forever, Dalt."

Those words went down rough as whiskey on a sore throat. Dalton fisted his right hand. It wasn't anger that drove him to tighten the grip; it was desperation. "I'm doing what I need to do for me. I'm sorry if the world disagrees."

Warren dropped into the seat across from him. Dalton hadn't bothered to rise from his own chair at his brother's challenge—and that's what that wide stance had been, a challenge—he hadn't bothered to meet him eye-to-eye and toe-to-toe. That's what brothers were supposed to do. But Dalton didn't respond in kind anymore. There wasn't the energy in his bones.

Clear blue eyes studied him from across the table, filled with just enough pleading to cut right into Dalton's heart. "We're all worried about you. It's been over a year since we lost them."

Dalton cringed from his ears to his feet. Over a year. One year, four months, two days. It didn't matter. The pain was the same. It never left. It never gave him rest. "Warren, I need to be here."

Warren threw his hands up and let them clop onto the tabletop. The cans shivered in response. "Why now? You were home for months after the funeral. We all thought . . . well, we thought you were doing fine."

Doing fine? Dalton hadn't even known what fine was.

Warren continued. "And why *here*?" He pointed to the window—the window Dalton loved, where he watched the dolphins in the mornings while guzzling mugs of hot coffee. Sailboats in the afternoon and the occasional luxury yacht in the evenings. The window where he'd watch fish jumping in the glistening sea while a blazing ball singed the horizon. And then there was his favorite—the seabirds that landed on the swaying branches of the weeping willow tree off to the left edge of his property. Mornings he'd drink coffee, eat a cinnamon roll, and decide which room to paint or what trim work to strip and stain. There was life here, if only the tiniest shreds of it. And even if it wasn't his life.

A hand waved in front of his face. "Hey, earth to Dalton."

Dalton tuned into the conversation. "What?"

A long, surrendering exhale from Warren said it all. Dalton's baby brother was getting weary of hitting the brick wall of Dalton's determination. Warren rubbed his palm over the scar above his right eye. A nervous tick since the day Dalton had given him the mark, compliments of a runaway baseball. "Why here?" His words were softer, though he was losing his patience. "On this tiny little island that's harder to get to than the inner circle of hell? Why, Dalt? It's like you're pushing everyone away."

Dalton pointed to the table. "I made you coffee. Gave you a bed to sleep in last night."

Warren shoved up out of the chair, and this time there was no intimidation in his motions, just disappointment and relinquishing surrender. "Mom said this was futile." He planted his hands on the countertop, his back to the table.

Dalton chewed his cheek. "I've been thinking about selling the business."

Warren spun from the window where seagulls scoured the shoreline. "Are you serious?"

What was that tone? Disgust? Disbelief? Dalton couldn't place it.

"You can't sell. You love the business. When you're not wallowing, that is. You and Melinda built it from the ground up." Ah yes. It was definitely disgust. "How can you even think of selling out?"

You and Melinda built it from the ground up. That was an understatement. They'd planned through college—her getting her business degree, him becoming a landscape architect. They'd drawn up plans a thousand times while laughing and eating cold pizza and dreaming about "one day." He'd use graph paper, and they'd carefully lay out the building, the grounds, the courtyard for welcoming customers, and the gazebo where a bounty of flowers and foliage would let each client know their dreams could easily become reality by allowing Reynolds Life-Scaping to partner with them. Melinda was the visionary; even the name had been her idea. "We don't just landscape," she'd said. "We make people's lives better. We Life-Scape." Dalton had been the elbow grease, and together they'd made it happen. Right down to the smallest detail, the tiniest bluebell bulb and bud of baby's breath. "I'll come back when I'm ready. Not before." It was obvious that discussing the idea of selling with his baby brother would go nowhere.

"We need you back at work, Dalt." This was a tactic. One Dalton recognized. Everyone needed him after losing Melinda and Kissy. Their baby girl's name was Krissy, but she'd insisted—at a very grown-up three and a half—that everyone call her Kissy. She'd had Melinda's blonde hair and zeal for life. She had Dalton's slightly crooked nose and love of digging in the dirt. Kissy used to find earthworms with Dalton, then search out her mother. She'd chase her around the house, with Melinda screaming and Kissy relentless in her pursuit. High-pitched little-girl laughter filling the air.

Everyone needed Dalton after losing Melinda and Kissy. His parents. The staff. Even his brother. For several months he'd thrown himself into work, into the business, into his hurting extended family. And then one day he up and left. No wonder they were worried about his sanity.

"You're doing great without me," Dalton said.

Warren shook his head. Dalton knew he'd like to argue, but the business had actually grown in the past months. The office ran smoothly with Warren at the helm, and the plants and flowers and inventory were chugging right along as if life hadn't come to an abrupt, violent, and screeching stop a year ago.

Warren took a long drink of his coffee. "Nothing I can say is going to change your mind, is it?"

Dalton didn't have to answer.

Warren strode across the kitchen and retrieved his duffel bag. "Thanks for letting me come."

"Next time, stay a few more days. We can plan an offshore fishing trip."

Warren stopped on his way to the front door. He angled to look at his brother. "Yeah. Maybe the work will get to be too much for me, and I'll move in with you."

That was a cheap shot, and Dalton knew Warren regretted the words as soon as he said them. "I'm not asking you to understand, little brother. Run the business, don't. Up to you. No pressure. If you decide you want to step down, I'll contact a business broker to list it."

Warren gritted his teeth, probably so he wouldn't say all the vile things he must be thinking. "How can you be so complacent? It's your life's work."

Easy, Dalton thought. *My life is over. No need to court what's already dead.* Instead, he said, "Come on. I'll drive you to the water taxi."

One hour later and after a quick lunch at the Dive, a combination dive shop and burger and seafood joint, Dalton returned home. He'd heard a storm was coming and wanted to check in on the Barlows, the couple who'd hired him to redo the small cabin two doors down from their beach house. Coastal storms were something. Usually, the lights would go out first, the wind would howl like a scorned lover, and the tide would rush in with such force, it let a person know just how small he was in the grand scheme of things.

After helping drag the Barlows' patio furniture into their screened and covered lanai, he folded his patio chairs, stacked them against the cottage and overturned his small patio table. He was just heading inside when he saw her.

The new neighbor. Dark hair pulled back in a ponytail that seemed incapable of holding the long strands. She was standing on the small awning-covered porch and staring up at its ceiling. What was she looking at? Cobwebs? A wasps' nest? Her hands on her hips almost gave shape to the oversize gray T-shirt that landed just above her knees. Her legs were covered to midcalf in black stretchy pants—the kind Melinda wore for yoga—and her feet were bare.

He started to yell that a storm was coming. That'd be a great way to meet a new neighbor. Dalton took a few steps toward the edge of her property. But before he could get within earshot, she dropped her hands and disappeared inside the glass door.

He stood there for a few moments as the sea grew angry. Above, the sky answered with a rumbling boom. The lightning would arrive next, ushered by a chilling bite of Gulf wind. Rain, he predicted. Lots of it.

The house he stared at was an interesting one. Old. But built in a style that suggested money, opulence, even whimsy. He'd heard it had been built by William Baxter, the circus tycoon who'd single-handedly helped build this part of the state—if the monument to him at the island's center was accurate. Dalton pondered how many bedrooms the place had. He'd seen it only from the outside, but counting the upstairs windows—something he'd done a time or two—suggested at least ten bedrooms. One shabbily clothed, scrawny woman and ten bedrooms. Curiosity about her niggled at his mind, but his thoughts returned to his brother, Warren, and all the talk about home and family. Home. Dalton was beginning to wonder if there was a home for him anymore. He'd stayed in their house after Melinda died as if one day, magically, it would feel OK to be there. That day never came, and with the passing months, his loneliness had spiraled down and down until he'd known he had to do something to shake off the grave clothes he wore. Even now the idea of going back to their home in Jacksonville chewed through his stomach like a hungry piranha.

He liked the glassed-in sleeping porch on the back of the neighbor's massive house best, he decided. The circus house was sandwiched between the tiny cottage he was remodeling and the small home the Barlows lived in. They'd purchased both properties at the same time, hoping her sister would move into the cottage, but she'd fallen sick and hadn't gotten the chance. His first project had been to paint the exterior walls cream with crisp-white shutters. The cottage and the Barlows' home gleamed like sparkling jewels on either side of the mansion. Even so, it was the mansion that drew attention from passersby. It was a soft shade of something between salmon and terracotta. He'd learned an infinite variety of colors from Melinda after planting the wrong *shade* of pink roses in a client's garden and costing his business a few grand.

Anywhere else, the color of the house might look strange, but here, on the beach, where colorful coral met greenery and sand and sea, this shade of salmon was perfect. White trim highlighted each nook. The terracotta roof was varied from dark tiles to pale ones, giving the over-all home a natural feel, similar to the bricks in a fireplace. The shades complemented the hulking design that was tempered by the almost whimsical turrets, one off-center at the front of the home and three off the back. Those three were covered patios overlooking the beach. Arched doorways led into the house, and Dalton hoped one day to get a glimpse inside.

The first jolt of blue-white lightning sent him inside his cottage after his eyes roamed the landscape as if it had been his job to button up the neighborhood. He took in the entire circus house and the snippet of the Barlows' home he could see from his vantage point.

Dalton had a fresh stack of library books, and since moving to the island three months ago, he'd rediscovered his love of literature. He'd started with Hemingway but quickly moved on to newer works by Cussler and White. Dalton had just settled into the fourth chapter when he heard the wind pick up. Carried on the rushing gusts was the unmistakable sound of a woman's scream.

CHAPTER 3

Special Ingredient

Dalton tossed the book and rushed to the back door, uncertain of where the scream had come from. He scanned the beach quickly. If someone was fool enough to try to swim in this mess, he was fool enough to rescue them. But his gut told him the sound hadn't come from the water.

He jumped off the porch, and his feet hit rain puddles. The wind stung his eyes, powerful enough to kick up sand and pelt his face. He squinted and tried to shield his eyes, which instantly felt full of gravel. All along the beach, he could see nothing. That's when the sound came again, off to his left, and he turned and ran toward it, the rain soaking through his shirt and chilling his body. As he neared the circus house, he saw her. Her arms were upstretched, her fingers in a death grip holding on to the side of the low awning that covered a small patio beside the sleeping porch.

"What in the world are you doing?" he screamed over the deafening wind.

She jolted, head turning and eyes filled with fear. All he could see was eyes—giant, and such a dark brown, they nearly looked black in the squall. She gazed over her shoulder at him, at nothing. He couldn't tell.

The wind gusted and almost brought her off her feet.

"Are you crazy? Get inside!"

But she only dangled there, toes trying to get traction, mouth a straight line, eyes blinking back the constant stream of water flowing off the edge of the low roofline and drenching her.

"It's . . . it's going to . . . fly off." Her feet shuffled beneath her, and suddenly Dalton realized what the woman was doing. His heart dropped into his stomach. He quickly examined the broken beam that held the awning in place. Without its support, the whole thing could be lifted in one strong gust. Instantly, he took the spot beside her and clamped his hands on the metal awning just as the wind tried to snatch it away from them.

The angry squall screeched and groaned over them. He didn't look at his neighbor's face, but her white-knuckled grip was hard to ignore. They couldn't stay like that. Too much lightning. Too dangerous. "Listen to me," he shouted, over the roar.

Her head jerked, and he saw that the elastic holding her ponytail was barely holding on. It clutched the ends of her hair.

"I've got a two-by-four I can use to shore this up."

She jerked a nod, but her look was blank—big, brown eyes blinking away the water and sand that flecked her eyelashes.

"I'm going to run over to my cottage. Can you hold it for a minute?" A clap of thunder. A fresh gust.

"I . . . I think so."

When the wind died long enough to take a breath, Dalton ran full force to the cottage and hurried inside the small shed where he found wood, nails, and his hammer.

He practically dropped the hammer going back to her, since everything was soaking wet and slick enough that it made gripping the tool difficult. She looked small as he neared, thin arms holding the weight of the entire house. He dropped the hammer into the belt loop on his jeans and put the nails in his mouth, then arranged the two-by-four for best support in a diagonal over the cracked beam. He started the nails, then hit each with one solid hit that leveled the nail head with the wood.

After the second, he heard her mumble, "Holy moly."

Dalton almost had to chuckle. It was a carpenter's trick. If the nail was hit in the right spot, it would sink like a broken submarine. Right into the wood. Great bar trick to impress girls. In college he had a buddy who carried around a hunk of wood in his car for just such opportunities. It was also handy when one needed to sink several nails in rapid succession so a Gulf storm couldn't blow away an awning and an odd young woman too stupid to stay inside.

"That should keep it." He hooked the hammer in his belt loop as she ducked under the awning.

"Thank you." She tried to push the mop of wet hair off her face, but much of it was plastered to her pale cheeks.

"No problem." He started to jog back toward the cottage, but a bolt of lightning struck overhead, and he jumped back, landing under the awning beside her.

The woman smiled. "I'm Charity."

"Dalton."

She shifted her weight from one bare foot to the other. "Um. I saw you yesterday."

He nodded.

She raised a finger and pointed at the back door into the windowed room Dalton liked from the outside. "I can make some tea or coffee. Until the storm passes."

She was offering him refuge inside. Charity chewed her cheek as Dalton scrutinized her, the thin veil of friendliness hiding a deep-seated lack of confidence. She looked needy but like she didn't know it. There was gray dirt under her nails, even after the rain bath. Of course, he often had dirt under his nails, but it was good, rich earth, not pale gray . . . whatever it was. She was soaking wet, and in the rain and wind and fierceness of the storm she seemed almost helpless. Why would anyone in her right mind choose a gargantuan house like this . . . alone? Then again, maybe she wasn't alone. Maybe her family was coming from wherever, and she'd just arrived a couple of days early. Great. Happy family and kids yelling outside his window. That, he wasn't sure he could handle. He had a hard time even going into town. The constant laughter of kids got to him.

"Are you alone?"

The question must have frightened her. The woman took a full step back. But the look in her eyes faded, and she squared her shoulders as if readying for a fight. "Yes." Her head tipped, and she reached down and scooped up a broom resting beside the back door. She clutched it between her hands like a shield across her body. "I've been living in New York City for the last several years."

Her eyes narrowed just barely, and Dalton realized the New York City statement was to let him know she'd not be a victim; if she could survive there, one lone neighbor with a hammer posed little threat. "No, thanks."

Her face flickered with confusion. "What?"

"No, thanks, on the tea or coffee." And with that, he ducked into the storm and jogged to the back door of the cottage.

Once there, he glanced over to the circus house to see if she'd gone inside.

She held the broom beside her, as if deciding the merits of sweeping, but her gaze remained on Dalton and the little cottage. Her head of dripping hair was tipped ever so slightly, and in the flashes of quick-fire lightning, he could feel more than see the curious frown on her face. Again, he thought how she looked small against the massive house. But Dalton was through with working out other people's problems—and problems no doubt surrounded this woman. He had his own issues to tackle and knew that if he didn't start making some progress, the despair was going to swallow him, drown him, take him so deep, he'd never return. And the worst thing was, he didn't hate that idea.

He'd known he was in trouble when he realized there was a part of him that wanted to die in the sorrow. He knew he'd gone too far. Now he had to fight, dig, claw his way out. Because the darkness had become comfort. And if Melinda were alive to see him, she'd be ashamed.

⟡

Summer of 1995

"Charity, do you remember what I taught you last year on the potter's wheel?" Her gramps smiled down at her.

Charity rose from the little couch Gram called a settee, her heart jumping into her throat. "Yes, Gramps." She'd been watching him make a set of dishes for a lady who lived up the road.

The scent of freshly made gingersnaps floated through the doorway and into the room. Gram was on the other side of the wall separating the pottery studio from the kitchen. Charity could hear Gram humming as she worked.

Charity's mouth watered for warm cookies, but nothing would distract her right now. Not even Gram's crispy sweet treats. Charity had been itching to get her hands on some clay and sit at her gramps's wheel, but she was old now—eleven—and when you were old, you were patient. So she'd sat on the settee, her hands neatly folded in her lap. Charity didn't know what *settee* meant; to her it was a couch made for kids her size. It was covered in crushed red velvet that crinkled and tickled her skin while she rested there. She always watched Gramps intently, silently praying that one day she'd be as good at pottery as him. She chewed the inside of her cheek as Gramps worked the piece, his hand wet and the wheel spinning at the perfect speed. Today, she'd be diligent because yesterday she'd fallen asleep, lulled by the constant spinning of the wheel and the soft hum that accompanied the movement. Fell asleep. Like a baby taking a nap. She'd been embarrassed because she was grown-up now, and grown-ups didn't take naps. It was important for her gramps to know she took the business of pottery seriously.

"Do you remember what I told you about the clay?"

"To listen to it?" She knew, but she wasn't certain she understood.

"Do you know what that means?"

"Mm hmm." But her mouth twitched, and Gramps grinned and picked her up like she weighed nothing and sat her on the very edge of the settee. But then he reached to the arms and dragged the settee closer to his wheel.

"I want you to watch me first. Then it'll be your turn."

She'd been watching him for days, but that was OK. She loved watching. Only now her hands would itch to feel the clay, the slippery water, the movement.

"I'm going to make a piece; then you're going to make the same."

That was a big order. Her gramps was a master at this, and she was just an almost grown-up kid sitting on a settee. She forced a nod and pushed the stringy strands of her hair out of the way. "OK. What are we making?"

He dropped a good hunk of clay onto the center of the wheel. First, his hand wobbled at the sides of the gray-brown clump as it spun and spun. He dipped one hand in the water and crowded his upper body around the clay until there was no wobble, only smooth turns.

"What are we making, Gramps?"

He looked up at her with a smile, and she was sure that pixies and fairies must be playing just behind her, the way his eyes sparkled. "You tell me."

She thought hard. Needed to get this right. Gramps said the clay liked to be consulted on what it would become. A beautiful vase popped into her head. "A vase!"

Gramps's approving nod warmed her, fueling her desire to create her own piece.

"Yes, I believe it's a vase."

His hands were slick with water from the little cup nearby, and his attention went to the piece. Once the edges were smooth, he dipped his thumbs at the top in the center, first one, then the other, right into the mound. In response, the clay expanded gently, its shape being coaxed by soft caresses. He made it look so easy. But it was hard. Just getting the clay to spin without wobbling was hard. But it was wonderful, too. After a little time and more water, more gentle touches and more spinning, the vase's shape came into full form. Gramps finished by using a sharp tool to notch out a design. He cut the vase from the wheel and supported it by its bottom. He held his creation at arm's length and inspected the piece. "Good," he uttered and placed it carefully on a shelf to dry.

When it was Charity's turn, and she'd coaxed the mound of soft, cool clay, her thumbs worked from the top, creating grooves and then an indentation. Her heart hammered, and her shoulders ached as she kept her fingers at the right angle to make a copy of her gramps's vase. After two attempts and her back aching, Charity found her sweet spot. Her movements became soft enough to produce a perfectly round vase. Its sides rose like magic as she spun the wheel, trying to not get so excited she'd crush the delicate walls.

"Water," Gramps instructed.

Charity dipped her hand again, spreading the moisture over the piece. The water traveled quickly, as if it were in a hurry to help. Cool wetness covered both her hands now, making them slick and smooth and making her feel one with the piece, like it took them both to create the vase, like they were partners, meant to be together. By the time she finished, there was sweat on her brow. "Do you want to score it, like I did? I can show you how to hold the tool."

She knew Gramps meant well, but she'd finished the vase, and it was perfect. Still, she didn't want to disappoint him. He used the cutting tool to remove her vase from the wheel. "You know what? I think yours should stay just like this. It's happy, Charity." He lifted it to sit on the shelf beside his. If Charity had ever felt a more proud moment, she couldn't think of it. There on the shelf, her vase sat beside her grandfather's.

∽◊

Present day

Charity had discovered that life was filled with important moments. They were brightly colored confetti strewn on a landscape of gray. Each one, its own miracle. Sometimes, those moments passed quietly. But a few—a glorious few—were recognized immediately for their inexplicable but undeniable significance. They were bombs of promise. When Charity found the royal-blue-lined leather bag with the golden tassels the day after the storm, she knew she was in the crux of one of those moments. It was in a cabinet in the small pottery studio where as a child she'd watched her gramps work his magic.

She'd saved the studio for last after divesting all the cobs in the entire house and then unpacking and cleaning and ignoring the phone when Emily Rudd, potential friend, called.

Her gramps's pottery studio rested behind a half wall by the kitchen. Charity knew herself well enough to know that once she started doing any pottery work, little else would get accomplished. She'd saved this as the dessert after dinner. It had been a first-class dinner, though. She'd dined on memories and dreams of twenty years ago, letting them play out in her mind, indulging each and every one. The big house was already beginning to feel like she remembered. Except it was quiet. Too quiet. That was a pity. She missed the sound of her gram humming in the kitchen and the low, melodic tone of the wheel as Gramps worked.

But she was alone here, her clothes filling only a tiny corner of the master bedroom closet, opposite the wall that overlooked the Gulf through floor-to-ceiling French doors and a private balcony.

Her dishes remained in a box because Gramps had dishes. Some were new, but some were old, like the metal drinking glasses that used to be various colors of the rainbow but now sported darkened spots that suggested their age. There were Fire King coffee mugs and dainty china tea sets. Wooden salad bowls and a wide platter Gram had purchased when a restaurant was going out of business. Stainless steel pots and pans were a newer addition to the collection of iron skillets Gram had preferred to cook in.

Charity wished she'd gotten her gram's skill in the kitchen. She cooked, but Gram had been a master at blending and mixing ingredients. Charity tended to fix simpler fare. No, she hadn't inherited her gram's kitchen ability. She'd have to do with Gramps's gift for making pottery. But for her, that was more than enough to be happy. Even if she wasn't as good at it as he.

The clay in the small room caused the space to smell like earth and life and every perfect thing. She flipped the light and there in the center like an antique jewel was the seat and the wheel. She stepped inside, feeling both the nostalgia of the special place and a claustrophobia she hadn't expected. Had this room always been so small? One tiny window overlooked the Barlows' house. She tried to force it open, but the frame wouldn't budge. Charity dropped onto the seat and took in the room. Two bookshelves lined the two remaining walls, their wood splattered with dried clay from decades past. Along the lower shelves, she found a few pieces unfinished. One half-painted, another cracked—seeing them made her miss her gramps. A couple were in good repair and Charity toyed with the idea of glazing and firing them in the kiln that sat in the mud room beside the sleeping porch.

On the opposite wall was a wooden counter, it too was scarred with drops of clay and housed her gramps's pottery tools. Sponges and chamois, potter's needles and calipers. Above the counter was a cabinet. It likely held more tools, but as Charity stared at the faded, peeling paint on the wood, she wondered why she'd never noticed the cabinet before. She didn't remember it. Didn't remember it at all.

Curiosity sent her to it. Her fingers closed around the handle, and she pulled. The cabinet doors opened with a groan. The inside was empty except for what looked to be a full suede bag that sat on a round bottom. When the hair on the back of her neck stood up, Charity knew there was something unusual about this moment in time.

She reached with both hands and carefully lifted the bag, then placed it on the counter. The top had a drawstring and was pulled closed with a gold cord with golden tassels on the ends. Charity lifted the edge of the cord and rolled it between her fingertips. The sheen was still on the tassels though the bag had likely been in the cabinet for ages. The suede was smooth and fresh—not what one would have assumed of a bag that seemed so old. It looked expensive, one that might have been carried by a king or perhaps one that brought gold to a child in a manger.

Charity slowly tugged the bag open, half expecting to find gold, half expecting fairies to come flying out in all directions. But as the bag opened fully, she frowned. Inside, held dearly by the dark-blue satin interior, the bag was full of . . . dust? Or perhaps sand. Charity couldn't tell what the light-brown substance was, so she slipped a finger inside to test the texture. Her finger swirled in the mix. It wasn't quite sand, but it wasn't fine enough to be dust. It was soft, cool to the touch, and when her fingertip scraped on something in the bag, she jerked out her hand. Her finger had left an indention and there, at the bottom of the divot, she saw a warn edge of paper. Charity dove in with her index finger and thumb until the small piece of onion skin paper was free. Clutching it closely, she read the words,

Charity,

Add one scoop to each special order.

Love, Gramps

She spun and looked at the wheel behind her, then back at the paper. It crinkled as she swiped the ribbons of dust still obscuring some of the letters. Her heart hammered inside her chest. Gramps had always done special orders for folks in the area. But he'd never told her about a bag filled with a mysterious substance. Charity held the small, handwritten note to her heart. Gramps wanted her to continue in his footsteps, to make special orders for the islanders. Of course, she still wasn't half the potter he'd been, and she knew no one on the island except Emily Rudd, so really, how many special orders could she expect? Still, this was a treasure. A personal message from her gramps. Having it in her hands caused the ache in her heart to settle a little deeper.

The knock at the front door drew her attention when it rose in volume. The intense banging must be someone with little patience and less manners. Charity gently placed the note in the top of the bag and tugged the drawstrings until the opening closed like a portal. She hurried to the front door and its persistent knocker on the other side. Once there, she realized her skin was clammy.

Charity took a deep breath, spread her legs, and jerked until the front door opened. Dalton offered a white smile, contrasting with his Florida tan and green eyes.

"Yes?"

His brows rose, and he lifted the beam he'd had resting against his collarbone. "I thought you could use this."

But Charity's thoughts were in her pottery shop, and her mind was deep in a bag of sand or dust where her gramps had seen fit to leave hidden notes. "Use it for what?"

Dalton frowned. "You're kidding, right?"

Charity pressed her hands to her cheeks, still feeling a little off-kilter. Apparently Mr. Bright and Cheery noticed, because he started to step forward, his smile fading to concern. The beam shifted, and he had to wrap an arm around it before asking, "Hey, are you all right?"

Charity gazed up at the porch ceiling, blinked a few times, noticing the beam supporting the span above. "Oh. You brought me a beam."

He must have been expecting more of a reaction because those brows tilted again. "I'm not certain the broken one can take another good storm. Even with the two-by-four reinforcement."

"Come in." Charity stepped aside.

Dalton situated the beam against the front porch wall and followed her. "Is that your phone ringing?"

"Huh?" Charity tuned in to the sound she'd been ignoring for the last few days. "Oh, um." She didn't want to talk to Emily right now, and she was certain that was who it was. No one else she knew had the number. But when Dalton kept staring at her, she excused herself and headed for the kitchen.

The phone stopped ringing as she reached for the receiver. Charity stared at the flashing red light and waited until the answering machine beeped. She hit the playback button.

Emily Rudd had left a message. She wanted to get together. Oh dear.

∞

Dalton waited at the front door while Charity answered the phone. She was odd. That was the only way to explain it. He wasn't even sure she'd heard the phone until he mentioned it. He'd never been inside the house, so stepping in should have been breathtaking, except he hadn't been able to take his eyes off his curious bird of a neighbor. She had on another knee-length T-shirt and stretchy pants. Bare feet, unpainted toe nails, pale skin.

With her gone, he took a moment to glance around the house. Marble floors bounced the light onto the walls, and large windows flooded the room with luminescence. A round stairway led to the second floor. Off to the left of the entry was a library, filled with books and tall ceilings. He loved to read. Little did he know the next-door neighbor had a stash like this. Against the opposite wall, a stone fireplace decorated the space and invited visitors. He could easily see most of the lower level of the home from his vantage point. It had to be a hundred years old. He was staring up at the detail work on the top of the stair rail when she reentered the room. His gaze followed the railing down down down to the bottom, where a carved figure held the railing and stood on the first marble step. He squatted down. "Is this a bear . . . in a dress?"

Behind him, Charity giggled. "Yes."

He suddenly became interested in what manner of creature held the opposite post. Dalton moved to it. "A lion on a round platform. Like at the circus?" He turned to face her.

Charity was smiling—at first—and he noticed a spark in her eye as she said, "Just like a circus."

His gaze drifted around the home, looking for more hidden additions.

She moved to stand beside him and pointed out a carved image of a circus train car over the front door. "When the original owner built the house, he had everyone at the circus add his own touches. He gave the plans to the builder, who, from what I understand, practically had a heart attack trying to figure out how to make some of the creations come to life."

"Wow." Dalton glanced over at her. "Do you know where all of them are?"

She shook that head of long, dark hair. "Nope. I still find things. Or I guess I should say, I'm finding things again. I hadn't been here for twenty years."

"So you didn't buy the house from George Baxter?"

Her eyes lit up. "My grandpa. You knew him?"

He hated to make that fresh fire burn out, but no, he really hadn't. "I only met him a few times. I hadn't been here long when he passed. I'm sorry for your loss." And even though George Baxter had been friendly, even inviting Dalton in once, Dalt had declined. Those first several weeks of being there on the island, he'd been consumed with self-pity and had only wanted to be left alone.

Giant brown eyes left his and settled on the floor beneath them as if drawing strength out of the marble.

"I wish I'd gotten to know him." That was true. He'd heard great things about George Baxter from the Barlows and Mrs. Cready.

Charity remained silent. Not much for conversation, apparently.

"The beam needs to be replaced. Soon, if you want to keep that little covered porch."

"Thank you for buying it."

"Do you have someone who can do the work?"

She chewed on her index fingernail. "In the kitchen," she said, so he followed her.

Surely she didn't keep workmen in the kitchen. Or maybe she did. Charity pulled a drawer open and searched tiny pieces of paper while mumbling, "Plumber, electrician, masonry." She turned and looked at Dalton. "I'm not great with building, but I don't think any of these are right for beam installation."

Dalton laughed and joined her at the kitchen drawer. "How about a seamstress?" He held up a card with a knitting needle on it.

Charity chuckled. "Here's a good option, pest control."

"I can do the beam."

Her gaze floated up to meet his. "Are you a carpenter?"

"No, but I'm more qualified than your seamstress or the bug man."

Again, the smile on her face. It was nice. Conversation, the warmth of another human being. When she hesitated over his offer, he added, "I can give you references if you'd like. But it's a small beam, really not that big a deal."

"I can pay you. Just tell me what the going rate is."

"Deal," he agreed, because he figured if he told her no charge, like he'd planned, she'd run him out of the circus house, and he'd never get the chance to see that upstairs with all those rooms he'd seen from below. "It's a two-man job, and I've got a guy here on the island I use sometimes for an extra pair of hands. Will that be OK?"

"Whatever you need." Sometimes she seemed too trusting, sometimes not trusting enough.

"OK, well, I'll haul the new beam around back and be here first thing in the morning."

She followed him to the front door. He was filled with questions but figured he'd exhausted her conversation quota already. Some people, he could just tell about them. She was one of those. Quiet, watchful some moments, completely oblivious at others. As if there were no middle ground with her. She was either full speed or dead stopped. And it was not like he was looking to make friends, but he'd always been a social kind of guy. That was before. And before and after were two different worlds separated by a cavern of torment.

As he hauled the beam to the back porch, he knew it'd be a good idea to branch out and get to know his neighbor. He just wasn't certain he could do it.

CHAPTER 4

The Garden

Harold Baxter turned on the light that illuminated the long set of wooden stairs. He cast a glance behind him at the Birmingham apartment he'd called home for more than two decades. Trophies lined the living room wall, a tattered quilt sprawled across the sofa because old men got chilly easily, and he was an old man now. At seventy-five, he could finally admit that.

It's not that Harold didn't want to grow old; he just hated the limitations age brought. He rubbed a hand over one knee, gazing down at the stairwell that would take him to the dance studio below. He used to take those stairs two at a time. Had never even considered them as a worthy adversary. Now he dreaded that first step where his aging knees would crack and pop and even groan in protest. The stairs had never seemed so long, so steep until lately. It'd be better once he got his body moving. It was merely the first trek down the steps that he dreaded.

He wasn't one to feel sorry for himself, so he focused on all the things for which he had to be thankful. He'd realized his dream and opened his own business some twenty years back. Before that he'd been a bit of a drifter, the only real anchor in his life, his brother George.

His thoughts had been on George lately, though he hadn't spoken to him in over five years. He needed to reach out. Needed at least to try. Again. After all, they were old men now. But even as he took that first step, he knew the idea of reaching out to George was one steeped in selfishness. Harold missed George. Still. Even after all this time.

When he reached the bottom of the stairwell and moved across the dark studio, he wasn't surprised at the welling of emotion. He'd miss this place, too. The smooth feel of the beech wood sprung floor, the way soft light bounced off the warm walls. The sounds of voices and laughter as couples floated across the space from 5:00 p.m. till midnight. The music. Maybe he'd miss the music most of all. To Harold, music was life.

A rap at the front door drew his attention. Harold unlocked the door, then went to the long picture windows as his attorney, Phil Borland, shook the rain from his coat and stepped inside.

"Coffee?" Harold asked as he pointed to the pot on the long, help-yourself counter. He'd programmed the coffee maker last night, and now the scent, fresh and inviting, filled the room.

Phil shook his head. "I have to be in court in thirty."

That was his way of telling Harold he didn't have time to get dragged into another debate about how they could save the studio. Harold's bushy brows went up. "I've got to-go cups."

Phil fought a grin. He was a softie, despite being a high-powered Birmingham attorney. "OK. Half a cup, I'm cutting back."

Pleased, Harold poured the coffee. Just a little more than half because folks should always have a little too much, rather than not quite enough. He handed over the steaming cup and knew there was unrealistic hope in his eyes when he said, "Any good news?"

Phil sighed. "Harold, you signed over the business. We've been over this. There's not much I can do."

They'd been over and over and over it. When Harold took on a junior partner—young Ephraim Conner—the spirited young man had said all the right things. They'd worked together for three years without incident. "He lied to me, Phil. I had no idea those papers were the business."

Ephraim had told Harold he'd needed his signature on an agreement between the dance studio and the local television station. Harold trusted him, and there had been no reason to doubt him. In three years, Ephraim had never given him a shred of a reason to think he was anything but honest. In fact, he'd started thinking of him as family, the son he never had.

Phil glanced at his watch. "Look, there's nothing *I* can do. However—"

Harold perked up.

Phil took a long drink of his coffee, his eyes fast and piercing, moving around the room in that way attorneys had. Finally, he continued. "I've got you a meeting this afternoon with Tray Sharples."

"He's kind of famous."

"He's had some success with situations like this, cases of coerced elderly people. No offense."

Harold bent his knees, straightened them. "None taken. It's no sin to tell an old man he's old. You think Sharples can help?"

Phil shrugged in a noncommittal way. "I don't know. You're a businessman, Harold, not some little old lady sitting at home counting her coupons and storing money in a mason jar. It's not going to be easy to prove you were tricked into signing over your entire business."

"I'd planned to sell it to Ephraim, eventually."

"That only makes it harder to prove you didn't sign it over, then change your mind. He'd been making payments on the place. He played this smart."

"He's a crook and a liar. And I extended too much trust."

"Live and learn, I guess. Anyway, Tray Sharples is your best shot. And he's meeting you as a favor to me. So, don't waste his time with a bunch of details he can't use. Cold, hard facts. He'll want *some* details, but let him ask. Don't volunteer everything. Maybe he'll see something I didn't." Phil took a step closer and placed a hand on Harold's shoulder. "I don't want to see you lose this place."

Phil had brought his momma to Harold's Dancing on Air Studio six years back after Phil's daddy died, and his momma didn't leave the house for weeks at a time. Between the big band music and the nostalgic atmosphere, Laverne Borland had found her zest for life again and was able to move on. In the bargain, Phil met his wife Mitzi, a Chicago transplant who loved all things from past eras, including the dances.

Harold's lips pressed together. "How can I ever thank you?"

Phil smiled. "No need. He's carved out three hours this afternoon. Meet him at the dining room in the Four Seasons Hotel. Three p.m. Don't be late."

With renewed hope he hadn't felt for weeks, Harold nodded. "I'll be there, God willing, and the creek don't rise."

Phil chuckled. "No rain in the forecast, so I think we're safe."

Harold watched Phil leave. He knew the attorney had done all he could. It just hadn't been enough. Maybe hotshot Tray Sharples could help him. He hoped so; quite honestly, if he lost the studio, he'd have nothing left.

Just as he was getting ready to flip the **OPEN** sign, he remembered to go get the mail. It had sat for a few days while he'd stared out the upstairs window of his apartment wondering how he could ever survive losing the place. He'd have no home, nowhere to go. And he was an old man now. His savings account had about $11,000 in it, and that wasn't much to start over with. But he supposed he should be grateful that he wasn't completely destitute.

Outside, the air was warm and already balmy as the morning dew of downtown Birmingham was replaced by the early sun. Not a cloud in the sky. Harold drew a deep breath and gave thanks for the air in his lungs, for the fact that his own legs could still carry him to and fro and for the fact that he'd made a difference in the lives of so many people who'd walked through the door of the Dancing on Air Studio. That was something that could never be taken from him.

He crossed the empty street and opened his mailbox. A small stack of bills and advertisements greeted him, but there in the pile was a handwritten letter. He plucked it from the box and held it closer.

The return address was Gaslamp Island, Florida. The letter was from his brother, George.

Harold left the other letters where they lay and rushed back to the studio, tearing the envelope open as he went. When he noticed the world going dark around him, he groped for a chair that sat just inside the front door. After a deep breath, Harold willed the world back into focus and unfolded the letter.

> Dear Harold,
> This is no way for brothers to end up. I haven't laid eyes on you in twenty years, and we haven't spoken in six. You called that Christmas Eve, but I couldn't talk. I'd allowed myself to be swallowed up in my grief, and because of it, I pushed everyone away. I hardly even see Ellen Marie and Charity anymore.
>
> But I didn't write this letter to complain or to talk about all the things I did wrong. I wrote it to apologize. You're my brother, Harold. And I miss you. I know it's not like me to reach out for help, but I need help right now. I need you. I'm dying.

Harold tried to choke back a sob that echoed off the walls of the studio. He read and reread those last two words. *I'm dying.* A trembling hand went to his mouth, where tears ran over his fingers and dropped onto his lap.

I don't know how long I have left, but I need you here. Will you come? We have to mend this thing between us. We have to fix the wrong and bring it all out into the open. Hidden things fester. Hurts need air; they need oxygen; then they can begin to heal. I need to know we can heal this, Harold. Too much hangs in the balance. I love you, brother. No matter what happened, I've always loved you.

Your brother forever,

George

The letter dropped into Harold's lap. He dragged the words into his heart and wished he could conjure the image of his brother, but it had been so long. So long since he'd seen him or even heard his voice. It wasn't supposed to be this way—one of them deathly ill before they reconciled. He used the back of his hand to swipe his cheeks. Once his legs were steady enough to carry the new weight—the weight of knowing his brother was dying—he crossed the studio and grabbed the phone.

On the other end of the phone line a woman answered, "Delta Airlines."

"I need a flight to Sarasota, Florida, from Birmingham, Alabama. Today, if possible." His voice sounded foreign, filled with despair and a barrage of echoes from the past, voices and murmurings that told him he didn't deserve his brother's forgiveness.

"We have a three p.m. direct flight. May I book that for you, sir?"

Without hesitation he answered yes. He'd leave a message for Phil to cancel the appointment with Tray. Some things were more important than business. Family was one of those things.

Charity woke with her head in a fog. It was 8:00 a.m., and there were hammering, sawing, and other carpentry noises rising from her back side porch and interrupting her sleep. She looked out her window and saw nothing but porch roof. She stumbled to the bathroom, splashed some water on her face, and headed downstairs to make muffins for the workmen.

She'd questioned the muffin idea but kept telling herself that's what Gram would do. Since she hoped to become a part of the island's community, it seemed a good idea to cultivate a What-Would-Gram-Do? System, since Charity was socially inept.

Unfortunately for the beam installers, Dalton and his helper, she burned the muffins, so her idea of thanking them with treats went right out the window with the smoke in the kitchen. She was still fanning the smoke when a knock on her back door startled her. She tossed the kitchen towel on the counter and pulled the door open to find Dalton standing there. A tool belt hung low on his hips, and a red bandana caught the sweat on his neck. "Morning." He sniffed the air.

"I was making lemon muffins," she said and waved a hand behind her in the kitchen.

"Beam's done. If you have a broom, I'll sweep up. We left a mess of sawdust."

"Do you want coffee?"

He crossed his arms over his chest. "Do you want to see your new beam?"

She followed him out. He stopped short of the awning and knocked his knuckles against one of the windows on the sleeping porch. "This is a really cool area."

She placed her fingertips on the sill and looked in, her gaze trailing from the far wall down to the marble floor. She'd never seen it from this angle. "I'm planning to turn it into my studio. The one my gramps used was tiny, smaller than I remembered, and kind of hot. I think he chose it because it was right by the kitchen, and that's where my grandma spent most of her time."

He used his index fingernail to scrape at some old paint that littered one corner of the window. "Did she make lemon muffins?"

"Sometimes. But she didn't burn them."

"I'm sure they'll taste fine." With the strip of paint removed, Dalton used a shop towel to wipe his fingerprints from the spot.

Charity hid a grin. "Don't bother cleaning off your fingerprints." She pointed to the row of long, wide windows. "They're covered in salt and dust."

He leaned back. "So they are. What kind of studio are you turning this room into?"

"Pottery," she said.

"It'll be a great place to work. Lots of sunshine and the beach view."

She was just getting ready to tell him that whenever she was working, her gaze was so focused on the project, she could face a blank wall, but Dalton had already stepped away. He rounded the corner and pointed up to the roofline of the porch. "Here's your new beam."

Charity followed and craned her neck. She examined the work as if she had a clue what she was looking at. "Nice job. And don't worry about sweeping. I'll get it later. Should I write you a check? I've got some cash, too."

"Either is good. What about those muffins?" Dalton gathered up his few remaining tools and slipped them into spots on his belt. Though he was nonchalant about the way he lifted, dusted, and placed his work gear, she had the distinct feeling he was giving her time to answer.

"You can't be serious about wanting to try one. Did you see the smoke coming from the kitchen?" When he shrugged, she raised her hands in the air. "OK, but they'll be terrible." Shaking her head, Charity went back inside. Dalton followed.

"Your helper? Did he leave?" Charity asked as she poured two cups of coffee. Her hands were sweating because she was lousy at small talk, and her voice tended to crack on words.

"Yes. I would have introduced you, but he was in a hurry. Kid's ball game today."

She set the coffee on the long, wooden butcher block that doubled as a kitchen island.

Dalton had placed his tool belt on the gray-and-white marble floor as he'd entered. Now he lowered himself onto a padded leather bar stool. "Coffee smells good."

How could he smell anything over the charred muffin scent? "It's an Ethiopian dark roast." Charity took the plate of muffins from beside the stove and placed them on the table with a sigh.

"They don't look so bad."

The edges of the paper cups were burned, and the underside of each muffin was black. "The frosting is disguising what's underneath."

He snagged one and peeled away the paper. "You just have to know how to eat them." His fingers scored a line halfway up the muffin. He carefully peeled away the burned section and then showed Charity the bottom. "See, good as new."

She sat across from him and watched as he took a huge bite.

"Mmm." His eyes closed, and Charity swallowed. Lemon frosting clung to his upper lip, and when he opened his eyes to smile at her, she rose quickly and brought him a napkin.

"Do you burn a lot of your food? Is that why you don't mind the taste?" The words popped right out of her mouth like popcorn in a hot skillet.

He laughed and swiped the napkin across his mouth before taking another bite. "No," Dalton said around a mouthful of muffin. "But my wife did."

Divorced? Charity chewed her lip wondering if she should ask. Her eyes trailed down to the ring finger of his left hand. Wide gold band. No, not divorced. A certain sadness rested on his shoulders. "Your wife is . . ."

"Gone," he answered.

Dead was what he meant. He didn't need to say it for Charity to know. "I'm sorry." Though the two words were small, they needed to be said, because whatever sorrow Dalton still felt was as palpable in the room as the scent of scorched lemons. And sorrow was one thing Charity understood.

His eyes settled on her. Green as a stormy sea and lonely as the ocean at night. "Thank you, Charity."

The moment stretched, but the silence wasn't awkward. It was comfortable in the cool kitchen with the beams of sun splashing the windows and the warm, solid wood of the butcher block to lean on. And for some reason, the comfort of the kitchen made her want to talk. "When I was in college, one of my roommates was killed in an accident. This woman who'd gone back to school after raising her kids called me. My roommate and I both knew her from classes. She said, 'I'm not going to ask how you are or how you're coping.'"

A shadow of a frown crossed Dalton's face, but he leaned forward, his forearms pressing into the counter.

Charity took his interest as an invitation to continue. "She just said, 'Tell me about your roommate.' For about an hour, I talked on and on."

"It helped?" His words were barely a whisper over the hum of the refrigerator and the sounds of the ocean beyond the kitchen window.

Charity pulled her mug to her and cradled it. "I just talked. I mean, the woman hadn't really known her very well, but there was something so pure and profound in the request. I can't explain it. Yes, it helped."

Dalton's body language shifted. He'd been lucid, pliable, but when she spotted a tear glistening in the edge of his eye, he leaned back, stiffened, and glanced up at the ceiling for a few long seconds.

"Anyway," Charity said on a long exhale. "If you ever want to call me and tell me about her, I'd like to hear. I won't ask how you're doing or how you're coping."

"Thanks," he mumbled, but the word seemed as if it had to fight to get out of his throat.

Charity peeled the paper from a muffin and removed the bottom half, "Like this?"

A shard of a grin touched his mouth. "Now, take a big bite."

She closed her eyes and dove in, knowing she'd leave lemon frosting on her lips. Still warm from the oven, sweet, tart. "Hey, these aren't too bad."

He chuckled and offered her his dirty napkin. She waved it off and grabbed a fresh one from beside the sink.

"Are you staying here long term, Charity? Or just getting your grandfather's estate in order?"

It sounded so big. Estate. To her he was just Gramps, the pottery master, the teller of bedtime stories, the dancer who was light on his feet and quick with a laugh. "I've moved here. Permanently."

The green in his eyes darkened by a tiny margin. Maybe he was trying to figure her out. "You just up and moved?" And yet there was a thread of envy to his tone. "Did that make the people around you crazy?"

What did he mean? "No. I mean, I still have my apartment in New York—at least until the end of the year. It's all packed up, though. Full of boxes." She focused on her cup. "It wasn't hard to come here."

"Because this was your grandfather's place? It's really incredible, Charity. A mansion."

"A lot of work, too," she added. "Of course, I can cross beam replacement off my list of chores. Beyond that, I don't know where to begin."

"No problem there, the house will dictate what you do when."

"That sounds frightening."

"If you'd like, I can help you make a list of some of the things I think will need to be done. There are plenty of skilled workmen in the area. I know you've got a drawer full of them."

"OK, yeah. That would be helpful."

"And I'm for hire on some things."

She pointed at him. "Like beams?"

He nodded, the earlier tension gone from his body, replaced by the comfort of a common goal. "You've got some vines climbing the side of the house. They're going to need attention unless you're interested in an indoor garden sprouting through the eaves. That's something I can do."

"Great, you're hired. Anything else you'd like to take on?"

"Thought you'd never ask." Suddenly, without any warning whatsoever, he shifted from casual to serious. And excited. His eyes flashed with a new light as he dug a folded piece of paper out of his back pocket.

Charity leaned back a bit.

"You've got this . . ." He sprung from the chair and went to the wide back window, arms stretched from side to side as if trying to hug the universe. "Incredible tropical-inspired garden that is literally falling apart."

Charity rose and walked slowly toward him when he motioned for her.

"There're vines overtaking the perennials around the gazebo, and weeds are practically running the place. I mean, underneath all this mess is probably one of the most beautiful gardens on the island."

Charity chewed her bottom lip, remembering the garden her gram and gramps had created, tended, cared for. Loved. She'd sit in that garden and watch butterflies and honeybees, lie on her back and make puff animals out of the clouds, imagine pixies and the tinkling sound of their music.

Dalton was talking. She should listen, but her attention was lost to yesteryear and the faraway scents of fresh earth and gardenias.

"That magnolia tree is covered with bugs. But this is all repairable, Charity."

At the sound of her name, she tuned in to his words.

"I can resurrect this for you. I'm sure of it."

Resurrect the garden. It was another part of Gramps and another thing that could help her feel closer. A hammer pounded in her chest, thoughts and ideas and memories colliding with the fantasy of a grown-up Charity sitting outside, beneath the magnolia on the concrete bench or in the gazebo sipping coffee. Resurrect the garden. The more she thought about it, the more excited she became. She could tell him to get started right away. She didn't care what it cost. Resurrect the garden. Just as she was opening her mouth, he said the unthinkable.

"And that incredible weeping willow. I've never seen one so large. I can carve a perfect path to it and clean up all the brush around it, scrub down the rocks on the short ledge that frames it."

Ice shot down Charity's spine.

"Those branches have to be trimmed or they're going to start breaking off. I'm sure some of them are dragging on the ground."

She stepped away from him, cold and wet from a sudden sweat. "Stop." Her hand came up. It was trembling. To her surprise, Dalton stopped talking. Instead of arguing, he stood there, waiting for her to say something.

She pulled a calming breath, slowly lifted her other hand until they were both level, a perfect shield protecting her. From the look on his face, her hands were even more effective than one of Emily Rudd's handbags. Seconds ticked by. The clock on the far wall counted each one. After what felt like an eternity, she said, "I don't like the weeping tree."

A frown deepened the lines on Dalton's forehead. "Why?"

Charity closed her eyes. "I just don't." She hadn't realized she was shaking her head until strands of hair cascaded over her shoulders.

Dalton examined her with a new look, one of concern. "You just don't?"

This was the part where he'd tell her she was being childish. He'd say to stop acting like a spoiled little brat and act like a grown-up. Well, she'd heard that for as long as she could remember. She dropped her open hands and pressed them against her sides. "I just don't."

He glanced out over the garden. "OK."

She was ready for the fight. She'd been pushed and shoved her whole life, and this was her house and her garden. "I don't have to explain anything—"

He cut her off. "OK, we leave the willow, the brush, all of it past the rock edge. You got a dry erase marker?"

Her mouth was hanging open, and apparently, she was just supposed to skip the whole discussion about the willow tree—which of course was what she wanted—and not at all what she expected.

He snapped his fingers. "A dry erase marker?"

She pointed to a drawer behind them. He pulled it open, then returned to where she stood at the window.

"Look." He used the dry erase to section off the garden areas by drawing on her large kitchen window. Roses along the left side of the house, low flowering ground cover in the center. And to the right, where the massive weeping willow sat alone, like a sentry guarding a path to another dimension, he drew a thick square, then scribbled it in, blotting out the tree and its immediate surrounding area. Gone. Just like that. Gone, but she could still have her garden.

His voice softened, and she liked the sudden change. It was a low hum beside her as he named specific plants and flowers and shrubs, all the while drawing little curlicues and zigzags. "Charity, it would be an honor to work on this. Some of this flora is . . . well, things I've never actually *seen* growing. Cut plants and flowers, sure, but these are from various tropical regions all over the world, all growing here in harmony. It's a landscaper's dream."

A thought struck her, one she didn't like. "Is that why you came over here in the first place?"

"What? No. I couldn't even see it for all the tall weeds." He pushed the top on the marker with force. "If you don't believe me, come over to the cottage. At the angle it sits, I see the back of your house from my back patio. I will admit to counting the windows on the second floor and wondering how many bedrooms were up there. And I really like the way the sleeping porch is lit up at night. It glows. Your side porch is adjacent to my house, so of course, I see that."

Her hand up went up again. This time to stop his string of confessions. More, she did not need.

"I drew up some plans while Manuel and I took a break." He retrieved the folded paper from where he'd placed it on the table and showed her the idea, but not before folding back the top right edge, removing the willow from her view.

She took the paper and studied it. He'd drawn swirls for bushes, smaller ones to represent the roses in the rose garden; the concrete benches were drawn at haphazard angles, but he'd fully represented the nice spots to sit and enjoy the shade. "You're a landscaper?"

"Landscape architect. I swear I won't do any harm to the garden's integrity."

Her brows rose. "Harm to that mess? I think we're safe."

"So that's a yes." It was a question and an answer.

She consulted the page before her. It didn't speak, but from the corner of her eye, something flashed outside, causing her to look out on the garden. She tried to focus, but the sun bounced off the water beyond her yard and seared her eyes. That's when she remembered that sensation. From when she was a girl, when she'd scorch her eyeballs to catch one glimpse of the gossamer wings and hear their tinkling sounds. "Pixies," she whispered. When the scent of cinnamon entered her nose, she placed the paper flat on the counter. She took a deep breath and faced Dalton. "Yes. Do it. All of it. I don't even care if some plants have to be shipped from . . . wherever." She thought a moment. "All of it but the weeping tree."

"I'll get started tomorrow morning. Charity, if it's not too personal to say so, I think George Baxter would be really proud of you right now."

Charity's mind went to her gramps. He'd always been proud of her, even when she didn't deserve it. But this, yes, this would make him happy. Her heart was light, filled with excitement and a sensation she couldn't quite name. Maybe it was magic. Maybe it was hope.

∽๑

Harold Baxter clutched the suitcase between his aging fingers. Stopping at the edge of the driveway, he closed his eyes and prayed. He hadn't remembered the ride on the water taxi being so long. He was tired, already. When he started to sway, his eyes flew open to stabilize him. The letter pressed against his heart in the shirt pocket where he'd stored it. He itched to read it again, but his heart wouldn't let him. One shaky breath later, he took a step toward the front door, leaving everything else behind. His business, his life. Earlier this morning, the situation at Dancing on Air had seemed surreal, both unbelievable and a bitter betrayal. Now it hardly mattered. Oh, the difference one letter could make. He was urging his feet forward when he heard a voice.

"Hey, do you live in that big house?"

Harold had to refocus his attention to even be able to answer. Slowly, he turned to see a teenage girl standing behind him. Her feet were bare, her shorts, cut-offs. But it was her deep tan and long, sun-blonde hair that made her an unmistakable island inhabitant, not a visitor. "No, I . . ."

She tilted her head so that the breeze would push her hair behind her, out of her face, as if the wind were an extra set of her own personal hands. Bright-blue eyes waited for him to give an answer he didn't even possess.

"My brother owns the house."

The girl crossed her arms over her chest and nodded, and her gaze trailed to the small suitcase he carried. "Cool place."

He turned back to the dwelling. He had to agree with the girl. It was a cool place. Pushing both the past and the future aside, he turned to her, and his mouth opened. She was gone. He glanced down the road in both directions. *Gone.* He heaved a sigh and headed for the door. Maybe ghosts appeared in the form of teenage girls. With regret as his tailwind, Harold set his feet in motion, making the long trek to the door, a journey he should have made a long, long time ago.

⤬

Charity had enlisted Dalton's help to move the potter's wheel to the sleeping porch. She'd also brought the bag of Gramps's special ingredient, though she'd not had a request for any special orders, so it sat unused on the bookcase behind her. The garden and the ocean lay beyond the window and, true to his word, Dalton was spending each morning trimming her overgrown yard. Then he'd return to the Barlows' cottage and work there the rest of the day. He'd grabbed the water taxi today to head to the mainland and had even invited her along, but she'd declined the offer.

Just as she was refilling her mug of coffee, someone knocked on the door. She glanced at the wall clock. Too early to be Dalton. Maybe it was Emily Rudd. Charity had grudgingly agreed to go out with Emily and a couple of her friends who would be visiting the island soon. Though Emily hadn't referred to it as a double date, that was the impression Charity had gotten. Well, this would be her chance to bow out gracefully. Always better to do those things in person. She was just forming her rejection speech when she tugged the door open.

A sudden intake of air forced all the thoughts of Emily and double dates aside. The older man standing on her front porch was too familiar to be a complete stranger, yet too much a stranger to be someone she knew. He stared at a crumpled letter in his hands and when he looked up to her, her grandfather's eyes were looking back.

Air hissed from her lungs, and she grabbed the doorframe to steady the suddenly shifting room. Her fingers were cold against the wood, no blood reaching her extremities; it all seemed to be swirling around her heart and surging into her head.

His hand trembled as he reached out to her. "Please. Please tell me I'm not too late." His voice was low and graveled with concern, each word its own plea, as if life and death hung in the balance.

Charity's mouth was desert dry, words seemingly unable to form in her mind.

He lifted the letter as if it held every secret. "Please."

But when she still didn't answer, she watched the weight of all he carried rush over him. He seemed to be held together by glue and string, and suddenly it was all unraveling. Words poured out of him. "I got here as quickly as I could. But the letter sat in my mailbox for a week before . . . before . . ." His pleading blue eyes closed. His shoulders quaked, and there on the front porch of her circus house, the man broke into sobs.

When he swayed, Charity moved to place an arm around him. She slid the suitcase from him and set it on the porch floor. She didn't dare touch the letter in his other hand, for it seemed the catalyst for the splay of emotion. But this man seemed so *familiar*. She stood there with him as he mumbled words she couldn't decipher. He was taller than her, nearing six feet, but his shoulders held the loose skin and boniness of age, a man who'd once been broad and strong but had succumbed to the rigors of a long life, time taking its toll and gravity dragging his flesh.

He sniffed, and once he seemed to be slightly more stable, Charity patted his shoulder and moved out of his personal space. She stayed close though, lest he sway again. "I'm sorry." He rubbed at his watery eyes with the back of his hand. "It's just that I—" Finally, he said, "I'd like to speak to George. He's my brother."

CHAPTER 5

The Letter

Charity's knees weakened beneath her, eyes going wide. "Uncle Harold?" And that's when she realized she was unmistakably looking into the eyes of her gramps. Same almond shape, slightly turned up at the outer edges, same sparse lashes. Same shade of blue, pale like the sky in springtime and warm as sun-kissed berries.

He stared for a few long moments as the past played in his eyes. She could practically see him searching to find the child he'd known in the woman who stood before him. "Charity?"

She closed the distance, this time hugging him, clinging to his neck. Her eyes squeezed shut, and it almost—*almost*—felt as though it was her gramps hugging her back. It comforted her but at the same time caused an even deeper ache. A wail of a cry left her throat—it was a foreign sound, something that had clawed its way up from the deepest parts of her stomach, something filled with hunger and despair. No one—*no one*—but Uncle Harold could understand what she'd lost in losing her gramps.

She heard the crinkling sound of paper near her ear. It must be the letter, the thing that had brought him here. He shifted for a moment and must have shoved the page into a pocket because now he was stroking her hair, trying to soothe her. Charity pressed her cheek to his chest. Typically, she wasn't one to draw strength from the touch of another human being. Growing up in a house where her mom rarely touched her had caused her to stop needing that. But her gram and gramps had always been rich with the ability to show their love through touch, and right now, it was as if she'd die if she had to step away. But then a thought struck her. Uncle Harold had asked to speak to Gramps. That meant he didn't know. She pulled away from him because she'd have to tell Uncle Harold that his brother was dead. Charity opened her mouth, expecting words, but none came.

Harold squeezed his eyes shut, his brow creased with age lines creating deep crevices in his forehead. His mouth pressed into a straight line, and he shook his head back and forth. When his eyes opened, he said the saddest words Charity had ever heard. "I'm too late." The words left his mouth and gathered power as they fell, landing on the porch floor like bombs.

This was where Charity was supposed to confirm that Gramps was gone. But there was no strength left in her. The world around was hazy, her power stripped and lost in the moment. "He, uh, he—"

Harold placed a firm hand on her shoulder. "He's gone."

She nodded, fighting the tears again, and fighting the need to cling to a man she hadn't seen for twenty years. But as he lifted her chin to look her in the eye, Charity felt something else, too. Fresh as morning rain and cool as a conch shell, she felt a connection to her gramps that only Uncle Harold could bring. It was like having a little bit of Gramps back at the house. When her gaze landed on his suitcase, an overwhelming sensation hit her. He'd come to stay . . . at least for a short time. Hope unfurled in her stomach.

Realizing that George was gone, Harold suggested he should leave, but Charity insisted that he stay, at least for the night. She placed his suitcase on one of the beds in an upstairs room, and she left him to freshen up in the powder room downstairs. He couldn't escape, her mind teased, what with his suitcase here. For good measure, she turned off the light and closed the bedroom door. She'd refrain from saying in which room she'd placed his things.

Childish as it was, she'd lost her gramps quite suddenly, and she refused to lose her uncle in the same—or any—manner. He was here. And they had so, *so* much to talk about.

After making coffee and listening as the water ran in the powder room near the kitchen, Charity took two mugs from the cupboard. Her fingers glided over the smooth pottery—perfection, forged by Gramps. Her work was never so smooth, so exact. She was heavy-handed, at best. Not the clay-whisperer her gramps had been.

Uncle Harold met her in the kitchen and sat at the butcher-block island. Neither of them drank the coffee. "The old home place looks good, Charity, You've taken care of it."

She shook her head. "I've only been here a little over a week. Gramps was the one."

Harold's gaze dropped to the mug. "How long has he been gone?" The words caught in his throat, and Charity cleared hers as if that might help.

"A little over four weeks."

Harold shook his head, aging blue eyes meeting hers. "No. That can't be." His look was faraway, eyes darting back and forth over the crown molding anchoring the ceiling to the wall behind her. He brushed a hand over his face and withdrew the letter from his pants pocket.

Curiosity caused Charity to tip forward in an attempt to read the envelope. She couldn't from her distance.

Harold tapped the letter. "It's impossible, Charity. The letter only reached my mailbox a week ago, and the postdate is from a few days before that. I dug it out this morning."

"And you believe it's from Gramps?" Her hands tightened around the mug. "What's in the letter, Uncle Harold?"

Harold slid the envelope closer, a sad, protective motion to cling to what was already lost. "He wanted to reconcile."

Charity remembered hearing that there had been a feud between Gramps and Harold all those years ago. But a letter sent from her gramps after he'd passed? No, that was impossible. And surely Harold hadn't meant reconcile from the fight way back then. "How long has it been since you were here?"

He looked away, focusing his attention on the floor as if it were the only place he had a right to look. "Twenty years."

Gramps and Harold hadn't spoken for that long? What on earth had brought such a close relationship to that? Then again, she'd watched her mother quarrel with a friend, a neighbor, and dramatically say she'd never speak to the woman again. And she hadn't. It was as if she'd cut the woman away from the fabric of her existence. But Gramps wasn't like her mother. At least she didn't think so.

"What happened, Uncle Harold?"

He shook his head, stress playing against the wrinkles of his face, causing them to deepen. "I made a mistake, Charity. A terrible mistake, and George never forgave me for it. At least not until I got the letter." There was so much sorrow on his shoulders, Charity decided to put the pieces together on her own and not question him further. She recalled Harold being there when she was eleven. He had been going into business as a dance instructor, and she remembered her gramps giving him lots of advice about business and money.

"I didn't deserve forgiveness. It happened the year your grandma died. He . . . was never the same after that."

"So you spoke to him? But you two didn't reconcile?"

Harold shook his head. "I tried to speak to him, especially in the first few years. He wouldn't answer my calls at first; then he got where he'd answer, but I could hear it in his voice. My calling only hurt him more. About six years ago, I quit calling at all. Figured it was best."

She knew her gramps hadn't been the same after Gram died. He'd even stopped asking her to come visit for the summers. "He didn't talk much to me on the phone, either. It always seemed like a chore for him. Mom and I moved to New York, so it was more difficult to see Gramps. I missed him, but what I really missed was how he'd been before Gram died. And that made me feel guilty."

He patted her hand. "You were a child. But you always were one to carry more responsibility than you should. Your momma? She doing OK?"

"She's fine." Charity rolled her shoulders in an attempt to loosen the tight muscles. "Back then I'd hoped we'd move closer to Gramps, not farther away. Sometimes I wonder if she moved us to New York to get back at him."

Harold frowned. "Why would she do that?"

"She wanted him to turn all his finances over to her." The words tasted vile in her mouth, but she'd long ago stopped making excuses for her mother.

"What? Why would she do that?"

Charity shrugged. "She said Gramps was in shock, that he needed help. He refused to turn anything over to her, and we packed and left."

Harold reached over and patted Charity's hand. "Your momma isn't a bad person, she's just—"

Charity could see him searching for words to soften the cold truth. "Self-centered? Narcissistic? Out for No. 1?"

His head dipped. "It's not my place to say."

"It's OK, Harold. I know what she is. And I know—in her own way—she loved Gramps. She even loves me."

He smiled, the years of hard-learned lessons highlighting his wrinkles. "People can't give what they don't have. But your momma loves you, I'm sure of it."

"It's nice to know someone understands." A long exhale left Charity's mouth. "For a family who loves so deeply, we sure have a way of messing things up."

Harold chuckled. It was good to see him smile, to see his teeth rather than the worry and concern of a straight, colorless mouth. Like her gramps, his eyes twinkled when he grinned. An ache settled deep in her chest. Having Harold here was one of the best gifts she could have hoped for. It was also one of the most painful.

$\sim$

"So, you still don't know what's in the letter?" Dalton had dark dirt under his fingernails when he'd shown up at her house. He'd been as excited as a schoolboy with a get-out-early card. He'd rambled on and on about the plants he'd purchased, but Charity had split her time between thinking she really needed to brush up on her local flora and fauna and wondering if Harold was settling into his room or sneaking out. Her uncle had been exhausted after their conversation, and she'd told him to rest upstairs while she got something for dinner. But Dalton had arrived just as she was going to the market. It hadn't taken him more than five minutes to realize something was wrong.

For whatever reason she couldn't explain, she launched into the whole thing, even how good and strange it was to look at Harold and see glimpses of her gramps. Also, that he was carrying a mysterious letter presumably from her gramps.

She plopped onto a concrete bench in the backyard, where Dalton had placed his day's findings. Already, the garden was taking shape. She purposely sat so that she couldn't see the willow. "I have no idea what's in the letter, except that Gramps wanted to reconcile."

"Wow, and I thought my day had been strange."

Charity leaned back, resting her hands flat on the warm concrete. Dalton sat on the ground a few feet away, still examining the plants he'd acquired on the mainland. "What do you mean?"

He was elbow high in a bush speckled with tiny purple flowers when he stopped digging to look up at her. His eyes took on the purple hue, causing them to seem unearthly. They were beautiful eyes, she realized.

Dalton rubbed a hand over his forehead, leaving a swipe of rich, dark earth along his hairline. "I got a call from my brother-in-law. He wants to send me a package here. He had some things at his house that belonged to Melinda and Kissy."

Something in Charity's stomach dropped. She'd once rode the fastest elevator in New York and had been forewarned that from the top floor going down, it feels as if everything inside you is falling. She felt that now as she mouthed the word, "Kissy?"

Dalton paled. Slowly his gaze went to the shoreline that was far off but adjacent to where he sat on his knees huddled over a flowering bush and where she faced him, perched on a concrete bench. The breeze played in the long strands of greenery housing the small purple flowers. "Kissy was my daughter."

Charity's heart dropped. She suddenly hated the word *was*.

"She was with my wife when . . . when   "

The invisible punch to her stomach caused Charity to come off the bench. "I'm so sorry." Before she could stop herself, Charity was on her knees, face-to-face with the man who'd suffered more than anyone should, yet who chose to resurrect a neighbor's garden rather than wallow in his pain. "Dalton." She reached right over the bush and touched his shoulder. He was warm beneath his shirt, though his heart was likely a frozen clump of dead coral. "I'm so, so sorry." The thought swirled in her mind . . . losing not only one's soul mate but also one's child. Though she had no children of her own, she couldn't imagine anything hurting more than that. She dropped her hand from him and stared down at her fingers—such a pitiful excuse for a condolence. When she felt the onset of tears, she blinked rapidly, small purple flowers dancing on the greenery. She bent at the waist and sniffed. "I like these," she forced from a tight throat.

When her eyes met his, Dalton was smiling. It was faint, barely there, but a smile, no doubt. "They're fragrant."

She nodded, breathing deeply and letting that scent enter her body. "Then plant them where I can smell them as I sit in the garden." Floral sweetness mingled with all the other smells around them—the rich soil; the salty air, which always held the faint scent of fish; and Dalton. He was still looking at her, and for some, the moment might have seemed awkward, the two of them hovering over a bush and sniffing the world around them, but it wasn't awkward. It was right. In Charity's thirty-one years, she'd come to understand something. Some moments were golden; they were designed and orchestrated by an invisible hand, and they were meant to be more than moments. They were meant to be memories.

"You'll find them most fragrant in the morning," he whispered as if he understood her need to relish this span of time where he'd brought her flowers and inadvertently told her a precious secret, something she was sure he withheld from most strangers, that he'd said good-bye to his wife and child on the same day.

She knew she'd remember it always. How her heart shattered for Dalton. The touch of early-evening sun on her cheek, the feel of the thick grass around her, the streaks of sun in Dalton's hair, the fact that on a floor above them, her uncle rested. It was as if Gramps kept giving her gifts. First the house, then the garden—the place Dalton was beautifying layer by layer—and now her uncle Harold. Maybe Dalton was a gift, too. Someone who understood pain. Someone who understood loss and regret. When she'd first arrived at Baxter House, she'd felt like she was trying to capture a reflection. Gramps was gone. She saw him everywhere and yet nowhere. He'd become the echo at the end of a cistern, a sound that reverberated back, though its source was long past. Now she felt like each and every new day had the potential of offering a little more lightning in a bottle. Gramps really was everywhere. Maybe she'd finally learned to look for him. She pointed to the gazebo that sat near the center of the garden and offered a perfect view of the Gulf. "There."

Dalton followed her gaze.

Charity found herself smiling. "Right there is where I'll sit and have my morning coffee."

"Good, because that's exactly where I'd planned to put these." He went back to work, his hands digging into the dirt.

Charity returned to the concrete bench, satisfied to watch him. There was something calming about the way his fingertips roamed over the plants, touching, testing their soil, removing the dead flowers. She gasped when he ran a pocket knife around the inside of a black plastic container and lifted the entire plant, roots, dirt, and all out of the pot.

He stopped, the plant dangling in midair like the carnage from an ax murderer, bits of dirt—the plant's life source—dropping onto the ground. "This one is going beside the house. I've already got the spot ready."

She supposed she should close her mouth lest a seagull fly inside it. Was that how Gram had handled plants? She couldn't recall. It seemed violent from the man who so lovingly stroked the leaves and flower petals.

"By the house," he repeated, brows rising. "Is that OK?"

She nodded, closing her mouth. "Do you always just yank them out of the pot like that?"

He chuckled. "Pretty much. Sometimes you have to cut away some of the roots." With that, he showed her the bottom of the black container where stringy white roots clung to the pot.

She nodded. "OK. I'll leave you to it. I gotta run to the market and grab something for dinner." She watched as he walked to the back of the house.

He was just placing the plant in a hole beside the corner of the sleeping porch when he looked back at her. "Dinner?"

"Well, I'd planned on grilled cheese and strawberries."

He winced. "Not together, I hope."

"No, but when I was in town yesterday, the farmer's market had these beautiful fresh strawberries. They're half the size of my fist." Her mouth watered at the thought. "Anyway, I have company now, so . . ." Her shrug filled in the blanks.

"Listen." He placed the plant in the hole and returned to her while dusting the earth from his hands. "I caught some snapper yesterday. It's more than I can eat. Why don't I bring some over for you two?"

A bumblebee buzzed past the side of his head, causing Dalton to duck, swat in a halfhearted manner, then grin when the bee settled on a flower bud at his feet. Why his gesture defeated Charity's common sense, she couldn't say. But it had. And before she could think twice, the image of Dalton at her dinner table overwhelmed her better judgment. "Only if you'll join us."

He stilled. Eyes the color of ivy in the sunshine considered her. "I wouldn't want to impose."

Ah. He thought it was a pity offer. In light of their discussion about his wife and daughter, she figured he was used to disingenuous offers of meals. The fact saddened her to the core because he really was a nice man, and nice men shouldn't have to feel as though people only wanted them around for the purpose of making themselves feel better . . . like they'd done some gloriously charitable deed. She cocked a hip. "That's silly, Dalton."

Dalton held her gaze. "I'll just drop the fish off in about an hour."

But Charity wasn't ready to give up on him. "My gram had an award-winning recipe for grilled snapper. Most delicious snapper you've ever tasted. I swear, it'll ruin you."

He remained silent.

"Please come."

Dalton chewed the inside of his cheek, his hands firmly splayed on his hips. "OK. Shall I bring over some ears of corn for the grill as well?"

She nodded. "Three."

A muscle in his cheek twitched. "Three it is."

"And I promise not to burn anything." She tapped her index finger to her chin. "I mean I promise to *try* to not burn anything."

"See you in an hour." Dalton walked home. As soon as he closed his door, Charity spun from her spot and headed inside, praying her gram's recipe was somewhere in the kitchen.

Before she could tear apart the drawers on the hunt, there was a knock at the front door. She passed the hallway and gave the library a half glance. Maybe Gram had a recipe book on the shelf somewhere. Charity pulled the door open to find a roundish woman in a floral print dress and high heels. Her hair was piled on her head in a loose bun with strands of gray running in zigzags across it. A chubby hand reached up to wrangle the faded strawberry locks. Tangerine lips smiled, and when they did, Charity noticed that a swath of the orangey color had found its way to her two front teeth.

"Are you Charity Baxter?" A pumpkin-shaped face held eyes that seemed too small for the space. But they were kind eyes, dark in color, and if Charity wasn't mistaken, hopeful.

"Yes, ma'am."

"Perfect." The woman strode inside as if invited, and this caused Charity's warning bells to toll. "Can I . . . can I help you?"

The woman turned to face her. "I'd like to place an order." She leaned forward so close, Charity could smell the faint hint of failing perfume and sweat. "A special order. My name is Gloria Parker." Each word was spoken carefully. Deliberately.

When Charity didn't answer, the woman glanced around the foyer. "This is George Baxter's house?"

But she said it as if she already knew and was informing Charity of the fact. "Yes, ma'am."

"And you do pottery pieces. Just as he did?"

Well, no. In fact, her work wasn't nearly what his had been. "Yes. Pottery." That was all she could declare without feeling like a fraud.

"I was under the impression you'd continue his work."

Her gramps had done special orders on the island and even a few on the mainland for years. And yes, Charity wanted to, but she'd never expected her first client to show up without any solicitation.

"I'm interested in dinnerware." The woman folded her hands in front of her. "Something simple, not too ornate. A lovely neutral color. I was thinking taupe with a heavy glaze."

Dinnerware. Oh wow. This could be a fabulous way to launch her island pottery business. Would the woman want a setting for ten? Twelve? A full set? Including platters and salad bowls and perhaps even drinkware?

"You can do that, right?"

Charity realized she hadn't answered. "Yes. Yes, of course. What size setting were you looking for?"

The woman's thinly drawn brows dipped. "Not an entire setting. A plate."

All the fun of inventing a unique set of dishes evaporated. "A single plate?" She tried not to sound disappointed, but her voice betrayed her.

"Yes, dear. It's very important to me." The brows—like miniature chopsticks drawn carefully above her eyes—rose until the woman's face resembled a child's. Someone who was standing at the window of a candy store but wasn't strong enough to pull the door open and step inside. Her eyes went misty for a moment, and she stepped away from Charity to look out the front window where palm branches swayed in the breeze. The woman's car, some type of large white sedan, sat in the driveway. "I'd hoped you could help me."

There was a plea and a sadness in her tone. Also, the sound of a woman giving up. Charity moved closer to her. "Did you say, taupe?"

The woman turned. "Yes. But any neutral color will be fine. Or perhaps not a neutral. Something bright and colorful."

For someone who so desperately wanted a plate, the woman seemed far too agreeable. And in that instance, Charity felt the weight of her own situation. The idea of filling her gramps's shoes seemed as insurmountable a task as emptying the Colorado River with a drinking straw. Sweat broke out on her forehead. "You know, Gramps—George—left some inventory here. I'm sure I can find a beautiful plate—"

A meaty hand gripped Charity's forearm. "Oh no. That would never work. It has to be made for me."

Charity decided it was time to stop dancing around the crazy tree and just agree. "OK. I think taupe will be lovely. Not too ornate. I'll have it ready in about two weeks."

The woman's face lit up. "Wonderful. I can't thank you enough."

They exchanged information, and Charity watched her leave without bothering to give her a price. No need to, if the woman was expecting a work of Gramps's caliber, it was possible she wouldn't even want the plate after seeing it. Still, Charity would do her best. She'd pour her heart and soul into the plate as if it would be the only dinnerware used by the queen of England for the rest of her life. Gramps had taught her to do everything with excellence. She just wished her own level of excellence measured up to his.

∾੭

Harold had napped, showered, and changed into a nicer pair of pants and a button-down shirt, so Charity felt the need to change as well. Though she rarely dressed up, and never for dinner in her own house, she donned a pair of new jeans and a dark-pink, short-sleeved sweater. Around her neck, she placed a locket she'd found in her gram's jewelry box. Gramps had left it full of costume jewelry, and she suspected he'd known she'd one day treasure sifting through it. She left her shoes off. No sense in going too hog wild—as Gramps would call it.

"So, this young man of yours," Uncle Harold said as he entered the kitchen carrying the set of dishes Charity had discovered in a box marked Unclaimed order.

"He's not *my* young man." Her knife hovered over the strawberries she was trimming. "He's the neighbor who is rehabbing the garden. I hope it's OK that I invited him. Fresh snapper is hard to turn down."

"I'm glad you did. Good for both of us. Probably for him, too."

Charity couldn't imagine why her uncle thought that, but at least he wasn't upset. The truth was, they needed to get to know each other all over again, and Dalton seemed a good buffer. Harold poured himself a cup of coffee from the carafe on the counter. "Is he a full-time resident?"

"No." Charity placed the strawberry knife on the counter, where it left a small, red stain. "He lost his wife and child a year ago. He's fixing up the Barlows' little cottage."

The mug stopped halfway to Harold's mouth. "How awful. I can see why he'd need a friend."

Charity nodded. She felt strange about admitting Dalton's secrets so readily but thought it might make for an easier transition if the subject came up. One thing she already knew about Dalton Reynolds was that he hated the looks of first horror, then pity at the mention of his lost family.

She placed the bowl of freshly trimmed strawberries in the center of the table where their scent rose and beckoned. Her uncle's words rang in her thoughts. *I can see why he'd need a friend.* She liked the idea of being Dalton's friend. Funny how she'd been hoping to do better on the friend front and was really committed to attempting a relationship with Emily Rudd. And here, out of the blue and thanks to her gram and gramps and their irresistible garden, a friend had been dropped right in her lap.

"You ever hear strange noises in the house?" Harold asked as he started chopping the ingredients for the salad Charity placed before him.

"Sometimes I think I hear footsteps and music. It's far off, barely there. In fact, I think it's most likely my imagination."

Harold grinned. "Good imagination you've got there, girl. I think I heard your music, too."

"I smell tobacco now and then. And cinnamon. Like Gramps is standing right behind me, and his scent is drifting over my shoulder and into my nose."

Harold lowered his head. "Guess he'll always be here."

Charity could see the top of Harold's white head and the bottom of his face, where his chin quivered. She reached across the counter and placed her hand on his forearm where springy hairs tickled her palm. "And now you're here. I'm so glad you came."

His eyes came up to meet her, saying so much more than words could have. He patted her hand. "Thanks, Lil' Bit. It was worth the world to get here."

And had he given the world to get here? The look on his face suggested so. "Is everything OK at home, Uncle Harold?"

"Ah, nothing for you to worry about."

He was a bad liar. Must run in the family. "Can you tell me?"

His mouth stretched into a straight line. "Nope. I'm here to spend time with you. Not talk about crusty ol' business." He pointed a crooked finger at her and closed one eye. "Now, not another word about it, girlie. OK?"

She gave him a salute. "Yes, sir."

Dalton returned to her house smelling like a man who'd showered and readied for a date. His fingernails were clean, she noted, and resisted the urge to tuck her own in the pockets of her cooking apron as she let him in the back door. Because mercy was shining on her,

Charity had found Gram's recipe box, dusty and sitting like a sentry on a shelf in the library. It was filled with recipes, all written in Gram's own hand.

Recipes she'd try, each and every one.

Dalton held out to her a bouquet of wild flowers wrapped in a wet paper towel. She suddenly hoped he hadn't misinterpreted her invitation. But of course he wouldn't have, because his heart was far away, lost in another life with the family he'd had to say good-bye to.

"These are beautiful. You shouldn't have." They smelled like the floral warehouse she used to sneak into in New York. It was on her way home and something about the rows and rows of fresh blooms always made her feel warm inside despite the cold in the chilled warehouse space. She'd step through the long plastic strips and be transplanted from crowded and greasy city streets to a dimension where fairies and pixies rested on gerbera daisies while plotting their next adventure. Lilies, ferns, bursting pots of baby's breath, all in neat rows, filling the world with color and scent.

"I thought you'd enjoy them. But don't thank me. They're all from your backyard. You could say I stole them."

She used a deep green vase for the flowers and filled it with tap water.

Dalton watched her. "Did you make the vase?"

She moved the strawberries and placed the flowers as the table centerpiece. "No. Gramps. His mark is on the bottom. Pretty much everything you see here—potterywise—was made by him."

Dalton nodded.

"I'm just getting started." She felt the need to explain. She'd done a few pieces but hadn't fired any yet, so nothing was finished. "I have a special order."

At that moment, Harold reappeared in the kitchen. "A special order. You don't say?" His eyes twinkled, but he looked away from her quickly.

"Uncle Harold, Gramps left me a bag with a note inside. It says to use one scoop on each special order. Do you ever remember seeing a bag like that when you were here?"

Harold's long hands dusted the thighs of his pants. If Charity wasn't wrong, he looked a tad uncomfortable. "I can't say as I do."

He turned from her toward Dalton. "So, you must be the gardener."

Dalton laughed. "Yes, sir. You must be Uncle Harold."

Harold gave him a mock glare. "Harold to you. We're not that friendly yet."

The two men shook hands and launched into a conversation about fish, lures, the weather, and boats. Charity watched in awe. Men. It seemed so easy for them. Why couldn't she have had a lovely, nonstrangling conversation with Emily Rudd? *Because you're hopelessly awkward and don't know anything about the things women discuss.* In fact, she really didn't know *what* women discussed. Recipes, maybe? No, that seemed like a horrible cliché. Restaurants? She took the baked potatoes from the oven, burning her finger on the foil. "Ouch, ouch, ouch." As soon as she said it, she wished she hadn't.

Both men stopped their conversation and came over to her, Harold grabbing her hand and inspecting the damage. "Hurts like a son of a gun, doesn't it?"

Dalton hovered over her right shoulder, and the kitchen suddenly felt too hot. "Be right back," he announced.

"You subscribe to that theory about rubbing a burn in your hair?" Harold asked.

She had to laugh. Her gram had told her that from the time she was tiny. "No, I do not."

"Me neither," Harold admitted with a half smile. "I think it makes you feel stupid and you forget about the sting."

Dalton came back inside with a snippet of gooey plant matter. Without invitation, he took her hand in his and rubbed the clear jelly oozing from the amputated plant piece on the meaty part of her hand. Instantly, the burn cooled. "Aloe?"

He looked over at her and winked. "Hello."

She rolled her eyes and withdrew her hand. "Not hello. Aloe?"

"Cures what ails you." Dalton took her spot at the potatoes and placed them on a plate, then carried them into the dining room, where the table was lit with an overhead chandelier that looked like it held flickering candles.

Charity watched him. He made himself at home so easily. She wouldn't want it any other way. If she invited someone to dinner, she wanted them to feel like family. But it was so effortless for him. She could learn from him.

He arranged the potatoes by the stack of plates, then turned to face her. The soft glow caught in his eyes as if those sparks were meant to bounce off him. As if the light had been awaiting his arrival. He likely altered everything he touched. Dalton squared his shoulders and gave her a smile. This fit him, helping someone prepare the table for dinner. Her heart squeezed as she wondered how many meals he'd sat at alone in the last year. Still, there was a granite quality to his posture, and what else but granite could survive the storm he'd lived through?

Harold stepped to the table. "Taters are gonna get cold."

Charity giggled. Taters. She hadn't heard them called that in a long time.

They helped themselves to grilled snapper, potatoes, and crusty bread she'd planned to make into croutons. They ate the strawberries right out of the large bowl, using their fingers and letting the juice have its way. They forgot about the salad. It sat wilting in a salad bowl on the kitchen counter.

Dalton leaned back from the table. "That was incredible."

"Gram's recipe. She really did win awards with it."

Dalton drained his water glass. "There's only one problem. You promised not to burn anything."

She sucked in a breath; the fish had been perfect.

Dalton grinned and pointed to her hand.

"Oh. Yeah, that." The last thing she wanted was all the attention on her again. She turned to her uncle. "So Harold, let's talk about Gramps's bag I found." Charity wasn't done with her questions. Harold knew something—of that she was certain.

He pushed his plate away and smiled.

"I'm supposed to put one scoop of the special ingredient into the special order per Gramps's instructions."

"Good. That's good."

"Any thoughts as to what's inside that sack?"

He folded his hands over his stomach and leaned back in the dining room chair. "Nope."

She opened her mouth to continue the interrogation, but Harold yawned. "Listen, kids, I'm not tired, but I don't want to help clean up this mess, so, I'm going to force a couple of yawns and wave good-bye while I head up to bed."

Same old Uncle Harold. Honest to a fault. Charity rose and caught him by the arm. "I'm so happy you're here. I hope . . ." But what to say? Fact was, she wanted Harold to stay. As long as he wanted. "I, um, hope you sleep well."

He patted her cheek, his soft, blue eyes watery and saying all the things she wanted to hear. "Good night, Lil' Bit."

Her heart practically sang as she watched him walk up the stairs. Lil' Bit. The nickname could have come straight from Gramps's mouth.

Dalton helped clean up from dinner, but it was quick work, so he poured them both a mug of coffee and suggested they sit in the garden. The night was quiet with soft, rolling waves of indigo ink pressing toward the shoreline. "It means the world to you that he's here, doesn't it?"

Charity had no poker face. She was as easy to read as a pop-up book. "I already feel like I'm losing him, and I don't even know when he's leaving."

Dalton sipped his coffee, then pointed to a spot far out in the water. "See the light of that buoy?"

Charity squinted. "Yes, but only when the waves are just right."

"Whether you see it or not, it's always there. Don't be afraid of losing your uncle, Charity. He's here. And even if he wasn't, he's—" Dalton took a tiny step closer to her and placed the tips of his fingers over her heart. "He's *here*." He tapped her breastbone.

"Thank you," she whispered. The gentle rush of waves created a rhythmic lullaby. A half-moon shone above, dropping silvery light on the ocean, giving it form. With the rise and fall of the soft waves, it looked like the shoreline was breathing. "I used to believe this island was alive."

Dalton stepped into the gazebo and sat down. He moved to one side, leaving her room to sit beside him. "It is alive."

"No, I mean, like a living, breathing organism with a mind and a soul and plans and dreams. I thought it was magic. A place where fairies from another realm came to live and play."

Dalton remained still, but out of the corner of her eye, she could see him dwelling on her words, as if testing them to see how much validity lay in them.

Charity sighed. "I used to believe in magic." Without wanting them to, her eyes drifted to the willow tree. "But then I learned that magic can also be destructive. And one day, I stopped believing in any of it."

Tension rose off him, and Charity could only wonder why. Maybe she'd said too much. Maybe their friendship didn't have a strong enough foundation for confessions about magic.

But then he spoke, and his words were soft. "You still believe in magic."

She tilted her head to look at him. He struck a handsome profile in the reflection of light from a silver moon and beams on the water.

"You believe in magic, or you couldn't create vases and pots out of a hunk of mud." He didn't look at her when he said it but rather kept his eyes focused on the water's edge. He shrugged. "I believe in magic, too."

Dalton rubbed his hands on his thighs and exhaled a long breath, the way someone does after admitting something he wishes he hadn't. He felt exposed now. It was almost palpable. In a quick movement, he was on his feet. "Good night, Lil' Bit."

She couldn't help but chuckle. "Please. That was a nickname from childhood, one I'd hoped would be left there."

"That's the thing about when our past catches up to us. We don't get to choose what stays behind and what follows us." Grass crunched beneath his feet as he slowly walked away. He disappeared beyond the edge of her house. His cabin was dark, devoid of any light, and as Charity sat in her garden alone, she realized that the past has destructive power. Incredible power. But there was one thing, one tiny thing that kept that power from ruining everything. Hope was its foil. As long as there was hope, there was promise. And promise was enough to light all the stars in the sky.

CHAPTER 6

Epic-Fail Date Night

Uncle Harold left the following morning—much to Charity's sorrow—but when Charity begged for his return, he promised to come back as quickly as he could. He'd claimed he had business to take care of in Birmingham, but Charity had the feeling that things for him—like her—were swiftly changing, a churning whirlpool one could only hope to navigate and not drown in.

In the days that passed, she made her first special order. It felt great to have completed the commission, but the plate looked ordinary. Lovely but ordinary. She wasn't sure what she'd expected. Just . . . *something*. She'd also watched Dalton work in the garden, and though she'd admitted too much—about believing in magic and all—she hadn't run him off. Their friendship continued to blossom . . . like the garden.

After completing the plate, she received five more special orders. All as weird as the first, and she'd taken care to add one scoop of Gramps's special ingredient to each. There was a local businessman who wanted a name plaque for his office desk, a young man who wanted two wine goblets—he'd told her he was planning to propose to his girlfriend. Wine goblets made from pottery. Not crystal, not etched glass. Pottery. Maybe they were outdoor enthusiasts. Hiking and backwoods and all. She had no clue, but like the others, he was thrilled when she agreed.

She was firing the last few pieces when she glanced at the wall clock: six fifteen. Charity was already running late when there was a light knock on the front door. If she hadn't been passing through the living room, she'd never have heard it. She threw her hip into tugging the door open to find a tiny wisp of a lady on the other side. Charity was instantly drawn to the kind, gray eyes. A strong wind rushed at them from around the side of the front porch, and Charity wondered whether the small woman could withstand its push. She had two thin sticks for legs and a plain yellow housedress dusting her knees. Her feet were clad in Oxford shoes and spread just enough to steady her. Between the folds of her sagging skin lay the unmistakable marks of a life well lived. Wrinkles turned her face into an interesting roadmap of trials and triumphs, and Charity liked this woman instantly.

"Are you Miss Baxter?" The woman's voice was bumpy at best but also filled with emotion and gentle as a butterfly's flutter.

"Yes, I am."

A handbag hung from the woman's arm and swung like a pendulum as she spoke. "Oh, lovely. I live just down the way. I've been looking forward to meeting you." Thin brows rose as she peered past Charity to look inside the house.

Where had Charity's manners gone? She motioned behind her. "Please come in."

The woman licked her thin lips as if contemplating the offer. "No, no. I don't want to impose." She leaned forward and whispered, "Are you George's granddaughter?"

"Yes, ma'am."

A single nod of the woman's head had Charity wondering what cryptic message might follow. The eyes that had been soft were now intense. "I'm Mrs. Gorben." She cast a glance behind her as if there were eavesdroppers listening from the bushes.

"Nice to meet you. I'm Charity."

Her hands came together in front of her. "Of course you are. And Charity, you're continuing your grandfather's work? Correct? You take"—she leaned forward again—"special orders."

Charity bit back a smile and thought about how any onlookers might just think she was dealing drugs, the way people seemed to be so cautiously nonchalant, which never worked. As soon as someone begins glancing over his shoulder to see who's listening, it tends to draw attention rather than avert onlookers.

"Yes. What are you needing? I've just finished the orders I had, and I'm looking for something to sink my teeth into."

This seemed to please the woman, evidenced by a smile that made all the lines on her face curve. "A candy dish." But after she said it, her voice drifted off, along with her gaze. She looped both hands through the handbag and held it tightly. "I'm . . ." The next words seemed to slip away as if she couldn't remember what she was going to say.

"Ma'am?"

Mrs. Gorben blinked. "I'm lonely, dear." It was a matter-of-fact statement delivered in a matter-of-fact tone. One Charity might even doubt had it not been for the lost, emotion-filled look in her eyes just before. "The house is too quiet since my husband became bedridden. I'd like a candy dish. A big one, the kind people use on Halloween when there's lots of laughter and lots of children. Is that too much to ask?"

Charity wasn't sure what she was asking. A candy dish, sure, but what did that have to do with being lonely?

The woman winked. "I like to sit on my porch in the early afternoon and watch the children walk past from school. Right on the bus route, I am. Close to your house, in fact. Last week, one of the moms sat with me while it rained. I had a little dish of candy. Do you think it's OK to give pieces of candy to strangers?"

Charity's heart was heavy with emotion. "I think it's very nice." She set her mind to creating a beautiful candy dish worthy of the sweet lady before her. "I can have it for you in two weeks."

"Oh, that long?"

"I'm sorry. But it takes time to create, dry, and trim the piece, then glazing and firing. But I'll rush it as much as I can. How would that be?"

Thin cold fingers snagged Charity's hands. For an old lady, she had one tight grip. "Wonderful. I'll return in two weeks' time."

Charity watched her leave, then ran upstairs and changed clothes quickly. She smeared on a bit of makeup because she'd be sitting all evening staring at pretty Emily Rudd and their two dates. Dates. The idea shouldn't make her want to dry heave, but it did.

And a blind date was even worse. She pulled the light summer sweater out of the White House Black Market bag and dug deeper for the shoes. Though Charity had lived most of her life in New York, she'd never been doted on by a store stylist the way she'd been a couple of days ago when visiting the small mall on the island. Brandon—"call me Bran"—had led her through the store grabbing items and telling her she had a great vibe. Some $631 later—and that was with a significant coupon Bran produced from the pocket of his linen pants—she had a complete outfit that she loved. And that fit her vibe. Brandon gave her his business card and told her he loved being a personal shopper and to call him any time she needed threads.

She bolted down the stairs two at a time when she heard another knock. She paused at the bottom, her hand on the bear's head. Back door. For some reason that made her smile. Only Dalton used the back door. "Come on in," she hollered, her black sandals dangling from her hand. In her other hand was an empty leather handbag, smaller than the one Emily toted around, but stylish and fitting her vibe and most certainly a shield Wonder Woman would envy.

Dalton was wiping the sweat from his forehead and cheeks with a shop towel. He'd been toiling intensely the last several hours in her garden and now smelled like man and work. She stopped just inside the kitchen doorway when Dalton's bright-blue eyes found her over the towel. He didn't speak, but there was a look in his eyes that inched across the marble to her.

Suddenly, the room was hot. Tendrils of fear rose and bloomed on her face. "What?" She croaked the word because if Dalton—someone she knew—was staring at her like she was some kind of alien, her date might actually run in the other direction. And here, she'd thought Bran had done her a favor.

Dalton closed his mouth, swallowed, and let his eyes trail down to her bare feet. "I've never seen you cleaned up like this."

She tried to focus on his words. He didn't sound appalled. She bent and set the shoes on the cool marble floor where she'd be able to shimmy her feet into them. "I'm going out with Emily Rudd."

Dalton's brows rose slowly, a grin toying at his mouth.

She huffed. "It's a double date thing. Something she set up." Charity chewed on a fingernail. "I'm not great with *social*."

Dalton stepped closer. "Well, don't ruin your manicure." When he got to her, he took her hand in his and studied her fingers.

She still had clay under the nails.

He led her to the sink, turned on the water, tested the temperature, and then started scrubbing. The room was a tight ball of oxygen-deprived space. Her gaze left the sink and all that cool water where Dalton's hands rubbed over hers. In the reflection of the window, she could see the concentration on his face. He reached for the soap, and the muscle in his upper arm stretched and then bulged as he grabbed the nail brush sitting nearby. She hardly ever used the thing, but Dalton handled it like a pro and scrubbed at the ends of her fingertips.

"Am I rubbing too hard?" His voice was a whisper against the long strands of hair that separated his face from hers. She tried to focus on him in the window but couldn't quite make him out in the fading light.

"No." Water ran in cool rivulets over her hands and wrists causing everything to feel fresh, alive.

Dalton's eyes looked different inside the house. Often, he'd show her plants and shrubs he was introducing to the garden, and there in the sunlight, his eyes were a green starburst. Here in the kitchen, with the overhead sink light playing off the colors, his eyes were softer. Warm. Trustworthy. And some of the sadness that swam in them was gone. If not gone, at least well hidden.

"Do you think you're ever going to tell me about your wife?" Charity didn't know why it was suddenly important to know, but it was.

He blinked but didn't look away. "Maybe."

She could live with that.

He shut off the water. "You think you can have a good time tonight? Now that your date won't have to wonder what's creeping under your fingernails?"

She half smiled. "Maybe."

Dalton handed her the kitchen towel. "You look nice, Charity. Take a deep breath and have fun."

She pulled a long breath but didn't let it out until tiny black spots danced in her vision.

He nodded toward the backyard. "I finished the right section of the garden. I'm going to replace some pavers, and there are a few tools I left in your sleeping porch. I didn't feel like hauling them back to the shed, and it might rain later. Can I stash a couple more things in there tonight?"

She shrugged. "Sure." Charity had gotten used to Dalton coming and going through the sleeping porch and the kitchen. He never messed with her pottery stuff and always made coffee, so he was golden. "I'll just leave the doors unlocked when I leave."

A frown creased his brow. "Don't do that."

She dropped the towel on the counter. "It's no big deal. Half the time, I forget to lock the sleeping porch anyway."

He rubbed a hand over his face. "I've been meaning to talk to you about that."

There was a look in his eye. Something she didn't like. Something territorial. She knew that tone. It was one used by people who wanted to control. But this was Dalton, and though she didn't know him well, controlling and overbearing didn't ring true. And yet . . .

"You've been meaning to talk to me about my sleeping porch being unlocked?" Her voice was strained.

"I figured it probably wasn't too big a deal since there's a lock on the kitchen door, but I've actually found that one unlocked before, too. Twice, in fact."

Apprehension crawled over her flesh, causing her new sweater to itch. "And this concerns you, why?" An unsettled feeling took root in her gut, causing her to gauge his every movement as he took a small step closer. The kitchen light caught in his eyes, and she saw something there that she hadn't expected. Honest concern.

"Charity, you live alone." He motioned around him. "In this massive house."

This had been her childhood summer home, and of all the things it was, scary wasn't in the mix. She felt perfectly comfortable here. "Yes, on an island where zero crime happens."

The muscle in his jaw flexed. "Crime happens everywhere."

For some insane reason, that sentence, and the look accompanying it, ended her discomfort with what she'd thought was nosiness. "You're not very trusting, are you?" she said.

"I know people can do bad things. Maybe you're too trusting."

She tried to smile. "Probably. I let you in."

This caught him off guard, and he chuckled. "My point exactly."

Charity went to the kitchen drawer and found the spare keys. She removed one from the ring and tried it on the kitchen door; then she held it out to Dalton. "Here. The sleeping porch will be unlocked, but in case you need anything in the kitchen. I'll start being better about locking up." She didn't even know why she wanted to do this for him, but she did. It was kind of sweet that he worried about her.

⁓

Dalton felt a sudden rush of relief. He took the key from Charity but failed to mention that he'd seen someone skulking around her house a few nights before. It was after her Uncle Harold had left and so late at night that Dalton had first thought his eyes were playing tricks on him.

But the shadow had run from the beach area to the far side of the house and disappeared. He'd run out front to see if the person was in the road, but there was nothing. The next day he'd checked for tracks. Again, nothing. Sometimes he had to wonder if his imagination was drawing him down a rabbit hole.

He watched Charity leave when the attorney, Emily Rudd, pulled up in her sports car. Some red exotic that probably cost more than the cottage he was living in. The night was a quiet one, complete with a Hemingway he finished as the night dragged on. Beyond his small window, the surf hummed. When he heard a car door and the unmistakable sound of Charity's laughter, Dalton peered out the front window. There in the drive was a car he didn't recognize. It was midnight, and he knew he should just go to bed. He hadn't been staying up to make sure Charity got home OK. No. When he heard her laugh again and focused on the silhouette of her and a guy just stepping into the pool of light from the porch lamp, Dalton's hair rose on end. Had Charity just stumbled?

He grabbed his shirt and pulled it on as he slipped out his back door. He went straight through the sleeping porch and unlocked the kitchen. He was at the front door just as Charity was muscling the mahogany giant open.

Dalton smiled. "Hey there." He smelled alcohol.

Charity's glassy eyes focused. "Dalton?"

His gaze trailed to the man with his arm draped over Charity's shoulder. The guy glowered at Dalton.

In response, Dalton thrust a hand out in front of him. It fully blocked they guy's entrance. "I'm Dalton."

Reluctantly, the man shook his hand.

Charity leaned on the doorjamb. "Dalton is my—"

"Brother," he finished for her and gave such a wide smile, the guy leaned back a little.

Charity giggled.

"Been drinking, sis?" There was a tightness to his tone.

She brushed her hair from her face. "I might have had a couple of glasses of wine."

"Or a couple of bottles?" Dalton took her arm and directed his next words to the date who—by the look on his face—had already kissed his plans for the rest of the night good-bye. "I can take her from here. Very nice of you to see her home safely." There was only a moment of challenge. Men were good at sizing up their competition, and this kind of man was good at cowering when he knew he was bested. Dalton didn't often rely on his intimidation power, but when necessary, he had no problem bringing out the grizzly bear in his personality. And if the dude in the dark suit thought he was taking one step into Charity's house, he'd be searching for his teeth between the porch boards. "Good night."

One last glance of challenge, and the rodent crawled back into his hole. He was halfway to the driveway before hollering back at her. "I'll call you."

Charity waved, but he was scurrying to his car. She turned to Dalton. "I'm not much of a drinker." She tossed an arm over his shoulder.

"Your posture would suggest otherwise."

"I was nervous." She used a stage whisper to tell him this, even though he was less than a heartbeat from her. He could smell wine on her breath. It mingled with something sweet. A scent he couldn't place but liked.

"Let's get you some coffee." He started to head into the kitchen, but she stopped in the dining room, deadweight coming to an abrupt halt. "Did Uncle Harold tell you how we used to dance here in the dining room? That's why the table is over there." Her hand flopped toward the table as if he needed it pointed out. "Gram and Gramps loved to dance. Uncle Harold taught them." Her shoulders began to sway, and though Dalton didn't like seeing her in this state—eyes glassy, thoughts undoubtedly foggy—he also knew that sometimes a mind could more easily trek down memory road with a bit of liquid lubrication. Charity's eyes misted. "I miss my gram and gramps. Is that silly? For a grown woman?"

"No." He understood. He missed Melinda and Kissy, and sometimes it wasn't just the thought of them, it was a scent, a feeling, a sound he missed most of all. He'd pass a playground on the way home from work, and he'd hear the laugh of a small girl who sounded like his daughter, and he'd scan the crowd, searching. But she was never there.

Charity planted both hands flat on the table. "Did you ever want to just be little again?"

He wanted to just stop aching. Wanted to quiet the demons. He touched her shoulder. "Little was probably simpler. Do I ever want to go back to a time that was simpler?" He hadn't meant for the tremor to pass through his hand and to her shoulder, but it did. "Yeah. Every day I want that."

Charity turned to face him. "Dalton?"

His nose tingled because there was something so honest in the look she was giving him, so pure, he'd be forced to tell her whatever she asked. Her honesty demanded it. "Does it ever get any easier?"

His throat closed.

"Does the grief ever let up?"

Tears tried to spring to his eyes, but he'd gotten good at swallowing them, drowning the emotion. He'd done it for a year. But the peculiar woman before him frowned. She saw through him, and she obviously didn't like how he'd already answered her honesty with a slap of deceit. Because behind that swallow and that closed throat, he was hiding. So he did the only thing he could do. He pulled a deep breath, let it hiss from his lips and let the first tear come. It filled his eye, then trickled onto his cheek. There, it trailed over his face and jaw.

Charity said nothing, but she watched the tear as it slid down and down until it could keep its hold on his chin no longer. It landed on the floor below them.

Another followed. And a third. And just the few tears felt strangely cleansing. They stood toe-to-toe in the dining room that used to double as a dance floor back when Charity was little, and love and laughter filled her life. She was grieving, too, he realized, maybe as much as he was. So he didn't brush the tears away as they filled his eyes and fell. His breathing was slow, his pulse normal, but his tears were full, and he wasn't ashamed to cry them.

Two streams ran the length of his face, the tears finding an easier and easier path as they dropped one by one. There was no sound in the room save for their breathing. Inhales and exhales. And something about it was sweet. Though he tasted despair, he also tasted something new. Something fresh and tinged with hope. He'd mourned. For over a year he'd mourned. But now he was getting the chance to grieve. The two were different. One was a sorrow for all that was lost. The other was an understanding that life had to go on.

Several minutes passed. Finally, Charity smiled. Dalton smiled back, his cheeks cracking with so much salt water dried on them. She swayed, and he said, "You better get to bed."

She yawned. "I am sleepy."

When the wine on her breath hit him again, he remembered how tipsy she was. "I'll lock the front door."

"Just like a big brother." She moved to the banister and rested her hand on the bear's head. "Everything's a little blurry."

He glanced up at the tall round staircase above her. "I'll probably regret this, but I'll walk you up."

"OK." She threw her arm over his shoulder again and hung on. "But don't wake up the ghost."

He stopped midstep. "What ghost?"

"Ssshhh. He lives in the attic. Sometimes I think I hear him walking around and sometimes I hear music. Uncle Harold heard it, too, so stop looking at me like I'm bonkers."

His heartbeat tried to increase, but he stilled it. People always talked about ghosts in their attics and footfalls and music. Normal, right? Common. Still, the hair on the back of his neck prickled, and he made a decision to check out the attic at first opportunity.

He'd never been upstairs, and the French doors leading to the master suite were as solid as two wooden walls. He deposited Charity inside and turned to leave as she made her way across the floor, only twice zigzagging. He heard her yell at him from the en suite bathroom. "Don't leave, Dalton, 'K?"

Almost escaped. He closed his eyes and shook his head. When he heard water running, then the unmistakable sound of something crashing to the floor, he turned but opted not to go running to her rescue. "You OK?"

"I knocked some stuff over while brushing my teeth. My mouth tasted like vinegar. I spilled water on my new pants."

He sat down on the corner of the bed. When she came out, he stood and faced her, then quickly spun around away from her. She was wearing a long T-shirt, and below it were only legs.

"I have on shorts," she said, a half laugh in her voice.

Well, that was a relief. How had he signed up for babysitter of inebriated next-door neighbor?

She made her way to her bed and pulled back the covers. Before she got in, she faced Dalton. "Will you stay with me for a little while?"

Cold shot down his spine, causing every excuse he could gather to swirl into his head. They fought for position, and he could easily give her thirty reasons why he couldn't—wouldn't—stay with her for even a few moments longer.

When he didn't answer, she sighed. "It's OK. I shouldn't have asked." Her gaze went to the second set of French doors that overlooked the dark ocean beyond. "I've spent most all my life alone to one degree or another. Have you ever seen those people who seem to thrive on human touch? I've never understood that. And at the same time, I've always envied it. When I was little, I'd hold my own hand crossing the street because I knew my mom wouldn't."

A small piece of Dalton's heart broke for her. A young woman willing to risk herself to feel. He could take a lesson. Life had always shown him love. His parents, then Melinda and Kissy. And here he was closing off emotion when Charity was searching for it, hoping to find and even understand it, a woman who'd maybe only been shown love by her grandparents, and that was only for the first eleven years of her life.

He didn't remember lifting his hand to stroke her hair, but there it was, fingers threading through the strands. Soft, silken. It was delicate, like her. Delicate but still strong. "I'd love to stay for a while." The words had no choice but to leave his mouth.

She seemed to drink them in. When she slipped under the covers, he caught a glimpse of hot-pink shorts covering her bottom. Dalton looked away until she was throat-high in blankets. She'd scooted over, making room for him. His feet were already bare, so he stretched out on the bed on top of the covers. She didn't seem to notice. Or mind, as she turned to face him, tucking her hands against her cheek.

It made her look angelic, with her big, dark eyes and long, dark hair splayed across the white pillowcase. He should say something.

She beat him to it. "I'm not a very good potter. But I thought that coming here, using Gramps's wheel and tools and kiln, I thought maybe I'd be better."

"Are you?"

She blinked. "I think I really am. I've had six special orders, and when Mrs. Parker picked up her plate, she was thrilled. It really was pretty, Dalton. Beautiful, in fact."

Her words were soft brushes of air against his cheeks. He needed to not concentrate on that feeling, so much like angels' wings. "That's great, Charity. What else are you working on?"

"A desk placard, a set of wine goblets—"

"Wine goblets? Good Lord, I hope you don't feel the need to test them out."

She giggled. "I really don't drink."

"That's what all the lushes say." When her face pinched into a frown, he placed a hand on her shoulder. It was there or the waist, and his hands didn't need to be that low on her body. "I'm teasing you, OK?"

"I was nervous. When I'm nervous, I don't eat."

A bit of her hair rubbed against the skin on his throat, and that sensation was one he didn't need, so he drew an index finger along her hairline and brushed the strands over her shoulder. "So, you hadn't eaten since lunch?"

"Yesterday."

He frowned.

Charity shrugged one shoulder causing the blanket between them to tug. "When I'm working, I lose track of time."

"You can't go without eating, Charity. It's not healthy."

"And it makes me loopy drunk after two or three glasses of merlot."

Her eyes were getting heavy; he could tell from the languid way they closed and opened. "I'll do better about eating," she said on an exhale. "And I'll lock my doors. Geez, you really are like a big brother."

Right now, not as much as he'd prefer. "Turn over," he commanded, and for a moment her eyes sprung open, but she soon obeyed without any question. She scooted around, bottom wiggling and getting comfortable on the bed, and once she was, he gently looped an arm over her shoulder and, with dogged determination, pulled himself alongside her so that the only thing between them was clothing and blankets.

It was a few seconds before she released the air in her lungs. She must have sucked most of it out of the room because she exhaled and exhaled and exhaled, every last bit of tension leaving her muscles with the motion. "Dalton," she whispered. "Will you talk to me?"

Of course he would. What else would two people do while stretched out on a bed? He ran his hand along her hairline again, hoping to remember the feel of it tomorrow. Because come tomorrow, he'd never ever be stroking it again. "My wife's name was Melinda, and we met in high school. She was a cheerleader, and I'd been on the football team since Mighty Mites. Her hair was the color of sunshine, and I swear she had the moon and stars wrapped up inside her soul. For me, it was love at first sight. She was new to the school, and I tripped over a helmet looking at her across the field. She laughed at me. But she also came running over to see if I was OK. Her dad was a banker, and she was an only child. She loved skiing and had always wanted to go to Europe. We were planning to on our fifteenth anniversary. That gave us time to save up. We wanted to spend a month there, have her folks meet us for the last two weeks and bring Kissy."

Dalton stroked her hair again and talked on. Even after he knew Charity was soundly asleep, he went on talking about Melinda. No more tears came. He just talked—everything about her—from her favorite pizza to her irrational fear of house spiders. It helped, the hollow place in his heart filling with memories rather than grief. It felt as though he'd righted a wrong. He hadn't talked about her enough since she'd died. All the people back home just wanted to know about the death—and he'd finally shut down. Just giving pat answers that didn't even always align with the questions. He'd given something back to Melinda tonight. Something she deserved.

He'd thank Charity for that tomorrow. But not until he scolded her about being too trusting with strangers.

Charity woke with a jackhammer in her head and a smile on her face. She sat up, smelling bacon and fresh coffee. Forcing her mind to clear, she leaned up to a seated position, eyes raking in the room as if she'd never seen it before.

Pieces of the night fell together. Dalton. Here. Beside her and now downstairs in her kitchen making her breakfast. She bolted from the bed and rushed down the steps refusing to regret what had happened. Something about it seemed right.

She found him in her kitchen, humming as he cooked.

"I bet you're hungry," he said, glancing behind him as if he'd known she was standing there, though she hadn't made a sound.

Charity dropped onto the nearest bar stool. Suddenly, her words were gone.

Dalton faced her and put his hands on his hips. "Don't worry. Nothing happened. Lucky for you I was here, because all that regret you're feeling right now would have been well founded if that poor excuse for a date had hung around."

Charity chewed her fingernail. She hated to admit it, but the guy had kept shoving glasses of wine in her direction. Not that she was without fault. He hadn't poured them down her throat.

"Can we just forget about the whole night?"

Something sparked in Dalton's eyes, as if her request had pricked his feelings. Then she remembered. He'd talked about his wife, Melinda. His voice had carried Charity from this world to a dream world with words about her. It had been beautiful. It had been raw. A frozen moment in time when he'd been able to let go of all those emotions that kept him from just talking about her. What a rare moment for both of them.

He returned his attention to the scrambled eggs.

"Dalton, I'm really glad you were here with me."

This time, he didn't turn around. "Me, too."

With his back to her, Charity took a moment to really look at him. He was tan from hours in the sun. He knew his way around a spatula and wielded it with finesse. He didn't deserve the sadness life had dealt him.

And she didn't deserve a friend like him.

⁂

After a few weeks of Saturday morning breakfast with Dalton, Charity wondered if her next-door neighbor had ulterior motives. Maybe he didn't just enjoy her company on lazy Saturdays when work could wait, and the morning sun on the gulf beckoned. After her epic-fail date night, Dalton had been popping over bright and early on Saturdays. Only Saturdays, and he usually arrived with all the makings of a great breakfast. As far as ulterior motives went, she figured he was making sure she got at least one decent meal a week . . . given her propensity for grabbing little bites of this and that, rather than cooking full meals. But in a short amount of time, Uncle Harold would be back, and she'd be cooking meals again. He'd planned on only being gone a week, but that had stretched to two, then three.

As they ate, she'd told Dalton all about the sweet old lady and the candy dish she'd picked up the week before. "She lives across the street at the end of the block." Charity scraped the last of her eggs into a small pile and scooped it up with her fork. "I hadn't noticed where she lived until yesterday when I was out front, and I saw the school bus go by. I watched it and was thinking about her and how excited she was to get the dish, and when the bus pulled away from its stop, I noticed several parents gathered on one porch."

"Her house?" Dalton looked up from his plate. He grabbed another biscuit—homemade by him the night before—and spread butter on the two halves.

Charity nodded. "Her house." She shook her head no when he offered her half of the biscuit.

"I guess she's not so lonely now, huh? When was the last time you went to town?"

"Uh, what's the date today?"

His brows rose. "If you have to ask to know, you've been cooped up too long. Today, we're going to town."

She shrugged her agreement. She liked going downtown. It was the perfect combination of an island paradise and a small-town main street. Cobblestones and lampposts. Rocking chairs in front of a marine store and brightly colored beach umbrellas for sale at the hair salon.

Just as they were planning to leave, the phone rang. Charity turned to face the offender on the kitchen wall. It was her mother. She knew without having to answer, and though relics like this one didn't have personal ringtones, there was a distinct frustration vibrating through the line and into the room. She lifted the receiver cautiously. "Hello?"

"Charity." Her mother's voice was as curt as the obnoxious ring had been.

"Hello, Mom. How are you?"

"Really? That's how you want to play this?" A heavy exhale—worthy of Broadway—shuddered through the phone line. "I'm fine, Charity. And how are you?"

"Good." *Boundaries,* Charity reminded herself. Where Ellen Marie Baxter was concerned, there had to be boundaries. Otherwise, her mother would steamroll right over her.

"Now that the pleasantries are out of the way, perhaps you can explain why your pottery shop is closed?"

That's why her mom had called. Not to check on her, not to see if she was doing OK. Charity choked back the hurt that tried to lodge in her throat, though she knew it shouldn't. She'd only spoken to her mother once since Gramps had died. He hadn't wanted a funeral. "I'm sorry. I should have called you."

"Yes. You should have. I used up one of my last favors at the newspaper to get your little shop some much-needed publicity, and what do you do?"

Charity closed her eyes.

"Veronica called me. She'd been planning to do a nice piece about the shop and had carved out an *hour* to spend with you. And you show your gratitude by closing the doors and not even bothering to let me know."

So that's what this was *really* about. A favor at the newspaper office. Her mother's embarrassment over not knowing her daughter had closed her business. "I'm sorry. It's just that after I heard about Gramps—"

"Oh please, Charity. Don't play the grieving granddaughter card. You hadn't even seen him in three years."

Charity bit into her cheek and counted to three silently. Yes, the words stabbed like daggers, but that was partly because her mother was right. When Charity saw Dalton making his way to the back door, she covered the receiver with the palm of her hand. "Please stay. I'll only be a minute." She knew that to be true because no matter how angry her mother was, she never kept Charity on the phone for more than a few minutes.

He nodded but turned away to give her privacy.

"Who are you talking to? When are you coming home?"

Home? She'd already started to think of this as home.

"Are you listening to me, Charity Monroe? When are you returning to New York?"

How to answer that? She still had her apartment. But with the shop closing, she had no business there. Her business was here. Not the New

York set, but the Mrs. Gorbens who needed candy dishes and the Mrs. Parkers who needed taupe plates. Her business was special orders and the people who wanted them. Her spine straightened. "I'm not coming back, Mom. I'm going to live here. For good. I love the island, and I've already started doing some business here."

Laughter filled the phone line. "Live *there*. You won't last six months. You're New York, Charity. Not tiny Florida island."

Across the room, she caught Dalton's eye. He was smiling. It gave her strength. "In fact, I think you're wrong, *You're* New York, Mom Always were. But me? Not as much. I always loved the island and this house."

But then her mother said the unthinkable. "Really, Charity? What about the willow tree? Do you remember what you told me about it? You said you never wanted to see it again. Is it there? Are you trimming the branches?"

She must have gone pale because Dalton—face awash with concern—had moved to stand at her side. He placed a hand at the small of her back, eyes studying her every movement.

Charity found her strength in his touch. "I'm hanging up now, Mom. It doesn't mean I don't love you, I just need to go. I have plans. I love you. But I'm staying on the island. Good-bye."

The silence in the room echoed as if trying to scrub away the stain of her mother's words. Dalton's hand moved ever so gently back and forth over the small of her back. "We can go to town another day," he whispered.

She tilted her head back. "No way. I want ice cream and to visit the farmer's market. I want to walk the marina and maybe buy some fresh fish for dinner. I want lunch at an outdoor bistro."

Dalton's chin dipped. "You OK?"

She thought a moment before answering. With most people, a static "Yes, I'm fine," would do. But not with Dalton. Charity exhaled.

"She can be such a difficult person. I'm not naïve. I know what she's capable of."

Dalton stayed silent. His only encouragement to continue was the light press of his palm to her back.

"And that's the problem, Dalton. I *know* what she's *capable* of. Then there are these glorious little glimpses of goodness that give me hope for her."

"That's not a problem, Charity. You're a good daughter."

She dropped her gaze. "I'm a fool. But I'm just not ready to give up on her. She's my mom. And until Harold showed up, she was all the family I had left."

Dalton stepped away from her, a smile appearing on his face. "Let me get this straight. Marina, lunch, farmer's market. Whatever the lady wants . . ."

They left, with the sun shining down on them as soon as they stepped from the door. Charity chose not to think about the willow swaying in the salty breeze out back. If no one tends it, no one can be hurt by it, she told herself over and over again. She needed the constant reminder because deep in her mind a tiny voice whispered that all the tree was and all it was capable of doing would soon wreck her world again.

CHAPTER 7

The Ghost

If someone could take a snow globe filled with tiny miniature pieces of a quaint small town and add sand and boats, palm trees and bait stores, and then shake the dickens out of the thing and let all the pieces land where they chose, well, that would be Gaslamp Island's downtown district.

A flat-roofed Florida house converted to a chiropractic practice next door to the marine salvage store. The ice cream shop beside Bessie's Bait and Tackle. The hub of downtown was the general store that sat adjacent to Founders Hall, where dark, rich wood was visible from the floor-to-ceiling windows. The hall was the gathering place for all things Gaslamp Island.

Charity was glad Dalton had suggested walking. It wasn't more than six blocks from home, and she'd used the time to let the remnants of her conversation with her mother roll off her in waves. Side by side, they headed to the long strip of downtown. At the far end—and just past the bright-white tents marking the farmer's market—the horizon and the Gulf ran in a perpendicular line as if suggesting each person pause, take in the view, then hit every shop in town and spend, spend, spend.

When they reached the green awning–covered sidewalk, a white brochure was shoved into Charity's hand. She read the words, *Save the Hall*, then glanced up to see who'd given her the page. It took a moment to realize who the woman was. If it hadn't been for the tangerine lips, Charity wouldn't have known her. "Mrs. Parker?" It was the taupe plate lady. Her first special order.

"Charity, dear. Goodness, I was so busy with my task, I didn't realize it was you."

Charity oomphed when the woman grabbed her by the shoulders and drew her into a bone-crushing hug. Papers were mashed between the two.

The gray threads were gone from Mrs. Parker's hair, and the strands had been cut into a stylish bob that accentuated her small eyes. Mrs. Parker touched her locks. "You like the new 'do? Nancy down at Studio Gaslamp did it. She's a marvel."

Charity shoved the paper at Dalton. "*You're* a marvel, Mrs. Parker." The woman looked forty pounds lighter and fifteen years younger. How was that possible?

Mrs. Parker placed a hand on her hip and wiggled back and forth. "Thank you, dear. I feel great. Sassy and sexy enough to keep the fishermen on their toes." Her gaze trailed to Dalton. She thrust out a hand.

Dalton extended his as well, but once they'd made contact, Mrs. Parker drew him into the same type of lung-squeezing hug. "You must be Dalton Reynolds. We haven't been formally introduced. I'm Gloria Parker, but these days folks call me Glorious." As she released him, she laughed. He joined her.

Charity remained stunned.

Glorious Parker—seeming satisfied with her dramatic introduction—frowned as she turned her attention back to the crumpled papers in her hand. "We have a problem. A serious, disastrous problem." Her brows tilted into a frown, but her smile and general joyfulness couldn't quite be contained. Though she was undoubtedly giving it her best. "It's the hall."

Dalton and Charity remained silent as Glorious Gloria's hand fell like a block of concrete onto Charity's shoulder. "There are structural issues, and if we can't raise the money quickly, we'll have to find a new venue for the Founders' Day Ball. It's in September, you know." The frown disappeared at the mention of the party.

Dalton withdrew his wallet and pulled out some cash. He held it out to Gloria, who took it and tucked it inside the *V* in her shirt. "Good job, young man."

But he'd looked away, lest his gaze unwillingly trail to the open throat where money rested between a bra strap and flesh.

When Gloria was called away, Charity turned to Dalton. A high-pink hue brightened his cheekbones. "Are you blushing?"

"Aren't you? She took that money and tucked it in her bra."

Charity giggled. "I saw that. You know there's a store out on the beach, and they have a sign saying they no longer accept sock or bra money."

He winced. "So what was with the look of shock on your face when you first saw her?"

Charity gazed down the street where Gloria Parker had already found new victims. "She looks completely different. She's lost a ton of weight. I'd wonder if maybe she was sick if she didn't seem so—"

"Vibrant?"

Charity nodded. "Yes. Vibrant. And thinner."

"Well, it's been a few weeks since you've seen her, right?"

"Not long enough to lose that much weight."

Dalton thrust his hands in his jeans pockets. "I don't know about that. I heard about a woman who lost two hundred pounds in just a few hours."

Charity rolled her eyes. "OK, I'll bite. How she'd do that?"

"She divorced her husband."

Charity laughed as a fresh breeze grabbed her hair and tossed it in multiple directions.

"Now, where to, first?" Dalton asked.

Her brow furrowed in concentration as she took in the area.

"Not a hard question, you know?"

It's not that Charity didn't know her mind; on the contrary, she knew exactly what she wanted to do. It was just that when anyone else was involved, she always let them choose. "What do you think? Lunch or shop or farmer's market?"

His gaze was flat on her. "I think I told you to pick."

And why not? She could pick. She always chose things when she was alone. But she wasn't alone. "Farmer's market, then down to the marina and the pier, then lunch." Without asking what he thought of the idea, she turned on her heel and headed to the end of the street, where the farmer's market was set up, anchored by white tents and homemade signs.

They passed Aldo's General Store—which was mostly an old timey convenience store with a few rows of groceries. It was a bustle of business today as Aldo held packages for locals who shopped the farmer's market. A woman with a box struggled with the front door to the store, and Dalton slipped around Charity to help her.

"Thank you," she said, smiling.

Charity looked beyond her. Inside the store, lined up against the wall were multiple boxes, each marked with a name written in marine-blue Sharpie. "We better hurry, or everything will be gone from the farmer's market. It's nice that Aldo keeps people's purchases here."

Dalton rubbed his chin. "Yes. From what I hear, it came from the days when everyone gathered downtown on Saturdays."

Charity glanced around her at the steady stream of locals and tourists—easily distinguished by their attire—milling about the town.

No one in a hurry. No one rushing to leave. "Not much has changed, I'd say."

Dalton nodded. "True. It was a different time, then. Folks dressed up to go to town. It was an occasion."

She eyed him. "You know a lot about it."

He nodded. "Read a couple books about the island's history. I read a lot."

"So that's how you spend your time when you're not stealing flowers from my garden and sitting on the rock ledge looking at the water."

He stopped and turned to face her. "I only stole flowers once, and that doesn't count because they were for you. But what do you mean about sitting on the ledge?"

She tilted her head to look at him. "The ledge out near the willow. I've seen you out there. Late at night. At least three times."

Dalton placed a hand on her elbow. "Charity, I've never sat out there."

Her mind drifted back to the last time—only a few nights ago—when she'd been working late out on the sleeping porch, and she looked up to see Dalton's silhouette—she'd thought it was Dalton, walking from the opposite side of the willow and sitting down on the rock ledge to look out at the water.

His hand squeezed a little tighter. "Charity, are you locking your doors at night?"

"Yes. I am." And with the edge in his voice, it seemed important to be doing just that.

"What about your ghost? Any more noises?"

"Footfalls, but they seem so far away. Like I'm imagining it. And music, still the music, but it's soft, faint . . ." She shook her head.

"Noises carry on the water, but unless you're leaving your windows open, I doubt that could be the source. Whatever it is, I don't like it."

She didn't mind the sounds. They weren't intrusive; they were far off and almost comforting. It was as if her gramps was in an upstairs room and just as Charity lifted her head, he'd come down the stairs and kiss her cheek.

"I'll be more diligent about knowing what's going on around the house at night," he said.

She could argue, but what she knew of Dalton was, he was stubborn. So why put forth the effort to disagree? He'd do it whether she wanted him to or not. "Oh! Mangos," she said and grabbed him by the hand to lead him to the first booth at the farmer's market.

∞

Dalton had to admit he enjoyed watching Charity rummage through items at the farmer's market. First, they'd only needed a small bag, then a grocery sack, then a full-on reinforced box that would wait for them at Aldo's while they watched commercial fishing boats and ate a late lunch. When she was at home, she seemed to sometimes forget about the tropical paradise around them, her head down, coaxing a hunk of clay into a beautiful vase or pot or bowl.

"Hey, I thought that guy was going to offer to give me his entire mango supply in exchange," Dalton said, baiting her. Charity was curious by nature, and she'd undoubtedly nibble on the proverbial carrot he'd just dangled in front of her. She was having a good day. He was giving it to her. That was the problem. Dalton had become a bit too preoccupied with Charity. And though he knew it was good to branch out from the small hole he was wallowing in, he needed to be cautious. He wasn't match material. He wasn't date material. He was—and would for the foreseeable future remain—emotionally unavailable. Best scenario? Find a match for Charity so they could remain uncomplicated friends. That opportunity presented itself when he'd returned to the mango booth while Charity looked at sunglasses and handmade jewelry. "Charity, did you hear me?"

She was inspecting a shark's tooth necklace at one of the last booths by practically holding it to her nose. "These are amazing. And what guy? The mango guy? In exchange for what?" *Carrot successfully delivered.*

"For you. Did you not notice he was flirting?"

She scrunched her nose and studied Dalton for a few seconds over the shark's tooth. "He wasn't flirting." She returned to inspecting the shark's tooth again.

"I bet you money he was."

"You can't bet. All your money is being saturated with sweat inside Gloria's blouse."

He winced but quickly shook off the memory of Glorious Gloria and her blouse. "Would it be so horrible if he was?"

She eyed him again. "Was what?" She'd already moved on from the conversation.

He cast a glance heavenward. "Flirting. I'll bet you a snapper dinner he wants to go out with you."

She placed the shark's tooth on the counter where she'd found it and faced Dalton. "You're hard to get a read on, Reynolds. First, you're all worried about me going out with the wrong kind of man." She poked him in the chest. "Not that I need a babysitter. Now you're hooking me up with a produce guy so you can get a few extra mangos and a free snapper dinner?"

He chuckled. "His name's Red. He's a good guy. I've known him since I've been here, and he likes to help out at the Barlows'. And he likes you."

Charity cast a suspicious glance behind her to the mango man on the first row. He looked down when she made eye contact. "He's watching us."

Dalton shrugged. "I told him I'd do what I could."

This time when she poked Dalton in the chest, it was hard enough to hurt. "Who made you Cupid? And what kind of big brother tries to set up his little sister on a date? Sick!"

A full out laugh came from Dalton's mouth. Across the lot, Red perked up. "You're like the little sister I never wanted." He mock-frowned. "Did I say that wrong? I meant always. Like the little sister I *always* wanted."

Something in the air changed. Charity's look became serious. "What about you, Dalton?"

His laughter stopped. Throat went dry.

The breeze caught Charity's hair. "You think you'll ever let me set you up on a date?" Her gaze dropped to his wedding band.

He'd speak if his throat wasn't filled with cotton. *With her*, was what she meant. In another world, they'd have been a good match. But not in this world. Not now. That kind of love had died with Melinda. "No, Charity, I don't think so."

Her chin quivered only slightly, and he knew she was regretting the words, unspecific as they'd been—the flash of hurt was evident.

⁓

Just move on. Charity shouldn't have said anything, but it seemed like an opportunity she didn't want to miss. Dalton was a grieving widower; she got that. But he was also a man with many years ahead of him and a lot to offer. To someone. Obviously not to her. She'd meant for the suggestion to sound like a general one, even if her heart knew differently. Unfortunately, Dalton had seen through her as soon as the words left her mouth. Aggravation tickled her scalp, so she sank her hands into her hairline and scrubbed the irritation away.

She cast a look behind her, this time considering Red as a potential date. He wasn't a bad-looking guy. Nice blue eyes, hair cut short, he'd made a couple of jokes while they'd been standing there, and though Charity couldn't remember them, she'd been entertained. She'd seen Dalton go back over after they'd purchased mangos, but it hadn't occurred to her to wonder why.

Dalton had become more of a friend than she'd ever imagined having, though working at socializing had been on her priority list when she came to the island. She also had Emily Rudd, but the sharp attorney hadn't been in contact much since the epic-fail date. At the same time, being set up by Dalton just felt weird, even though he was her friend. Her *best friend*. How had that happened? Well, since her list of close friends was small—microscopic, even—it had happened pretty easily. "Why such an interest in my love life?"

His face split into a smile. "You're too young and pretty to spend all your nights home alone."

She tipped a shoulder. "I'm not alone. I have my ghost. And what was that first part? Something about pretty?"

The sun caught the green in his eyes, making that kaleidoscope of colors she so enjoyed. "You're pretty. Pretty strange, pretty obnoxious. Shall I go on?"

"Nope. All I heard was pretty." She chewed her lip. "He's a good guy, you say?"

Dalton nodded.

"I guess I could meet him for coffee."

"Coffee? No wine so you can get slobbering drunk and—"

She placed her entire hand over his mouth. "Coffee."

"Great, you owe me one snapper dinner," he said around her fingers.

"What? How do you figure that?"

He gave a thumbs up to Red. "We made a bet."

She shook her head. "No, *you* made a bet; *I'm* making a date. Now, take me to the Ice House for lunch, or suffer my wrath."

They walked the distance from downtown to the Ice House. Back in the day when Gaslamp Island had been more of a working island, the Ice House provided ice for the fisherman. Resting on stilts, its two-story wooden structure overlooked the town on one side and the gulf on the other. Charity hadn't eaten there, but as they climbed the outside staircase to the hostess desk, she already knew she was going to love it.

The breeze on the stairs was powerful—much stronger than in town where the buildings and cars created a buffer.

They chose a spot outside after crossing through the clapboard-walled restaurant decorated with what looked like a hundred years of fishing gear and memorabilia. "Look," Dalton said, drawing her attention to the line of fishing boats crossing the gulf and angling to come into the marina where WAKE ZONE signs slowed the traffic. "Some of the commercial fisherman are coming in."

She angled her plastic patio chair to see the gulf. They ordered crab cakes because the server assured them they were the best in the state and pointed out a local award on the wall as proof. But Charity was fairly certain she'd eaten at three restaurants touting the best crab cakes in Florida while she'd driven three quarters of the length of the state on the way to the island.

They were just getting ready to order dessert when Gloria came bursting through the patio door. The commotion drew the attention of half the guests seated on the wooden patio; the others continued on with their meals unfazed. Behind Gloria stood a short pixie of a woman, and if Charity didn't know better, she'd swear it was Emily Rudd aged by thirty years.

"Charity, Dalton, this is Jeanna McDouglas-Rudd." Gloria leaned all the way to Charity's ear and whispered, "She's one of those feminist ladies who uses her maiden name and married name. Hyphenated. She's Emily's mama."

Charity bit back a smile. Jeanna McDouglas-Rudd was every bit the professional Emily was. Same short hair—hers was a bit longer and flattering to her pretty but aging face. Her skin was porcelain, and Charity could only wonder what magic kept it that way in the harsh Florida sun.

The two women shook hands. "Charity, I don't mean to interrupt your lunch date, but I have a favor to ask."

Dalton leaned back and grinned. "Oh, this isn't a date. She's drinking iced tea. On dates she drinks coffee." Under his breath, he uttered,

"Or wine." It was only for Charity's ears, but the little quiet announcement made her cheeks burn as if the whole restaurant had heard him.

She shot daggers at him and when she felt satisfied that he was pin-cushioned, she gave her full attention to Jeanna and Gloria. "What can I do for you?"

Jeanna dragged a chair over, and Gloria followed her lead and dragged one, too. They both sat down. "First, let me say that I am so thrilled you're continuing George's work. He was . . ." Sharp silvery eyes narrowed and, like a politician, she was choosing her words carefully. Charity could only imagine why. Was this the buttering-up treatment before sliding the turkey into the oven? Had she done something wrong already? The words coming from Jeanna's mouth were heavy with something. Good, bad, or otherwise.

"What I'm trying to say, Charity, is your grandfather was an important part of our community. We're all very sad he's gone."

In the reflection of those steely gray eyes, Charity saw honesty.

Jeanna swallowed hard. "We miss him."

For reasons unknown, the kind words about her gramps made Charity a little choked up. "Thank you," she said.

Jeanna flicked her hair and patted Charity's hand, chin rising and warring against the emotions she'd just shared. Back to business. "I'd like to ask you to consider hosting the Founders' Day Ball."

First, Charity's mind completely rejected the words. But as they settled in, tiny black spots of fear appeared before Charity's eyes. She couldn't host a ball. Cannonballs didn't float, sparrows didn't lift cement blocks, and Charity Baxter didn't host formal events.

Jeanna continued, unshaken. "I'd love to have it at Baxter House."

Charity's mouth turned to cotton. Sure, she'd heard of the ball, but it was never held in the summer, so all she'd gotten was pictures and a thousand stories from Gram and Gramps. It was a September event, and sadly, she had always returned to her mother at the end of August.

"You know William Baxter was the founder of the ball. He used it as an excuse to get high-powered friends with deep pockets to come this far south. We owe this island's entire community to him—the fact that we have a library, a medical center, a town square. All thanks to Baxter. The man who also built your house." She'd added that last line for good measure—to remind Charity of her connection to their founder.

Charity needed to say something because all eyes were on her. "Um, Mrs. McDouglas-Rudd—"

A crimson manicure waved in the air. "Please. Call me Jeanna."

"Jeanna, I know that my grandparents were incredible hosts. They loved parties and dancing, but I'm . . ." Awkward, socially backward, so many choices. Which one to fill in the blank?

"We wouldn't expect much from you, Charity. Just a willingness to open your home. The ladies of the league will do all the work." Jeanna folded her hands and placed them over her knee. And waited, a perfect smile set against her porcelain skin.

Charity was going to faint. Die, then vomit, then faint. She couldn't host a ball. She could barely host a blind date, and only then when Dalton scrubbed her fingernails for her. Dalton. She glanced across the table to find him focused on her. No suggestion in his eyes, no nod of approval, just listening, just being there. Still, it helped.

Her greatest dream had been to come here and assimilate into the community, to really feel a part, but if she ruined the ball—which could easily happen—she'd be a pariah.

Jeanna split her glances between Charity and Dalton. "Just think about it. There's a chance we can raise the funds and get workmen on the hall so that it's complete in time. Please, keep the idea in the back of your mind."

The hall. That was her way out. They were raising money, and Charity had money. She still didn't know exactly how much, but she could plan to meet Emily right away to discuss a sizable contribution . . .

sizable enough, in fact, to guarantee the work's completion. If, of course, Charity could afford that. "I'll think about it."

Jeanna and Gloria rose and disappeared through the patio door.

Far below, the water lapped hungrily at the beach. Movement of the boats in the harbor caused a scurry of troubled waves that sent layers of seaweed onto the shore and left them in zigzag patterns to bake in the sun, scattered over the sand. Far out, the water was silent. Solid. Never wavering, only rising and falling with the tides, flexing and releasing with the boats and wind. Symbiotic. An entity that was part of a greater whole, able to cooperate, to reciprocate with its peers. She needed to learn the art of synergy. Her whole existence had been swallowed up by first trying to please the few people around her—her mother, mainly—then by trying to fill the void left when one realizes that no amount of good intention can change another person's heart. People are people. Sometimes, they let you down. In fact, they often did.

Dalton shooed at a seabird that had landed on the weathered railing near their table. It was illegal to feed the seabirds. They became horrible nuisances, even biting fingers when unsuspecting tourists thought it fun to feed them. The feathered intruder landed again, this time hopping a bit closer. Dalton glanced at the tables around him, then pulled a tiny corner of bread from his plate and dropped it on the floor. He used his foot to scoot it through the railing and the bird dove when it saw it fall.

Charity had to smile. And then there were people like Dalton. Those who surprised you in the most glorious ways. He could coax a smile, fix a beam, and refurbish a garden. He did it all with no expectation of payback. Those kinds of people were builders; they built friendships and relationships and built people up in the process. She needed more people like that. Even more important, she was determined to be one.

Just as she made that assessment, the wind changed. Napkins and placemats tumbled off tables, their corners caught in the swirling breeze. A few littered the porch floor beneath; some dove right off the side of the railing. The new wind hit Charity square in the face and, had she been on the ground, she'd be scrubbing sand out of her eyes, but up here, above the sand and sea and above the noise of downtown and the eternal drone of boat motors, the wind was a lullaby. She closed her eyes, her thoughts becoming whispers on the breeze. Mrs. Parker came to mind, then Mrs. Gorben and her oversize candy dish. And for the briefest of seconds, it felt to Charity as if the breeze had been sent just for her. To caress her, to thank her, to tell her that she was doing the right thing.

For the first time in her life, Charity didn't care what her mother thought of her. She didn't care that she was a thirtysomething with a failed business and that she was only a mediocre potter. Charity had somehow pleased the pixies and the magic that made Gaslamp Island a mystical place, and those powers were sending her a message. She was Charity Monroe Baxter. And that was enough.

∞

Charity sat in Emily Rudd's office wringing her hands because that's what people did who hadn't been trained how to let go of their stress. She'd already told Emily she wanted to do her part to fund the repairs on Founders Hall.

Emily said that would be no problem and brought her a bottle of water. Emily smiled too brightly and walked around the office too softly for Charity's comfort. So instead of focusing on the attorney with the killer high heels, she turned her focus to the chandelier above them. *You've got cobs.* Charity blanched but recovered when she realized she hadn't said the words aloud, just in her mind.

There on a swinging vine from one tear-shaped crystal to another, she could practically see the cobs working to overtake the delicate chandelier.

Emily excused herself for a moment when her phone rang, then pressed a button on the dark, square phone on her dark, square desk and informed her receptionist not to interrupt their meeting again.

Charity chewed her index fingernail. When she noticed the thick layer of clay under her nails, she tucked her hands under her thighs— much like a small child would if she knew she couldn't keep her hand out of the nearby cookie dish.

"First," Emily said as she rolled a pencil between her finger and thumb, "I want to apologize about the blind date and all that. This is a small island, Charity, and we all know one another. Employers socialize with their employees, attorneys with their clients, but I feel as though I put you in a terrible situation, and I'm hoping you can forgive me."

Oh. That wasn't what Charity had expected.

Emily smiled, red-lined lips tilting. "And right or wrong, I hope we can still be friends."

"I'd like that."

Emily lifted her hands in surrender. "No more blind dates. I swear." She shook her head. "That guy was a jerk. I should have known not to trust my date to be a decent judge of character. He's a Steelers fan, after all."

Charity took in a quick gasp of air. She liked the Steelers.

"On to business?" Emily opened a folder but didn't move her gaze from Charity. "Are we ready to talk money?"

Charity nodded, but it was tentative at best.

Emily launched into a description of assets and bank accounts that had Charity's mind aching. Maybe some of those cobs could climb into her ear and insulate her brain. When Emily said the word *million*, Charity completely zoned out. There had been a number and the word *million* after it. What had that number been? Three? Five? What did it matter? It was more than she'd ever dreamed her grandfather's estate was worth. She'd been hoping for a few hundred thousand so she could maintain the house and keep the lights on and replace that expensive roof if it ever needed replacing—after all, hurricane season was quickly approaching. She'd figured two to three hundred thousand could pay the taxes and all other expenses for a good fifteen years.

"Are you all right, Charity? Do we need to take a break?"

Am I going to faint or have a heart attack right here in your office? I don't know. Maybe. "I'm OK," she whispered.

"Better than OK, you're a freaking multimillionaire."

And that's when the lights went out.

The world came back into view, and Charity found herself hunkered forward, chest pressed against her thighs, and she was staring at her feet. The laces of her Sauconys were threadbare, and the side of her foot pressed against the trim in an effort to free itself from its sneaker captor. She needed a new pair. But they cost $130, and she had to work herself up to spending that amount of money, though they typically lasted her two and a half years. Well, two years. Then six months of debating.

She pulled a breath and realized Emily's hand was flat on her back. Good thing that office chair had arms or she might have tumbled right off onto the floor.

She'd never have to fret over buying sneakers again. Her morning coffee roiled in her stomach, and though she didn't feel ready, she righted herself, Emily's office coming back into view. "That much money is . . . a little scary."

Emily took her seat on the other side of the desk after taking the lid from the water bottle and handing the drink to Charity. "It is. And you're right to be concerned. It's a lot of money."

Charity flew out of the chair, surprised by the rush that sent her practically airborne. "No, Emily. Three hundred thousand is a lot of money. Half a million is a lot of money, this is . . ." But she couldn't remember the exact amount.

"Five million, give or take. That's a collection of all of George's assets, minus, of course, your mother's trust and the Atlanta home he left to her and the house here on the island. It's in the two to three million range on its own."

Charity's butt was quickly reintroduced to the chair again. She'd dropped hard enough to force the air from her lungs. Almost apologetically, she said, "I knew the house was worth something, I mean, a lot, but—"

Emily cut her off. "Don't apologize for being wealthy, Charity. It's a responsibility, yes. But this is what George wanted for you. All of it."

She nodded because she didn't know what else to do.

"Do you have any plans to sell Baxter House? Or do you foresee that in the near future?"

A dark cloud passed over Charity. "Sell it? No. I already told you I'm staying here."

"The amount of money we're talking about would make it possible for you to live wherever you choose. Your dream life. New York, Paris."

Her heartbeat quickened. That was the problem with money. It changed everything but had no power to make any lasting difference. "*This* is my dream life. I don't want to live anywhere else."

Emily smiled. "Great. I just wanted you to realize you have options. You're not locked down to anything. George hoped you'd want to stay here, but ultimately, it's your dream that counts, not his—his words, not mine," she added.

The weight of her new responsibility sat heavily on Charity's shoulders. "What do I do now?"

Emily placed her folded hands on her desk. "The estate runs with little interference. George's investments are solid, and unless you choose to make changes, everything can continue on as it has. You've already got access to a couple of bank accounts. Use those for whatever you need and know that if you want to move some money around, you can." She leaned forward. "It's your money, Charity."

Charity should breathe. "But what do I *do*?"

"I think George would like for you to not be stressed out about this. Take a great vacation, buy a giant, blingy piece of jewelry you've always admired, have some fun. You're a smart woman. You'll likely purchase a few higher-ticket items; then life will go back to normal . . . just with great vacation photos and better jewelry."

Charity was pretty sure there was a joke in that statement somewhere, but her cloudy mind couldn't find it.

&

Two hours later and one banana split down, she returned home. It was evening now, and she went straight through the house and out the back door. Passing through her colorful garden usually coaxed a smile, a pause, a fresh appreciation of Dalton's work, but not today. She fully understood the word *shell-shocked*. She'd heard of a soldier once who'd lost his hearing for hours after a mortar round went off too close. The world must have been a frightfully quiet place for him in those hours. Knowing he had ears and knowing how important they were but being helpless to use them.

Charity also knew that if anyone in his right mind could see her fretting over being a millionaire, he'd laugh in her face and tell her to get a grip and stop whining. But she'd spent her entire childhood watching her mother chase wealth and worth. The two were different. So different. But in her mother's world, they were the same. How much of Ellen Marie Baxter was in Charity Monroe Baxter? Her mother had failed at finding that validation she'd desperately searched for. Now she was bitter—still beautiful but living off her husband's money instead of fulfilling her dream to make her own and rule the world.

Before Charity, the sea continued to breathe as the stars lit up the night sky. Above her head, the moon dropped broken glass on the water, creating beautiful, shimmering images. *That's where the fairies dance,* she used to think, *atop those moon-white shards.*

When she heard a noise behind her, Charity spun.

Off to her left, the willow tree inhaled the breeze as if it would release its hold from the ground and come to her. They'd find her buried beneath its branches and deem it an act of God. But Charity knew God didn't kill people. Evil killed people, and the tree was evil. It took. It stole. Just as she turned to head into the house, she saw a figure running across her yard. The scene unfolded in slow motion—first one person, then two. The second—taller, more ominous—gaining on the first.

"Oh, no you don't . . ." Charity heard as the second figure tackled the first. Dalton's voice. Scuffling. Another voice, this one higher, feminine. Young.

Charity closed the distance to the shadowed pile of arms and struggling legs. "Dalton! It's just a young girl."

He stood and dragged the teen to her feet. Once upright, Charity could see her face, eyes wide with fear but also determination. She was ready to bolt or fight, but Dalton kept his hold on her, making it impossible to do either.

"Can someone explain?" Charity was surprised by the authority in her voice.

The girl tried to jerk free, her long hair flying in an arc, but Dalton had her in a grip so solid, she'd have to remove her arm to get away. "This dude is assaulting me. Call the cops."

CHAPTER 8

Discovering Daisy

Daisy Voss knew better. But her swimsuit was cold, and she'd actually gotten burned at the beach—rarely happened—it had been a good day to work the crowd, and the hours had stretched. Her reward, a full stomach and an invite to sit with one of the families tomorrow. Tourists with their bags and coolers, always welcoming to the sweet local who showed their kids how to make sand castles. She'd become great at what she did.

With a full belly, she'd gone inside the house. But then she'd remembered leaving her jacket—her only jacket—at the pier, and she snuck back out. Big mistake.

She'd gotten too comfortable in the last few months with her living situation. At first, she'd counted every night a treasure because she'd gotten to sleep in a bed. But the days dragged into weeks, and when the lady moved in—of course she'd known *someone* would move in—she became lazy. She'd have to be more careful from now on.

Daisy squirmed again to get the guy to let go. He tightened his grip in answer. Daisy focused on the woman, the weaker link in the chain.

Charity Baxter crossed her arms over her chest. Oh, Daisy knew her name. Knew who she was. She was the idiot woman who'd ruined a really good thing by letting the stupid neighbor into her business. Now here Daisy was, caught.

Stay tough. You got this. She'd been on the run for over a year. A scrawny woman and a hulk weren't going to shake her up. "My parents are expecting me at home. If you let me go, I won't tell them you tried to attack me."

The guy's eyes burned, and the lady, Charity, stepped between Daisy and her captor. She touched Daisy. Daisy jerked away. "Dalton, she's freezing."

"Yeah? She's also a thief. I watched her sneak up the back stairs to the door on the third floor. I was just getting ready to call the cops when she came back down."

The woman seemed shocked. The set of external stairs were perfectly hidden from the front and back of the house, tucked into a little alcove opposite the nosy neighbor side.

"What were you doing up there?" Charity asked.

The dude gave her a little shake when she didn't answer.

Daisy mocked a smile. "Got lost. Thought it was my house."

The wind kicked up, and Daisy hated that her flesh shook with the cold. She felt bone-cold. From the inside out, the only kind of cold you got if you were sleeping in a ditch on the ground or if you spent too long in the Florida sun.

"Dalton, this is ridiculous. Look at her. Let's get her inside so we can sort this out," Charity said.

Oh. Inside. That gave Daisy time to plan. Good. Dalton looked incensed. Even better. Daisy grinned. "Yeah, thanks for the help, Dalt. You can toddle on home, now. We'll take it from here."

He answered Daisy by tugging her toward the back door.

Charity didn't know why, but her heart went out to the tough teen. Sure, she'd acted like she could handle herself, eyes spitting fire, mouth lashing insults. But there was something else there in her gaze. A hopelessness that could only be born of suffering. No matter how strong she acted, the girl was fragile in ways maybe few could understand. Charity was one of those few.

"What's your name?" Charity asked the girl as Dalton led her to a kitchen stool and deposited her there. Charity faced him. "Can you bring the throw from the couch? Also, Dalton, put some hot cocoa on the stove."

His mouth dropped open. "Shall we dig out the fine china and wrap it up for her?"

Charity gave him a flat stare. "If she was here to rob me, it would have been a bust. The door to that upstairs attic is locked from the other side, and I'm pretty certain all that's up there are boxes of junk. It was always the junk drawer of the house. Even when I was little."

The girl's eyes widened. "You grew up here?"

Charity nodded. "In the summers. This is my grandparents' place. Well, now my place."

"Cool," the girl said.

From the stove, "Oh, for Pete's sake."

Charity chose to ignore Dalton. "Will you tell me your name?"

"Daisy . . . Smith."

Charity nodded but wasn't convinced. Quite convenient to have such a common last name.

Daisy rolled her eyes and tugged at the shoulder of her thin T-shirt. There, tattooed just below her collarbone was the name Daisy encircled by a daisy and its stem.

Charity smiled. "OK, Daisy. Will you be honest with me?"

If I can, Daisy's eyes said.

"Were you robbing me?"

"No."

"Was this the first time you've broken into my attic?"

Daisy dropped her gaze. "No."

Charity bolted upright so quickly, it caused Daisy to throw her hands in front of her face, ninja style.

Charity clapped her hands together. "I knew it! You're my ghost."

Slowly, Dalton turned from the stove. The spatula was in his hand and hot cocoa dripped onto the floor. "She's *what*?"

"You sneak up there sometimes, don't you?" Charity's heart pounded, and rather than feeling like an upset home owner, she felt slightly tugged into this girl's world of mystery and intrigue where teens will do anything to escape their little brothers. "Is it like a hideout? You come here to get away from everyone?"

Again, the eyes dropped. "Sort of."

"Have you ever taken anything from there that wasn't yours?"

The girl's young face became troubled, and one shoulder tipped. "I uh . . . I don't know. I kind of feel like it's all mine."

That's when the world shifted under Charity's feet. Her heart dropped, her eyes widened. "Oh dear God." A hand covered her mouth. She should have known. The dirty sandals, the long hair uneven on the edges, the hollow area below her eyes. "You've been living there."

⁓

The next day, Dalton opened his cottage door to find a bright morning sun shining down on the green grass in his front yard. Maybe he needed to learn to mind his own business. He'd been a jerk to Charity last night after she'd insisted that the girl, Daisy, stay at her house. He'd spent the first half of the night tossing and turning and listening for any unusual sounds from the big house next door. Now, standing on his front porch, everything looked fine. He'd told Charity to keep her bedroom door locked and to sleep with a knife under her pillow. She'd practically laughed at him. He had to admit, mornings brought light, and light chased away the darkness, and OK, so fine. He'd probably overreacted. Still, he'd keep an eye on the girl who was undoubtedly a runaway. He knew the cost of not being careful.

He inhaled the morning air and turned his attention to his own musings. This was the kind of day a man could spend on a boat. The Barlows had a deep-sea fishing boat they wanted to sell. He'd taken it out on a few occasions, and if he was going to live here, live here for good, he'd up and buy it from them.

But he wasn't going to live here for good, he reminded himself. This was just a stop-off on his way back home, figuratively speaking. There was a business and an impatient brother waiting for him, all in Jacksonville.

He took a step into the perfect tropical morning with the sea breeze sneaking around the sides of the cottage and seagulls darting overhead, making their way to the shoreline on the opposite side of his house. One more step, and his foot tapped against something sitting on the front porch. His gaze trailed down and landed on a box. A flash of heat swept up over his head and bolted down his spine as if its very intent was to rip away the calm island morning and replace it with something else. He didn't have to look at the return address to know that the box had been sent by his brother-in-law and that it contained items belonging to his wife and daughter.

Dalton took several deep breaths, hoping for some form of equilibrium. His hands were trembling when he reached down and gathered the box in his arms.

Once inside, Dalton placed it on the table and grabbed the nearest kitchen knife. His heart beat wildly, and he knew he needed to slow its rhythm before going further, but the motion seemed impossible. He slit the edges of tape and folded back the sides of the box.

When his eyes fell on Kissy's favorite blanket, the same heart stopped. There, in the box, as if swaddling the other objects, rested his baby girl's pink-and-blue blanket. He'd planned to bury it with her but hadn't been able to find the soft, fuzzy thing, though he'd torn the house apart looking. That had been the first time he'd broken down, really broken down. That night, as if he'd let his little girl down, he'd curled up on the floor of her room and cried himself to sleep. It was the first and only opportunity he'd gotten to do that. Early the next morning, his parents had arrived with the same bewildered look he'd had since getting the news. Once his folks were there—Melinda had been like their own daughter—all his energy had gone into making sure his mom, with her heart condition, and his dad, with his eighteen years of sobriety, were OK.

Slowly, Dalton reached into the box, his fingers closing around the cool cloth. The motion caused a whoosh of boxed air to surge up to him. It still smelled like her. Fresh and summer and little girl. One corner was tattered from Kissy dragging the blanket around. Its edges frayed. He held it against his cheek as the tidal wave of memories came. Already he understood why it took his brother-in-law so long to get these items to him.

Cheeks wet with tears, Dalton folded back the side of the box that had reclosed itself as if it knew things of this nature must be revealed in layers. Light flooded the box, and his eyes couldn't decide where to land—the contents a mishmash of things they'd left behind on their last trip to visit Melinda's brother and family, only two weeks before she and Kissy died. There was a hat Melinda had purchased at a fruit stand resting beside a folded cloth shopping bag. One of Kissy's dolls and a coin purse of Melinda's. He withdrew the hat and held it against his chest. Melinda always kept a hat nearby while doing garden work— which was a lot of the time. On this visit, she'd planted a rose garden for their sister-in-law. Dalton had wanted to help, but she'd told him it was a project for the girls and for him and her brother to stay out of their way. It was the last project she'd completed. Dalton squeezed his eyes shut as if the motion would force the agony from his aching body. His soul was empty. His heart, shattered.

How the pain could still be so raw, so fresh, he didn't understand. It was like opening a door that had been closed and being propelled inside a room where the walls seeped with sorrow. In that moment, the hurt was as fresh and real as the day he'd buried them. How was that possible? Wasn't time supposed to heal? Some days he did all right. But out of the blue, something could take him right back to that moment, the moment he knew he'd live the rest of his life without his wife and child, and there was no warning, no premonition that he'd be emotionally wrecked all over again. Sorrow had more power than it should.

The last item he withdrew from the box was a tiny pair of hiking boots. Melinda had bought them for Kissy when they were going to walk a trail leading to a waterfall. Floridians rarely owned hiking boots, but in northern Georgia, rocky climbs were common for outdoor types like Melinda's brother and sister-in-law. They'd all worn jeans and sweatshirts and hiked the mountain trail. He remembered looking over at Melinda when she'd stepped into the sunshine where the surging waterfall lit her profile. He'd fallen in love with her all over again that day. Her mouth open and the mountain wind working its fingers through her hair. She'd laughed when he slipped on a rock and almost landed in the water. If he closed his eyes tight enough, he could still hear her voice, the laughter like bells. But with time, the sound was growing faint. Would it one day be gone? Perhaps that was the price you paid for healing.

He swiped his eyes and lifted the boots from the box. Scuffed toes, red cord laces. A tiny sound escaped his mouth as he reached inside one of the boots to find a wadded pink lace sock in the toe. He pulled it from the boot, wrinkled. It still had the imprint of his daughter's foot. Dalton pulled a few more breaths, but they were shaky, broken, and he knew if he didn't step away he might die right there. He set the boots on his table and took a step back, hands scrubbing at his face as if he could erase the emotions. He'd placed one of the boots too close to the edge, and gravity dragged it forward. In slow motion he watched the boot tumble end over end, the red laces streaks of crimson trying to catch up. It landed and left small clumps of dried mud in a splatter pattern on his kitchen floor. He knelt, eyes focused on the dirt. Some of the pieces still held the shape of the tread on the bottom of the boots.

He started to clean up the mess, but tears got in his way. Oxygen couldn't seem to reach his brain. Dalton grew light-headed. He swayed. His hand fisted, filled with clumps of dirt. With more force than he thought he possessed, he hammered his fist into the floor. Pain instantly shot up from his digits to his wrist and into his forearm.

He'd spent his life planting things in the dirt. With Melinda at his side, they'd dug thousands of holes and placed multitudes of plants, flowers, shrubs. They'd planted life. Never had he expected he'd place his wife and child in the ground. Where there was no life for them, where the nutrient-rich soil would erode away at them rather than help them grow. Unable to stand the pressure in the room any longer, Dalton rushed out the back door. He had no destination, but he knew he had to leave, or the sorrow was going to grow arms and legs and a mouth and swallow him whole. Through blurry eyes, he saw green swaying to the left of him. A giant sanctuary of moving limbs. A cadence like the rustling of strips of satin on the wind murmured against his ears. The muffled crackling grew with each breath of sea air. The willow tree. Feathery leaves reached toward him. Without slowing, he angled toward it as if the tree had beckoned him. His feet moved in a dream, one step after another until he was there, at the edge of the towering giant. With the sun on his back, Dalton parted the branches and stepped inside.

CHAPTER 9
Weeping

It was eerily quiet under the willow tree. Even the sound of the beach beyond was muffled to a whisper. Air left his lungs slowly as the wind tickled against the swaying branches, creating a sort of lullaby that made him want to lie down, made him want to sleep. Knees locked, he stood firm, but in the muted quiet and sighing of the branches, Dalton found himself swaying from side to side, moving with the tree, like a man caught in the waves, swept by each rise and fall of the ocean. Something tugged on his hand. He glanced down to see one of Kissy's boots dangling from his fingers, caught by one of the red laces. He cradled the boot. "I'm so sorry, Kissy." His voice was barely audible, broken words filled with too much breath. "Daddy couldn't protect you from everything."

Dalton dropped to his knees and wept.

He didn't know how long he'd been there when he felt the first gentle droplets of rain. Beyond the veil of the tree, he couldn't hear the storm, but fat drops landed on him, first on his head, then his shoulders and neck. It was cool. It was cleansing, and though he hadn't opened his eyes yet, he stayed there and let the water fall. Within a couple of minutes, his hair was drenched, so he tilted his face back and let the water land where tears had been only moments before. There'd always been something cleansing about the rain. He drew in the rich, fresh scent of moistened earth and let it replace the scent of memory he'd been clinging to since opening the box. His shoulders were soaked, and Kissy's boot sat on the ground somewhere nearby. With each passing moment, his heart calmed, his soul transforming into a pliable clay from the hard, crusty clump it had been. He felt like one of Charity's pottery pieces, an earthen vessel being molded, altered, and made into something useful. Masterful hands working with steady movements readying to place him in a kiln.

A chill ran the length of his body—invasive, growing talons and clawing its way through him. Dalton's eyes flew open. But there was no threat, just giant globs of water too thick to see through. In the gray haze around him, his eyes landed on Kissy's boot. Rain filled the opening, and the laces stretched out as if they'd been placed. He started to reach for the boot, but something stopped him. Where his skin had started to shiver, a warmth rushed over him like he'd opened the oven on Thanksgiving Day, and all the heat had surged out. The gooseflesh disappeared. The droplets changed from giant beads to tiny ones, fragmented by an invisible screen. Dalton had never in his life experienced such a fast shift in weather temperature, and though it begged his mind to question, he couldn't muster the energy. Something was happening. Something deep within him, and it was more important than an impending tornado—which was the only thing he could imagine able to cause such quick temperature changes. That's when he realized the warmth wasn't coming from outside; it felt like it was coming from him. From the inside out, he was heating the space around him.

He tried to focus on the world beyond the tree. Just for a moment, he needed to see the real world because everything about this was strange. Wonderful but strange. Like he'd stepped into a fairy tale. Like the real world waited just beyond the veil of willow branches. Without planning to stand, Dalton was suddenly on his feet. He took two steps and reached out to hold the branches aside. There, beyond the willow, the sun shone gloriously on the beach. There wasn't a cloud in the sky.

Dalton dropped the branches and looked up at the towering tree above him. Arches and curves created a perfect sanctuary over his head, and there, the rain continued to fall.

Sometimes it's in the most unsettling moments that the mind has the clearest thoughts. Dalton held a hand out and watched as the drops landed on his palm. He lifted the hand to his mouth and tasted. Saline.

"The tree is weeping." The words left his mouth simply. No fear in them, no curiosity. As if deep in his heart he somehow knew, somehow understood that of course the tree would weep for him. After all, he'd lost his whole world. The tears slowed, and now the sun was able to shine dappled light through the willow's branches. The heat from the sun was warm and powerful. His hand fell to his chest, where a new fluttering sensation stole his attention. His shoulders rose and fell. The weight of despair was gone. Not pushed aside, not hidden in a room in his heart, gone.

It hadn't been the pain and sorrow of losing his wife and child that had nearly made life unbearable. It had been the despair. The despair never left, never gave him rest, and it had never been far from the surface of his soul.

His hand ran from the pit of his belly up to his chest and back. The despair was gone. Dalton picked up the boot, and tears from the tree sloshed inside as he walked to the edge of the willow. "Thank you," he said.

But the tree didn't answer. It stood steadfast, gently moving in the coastal breeze. When Dalton stepped from under the tree, he realized that his clothes were still wet, but the tears were gone from the boot. The sun heated his skin, and his soul felt lighter. It was a glorious freedom he hadn't even known existed or could exist after losing Melinda and Kissy. Their names brought the memories. And the memories usually brought the despair, but not now. Now, though the pain of their loss was still there, he could think of them with the tiniest seed of hope.

He took a couple of steps away, then turned to the tree. "Thank you," he said again. Dalton heard a snapping sound and then a muffled scraping. He ran around the side of the tree, where branches moved apart because of the breeze. He got to the spot just as one of the tree's branches landed with a thud. "No, no, no," he whispered. His gaze went from the fallen branch to the climbing vines he hadn't noticed before. They threatened to choke the life from the tree. His eyes took in the overloaded branches and the weeds spreading out from the trunk, all stealing the nutrients from the willow. "No." His free hand went to one of the long branches, and he stroked it like one would a horse's neck. "Don't worry. I'll save you. I swear."

⊂☉

Charity had slept well knowing that her ghost was a teen runaway now resting in one of her upstairs bedrooms. Charity had just made coffee when Uncle Harold arrived. She watched from her front porch as he pulled into her driveway. Early June offered a balmy atmosphere, but the breeze off the gulf replaced the mugginess with salty sea air. She smiled and waved. This time, he'd brought two suitcases and his own car.

She carried Harold's things to his room and returned to find him in the kitchen. "Will you stay longer this visit?" Hope filled each word.

"I suspect." He turned from her and poured the coffee. "If you'll have me."

There was more to that comment, she knew. Maybe it had to do with her gramps and Harold's falling-out. It seemed a sensitive subject that closed him off and pinched the corners of his eyes. The last thing Charity wanted to do was cause him more pain. Besides, the letter from her gramps forgave whatever happened between them. If it was good enough for Gramps, it was good enough for her.

"Let's have Dalton over for dinner," Charity said.

"I can go to town in a bit and pick up some fixin's. How would that be?" Harold sat at the kitchen island across from her.

Charity nodded. "There's a girl staying with me. Very sweet but . . . kind of . . . standoffish."

"A friend's child?" he asked.

She leaned forward. "Pretty sure she's a runaway. Eighteen, though—she claims—so technically she's an adult."

"That makes her a transient, not a runaway," he corrected her. His brows were high on his forehead.

Charity didn't want to have to fight over this. Dalton had given her enough trouble last night about Daisy and the fact of the matter was, she was helping Daisy, and that's all there was to it. "She's staying with me, and that's the end of it."

A crooked smile grew on Harold's face. "Well, look at you. I don't remember you being so stubborn, Lil' Bit. You always seemed more of a people pleaser than a rabble-rouser."

She had to laugh. "That was then, Uncle Harold. I even stood up to my mother when she called and *ordered* me back to New York."

His arms spread wide. "Didn't know you had it in you." He winked. "This calls for a celebration. Steaks for dinner. My treat."

She sipped her coffee and considered her uncle. He looked as if the weeks away had aged him. "What happened in Birmingham?"

His gaze dropped to his mug, old fingers toying with the handle of the marine-blue pottery piece. "This here is a nice mug. Did George make it?"

She grinned. "I made it."

He closed one eye. "Proud of your work on this piece, aren't you?"

Sometimes he reminded her of Master Yoda from *Star Wars*. Insightful is this one. "I am proud of it." She motioned around her.

"It's this place. It's Gramps's wheel and kiln and the sleeping porch and the special ingredient—"

His eyes flashed, only for a moment, but she noticed. "There's special ingredient in this mug?"

"No. I only use it in special orders."

"And you've never had a special order for yourself?" He was fishing here. But for what, she couldn't say.

"Harold, what do you know about all this? Why would Gramps leave me a bag with an unknown substance inside and make sure I put a scoop in each order?" Mrs. Parker had wanted a plate. Mrs. Gorben had wanted a candy dish. Charity had received an invitation to a wedding from the young man who'd requested wine goblets. They'd all been overjoyed with their purchases. But why? It was just a candy dish. Just a plate.

"All I know is, your gramps would be awful proud of you, Lil' Bit." Harold tipped his head back, and the morning sun got trapped in the tear in his eye.

She reached over the table. "Harold, I know you have a business in Birmingham and surely a life there, but I was wondering if you could maybe stay here for a while. A few months maybe? I know it's a lot to ask. But when you're here, I feel . . . like I haven't lost my family."

Old men weren't supposed to cry. Still the tears came, and Harold fought them by pressing his lips together and swiping his cheeks with his aged hands. "I want to stay, Charity, so much, but—" His voice cracked, and he swallowed the words.

"Harold, what?"

He pressed his hands flat on the counter. "Things between your gramps and me weren't good when he passed. There are things you don't know. Things that might change your mind about wanting me here."

"Didn't Gramps send you that letter wanting to reconcile?"

He shook his head, no. "You don't understand. That letter was postmarked weeks after he'd died."

Charity tried to absorb the implications. What could that mean? Was it a fraud? "He didn't write it?"

"Don't know. I look at the words, and it's his handwriting, I mean, more shaky, but it has me convinced. I don't know what to make of it, Charity."

She squared her shoulders. "Letters get lost in the mail. If you believe he wrote it, I believe he wrote it."

He sniffed. "Why would you put such trust in me?"

She stood from the kitchen stool and moved around the island to be near him. "You're my Uncle Harold. You'd never do anything to hurt me."

They were interrupted by a knock on the back door. But as Charity moved away from her uncle, she was almost certain she'd heard him whisper, "I already have."

Dalton stood at her back door soaking wet, his dark hair matted to his brow and his clothes shining. "Did you run through the sprinklers?" But just as she opened the door more fully to let him in, she saw the look in his eyes. It was as if he'd trapped a chunk of sunlight and was trying to hide it. Uncontainable, it gleamed from his irises.

"I need to talk to you." It was a breathy few words. He reached in and took her hands. The motion drew her a bit closer, and that was when she noticed something dangling from one of his fingers.

Charity sucked a breath as she stared down at the smallest hiking boot she'd ever seen. Was this his child's shoe? No other personal item was more painful to see than a lost person's shoes. Shoes were life. They represented the journey, the travels, the destinations of their owners. They stretched to fit their master. They conformed to that person's shape. They carried the dust from where one had gone and pointed in the direction of the future. Shoes were life. And there was nothing sadder than a pair of shoes that would never be used by their owner again.

Barely able to move, she stepped aside as he strode into the kitchen. With both hands—as if it were a delicate porcelain doll—he lovingly placed the tiny boot on her kitchen counter.

"Charity, we have to talk about the tree."

Her mind tried to form a remark, but she had no words. All she could do was stare at that tiny shoe that would never again feel a little girl's foot. It looked so lonely there, without its mate.

"Charity." The word—almost a command—held more substance, so she dragged her gaze from the counter to Dalton.

"The tree."

What had happened to his eyes? They looked lighter.

Dalton straightened his spine. "I'm going to tend the tree. I know you don't like that idea, but—"

"You mean the willow. I told you to stay away from it," she said through gritted teeth. Her head spun. Didn't *like* the idea? She'd rather have him move away from the island and never see him again than have him working on the tree.

He came toward her. "You don't understand. Let me explain what happened. I went and sat beneath the tree."

Her hands fisted. He hadn't listened to her at all. He'd been under the tree? Charity placed her hands at the sides of her head where a pounding sensation drove her to move away from him. As she passed, she noticed that Uncle Harold was on his feet.

Harold's voice interrupted her wild thoughts. "I'm going to leave you two to talk."

Before either could answer him, he'd passed through the doorway, his feet echoing off the marble floor.

Charity yelled for him. "Harold!"

When he stepped back inside and paused at the doorway—ready to make a quick exit, no doubt—Charity motioned him into the room. "Look, you need to hear this, too. You're both going to be around, and I don't want to have to keep arguing about this. *No one* tends the tree."

"It's going to die, Charity." There was a pleading tone in Dalton's words.

There was nothing she'd like more.

Harold took a small step toward her, causing her to look at him. She'd expected to see understanding on his face, but all she saw was concern. "You'd let the willow die? Charity, I can't believe that."

Shame rushed over her, but quick on its heels, determination. "I know objects aren't evil, but the willow—"

Harold didn't seem to hear her. "Your grandfather loved the willow."

Her hands fisted with years of frustration. No one understood.

Dalton approached her. "Why do you hate it?"

Of course no one understood. She'd never explained. "There are a lot of poems and legends about willow trees. That you're not supposed to plant them at night, that if you cut yourself on a willow branch, it will cut everyone who touches it. But the one I always remembered was about trimming the branches."

"What about the poem, Charity?" Uncle Harold asked. "That's the legend you can believe in. I know George and Marilyn recited it to you a thousand times. I heard them."

The poem had played like a record in her head for years. But that was before her eleventh birthday and the last summer she'd spent here on Gaslamp Island. She tried to force the rhyme from her head, but Harold's voice interrupted her.

> *Will you come, sit with me.*
> *We'll tell our troubles 'neath the tree*
> *The tears we shed will surely be*
> *Water for the weeping tree.*
> *And in its shade our woes will fall.*
> *Pain and suffering, sorrow and all*
> *They'll fall like glistening diamond drops.*
> *You see, the tree, our pain, it stops.*

Dalton took ahold of her arm. "Charity, that's what happened to me. I sat under the tree, and I can't explain it, but . . . it gave me hope."

Her head hurt. Her stomach was sick. "No. The tree doesn't give. It takes. *I* was supposed to trim the branches." Charity felt the tears welling in her eyes. "When I turned eleven. Gramps gave me the task of trimming the branches, but the tree was so big, and I only trimmed the ones on the front. I let the back of the tree grow. I didn't like being back there where no one could see me."

Dalton shook his head. "OK."

"The legends. The one I always remembered was that if you didn't trim the branches, and if they touched the ground, someone you loved would die. My gram died after I went home that summer. It was my fault."

She heard something behind her and turned just in time to see Harold losing his balance, his face pale. She and Dalton both dove for him, her hand reaching out and closing around the sleeve of his shirt. His weight fell against Dalton, who helped him onto the nearby bar stool.

"Uncle Harold, are you OK?"

But his look was bewildered. A set of watery blue eyes darted around them. His gaze finally landed on Charity. "Oh, Lil' Bit." His age-rough hand cupped her cheek. "Your grandma's death wasn't your fault."

The look of absolution in his eyes caused her to want to believe. But her hard speculation shot it down. She'd carried the weight of her gram's death. It rested on her shoulders. Right where it was supposed to be. "Let's get you to the living room where you can lie down."

Before he could protest, Charity cupped her shoulder beneath his arm, and with Dalton on the other side, they helped Harold to the couch.

Once he was stretched out, and Charity had covered him with a throw, she cut her eyes to Dalton. "We'll talk about this later."

She knew he wanted to protest, but he was a wise man and also knew she'd met her quota of brick walls for the day.

When Harold mumbled, she bent closer to hear him. A crooked finger pointed at the chandelier fixture above his head. "You got cobs." Then he closed his eyes and slept.

⌒૭

End of summer, 1996

Charity's grandma's funeral was the first one she'd ever attended. Were they always so sad? Did the sky always cover the sun with clouds when the preacher spoke of the great reward waiting on the other side at a place he called Glory?

After the ceremony, they pulled the car into the driveway of her gramps and gram's house. Now that Gram was gone, was she supposed to just refer to it as her gramps's house? So many questions. Kendrick and Momma kept her between them, each holding one of her hands as they stepped from the car. Kendrick's hand was cold and sweaty, and Charity didn't like holding it. He'd pushed Charity away at first when her momma had suggested they walk to the front door of the big mansion like this. Momma always thought of how things looked, and she'd whispered to Kendrick they needed to make it look good. She dabbed her eyes with a napkin from McDonald's as Gramps opened the front door. Charity tried to pull away from Kendrick, but that only made him angry. He squeezed Charity's hand until she could feel the throbbing of her own heart in each fingertip. Charity had tried to ride with Gramps, but her momma had snagged her by the collar of her black dress and mumbled, "Oh, no you don't." She'd shoved Charity into the backseat.

There at his front door, her gramps looked sick. His whole head seemed covered with wrinkles that she'd never even noticed before. On the porch, he knelt to hug her, and she stepped into his arms and could have stayed right there forever. When Kendrick started talking—eyes sad and saying all those things people said when someone died—Gramps stood from his spot. Charity half expected him to scoop her into his arms, but he didn't seem to have the energy to do it.

Inside, Gramps made Twinings Earl Grey tea. Charity dragged its full scent into her lungs. On the couch was Gram's favorite quilt. On the side table, her reading glasses. Charity stared and stared at them, trying to gather all the magic she could, trying her best to will Gram back into the room. Surely, she couldn't be gone. Not really gone. Not forever gone.

With the grown-ups in the kitchen, Charity sat on the cold marble floor of the parlor and stared at the library. She reached behind her and dragged Gram's quilt from the couch and curled inside it.

Kendrick was talking about how he and Ellen were going to get married and how they wanted to help Gramps in his time of need. But Gramps's tone sharpened as he asked questions and apparently didn't get answers he liked. Charity's momma took over the conversation. She talked on and on about how she hadn't done right by Charity in the past, but they had changed all that.

Had they? Charity didn't see any difference in anything. If anything, things were worse for her. Momma spent every waking hour looking at herself in the mirror and asking Charity if she thought Kendrick still found her beautiful. Charity's momma was the most beautiful woman in the world. How she couldn't see that herself defied Charity's comprehension.

When the grown-ups started arguing, Charity knew she needed to interrupt them. She had to tell them the truth. It was going to change everything. With courage she could only have drawn from knowing a devastating secret, she headed for the kitchen. She stepped inside, still wrapped in the blanket and opened her mouth wide to admit the sin that had taken her gram's life. But she froze when three sets of eyes landed on her. Gramps's filled with pain, Momma's flashing anger, and

Kendrick's loathing her interruption, or maybe her entire existence. She lost her voice. She tried to croak out a word, just to get started, but no words came. Would Gramps look at her the way Kendrick and her momma did once he knew Gram's death was Charity's fault? She'd never survive that. Not from Gramps.

Charity's hands fisted around the quilt, and she ran through the kitchen and right out the back door through the sleeping porch and into the yard. Before her, Gram's garden shone like balloon bouquets of bright colors. Off to the right stood the weeping tree.

Charity's heart filled with anger—maybe hate, it was such an intense emotion. It propelled her forward. But she stopped, narrowed eyes darting from side to side, searching for a weapon. There, sitting on the ground by the shrubs at the back door sat Gramps's garden ax. She grabbed it up in one swoop and stomped toward the willow tree. It was her fault that her gram was dead, but it was the weeping tree's fault, too. If she'd only been brave enough to tend the tree and trim all the branches . . . but the back of the tree was scary. Why she felt no fear now, she didn't know.

Her hand was slick with sweat, and she swiped it on the quilt that was now slowing her, dragging along behind as if it knew she needed to stay away from the tree. But despair made her courageous, and she used the ax to part the branches and step under the tree. She stopped cold. It was darker here. Long branches arched over her head. There were bare sections of dirt below her feet. When the wind rose, and the branches answered by swaying, she lifted the ax high overhead and took five full steps toward the massive trunk. "I hate you," she said and swung with all her might until the ax lodged into the flesh of the tree.

Over and over again, she repeated the motion until her face was slick with tears, and her arms ached. She tried to focus her blurry eyes but couldn't. Sweat matted her hair to her head, and bits of tree bark speckled her black dress. Charity dropped to her knees, the ax slipping from her hand and landing on the ground. She pulled in a long breath, and as she exhaled, it was as if all the sorrow she'd ever felt or could ever feel had rushed to the surface of her being. A silent scream stayed on her face as she dropped to the ground and lay down beneath the tree. "I hate you," she whispered again and covered herself with the quilt.

Time passed, and the branches moved, but Charity refused to look out from under the quilt until she felt a tapping on the covering. She uncovered her head, half expecting pixies to be dancing atop her, but it was only rain. She wished the rain could wash away her guilt. She wished it could take her pain and make it disappear like she'd disappeared beneath Gram's quilt. But there were no fairy answers to her problem.

Soaking wet, Charity stood. When a warm breeze moved into the space around her, she lifted her arms wide and let the rain wash over her from head to toe. She stayed like that a long time. Until the rain stopped, and she knew it was time to go back inside the house. But as Charity stepped out into the bright sunlight, a shiver ran over her flesh. Something was gone. She hurried from under the tree, leaving the quilt behind, and ran to the door of the sleeping porch. There she stopped to take in the view behind her. The tree, speckles of color on the ground where her gram's quilt lay getting dirty. Charity was wet, and her momma would tan her hide for getting the dress so filthy, but it was inside Charity's heart that the real problem lay. The tree had stolen a piece of it. It surely had. Because Charity knew it was her fault that her gram was dead, but the guilt she knew should be there was gone.

CHAPTER 10

The Secret

For three weeks Charity mulled over what Dalton had said about the weeping tree. In that time, she'd allowed memories from her past to flood her. Again and again she'd gone over that day when she stood beneath the weeping tree searching for clues to things she couldn't understand.

In the end, she remembered that certain things had to be taken on faith. Like the hope she held that her mother could be a better person if she had the right motivation. Like the fact that Uncle Harold was harboring secrets, and in time, he'd share them with her. One thing Charity knew was the weight of secrets. But after Harold collapsed when she'd admitted the truth about her gram's death, Charity decided to trust that he would come to her when he was ready.

The house was quiet, like a mother who'd just tucked in her sleepy child. Daisy had turned in early. The girl had only been there a few weeks but seemed to be catching up on a year's worth of sleep. Then again, Daisy wasn't fond of Dalton, and she'd made a speedy exit when Charity told her he was coming over that night. She'd been steering clear of him since that first day when Charity had her bring her stuff—what little she had—from the attic and move it into a room on the second floor. Charity didn't believe Daisy actually *disliked* Dalton, but he'd been the one to catch her. She held a distrust that radiated from her body language whenever he entered the room. That lack of trust vibrated from Daisy's eyes, the blue in them turning to steel and narrowing whenever Dalton came near her.

Daisy would come around. Charity was certain of it. She was a frightened young girl who might have a good reason not to trust men. Soon enough, the two of them would be friends.

Harold and Dalton were already friends. From the first night they'd met in her kitchen, the two had quickly bonded. Charity's life was feeling fuller with Daisy and Harold staying there. She hoped it would remain like this. But sadly, she knew that the one constant life promised was change.

Uncle Harold had turned in for the night, too, and Charity was glad she'd be alone with Dalton for this conversation. This was something she needed to do. It was time to talk about what happened under the weeping tree when she was eleven. Because maybe, just maybe, she had it all wrong.

He arrived, and they made tea, then sat down in the parlor.

She wrung her hands as she told him her story about the weeping tree. From the funeral to the garden ax to feeling like the tree had stolen part of her soul, all of it poured out of her.

"I noticed some pockmarks on the trunk."

"Difficult to chop a tree with an ax the size of a steak knife."

It was warm in the parlor. She'd moved the settee so that it sat beneath the window, where sunlight could land on her in the day, and a dark blanket of heavy curtains could frame her at night. She'd grown to love both the parlor and the library in the passing weeks as she'd found so many treasures in each. First Gram's recipe box, then a stash of Gramps's cinnamon sticks. He was forever chewing on them from the day he'd decided to quit tobacco. She'd also found the tobacco stash hidden behind a dog-eared edition of Poe.

Dalton sat beside her, his elbow propped on the arm of the settee. "That had to be really scary and confusing for a child."

She shrugged. "The tree took my grandmother because I didn't trim the branches. Then it stole a part of my heart." That's what she'd believed for all these years.

He leaned toward her. "It didn't steal part of your heart; it just took your guilt away."

"It was mine to carry."

"So, you resurrected it on your own."

"What?" Charity's hands dropped to her lap.

"The tree took your guilt, but over time, you replaced it with new guilt about your grandmother's death."

Of course she had. "Like I said, it was my burden to carry. I didn't want it to go away—"

"Because it kept you company."

Her mouth dropped open. He was right. Guilt was her companion, her closest friend. It was the only thing that understood.

Dalton lightly placed a hand over hers. "Charity, I get it." His voice was whisper soft as if he knew the dangers of waking the demons in the room. "Believe me, I get it."

No. He didn't . . .

Dalton drew a breath. "When Melinda and Kissy were murdered—"

The world faded. Suddenly, there was no oxygen to fill her lungs. He hadn't said—

Then, he said it again. "When they were murdered, I was gone. Out of town. I could have come on home, and it wouldn't have happened."

She couldn't breathe. Spots appeared and disappeared before her eyes. But something deep within clawed through the haze. Her hand reached out and grabbed his. "Dalton, I had no idea."

"I do understand how you feel. How you felt that day. Melinda and Kissy walked into a convenience store during a robbery. The robbers panicked, opened fire. It wouldn't have happened if I'd been home. She wouldn't have even been in that part of town."

Charity lifted his hand to her cheek.

"I was on the phone with her before she stopped at the store. She'd gone across town to pick up a computer from my mom's house. I was supposed to have gotten it a week before but kept forgetting."

"Oh, Dalton." She pressed his hand against her cheek as if the motion could lift some of the pain.

"A retired policeman with a firearm slipped into the store and shot the two thieves before they could escape."

Still holding his hand, Charity clamped her fingers more tightly on his, to let him know he wasn't alone.

"The police chief in Jacksonville was a friend of mine. He knew where I was. He had the local police come to notify me. They arrived at my hotel room at eleven twenty-six. My brother, Warren, arrived two hours later to bring me home."

"Here I am going on about a legend and a tree when you've been facing this. I'm so sorry. I don't know what else to say, and those words fall pitifully short."

He withdrew his hand from hers, and she thought he'd stand and move away from her. Instead, he used the same hand to trail her cheek. "Loss is loss. Whether we're eleven or thirty-five. The pain is still the same. And it's debilitating if we allow it to consume us. But if we let forgiveness work . . ."

She shook her head. "I don't know how you've been able to forgive what they did."

"I had to forgive *myself*, Charity. For not being there. For not protecting them. If we don't forgive ourselves, we're ruined, and we're no good to anyone."

She tried to take that in, tried to absorb it.

Dalton gave her a weak smile and reached to pick up his teacup. "Unforgiveness is an anchor. It will tie you to the pain with a chain too thick to break. It will wind around your neck and drown you in the very water you need to navigate. I don't understand how the tree took my despair, but it did. It interceded for me, cried tears that eroded the unforgiveness in my heart. For you, it took your guilt." He took a sip.

Charity thought back to that day so long ago. For the first time ever, she could think of the memory and not have hate in her gut. "I remember a branch falling to the ground after I stepped out. I'd hoped the whole tree would collapse one branch at a time."

"A branch fell off after I'd been under the tree, too."

"What does that mean?" Charity squeezed her upper arms; she was suddenly cold.

"I don't know. Maybe it gives life but has to give up something in return."

She nodded and ignored the part of her brain that reminded her this was a *tree* for heaven's sake.

"I want to tend the tree, Charity. Will you let me do that?"

A tree with the power to take someone's deepest pain and turn it into something good. If Dalton was right—and somewhere in her heart she knew he was—the tree was a gift. Yes, she had no choice but to let him tend the tree. "OK."

"I understand why you were afraid of it."

"I understand why you have faith in it."

They sat in silence for a few long moments while the house cradled them in their new revelation. Dalton leaned back. "It's quiet. Since Daisy and Harold came, seems like there's always noise in the house."

Charity nodded and reached for her cup but knew the tea had already gone cold.

A half smile tilted his cheek. "You love it, don't you?"

She nodded again.

Dalton placed his tea on the side table. "But Charity, things probably aren't going to stay like this. You know that, right?"

"I don't see why not." She drew her bottom lip between her teeth and bit down.

"Daisy has been here for three weeks and you haven't even tried to find out where she came from or if anyone is looking for her."

Irritation skated over Charity's flesh. "She's eighteen. She doesn't have to answer to anyone."

Dalton leaned toward her, the chandelier light above dancing in his soft, green eyes. "So she says. What if she's lying? You'd be harboring a runaway. That's something the law takes seriously."

But Daisy wasn't lying. At least, Charity didn't think she was. But who was she kidding? She had her doubts about how much truth was in Daisy's admissions about her name and actual age. Not that it mattered that much to Charity. She understood what it meant to have a parent who was unbearable. If that was Daisy's case, she'd take on the law if she had to.

"Listen, somewhere out there, she has parents. If she truly is eighteen, then they have no power to make her go home if she doesn't want to. She has *parents*, Charity. Don't they at least deserve to know she's alive?"

That's when it hit her, Dalton's desire to contact the parents. He'd lost a child. He'd suffered the torture that Daisy's family might be going through. Charity had only seen things from the child's perspective; Dalton was seeing it from a father's. What if he was right? Reluctantly, she agreed. "OK. I'll try to get some information from her and see what I can do."

"Thanks." He drew her into a hug. Something she hadn't expected but at the same time was delighted by because now she and Dalton shared something far greater than the pain that had driven them both here to the island. They shared hope, fresh and blooming, as green and lush as the garden Dalton had resurrected, as surprising as the weeping tree that anchored the edge of her yard and watched over them all.

⁓

"So, I used your laptop and Googled weeping willow legends, and I found nothing about trimming the branches and someone dying," Daisy said and popped a potato chip into her mouth.

They'd just cleaned up from breakfast, and already Daisy was dipping into the potato chip bag. Teenagers.

Charity scrubbed the sink with a scouring pad.

"I searched everywhere." Daisy crunched another chip. "I'm talking a *lengthy* search."

Charity sighed. Last night at dinner, the whole story had unfolded for Uncle Harold and Daisy while they all ate steak and potatoes. It was a relief to know the details were finally out in the open. Like when you're a child, and you're terrified of lizards until someone hands you one, and you realize it has no power to hurt you.

But she'd tired of the constant inquisition from Daisy and had sent her on an errand right after breakfast to gather all the hurricane preparedness items she could find throughout the house. Hurricane Erika—which had been Tropical Storm Erika until yesterday—was headed their direction.

"So, who told you the legend?" Daisy was relentless in her quest. "Are you sure you didn't make it up yourself?"

Charity spun from the sink to look at her. "Make it up?"

Daisy shrugged. "You were a kid, right? I'm just saying that I did an exhaustive search online and nada."

Charity frowned.

Daisy reached into a box she'd carried down from the attic. A giant white candle was cradled in her hands. "Do we need these for the storm? There are several in here."

Charity came around the counter and took it from her. "Is that Gram's hurricane box?" She remembered her grandmother filling a large box with items for a storm. Lighters, candles, lanterns, iodine, a first aid kit.

"I guess so. So, where did you hear the willow tree legend about trimming the branches?"

Charity rifled through the hurricane box. "My mother. She's the one who told me the legend." She thought back. "No, wait. It was Kendrick. Yes, Kendrick—who lied to me on a daily basis, but my mother jumped right into the story with him, so I never doubted it."

Daisy refastened the clip on the bag of potato chips. "Why would they do that?"

"Sometimes they were mean." Charity went back to the sink of vegetables waiting to be chopped and arranged in a salad.

Daisy shook her head, sun-streaked hair flying around her shoulders. "Dude. That is messed up."

"Gramps had called and told her that when I visited that year, they were going to have some chores for me. When she mentioned the willow to me, I undoubtedly turned white as a ghost because it was so huge and kind of scary-looking. The hoax must have started right then and there." Did her mother even remember that Charity's fear of the tree stemmed from a lie she had perpetuated? Probably not; sometimes lying was as easy for Ellen as breathing. *White lies*, she called them. But there was nothing white about a white lie. They were black as soot and empty as an unused grave.

"All this time, you were scared of nothing."

"Don't go overboard with the sympathy," Charity said.

Daisy cocked her hip. "I've been on the street for a year. Sympathy is hard to come by. Sarcasm, though. If you need that, I'm your girl."

"Daisy, speaking of being on the street, don't you think it's time you told me where you came from? Is anyone looking for you?"

Daisy busied herself by examining items in the hurricane box. "Doubtful," she finally mumbled when Charity continued looking at her.

Charity's constant stare must have worn her down. Daisy huffed and propped her hands on the corners of the box. "My name is actually Daisy Voss, not Smith. I'm from Vale, Colorado, and I highly doubt my mother is looking for me."

Charity dropped onto one of the bar stools and motioned for Daisy to take the one across from her. "You and your mom didn't get along?"

Daisy's long blonde hair caught the light from above. She was too young and pretty to have lived such a hard life for the past year. "She was always moving different guys into the house. Couldn't seem to keep a man for more than a few months. Then this last guy, Bud, stayed on. He'd been there for almost a year when I realized he was looking at me."

"Looking at you?" Charity hadn't meant to repeat the words out loud; they were heavy and cold, and she didn't like where this was headed.

"Yeah, just looking at me, but it was the snakelike gleam in his eyes that freaked me out. Then one day my mom is pulling a double shift at the restaurant, and he starts rubbing my shoulders and talking about how beautiful I am." Daisy's eyes trailed to the window. "Next thing I know, he's trying to kiss me."

"Oh, honey." Charity understood what it was to feel unprotected in one's own home. But not in this way. Charity's mother had never allowed anyone—any male, whether he was Ellen's friend or lover—to say anything sexually inappropriate to Charity. Ellen might not have been a great mother, but she'd had moral lines she didn't allow anyone to cross. "Daisy, you must have been terrified."

She laughed without humor. "Mad was more like it. I told him to just wait until my mom got home. She was totally jealous of anyone even talking to him."

"What happened when she got home?"

"I told her. She just couldn't wrap her head around it. She told me I must have made a mistake. That I'd misinterpreted his friendliness. "

"And so you left?" Charity said.

"Yep. I was gone before the next morning. It was fall, and I knew I couldn't stay north through the winter so I sold my laptop, my cell phone, all my electronics, which I'd collected when my mom was dating a guy who"—Daisy made air quotes—"worked in an electronic store. I figured all the stuff was stolen, but nothing I could do about that."

Charity's heart ached for her. This was a far different situation from the one Dalton had suggested. "What about before Bud? Were things good between you and your mom?" Maybe Charity was grasping at straws, but she knew the debilitating power of losing what little family one had.

"Before Bud, she'd always been a good mom. I mean, not perfect, but good."

So there was hope for a reconciliation. If, of course, Bud was out of the picture. After all, she didn't want to see Daisy end up like her. A thirty-one-year-old still searching for approval that might never come.

Daisy ran a hand through her hair. "I bought a bus ticket and made it to Georgia. Then worked my way down here. I've been on the island for four months. Longest I've stayed anywhere since leaving Vale."

"If you want to call your mother—"

"I don't."

"There are legal things to consider. If you're eighteen, then no harm can come from calling her. I really believe it will help you move on, Daisy."

Daisy's gaze narrowed. "I told you I was eighteen."

"Daisy—"

"I said I don't want to talk to her. I'm not going home." Daisy's words were flat. "Look, I know that loser Bud has probably already moved on. But I'm not sure I can forgive her."

What if Daisy's mom had come to her senses and woke up to find her daughter gone? What if Dalton was right and Daisy's mother was crying herself to sleep every night wondering if her child was alive or dead? For all they knew, she might have thrown Bud out after having time to consider the situation. The problem was, they didn't know. Miscommunication was a deadly force. "You're an adult now. You don't have to go home. She couldn't make you. But maybe you could let her know you're OK."

"Like she deserves that." Daisy chewed her bottom lip. "Someday, I'll let her know. But I'm not in any hurry. If she misses me, good. She should have believed me."

"You're right. She should have."

"You know what?" Daisy popped up off the bar stool. "I'm done talking about this right now. You never answered me about the candles."

Charity came around the kitchen counter and stared into the box of Gram's hurricane provisions. July had started with a bang, the first potential storm bearing down on them and gathering strength in the Gulf of Mexico.

Daisy pointed to the ceiling. "There's more up in the attic room. You want to check it out?"

"Sure." Charity hadn't been up there yet. She reached over and took Daisy's hand. "I'm not trying to force you to do anything you don't want to, but I care about you, Daisy. Sometimes, a lot of hurt can be avoided if we hit a situation head-on. Does that make sense?"

Daisy shrugged and mumbled, "I guess."

Charity squeezed her hand and let it go. As they were leaving the kitchen, the wall phone rang. "What now?" Charity mumbled as she stepped away from Daisy to answer the phone. "Hello?"

"Charity, I'm coming to visit. There's something I need to discuss with you."

Charity's mother's voice sent a quick chill down her spine. She was coming to visit? "Mom, when?"

"I'll be there in an hour."

Charity shook her head to clear it. Surely she'd heard wrong. "Mom, there's a hurricane in the Gulf, making its way to us right now."

"Don't be so dramatic, Charity. It's expected to turn and hit Texas. And it's only a tropical storm, not a hurricane."

"No, Mom. That was yesterday. We're going to get at least the southern corner of the storm, and hurricane or not, it'll be severe on the island," Charity said, feeling a rush of flulike symptoms coursing over her body.

"Well, that would have been nice to know before I rerouted my flight from Atlanta back to New York."

And somehow, Charity felt like it was her fault that the storm shifted directions. "You're in Atlanta?"

"I *was* in Atlanta. I had to go see to that shack Dad left me. I swear it's falling in on itself. I'm driving from the Sarasota airport now. I'll be on the water taxi shortly." There was a frustrated sigh. "If you don't want me to come, Charity, just say so."

"No. Of course I want you to come. Uncle Harold is here, and you'll get to meet my neighbor Dalton."

"What's Harold doing there?"

"He came for a visit. It's so great to see him, like seeing Gramps, almost. And I have a house guest. Her name is Dai—"

"I need to go, Charity. It's starting to rain." Click.

Always such a loud click when her mom disconnected a call. Charity figured it was that she hung on her mother's every word, even leaning into the phone, cradling it closer so that she didn't miss anything, so when the click happened it was less of a disconnected phone line and more of a disconnected heart.

Slowly she placed the phone on its receiver. "We're having company."

Daisy chuckled. "Your mom?"

Charity nodded.

"She sounds like a real piece of work." Daisy cocked her head. A tiny dimple appeared on the side of her cheek. "And it doesn't sound like you're all that excited to see her. Miss call-your-mom-she-probably-misses-you."

Charity rubbed her hands over her face. "It's complicated with her. I mean, she's my mom. I love her. Really. But she's difficult."

"Yeah, I got that impression."

"Even as hard as she is to deal with, if I'd ever run away as a teen, I think she would have lost it. Sometimes moms love us, but in the only way they know how—which doesn't look like much when compared with the rest of the world. But maybe it's all they have to offer. In my case, my mom's too busy to offer much in the way of affection."

"Is she like a doctor or a lawyer or something?"

"Nope. She's a housewife." Charity was trying to get a visual of the motley crew that would be there for the evening. If nothing else, Daisy would get to see what a dysfunctional mother/daughter relationship looked like.

"OK. Heading into a hurricane. Smart lady."

One of Charity's shoulders tipped up in a shrug. "She doesn't let anything stop her. Not even Mother Nature. She's a bit of a hurricane herself. Come on, I want to check out the attic before Harold gets home."

༄

Daisy knew Charity expected the third floor attic room to be a dark, spider-infested place, but that couldn't be further from the space Daisy liked to think of as home. Even though Charity had given Daisy a room on the second floor—and she liked that, really, she did—her attic held a certain coziness that the other rooms of the house didn't. It was her space. Her own.

At the top of the narrow stairs, Charity flipped on a light. It was a few moments before she stepped inside. From the doorway, her eyes trailed the room. "Did you move the furniture around?"

Daisy scanned the space—a daybed along one wall, with a small, round end table nearby; the trunk in one corner; a fabric-covered chair by the small window that overlooked the sea; and everything resting beneath exposed rafters of dark wood. So, maybe there were bags and boxes tucked and stacked around the furniture, but she didn't mind. It made her feel safe, like everything was there to watch over her, protect her. There was even a wedding photo in a broken frame that Daisy had found and hung on one wall. "The room was like this. I didn't change anything. Except that." She pointed to the wedding picture.

Charity crossed the room to it. "There's one like it downstairs. It's my Gram and Gramps. This must be a copy."

Daisy pointed to the frame. "The corner was busted, but I tacked it together and hung it up. Seemed like it should be displayed. Not sitting on an old trunk."

Charity's gaze dropped to the bed, then the chair.

Daisy had never thought it was weird until now. Why would someone have a room set up like this when there were ten bedrooms on the second floor?

Charity knelt in front of the trunk. Knees bent and hands splayed on the warm, rich wood, she gazed over her shoulder at Daisy. "This was my grandmother's hope chest."

Daisy plopped onto the nearby chair when Charity opened the case, its rusted hinges groaning in protest. Daisy had already scoured through everything in the room. Nothing new there.

A scent like old books and dust wafted out of the trunk. She watched Charity close her eyes and inhale deeply; obviously she wasn't afraid of inhaling dust mites.

A folded quilt rested on one side of the trunk, the plastic box of photos on the other. "I've been looking for these," Charity said.

Daisy nodded, uncertain if she should admit rifling through the possessions Charity obviously adored. She pointed at the box as Charity lifted it from the case and placed it behind her. "Lots of cool pictures in that box."

Charity smiled. "I suppose they kept you company on a lot of long, lonely nights."

Daisy pursed her mouth. "It's fun to make up stories about the people in the photos. Who they are, where they're going. The ones with a dark-haired little girl in them—that's you, isn't it?"

Charity nodded. "The best times of my childhood were right here on this island." She pulled a deep breath. "Also the worst time of my life."

"When your grandma died?" Daisy pushed off the chair and slowly dropped onto the floor beside Charity. "I kind of feel weird about having gone through all this stuff now. Like I was intruding."

"You didn't go through everything." Charity sank both hands into the trunk. There was a clunking sound, then a scraping.

Daisy leaned forward and peered inside. "It has a false bottom."

Charity had already tilted the fake bottom up, and there below it, wrapped in a plastic bag, was another set of photos. "My gramps didn't even know about the false bottom. Gram told me on my last trip here because she'd planned to give it to me once I got older."

"So, she showed you all this stuff?"

Charity shook her head. "No. She never even told me where it was." She slowly opened the plastic bag. "I've never seen these pictures before."

"Why hadn't she planned to give the trunk to your mother?"

"Mom didn't want it. Said the musty smell irritated her allergies."

"Harsh," Daisy mumbled. "Well, it's yours now." She peered at a photo because Charity was laying them out on the floor. "Is this your grandpa?"

"Yes." Charity took the photo and pulled it closer. There in the picture, a young couple in love held hands with a Ferris wheel as their backdrop. "No. This isn't Gramps." Tension filled her words.

Daisy took the picture back and stared at it again. On the far wall was the wedding photo. Charity grabbed it and compared the two men while Daisy stared over her shoulder. "That's your gramps, right?" She pointed to the wedding picture.

"Yes."

"This guy looks the same to me."

Charity shook her head. "No. Look, Gramps wasn't this tall. Or thin. I've seen dozens of pictures of him as a young man." Sparks of electric energy flew off Charity, causing Daisy to want to retreat.

"They have the same eyes." Daisy pointed.

That's when whatever the mystery was must have registered for Charity because she started grabbing up pictures from the hidden box and looking at them, then casting each one aside. After a long time, she spoke. "They have the same eyes because these pictures are of Uncle Harold."

Daisy sucked in a breath. Without wanting them to, her eyes trailed down to the stack of maybe twenty pictures where Charity's grandma and her uncle Harold held hands, had their arms around each other, basically looking like they were totally in love. When she could look no more, Daisy cast a glance at Charity, who seemed equally shell-shocked. Her mouth hung open, and her skin had gone pale.

"It's impossible," Charity said.

"Why would your grandmother keep these? I mean, she loved your grandpa, right?"

"More than life."

"Or so you thought," Daisy added and tossed one of the photos at Charity's feet.

CHAPTER 11
The Hurricane

Charity gathered the photos to take downstairs. She'd tuck them in a drawer in her bedroom. There were at least a dozen photos in the bunch where Harold was hugging Gram. She forced away the questions and the trickle of impending calamity that niggled at her consciousness. There was no time to dive into the love life of her teenaged grandmother. After all, Hurricane Erika was getting ready to make landfall and right before it, Hurricane Ellen Marie Baxter was getting ready to board the water taxi.

There were definitely storms brewing. Charity just wasn't sure which one would do the most damage.

She flew down the stairs, hoping to leave all the questions behind— at least for a while—and ticked off the things she needed to do before the storm hit. She left Daisy in the attic and asked her to close things up when she was finished. The girl had gathered a few items to take downstairs to her room. Charity wanted to keep the attic locked after today.

Dalton and Uncle Harold had put the storm shutters on the downstairs windows, making the house mausoleum-dark. They'd likely lose power, for a few hours at least, a few days at most, so she'd sent Harold to buy more candles, but he'd returned with a gas-powered generator. Daisy had filled both claw-foot bathtubs with water, and Dalton had moved potted plants from her garden into her sleeping porch studio. She'd moved the bag of the special ingredient into the house.

Dalton arrived by way of the back door, toting a sleeping bag. She'd asked him to weather the storm with her, Harold, and Daisy. Now, with her mom coming and the scandalous photos upstairs burning a hole through her bureau drawer, she wondered if any of this was a good idea.

But the smile on his face as he pointed a flashlight at her and said, "Tag, you're it," melted her apprehension.

"Why the sleeping bag? I told you I made up one of the beds for you."

He brushed past her and paused at the kitchen window—the only one they hadn't covered with storm shutters. Dalton looked out over the garden. "No sense dirtying the sheets. I can sleep in the bag and save you the trouble."

She stopped beside him at the window. "Oh, didn't I mention *you'll* be doing the sheets?"

He chuckled. "Some hotel this is if I have to do my own sheets."

"Not yours, everyone's." She blinked innocently.

He bumped his shoulder against hers, then turned a watchful eye to the garden. He'd worked so hard on it, and she hated the fact that it had to suffer through Storm Erika. "Will Erika wipe it all away?"

"Nah. I've anchored everything that I can. The potted plants are the most vulnerable, but those are all—"

"On my sleeping porch." She tossed a look to the studio, where an array of brightly colored plants and flowers now gave the room a tropical feel and smell.

"Hope you weren't planning on working."

"How could I? I'll be busy washing bedding, right?" She sighed. "My mom's coming."

His chin dropped forward. "In a hurricane?"

"Yeah, seems ironic. No stopping Ellen Marie when she gets something in her head. Also," Charity checked the kitchen door and lowered her voice, "I found Daisy's mother."

"Really? That's great." Dalton placed the sleeping bag on the counter.

Daisy popped into the kitchen carrying a stack of old towels. "Whose sleeping bag?"

Charity had noticed Daisy's interest in things that screamed *mobility*. Backpacks, gym bags, sleeping bags, flashlights. Charity had started to wonder if Daisy spent most of her time readying for Charity to send her packing. She had watched the girl tuck food away—packets of ketchup, unopened sleeves of crackers, even a jar of olives. Charity hadn't talked to her about it because if the food items made her feel more comfortable, so be it. She also noticed the girl slept with everything she owned piled around her on the bed. There were empty drawers in her room, but she preferred her stuff to be within arm's reach.

Charity had asked her to keep quiet about the photos they'd discovered. She figured Daisy was good at keeping secrets—a year on the street had likely taught her the value of loyalty. Charity needed her loyalty in this. If any of it came to light while her mother was there . . . well, she didn't want to think about it.

Plus, Dalton and Harold were becoming friends, and she couldn't help but feel that this news of romance between her grandmother and Uncle Harold might darken Dalton's opinion of her uncle. After all, Dalton still wore his wedding ring and still seemed fiercely devoted to a woman who'd been gone for over a year. Loyalty. Dalton had it in spades. Besides, they didn't really know what those pictures were all about. And though Charity ached to know, she'd give Harold plenty of time before hitting him with questions. He still sometimes seemed like a skittish cat. Say the wrong thing, and maybe he'd bolt. She wasn't ready to lose him.

"Will the weeping willow live through the hurricane?" Daisy asked and stopped beside them to look out past the garden.

Concern washed over Charity. She hadn't even considered what a hurricane could do to the weeping tree. Her gaze fell on Dalton. He placed a hand over hers. "It'll be fine." But just as he said it, the wind gusted, sending a wave of forceful air over the garden and the tree. The shrubs and plants tilted as if trying to lie down and take cover. The branches of the weeping tree rocked, exposing the trunk and allowing loose leaves to release their grip and fall to the ground. The tree suddenly looked like an old, old woman, worn down by life, long hair split to reveal a pink scalp, frail body fighting to stand against the approaching storm.

Dalton whispered in Charity's ear, "Don't worry, the tree is strong." She never would have thought she'd be protective of the weeping tree, but here she was, wishing they could somehow anchor it.

She tried to pry her focus from the tree. Dalton picked up on it—he always seemed to—and changed the subject. "Everyone in town is gearing up for the storm."

"Are they?" The willow's branches swayed in the wind, tiny leaves releasing their grip and flying away from the tree.

He turned her to face him. "Yep. Do you mind if Mrs. Cready comes by? I saw her in town. She just returned from her sister's up north. I'm not sure she's ready to face a storm like this on her own. I'm fairly certain she hasn't had time to gather provisions."

"I don't mind." Charity wanted to meet her, but this probably wasn't the best time. On the other hand, she'd never turn someone away.

"She'll probably just wait out the worst of it—which should be around ten or eleven o'clock tonight, and then I'll drive her home. It's just a few blocks."

"There are beds ready. She's welcome to stay. I'm not going to send an old woman out in the rain at midnight."

"She was going to stop by the Barlows, then come over. I know they'll try to get her to stay there, but they only have one bedroom, so she'd need to sleep on the couch. But I figured if you don't want any more company, I'd ask them to insist."

"Dalton, she was Gramps's friend. Even kept the house up for him. I'd never let her sleep on a couch when we have plenty of room and a perfectly good bed. You did the right thing."

He brushed a hand through his hair. "It was weird. I just opened my mouth and heard myself saying we'd love to have her here. I don't know what came over me, Charity. This isn't my house. I had no right."

It was weird if one looked at it from the outside. But inside, within the walls of the circus house, it seemed perfectly normal. Just like her constantly saying things like "we" have plenty of room. Instead of "I" have plenty of room.

Who exactly was "we?" She'd pondered that thought a couple of nights ago when she couldn't sleep, and there were cookies and milk screaming her name in the kitchen. Was "we" her and Uncle Harold? Dalton? Gram and Gramps, who might not physically be there now, but whose essence marked rooms of the whole house? She'd decided "we" was . . . all of them. Daisy included. It was their home, not just hers. And after four cookies and a belly full of two-percent, she'd wiped the crumbs from her mouth and gone to bed, a smile on her face. "Chivalry came over you, Dalton. It isn't a crime. And you've been working so hard on the garden, I'm sure you've taken a bit of ownership in this place. You've offered up enough blood to the thorn gods to have a say in what goes on here."

"And you're too kind."

From behind them, "And I'm about to vomit. Could you two keep your sweet talk to a minimum while company is here? It's kind of sickening." Daisy spun and left the kitchen.

Dalton scratched his head. Charity shrugged. Sweet talk. Humph.

The first knock on the front door was Mrs. Cready, a woman who was both everything and nothing like what Charity had expected. She'd pictured her old and frail but more able to do the housework than Gramps had been. A stylish-looking elderly woman smiled on the other side of the front door, her hair wrapped in a plastic rain cover and her trench coat dripping.

Charity shook her hand and said hello.

"Goodness, I'd forgotten how dark the downstairs could be with the storm shutters in place. I'm Louise Cready. Your grandfather adored you."

Charity had intended to introduce herself, but that seemed unnecessary now. "Come on in." The wind was starting to howl, gusts becoming a constant press of electrified air. The streets littered with bits of trees and shrubs unable to withstand the forceful assault.

Daisy made tea, and the odd trio—a teen-something, a thirtysomething, and a seventy-something—sat in the parlor and sipped Earl Grey while the storm built. The men were working upstairs to make sure the windows were secured. No storm shutters up there, so they moved furniture away from the openings and placed large pieces of plywood against them. From the inside, it wouldn't stop the window from breaking, but it would offer some protection to the contents of the house.

"So, had you known my gramps for long before he passed?"

A reflective smile appeared on Louise's face. "For years and years."

She was an attractive woman whose light-brown hair was dusted with silver streaks, as if she'd requested that each shimmering strand be placed in a specific spot. If everyone could look this beautiful as they aged, no one would mind going gray. The entire hair-coloring business would lose an important niche.

Louise crossed her legs and sat back on the velvet chair. "We've met before, Charity. You just don't remember."

"When I was small?"

Louise nodded. She'd left her tailored trench coat at the front door to reveal a peach-colored pantsuit beneath, the expensive kind sold in those upscale boutiques that catered to wealthy older women. Trendy enough to look modern but elegant enough to hint at money. She wore her clothes well.

Louise stared up at the chandelier. "Goodness, it must be twenty-odd years back, now. Your grandparents were close friends of mine. Losing Marilyn was like losing a sister. Hardest thing I've ever gone through next to losing my husband."

Charity should remember this woman, who loved her gram like a sister.

Louise tilted forward on the seat. "Charity, you were very small. And when you came to visit, life was all about you. As it should be. Your visits were golden to Marilyn and George."

Charity did remember a woman coming by to visit Gram on occasion. A pretty lady, with blondish hair and . . . "You had a limp." It was coming back to her now.

Louise tilted her head and used her hand to brush the hair away from her shoulder. The light above caught the sheen of scarring along her neck. "And scars from a car accident. It happened on my way home from school my senior year. Not the greatest way to end a school year, I can tell you."

Daisy leaned forward. "You don't limp now."

Louise winked. "Time heals all wounds, or so it would seem." Her focus went to Charity. "Funny that you remember the limp but not the burns. I always thought they were so glaring."

Charity smiled, now recalling more and more bits of this woman and who she was to her gram and gramps. "I don't think I ever noticed them. Your eyes were so captivating. When I saw you, I couldn't stop looking at them. I thought you must have been a descendent from royalty or perhaps a mermaid or fairies."

Louise tilted her head back and laughed. "No. Descendent of a local fisherman."

But there had always been an air of intrigue surrounding Louise. That, Charity remembered well. She'd likely created it in her own head, but still. Such a lovely lady, but damaged, physically damaged, and to a young girl that had seemed horrifically unfair.

If Louise had been close to Gram and Gramps that many years ago, she must know Uncle Harold. Charity hadn't even gotten the chance to tell her that Harold was there. She opened her mouth to say so, but Dalton and Harold materialized at the top of the stairs announcing that the house was secure. All three women turned to face them.

Louise's teacup crashed to the floor as she jolted upright from her seat.

Daisy rushed to help her and righted the cup, where it continued to dump tea onto the marble floor. It was a miracle it hadn't broken.

Louise groped for the chair arms and clung to one as if it were the last tree in the forest, and she was the last leaf. Charity stood, too, but found herself unable to move as she took it all in. Dalton and Harold froze on the stairs, mouths agape and obviously wondering what invisible demon caused the woman to fly up out of her seat, toppling her teacup. Louise had a white-knuckled grip on the chair, whose material was beginning to pucker.

It must be Harold. From a distance he favored Gramps, and Louise looked as if she'd just seen a ghost. A delicate hand covered her mouth, but her other hand stayed in a death lock on the chair. "Harold," she whispered, and the word was so soft, so filled with uncertainty, that Charity thought perhaps she would disappear once she'd uttered it. The fog of a word drifted around the room, finding no comfortable place to land.

But its impact was felt. In like manner, Harold placed a hand to his mouth. "Louise," he said. Even from a distance, his eyes looked misty. He brushed his hands over pants, dusty from hours of work readying for the storm. Then his fingers combed through his hair, an effort to look his best, no doubt. Hand on the banister, he floated down the steps toward her.

Charity bubbled with her expectation of what was surely going to be a joyful reunion. Harold stepped closer to Louise, eyes scanning her face, half smile in place as if his mouth couldn't decide on joy or wonder. He reached his hands out.

Charity's heart thudded to an abrupt stop when Louise took a full step back, closing off her body by crossing her arms protectively.

And there, the room of onlookers hung in stilled silence as Harold's face changed from happiness to anguish. Charity's chest burned for him. Such a look of utter disappointment filled the space around his eyes, his mouth. Even his wrinkles seemed to deepen. They were the last flower petals standing against a harsh winter, and a final freeze squeezed their life.

Harold's gaze dropped, his mouth pressed into a line as if he could somehow recover the moment. His posture shifted from welcoming to conversational as he tried to speak, but his voice quivered on the first word, causing him to also take a step back and clear his throat. "It's nice to see you," he said, his voice fighting to sound solid. "It's been a long time."

Charity glanced at Louise, who'd also attempted some form of recovery. An emotionless smile appeared and disappeared. But the memories that floated across her face were as palpable as sea spray—cool, instant, and quickly vanishing. She'd released the chair, and her fingertips fidgeted at her sides. "I'm . . . I didn't expect to see you. You're . . . here."

"I just got back," Harold said.

Louise's confused eyes landed on Charity.

"This will sound strange, Louise, but Gramps sent for him before he died."

Fury blazed on Louise's face. "And you're only *now* arriving?"

Charity moved closer to her and placed a hand on Louise's arm. Her touch was gentle because it seemed as though Louise might crumble like the bits of ash on the end of a cigarette left burning too long. "Uncle Harold didn't get the message until after Gramps had died. He came immediately upon receiving it."

Louise forced a smile. "Immediately, huh? It was nice to see you, Harold." She turned to Charity. "Thank you so much for the tea. I'll be at the Barlows. Maybe we can get together after the storm. There's a lot I'd love to tell you about your grandfather."

They'd established that Louise would stay at Baxter House for the night, so her insistence on leaving couldn't be addressed without causing more embarrassment to the woman. So Charity took her arm to see her to the front door. Funny how, moments ago, Louise had seemed so strong, so elegant, and now she seemed as if a puff of air would disintegrate her. As they made their way through the foyer, Charity noticed something else, too. Louise's limp had returned.

৩

Ellen Marie Baxter had never driven in a hurricane. The wind didn't gust like New York storms; it simply stayed solid, forcing her to fight the steering wheel and causing her to squint into the oncoming pellets.

Hurricanes. She didn't see the big deal. She'd gotten on the last water taxi to the island, the sky a drab and boring shade of unimaginative gray. Leonard owned a suit that color, and she'd always hated it. When gray was the new black, she'd completely balked, refusing to wear such a tragedy. She'd been right, of course. Gray quickly became gauche, and all her society friends had to toss their purchases and return to their senses.

Ellen chuckled at that. All those thousands of dollars spent, only to be given to housemaids or sent to thrift stores. The poor? Let them wear gray. She swerved to miss a felled palm tree and cursed Leonard for sending her on this errand. It was in her best interest, of course. That's what she always told herself when he needed her to do something she thought ridiculous or unfruitful or simply an imposition. A pang of guilt pinched her brows. She quickly lifted her fingertip to scrub against the spot. *Botox,* she reminded herself. It wasn't that she didn't want to see Charity. She was her mother. But around Charity, Ellen had always felt like not quite enough.

And Ellen was sick and tired of not being enough. She'd never been enough for her parents, for her lovers, for Charity. Now she wasn't enough for Leonard and his spoiled brat daughters, Portia and Giselle. And Ellen already knew she wouldn't be enough for Portia's new baby, either. Harold, her uncle, was at Charity's house, but she didn't think that would change anything in her plan. He'd always been nice enough, though she hadn't seen him in decades. She flipped on the radio to drown the voice in her head, but with the wind, she could barely make out the station. All she heard was a grumbling, twangy country music horror that seemed to have *not enough* as the lyrics.

With the force of a woman with a new credit card, she swiped a hand across the radio, silencing it. *Not enough, not enough* echoed in her head.

She couldn't deny that something had sprouted in her stomach when Leonard told her to go to see Charity. A tiny little seed had broken open, exposing roots that sought to find fertile ground. It had surprised her at first, and then it had unsettled her. Finally, she'd decided to call it precisely what it was. She missed Charity. Missed having her an hour away. Missed knowing she could hop on the train and be at her door. Ellen even knew the reason why. Of all the people who had come and gone in her life, Charity was the only one who loved her unconditionally. Though Ellen felt like not enough for Charity, Charity had always made sure she was more than enough for Ellen.

Her stomach sickened as she pulled into the drive, and she forced her thoughts away from the self-examination she'd just put herself through. She focused on the house. This would be such a beautiful estate if it wasn't on this poor excuse for an island. If it sat in the Hamptons, she'd have fought Charity tooth and manicured nail to live in it. She and Leonard and the girls could have had lavish parties where all of the city would buzz about the place. She'd gut it, of course. Strip every ounce of that horrible circus interior. Make it glow. Make it relevant.

The wind howled overhead like a pack of ravenous shoppers zeroing in on a kill. She forced the car door open and left her suitcase in the backseat. Charity could come get it. The door slammed shut, and she barely got out of its way. Just like that, she was trapped. Cold whistled around her head as she made her way to the door, the only opening on the first floor not shrouded by metal shutters. The familiar feeling of being strangled by giant hands gripped her. Ellen took several deep breaths, only to find that when one breathed in a tropical storm, one inhaled more water than air. She coughed and stumbled up the front steps just as someone was swinging the giant door open.

A woman stepped out, her face and upper body covered by an umbrella that had no chance of surviving the onslaught of obnoxious wind—nice trench coat, though. From the safety of the front porch, Ellen watched her walk toward the house next door. She hollered after her, but the words disappeared in the rush of air. The woman hadn't even seen her.

Ellen huffed and turned her attention to the door, where Charity stood with an audience of onlookers. "My bag is in the car."

Charity seemed stunned for a moment but quickly recovered and ushered her in. The good-looking man behind her said, "I'll go get the bag." He smiled and reached a hand out for her keys.

Her heart did a little sputter and that charisma spark shot right into her gut. This must be Charity's neighbor. She'd mentioned him on the phone. She'd left the car unlocked but made a show of tossing her hair and searching out the keys. How old was he? Thirties, probably. She could still attract *thirties*, if she chose. But now it was harder to get younger men to notice her. Ellen painted on her brightest smile. "It's monstrous out there."

His hand was still waiting, so she placed the rental cars keys in his palm, making sure there was skin-to-skin contact, her fingertips brushing that delicate spot where the webbing of his fingers lay, her wrist gently scraping against the muscle at the base of his thumb.

He didn't seem to notice the connection, so she spun away from him and turned her gaze on Charity. They hugged, awkwardly, because Charity was all bony shoulders, hipbones, and elbows. She always had been. Ellen had told her the sweets would one day catch up, but wouldn't you know it? Mother Nature found it infinitely pleasing to make a liar out of her. Charity hadn't put on a pound. *Wait till you hit forty,* Ellen thought.

"You look great, Mom. I've missed you." Charity's heart-shaped face made her seem slightly angelic. She looked good, still young, her thirty-one years hidden somewhere behind her smile. Her eyes, filled with emotion, scanned Ellen's face.

Ellen patted her cheek, creating some distance between them. "You look good, too, Charity. Happy." That last word was a tad difficult to sputter because she didn't want Charity to be happy here. She wanted her to come home to New York. Truth be told, Ellen needed her. More than she cared to admit. Still, she wouldn't fight for that on this visit. No, that'd keep. This visit was about the family trip and the importance of Charity agreeing to go. Ellen would play nice. No ultimatums, no manipulation. They never worked on Charity, and Ellen had to learn more creative ways to convince her daughter. Charity was sweet, but she was nobody's fool. This invitation couldn't have been done over the phone because she needed to see Charity's face to judge her reaction. Leonard's girls hadn't been nice to Charity in the past. There was always the chance Charity would turn down the invitation.

An irritating question scraped at her mind. Was she putting Charity in an impossible situation? No. Charity was strong, level. Maybe she and the girls could actually get to know one another. Or maybe Charity would reject the offer. But that wouldn't bode well for any of them. Especially Ellen.

～♋

Charity sat in the parlor with her mother, who—in spite of the storm she'd come through—looked ready for a night out on the town. How Ellen Marie Baxter could always look so put together, Charity didn't know.

"Where did everyone go?" Ellen asked, casting a glance up the stairs.

"They're giving us time to catch up." Where had *Dalton* gone was more what she meant, but Charity knew her mom well enough to know she wouldn't ask that outright. Ellen Marie was always more interested in conversations when there were good-looking men around who could hear her bragging about how she'd gotten carded at a club or how someone mistook her for some celebrity. Charity had always believed her far-fetched stories until one day she realized that her mother had passed the half-century age mark, and there was no way, no possible way, someone had thought she was under twenty-one. If she'd been carded in the last twenty years, it had been done out of pity or as a joke. She was still beautiful, though. A striking woman who commanded the room.

Ellen Marie sat on the corner chair. She blinked and straightened her spine when Charity bent her knees and tucked her feet beneath her on the couch. The two women couldn't be more different. But Charity was learning to embrace who she was. She'd learned *that* since she'd been here, taught lovingly by the house, by the pottery. They gave her power. She was Charity Monroe Baxter and even being weighed and measured by her mother couldn't make her ashamed of who she was. *Vive la différence!*

"What brings you here, Mom? You said you needed to discuss something with me."

Ellen smiled. "I do. Leonard is taking us on a family cruise. Fourteen days in Europe. It's an absolute dream vacation, Charity."

"Oh, Mom. That's great! You'll have so much fun. We always talked about going to Europe. Seeing the Eiffel Tower, touring the Black Forest."

"Every port is incredible. All my friends are absolutely green with envy."

"You'll have to take a ton of pictures. I want to see everything when you return." She was glad that her mother was finally getting to live the life she'd always dreamed of. Even if Charity wasn't a huge part of it. Ellen was her mother, and Charity wanted to see her happy.

"You'll see everything, Charity, because you'll be with us."

The world screeched to a stop. "What?"

Ellen folded her hands over her lap. "That's why I came. To invite you."

Charity's first thought was to pinch her own arm to ensure that she wasn't asleep. "But . . ." But what? She couldn't very well finish that sentence. It went something like, *But you said it was a family vacation, and since when am I included on family anything?* Since her mother married Leonard, they had kept the two "families" separate on all except the rarest occasions. Even though they frequently invited all of Leonard's extended family over for holidays, there were years Charity never received an invitation. Not written, not spoken, not at all. "I didn't think Leonard and his girls liked me very much."

Ellen scoffed. "That's not true, Charity. You just don't have much in common, and I never told them they had to be something they weren't to make you feel comfortable."

Well, that's not what she would have wanted. And true, she was desperately awkward in social situations. Still, she was Ellen's daughter. Shouldn't she be invited to all the family get-togethers? Well, she could ponder that question later. They wanted her to go on a European cruise with them. That was . . . well, it certainly helped make up for the times she'd felt slighted when her mother suggested the two of them get together for lunch to exchange Christmas gifts. "Just us," her mother would say, as if that negated a family gathering. Why all these memories and old hurts were rising up now, she couldn't say, but her eyes were welling up. Maybe this was it. She'd always known her mom was capable of more. Maybe she was finally getting to see it. "I would love, to. Yes."

Her mother smiled, and it was the most beautiful thing Charity had ever seen.

A thought occurred to her. "And I won't expect you and Leonard to pay my way. I can do that myself."

Her mother waved a hand through the air. "The staterooms are already covered. You'll only need spending money."

"Thank you." Charity itched to hug her mother, but Ellen Marie wasn't a hugger. Charity'd gotten her once at the door, so they'd probably reached their hug quota. "You must have been really confident that I could go if he already paid for my stateroom. That was very generous of Leonard." And here, she'd always thought the doctor stuffy, self-absorbed, and cold.

"We had to lock down the tickets. It was filling up fast. Plus, we'd need the stateroom whether you went or not. You're rooming with Portia."

"Oh." Charity tried to get a mental picture of herself and the princess of a girl in the same room. "I'm surprised she'd agree to that."

Ellen laughed. "She'd be stupid not to. She's a complete night owl. And you prefer to go to bed early."

Charity still didn't see how that helped with the fact that Portia tended to treat Charity slightly better than a plague but worse than a rodent.

Ellen finally shrugged. "You'll be there to stay with Portia's baby, so she can go out at night."

Heat flashed from Charity's forehead down. "You want me to babysit?" And if she was staying with the baby while Portia partied, that meant she'd have the baby the next morning while Portia slept it off.

"This is a great opportunity for you to get to know the girls. I'd think you'd be happy, Charity. This is your *family* we're talking about."

Charity flew up off the couch. "Your stepdaughters have wanted nothing to do with me since you married. But now, suddenly, I'm part of the family? Because I can offer my babysitting services?" She had to repeat the words to make sure they were real. Hearing them again, from her own mouth, only made her angrier.

"Be reasonable, Charity Monroe. Think about someone else. What about me? I was looking forward to spending time with you on this trip."

"When, Mom? When I'm not babysitting?" She hated that it hurt so much, but it did. This was Ellen Marie Baxter 101. Why Charity always expected more from her mother, she didn't know. She really needed to learn how to let go of things.

Ellen brushed a hand through her hair. "Leonard will be playing golf while we're in Germany, and I thought we could spend the day together. Just us." It was the *just us* that did it. *Just us*—we'll get together for Christmas lunch at the most exclusive spot in Manhattan. *Just us*, her token day with her mother in payment for being the hired help while Leonard was too busy to entertain Ellen. Charity never wanted opulent lunches at Christmastime; she wanted to sit at the table with her family and eat Christmas dinner. It was never going to be that way, she realized again for the hundredth time. From the outside, Leonard's house glowed with holiday perfection, attention given to lighting every shrub in the yard, to the placement of every ornament on the tree. The perfectly spread, shimmering tablecloths and plates and glasses that sparkled like fairies in a windstorm. The few times Charity had been invited, she'd adored the feel of family—even if she was an outsider. She appreciated the work and thought that went into the entire thing.

But then the *just us* years began. And Ellen always said it like it was a treat, not realizing she was also stripping away the one thing Charity really wanted—that sense of family. And with more clarity than she'd have given herself credit for, she simply smiled down at her mother and said, "Portia needs to hire a nanny."

Ellen muttered, "No one can work for her."

"I won't be going, Mom." Charity left the parlor and walked into the kitchen, out of the fog of Ellen. At the sink, she gazed out at the forever wind and the garden. Off to the right, the weeping tree gripped the soil, its roots probably as deep as her sorrow. In her mind's eye, she could picture Dalton in the garden, Daisy sneaking potato chips from the pantry, her Uncle Harold grabbing her by the waist and spinning her around the dining room, humming music until her laughter took its place. Charity *had* family. Finally. And it had taken her mother's visit to make her realize it. She slammed a hand on the sink and started to go back into the parlor, but at the kitchen door, she stopped. Brushing her hair over her shoulder, she cast a glance behind her. Beyond the kitchen window, the yard and the edge of the weeping tree stole her focus.

Without a thought to what the wind would do to her, she marched through the kitchen, through the sleeping porch, and into her yard. The wind grabbed the door as she tried to close it, causing her to have to muscle her way. But some things were worth the fight.

Blocking her eyes from the wind, she stepped to the edge of the weeping tree, ignoring the sudden gooseflesh rising on her skin. Its branches swayed, dragged by the impossible press of strong wind off the Gulf. The ground beneath her feet was a mix of sand and dirt, and her toes sank into it. The trunk seemed to groan under the pressure of the storm, but Charity stepped closer. Above her, a mud-gray sky—the remnants of a great artist's pallet—cleared for a moment, offering a glimpse of bright-blue beyond the clouds. It was as if heaven were peering down on her, all the angels watching with bated breath in case the weeping tree sought its final revenge, releasing its grip on the soil and falling on her. A fitting end to a lifelong rivalry. After all, she'd taken an ax to its trunk as an angry eleven-year-old.

Charity's throat was thick. Emotions swirled like the leaves on the trees. "I shouldn't have tried to chop you down," she whispered. Memories rose from the basement of her heart. "But Gram and Gramps were everything to me. And in a way, they both died that day."

Around her, the wind stopped. And quite suddenly, she wanted—needed—to step beneath the tree. She swayed forward but caught herself. There, an invisible wall born from too much blame and too little trust kept her feet steadfast. She couldn't, *wouldn't*, step beneath the tree.

Tears filled her eyes, making the long branches before her swim in her vision. When she blinked, the tears ran down her cheeks in straight lines. "It felt like my world ended." The emotion was more than she could bear, so Charity dropped her head into her hands and cried. Minutes later, she opened her eyes. The tree was still there, and her feet were still unmoving, but something had changed. She glanced down to find a long, slender branch draped over each of her shoulders. A bit of air escaped her mouth. It was as if the tree was consoling her. "Thank you," she whispered, trailing a finger along one of the branches.

When the wind's short reprieve ended, she carefully replaced the branches that had been across her shoulders, lowering them to their spots where they shrouded the outside world. Charity walked back to her sleeping porch and cast a final glance to the tree before going to find her mother.

Back in the parlor, her mother stood up from the settee, looking uncertain. She had nowhere else to go, but she likely wanted to escape.

Ellen flinched when Charity grabbed and hugged her. "Mom, thank you for inviting me. I'm still not going, but Germany would have been a lovely day. I'm thrilled you're here. Let me tell you about Baxter House."

✦

Daisy had already decided she didn't like Ellen, Charity's mom. She had a way of dismissing people that set Daisy's nerves on edge. Later that night, as the storm worsened, they all huddled in the kitchen, and Daisy kept one eye on the window where the hurricane raged and one eye on Ellen.

Harold's generator hadn't been used, but it was gassed up and ready for the lights to go. To keep from thinking about Ellen, Daisy turned her thoughts to poor Mrs. Cready and how she'd looked almost frightened when she left. She'd tucked the umbrella against her upper body and fought her way to the Barlows' house next door. Of course, they hadn't actually seen her go inside. They'd all been distracted by Charity's mother.

Elbow on the table, Daisy propped her chin on her palm. "Do you think the Barlows are OK? It sounded like a tree fell by their house. Plus, it seems like we should make sure Mrs. Cready made it over there."

Dalton stood. "I can run next door. The wind died a bit, and the worst part of the storm won't hit for a while yet."

Daisy walked to the kitchen wall. "Do we have their number? I can just call." She picked up the phone and waited for someone to give her the number. When she realized there was no dial tone, she set it down. "Phone's out."

Charity pointed to the counter. "Use my cell. Their number is in the contacts list."

Daisy grabbed it and pressed the phone button, but when she saw the last called number, her heart stopped. She was staring at her home phone number. A gust of breath left her mouth.

All that talk about how Charity cared about her was just a lie. At the first opportunity, Charity had called her mom. Traitor. So she was just waiting to get rid of Daisy. She'd suspected as much. Who takes in a teenager by choice? "You called my mother."

Charity popped up from the bar stool, hands out in surrender. "Daisy, I didn't talk to her."

Daisy was lightheaded. Somehow, she dropped the phone on the counter and held on to the edge of the sink to stabilize herself. "You want to get rid of me."

"No. I don't. I just wanted her to know you're safe."

"You lied to me. I told you I'd let her know when I was ready."

Charity shook her head. "I shouldn't have done it, Daisy. When she answered, I hung up." Charity was pleading now. "I just had a weak moment and thought about how worried she might be."

Worried? She wasn't worried. She'd called Daisy a liar and picked a loser boyfriend over her own child. And maybe, just maybe, Charity wasn't any better. Sure, she'd been nice, but how long could that last? People didn't just open their doors to strangers. The newness would wear off, and before long, they'd wonder why they ever let a stranger into their house. But she'd so badly wanted to believe Charity was different. Daisy grabbed a flashlight off the counter and ran out of the room and through the front door. The rain had slowed almost to a stop, but the wind was relentless. She flipped on the flashlight and headed in the direction of the Barlows' house.

Wind blasted her face as she stopped on their front porch for a few moments and contemplated knocking. But she didn't really know the Barlows, and she'd only met Louise Cready earlier that evening. Daisy dropped her weight against their front door. She should have known not to get too comfortable. When you're comfortable, people have power over you. The power to let you down. When a curtain in the window moved, Daisy stepped back, expecting to see a friendly face gazing out at her. Instead, a fat, gray-and-mud-colored cat nosed the window.

Without taking time to think about it, she ran off the porch and toward the beach. When you get too comfortable, you count on people. And when you count on someone, they're going to let you down.

CHAPTER 12

Searching

Charity watched Dalton shake off the sand and come back inside. She'd stood on the front porch, waiting, wringing her hands while he'd gone down the steps to see where Daisy had gone.

"I saw her on the Barlows' porch. She must be over there."

Charity retrieved her cell phone and dialed their number, but a fast busy was the response. In her gut, a gnawing, angry thought ate away the last shreds of calm. She'd crossed a line with Daisy. The girl had trusted her, and she'd ruined it.

Dalton crossed the room and placed a hand on her arm. "I'll run next door and make sure she's OK."

Charity nodded. "Thanks, Dalton."

"Least I can do. This is my fault. I encouraged you to find her mother."

"Dalton, you had valid reasons. I just should have waited for her to want to call. No one can carry the blame for this but me."

"I'll be right back." She watched him leave and paced the kitchen floor while he was gone.

Ellen rose from her bar stool and poured a glass of water. "Have any wine around here?"

"No. I have caffeine-free soda."

Ellen sighed.

Charity could see that her mother was getting antsy. She'd watched her sneak out of the house and onto the front porch twice to smoke. That worried Charity. Her mom had always been a social smoker, only lighting up when she was in the company of smokers. Now she seemed hooked. "Does Leonard smoke?" The question came out of Charity's mouth before she could stop it.

Ellen's piercing eyes narrowed on her. "No."

Harold peeled an apple with a pocket knife, removing the entire red skin in one long spiral. "Bad stuff, that tobacco. George never did fully get over his addiction."

Ellen's frustration was thick enough to cut.

Dalton returned. "She's not over there. I'm going out to look for her."

Harold discarded the apple in midcut. "You're not goin' alone. I'll get my jacket."

꩜

Harold dropped into the seat of his car and headed north, since Dalton had said he'd go south. The branch- and debris-strewn road wound along the beach where a turbulent sea continued to pound the shoreline. Homes were dark, and Harold's eyes weren't what they used to be. Many of the colorful beach houses had been made hurricane-ready with window and door coverings. They'd also been abandoned by tenants who'd chosen to ride out the storm on the mainland. Maybe he should have suggested to Charity that their little group do the same. But it had only been hours before that the tropical storm had been upgraded to a full-blown hurricane.

His old eyes squinted, grazing along the landscape in an attempt to spot the young girl. Surely she'd find shelter. No one would be walking in this mess. Already the water was rising, swallowing the shoreline and crowding the homes. That was the thing about hurricanes: even if you survived the winds, you might find yourself fighting the flood waters. He stopped the car in the middle of the road. Off to the left, he saw something. Harold leaned toward the window, but it was only a runaway lawn chair. They'd secured everything back at the house, and with the lawn chair flipping and dancing, tipping end over end, he was glad they had. Rain pelted the windshield of his car as if giant buckets of water were being slung at him. This was an impossible task, he realized, shaking his head, his heart beginning to get heavy. It was a needle in a haystack, with the haystack in a giant vacuum cleaner.

Harold put the car into "Park," closed his eyes, and folded his hands. "Not sure if you're inclined to hear the prayer of an old man with more regrets than victories." His voice bounced around the empty car as if it had no purpose except to fill the moment. "Still, I'm going to ask. There's a girl out here somewhere. I'd sure appreciate it if you'd help us find her."

A palm branch smacked the side of his car door so hard, Harold jumped. He'd keep up the search. All night, if that's what it took, but he wouldn't give up.

It took another thirty minutes of driving up and down the beach road before he spotted something. Off to the right, out on the beach, sat a small shed. At first, he'd thought the light he'd seen from a broken window must have been a reflection from his own headlights. Still, he swung the front of the car around to get a better look, and there, the unmistakable slash of a moving light skittered about in the shed's window.

Daisy had left the house with a flashlight in her hands. His heart quickened. Surely this was her. His cell phone lay on the seat beside him, so he tried to call Dalton, but there was no signal. He stuffed the phone in his pocket and got out of the car. No sense calling her name, the sound would be absorbed by the roar of the wind and ocean. Before him, the sea had continued to rise, stealing the shoreline and creeping closer and closer to the row of houses and the small shed. Already, waves crested and brushed the foundation of the rickety little building. This was no safe place to weather a storm. He was thankful he'd gotten to her. With an arthritic knee screaming in protest, he ran toward the beacon of light, trying to keep the sand from slamming into his eyes.

Once there, he dragged the wooden door open and peered inside.

~∾~

"They've been gone too long." Charity paced the marble floor, her mother sitting on the settee with an unlit cigarette between her fingers. Charity headed for the front door. "I'm going out to look for them."

Ellen rolled her eyes. "Don't be foolish. You'd be as lost out there as the girl, and then they'd have to rescue you."

Charity stopped and turned to her mother, who was probably right. Her thoughts went to Daisy. "It's my fault she's out there."

Ellen stood and cocked both her head and her hip in that way that only she could. The motion conveyed more than words, assuring its receiver that whatever words were to follow could surely reduce a person to powder. "No, Charity Monroe, it's not *your* fault. *She* left. What kind of idiot runs out in a hurricane?"

What kind of idiot heads into one to ask her daughter to go on a family vacation to babysit? But Charity swallowed the comparison. A battle of wits was impossible to win when her mother was involved. "I broke her trust, Mom. I told her I wouldn't call her mother, but that's what I did."

Ellen waved the cigarette in the air. "Of course you did. She's a stranger, Charity. Not your problem."

Charity's hands fisted at her sides. "That's not why I called."

"Whatever. She's a runaway. There's no telling what kind of trouble could be following her. Of course, I don't want anything bad to happen to her, but honestly, Charity, what do you even know about this girl?"

How could anyone be so flippant about another human being? "I know she needs me."

Ellen placed the cigarette on a small table beside the settee. She crossed the room and placed her hands on Charity's folded arms.

Charity's eyes widened. Her mother rarely touched her.

There, on Ellen's forehead, a frown appeared. A *worry* frown. "Give it thirty more minutes; then head out into the fray, all right?"

Could she watch the clock for another thirty minutes? It was a lot to ask.

"Please," her mother said, the tiny lines around her eyes crinkling with the slightest hint of a smile.

Charity's heart melted. She'd try to rope the moon if her mother asked, even if she knew it was futile. It had bothered her for years that she'd do anything and everything to please her mother, to get the tiniest hint of approval from the woman who was so beautiful but so cold. But babysitting on a cruise ship had been the reminder she'd needed. She had the power to tell her mother no. Strength and self-reliance surged inside, and Charity opened her mouth to say she'd be back when they found Daisy, but her mother surprised her yet again.

"I know you feel helpless, not being out there looking for her. But when they return, they're going to be cold, soaking wet, and hungry. Let's do what needs to be done here, Charity. When we're done, if you insist on going out, I won't try to stop you."

Let's do what needs to be done here? Charity knew she must be frowning but couldn't help herself. Who was this woman? Her mother closed a slender hand around Charity's arm and pulled her toward the kitchen.

"Good to see your face, girl." Harold smiled at the frail, shivering wisp of a girl huddled in the corner of the shed, the light of the flashlight glaring in his eyes. "This ain't the best place to ride out a full-blown hurricane. You ready to head back?"

"There . . . there was a cat. She had babies, and I'd been feeding her scraps."

Harold scratched his head and glanced around the small, dark space. "There's no momma cat here during a storm like this. She'd have sensed it coming and moved her kittens somewhere safe."

Daisy removed the light from his eyes, but dark spots remained. He took a step inside the shed. "Now, I expect, you've had a bit of time to sit here and think about why Charity was calling your momma. I expect you know how much Charity cares about you, or she wouldn't have moved you right into her house. I expect you've thought about how she's grown more and more fond of you and that *that* could be the reason she tried to reach out to your mom. She's not looking to get rid of you. She don't need an excuse to do that. All she has to do is open the front door and say good-bye."

Daisy dropped her gaze to the shed floor. It was half covered with sand where decades of wind had forced a layer of the salty stuff between the rotting boards. A strong gust of wind slammed the shed, causing boards and roofing to creak. Harold looked overhead. A crack appeared near where Daisy sat. He motioned for her. "Come on. This place won't survive what's comin'."

Daisy stood and started to make her way over the floor strewn with boat parts and pieces of wood. She was almost to Harold when the roof caved in.

CHAPTER 13

Water Rising

"It's not the same," Dalton told himself as he paused on the front porch before entering Charity's house. The situation with Daisy couldn't be more different from the situation Kissy had been in. Still, the similarities haunted his mind. Kissy had been a helpless victim. So was Daisy. Kissy had trusted others to protect her. So had Daisy. And now Daisy was lost somewhere in the violence of a hurricane, and though Dalton certainly didn't feel about her the way he'd felt about his baby girl, the thought of losing her practically strangled him. It was an irrational response, yes. But it was also one he had no hope of controlling. To make the situation worse, he had the distinct feeling that Harold was also in trouble.

Dalton made his way into the house just as Charity and her mother were settling into the kitchen. He needed another flashlight, extra batteries, and a change of clothes. His jeans had gotten snagged on a tree branch and ripped. He stayed no more than five minutes, took the thermos of coffee offered by Ellen, and headed back out. On the porch he told Charity, "The storm's right over us. I'll check back every fifteen minutes or so in case either of them returns. Tell Harold to do the same. I'm going north now. I've covered all the area south unless she made it to town. If she did, she'll be fine. There are two shelters set up there. But I have a feeling she's north. With any luck, Harold has found her."

Before Dalton left, he bent and kissed Charity on the cheek. "Stay here."

Her gaze dropped. He leaned closer and reached to squeeze her arms. "Charity, promise me."

The smallest hint of a defiant frown pinched her brows. She was beautiful, standing there on her front porch and readying to run out into a hurricane to search for a girl he'd wanted to turn over to the police only a short while ago. Cold swept up his back and over his shoulders. It was a warning, a premonition of something on the horizon, something awful.

Finally, she relented. "I promise. I won't leave."

Relief flooded him.

"But *you* promise *me* you'll come back."

"I will." He grinned to lighten the mood. "I'm fairly certain the garden will need me tomorrow."

She swallowed. "The garden needs you all the time. More than it cares to admit."

Dalton winked and headed out into the storm.

Charity went into the house and found her mother bent over the fridge.

"It's not a chef's kitchen, but you've got enough to make a great pot of stew," Ellen said.

Her mother? Making stew? As if she'd heard Charity's thoughts, Ellen began talking. "Leonard is a workaholic. Always at the office. His practice has grown since we married, but I'd expected more time with him. We didn't need more money. Why wouldn't he want to be home?"

Ellen turned around, arms loaded with a variety of veggies from the refrigerator. She used her hip to close the door and spread the ingredients on the counter beside the stove. There was something warm and comforting about the kitchen and the way her mother washed vegetables under the running water of the sink, then lined them up on the counter. Sharp knife beside her, she chunked a pot roast Charity was going to attempt to cook for dinner one night into an iron skillet. She browned the meat, filling the kitchen with a delicious scent of garlic, meat, and onion.

"He liked for me to be home throughout the day." Ellen waved the knife in the air. "Oh, I would have been fine meeting the girls at the country club for a round of golf or shopping or even lunch and the spa. Most of them have a weekly routine that keeps them quite busy during the long hours of the day. But when I suggested to Leonard I find ways to busy myself—since he worked so much—he became angry. Apparently that's just what his wife—the girls' mother—had done before running off to the Caribbean with her Zumba instructor."

Charity sat down at the kitchen counter when her mother handed her a bunch of freshly washed carrots and said, "Bite-size pieces." Charity went right to work.

"So, you learned to cook? Don't you guys have a housekeeper who does the cooking for you?" She was certain her mother had mentioned a woman who took care of the house and meals.

"We had an older woman named Vivien, but Leonard let her go. He put me in charge of hiring the replacement. Sonia. She is French, a few years older than me, good skin. She watched me meander around the house for months before suggesting I join her for a chat in the kitchen while she cooked dinner."

"You two hit it off?" Charity tried to get a picture of her mother standing in the kitchen with the hired help. It was as strange as Ellen cooking while Charity sat chopping carrots.

Ellen smiled over her shoulder. "She'd led this incredible life. Poor but happy. Adventurous. She'd even spent a year on a yacht with a sheik."

"As his cook?"

"As his lover," Ellen corrected.

Charity could feel the heat rising to her face. "Oh dear."

"Bring the carrots." They dumped them into the pot of boiling broth. "Make another pot of coffee, Charity."

She did and tried to keep her focus on her mother's words rather than on the war raging beyond the windows. It was dark out, with only the single uncovered kitchen window to give a glimpse to the world beyond. "Look how high the water is," she said to her mom, pointing to the half-swallowed yard.

"Will it come into the house?"

Charity shrugged. Honestly, she didn't know. Dalton and Harold had placed sandbags around the exterior doors in the low areas. "I hope not."

"Well, at least we'll have good food and good coffee." Ellen blinked and turned away from the window as if doing so would make it all disappear.

Charity tried to smile. "Tell me more about Sonia."

⟨ ☙

You've lived a long life.

Harold couldn't explain why that thought ran through his head at the moment the ceiling collapsed, dumping lumber and gallons of water on them. It didn't matter that he'd lived a long life. What mattered was getting Daisy out of there. She screamed when Harold tried to lift the water-logged boards off them. Ten seconds sooner, and she'd have made it out of the shed. Instead, her icy hand had just brushed his when the roof caved, and the walls followed, trapping them beneath hundreds of pounds of debris. Already, water covered the floor, and Harold wasn't certain if it was from the deluge of rain or if the sea had risen that far. A boat motor held the roof a few inches above their heads, keeping it from crushing them, but Daisy's leg was lodged between it and some other large piece of metal that he couldn't identify.

His own body was twisted, and his knee throbbed with pain. Cold water brushed up on them, and Harold knew they wouldn't have much time to squirm out. "I'll shove. You try to get your foot out from under that mess, OK?" She was a brave little thing. First, ducking when the roof caved, now fighting like a wildcat to get out. He was just close enough to grab her hand and tug, but with his body also trapped, he had no leverage, and her rain-slick flesh didn't help. They worked and worked, trying to pry, counting to three and lifting, but the debris wouldn't move. And the rain continued. And the water was rising.

Daisy's face was smeared with dirt, and seaweed hung in her hair. "The water is coming up, isn't it?" Her voice cracked.

"Maybe it'll lift some of the wood, and we can scurry out."

"Maybe not." It was a hopeless statement. One from a child who'd seen too much on the street for her young years.

"I ain't giving up yet, girlie. And neither should you."

"I'm too tired to move." She lay her head back and rested it on the scattered pieces of wood behind her.

Harold's heart lurched when he realized the water was already halfway covering her body. "Well, we'll just rest a bit; then we'll start fighting again. OK?" He needed her to agree. This was rest, not surrender.

She swiped at her eyes. "I miss my mom." The whimpering sound broke Harold's heart. He reached for her.

"You'll see her again, young lady. I promise. We're gonna get out of this." He hoped it wasn't a lie. Everything in him wanted to fight, but if they had a chance at getting out, it would be when the water rose enough to lift the weight of the wood. That would also be about the time the girl's head would be nearly underwater.

"Can you just . . . I don't know. Talk to me?" Her hand in his was cold and quaking.

He pulled a breath. She was being as brave as she knew how. "I'll tell you about anything. What do you want to know?"

"I want to know about the car accident that caused Mrs. Cready's limp and scars. But first, I want you to answer a question."

"Fair enough."

"Were you in love with Charity's grandma?"

The words hit Harold with all the force of the hurricane around them. He opened his mouth, but no words formed.

"I saw the pictures. You and her, and you looked pretty much in love to me."

The words took him back to another time. A time when Marilyn Cort lived next door and was his best friend. A time when his little brother George was still more interested in frog-catchin' than girl-watchin'. "A long time ago, a girl my age moved in next door. It was a year after I'd had the mumps and spent a long time recovering. I'd discovered girls by way of a novel my mother had accidently left in my room while I'd been sick."

"Like a romance novel?"

"It was written by a woman named Jane Austen."

"Sure. I've heard of her." The boards groaned, settling into the rising water. Daisy tried to move but still remained trapped.

"Well, reading that book made me see girls in a whole new light. So, when Marilyn Cort's family moved in, I offered to show her around town. For months we were best friends, but one day she caught me reading that book and asked me to read some of it to her."

"Did you?"

"I sure did. When I was done, I kissed her."

"But she married George. Where was he? Did he know you two were in love?"

"No one knew we were in love. Except us. Our parents didn't mind all the hours we spent together because we were just friends." Harold kept one eye on the rising water.

"But where was George?"

"He was busy becoming a football star, basketball star. One day he was a kid, and the next he was a young man."

"But you were the one in love with Marilyn. Not him."

"Sometimes love ain't enough. Marilyn had lost her baby sisters in a horrible boating accident. That's why her family moved to my town. All she ever wanted was a big family. For the rest of that summer, she and I would take off for the creek, and I don't mind telling you that with our parents oblivious to what was going on, we, well, we . . ."

"Ooooohhhh." Daisy nodded. "Yeah, kids still do that. Not much has changed there."

Harold tried to brush off the embarrassment that warmed his cheeks. "Well, it wasn't until the end of summer that I realized there were consequences to what we were doing. Or there should have been. And that's when I got worried that maybe I couldn't give Marilyn that family she always wanted."

"So what happened?"

"I heard that men who had the mumps were sometimes unable to have kids. So, I took myself to Birmingham to a doctor there, and he checked me."

"You were sterile?"

All the pain of it rushed back to Harold as if there'd been no passage of time. "She wanted the one thing I couldn't give her."

"But surely she didn't just kick you to the curb. I mean, that's not love."

He nodded. "She didn't have to. I didn't go back." Even now he could remember the very moment he'd decided to walk away. To walk away from her, from their love, from everything. And even still, it stabbed his heart.

Daisy's sudden intake of air pulled Harold from the memory. He squinted in the darkness to make sure she hadn't gone under water. "You still with me, girlie?"

"I am. You just left?"

The water covered his torso, working its way to his shoulders. "I joined a dance troop headed out of town and sent a letter to my folks."

"You broke her heart."

"Had to. Couldn't let her pine for me. I can't say I expected George to carry the torch, but I'd hoped. At least I'd know she'd be taken care of by a good man." And for months, he'd gone to sleep each night fighting the desperate sinking feeling that his life was over. He'd destroyed it before it really began.

"Harold, that's tragic. Like Romeo and Juliet kind of tragic."

"About Louise's car accident—"

"Yes?"

He could hear the shaking in her voice. There was no fat on Daisy to hold her body heat in, and he wondered about hypothermia. "Louise and her brothers were driving home from school and wrecked. The car caught on fire. Louise was trapped inside. Using nothing but love and brute force, her brothers dragged her out of that burning car."

Daisy was quiet for a few moments. "Wow."

Harold was tired. The talking and confessions had worn him out. Maybe he could just close his eyes for a few seconds. But before he could, he saw something. He craned his neck. Over the rush of wind and the waves that were just cresting the tops of the boards and curling over their necks, he saw lights behind him and prayed it was salvation.

∽

Dalton was already thanking God when he spotted Harold's car. Without thinking about the depth of the water, he threw his truck into four wheel drive and drove to the shed, where he could faintly see the outline of Harold's arm, raised and waving to him.

He poured all his strength into moving the debris. Everything was slick, but as he shoved, so did Daisy and Harold, both of them using what energy they still possessed. The water was so high on Daisy that she had to lean up to get fresh air. Her head was tipped back, her face frozen in panic. They'd only moved the boards a few inches. And it wasn't enough.

Dalton would need to use the truck. Maybe he could roll forward and bump the debris. But that was risky, and time was running out. "I'm going to get the truck." He started to turn, and Daisy yelled for him.

He dropped to his knees beside her.

"Dalton, don't." Her blue eyes were round with fear. If the load shifted wrong, it would bury her.

She reached for him. "Take my wrists. Pull as hard as you can. Even if it jerks my arms out of their sockets."

All the air left his lungs. A thousand thoughts crashed through his mind.

She stilled. "Dalton. It's the only way."

He touched a hand to her cheek. Cold, soft as velvet. There was a smattering of tiny freckles across her nose. He'd never seen them before, but now in the glow of the headlights, they made her look like a small child. Helpless. Depending on him. He swallowed the emotions that gripped his system. "OK. I won't let you down," he whispered.

She smiled. "I know. Use all your brute strength and your love. Even if it's not love for me." When his powerful hands closed in a death grip around her wrists, she nodded. "We got this. Go!"

With all the strength he had, Dalton closed his eyes and pulled. He saw Daisy in his mind's eye, then his wife, Melinda. And then Kissy. When one hand slipped, he screamed and tightened his grip. When the debris finally released her, he tumbled to the ground. With the shifting of the load Harold was able to scurry out on his own.

Dalton jumped to his feet, and when Daisy stood on shaking legs, he wrapped his arms around her so completely, it made her quaking instantly stop. His quaking began. He took a sharp intake of air, and when he released it into the night, his tears mingled with the rainwater. There, he held her while Harold made his way to them. And he thanked God that they had cheated death.

~

"They're coming!" Charity and her mother had been waiting on the front porch when they saw the headlights from Dalton's truck in the distance. Harold's car followed, both turning into the driveway. Charity rushed out and grabbed Daisy in a crushing hug. "Is anyone hurt?"

The men were right behind her. "We're all fine—a bit shaken, but not hurt," Dalton said. They entered the house and left a puddle on the floor, all three wet and shivering. Ellen grabbed the stack of towels and wrapped Daisy in one. She rubbed her hands against Daisy's shoulders in an attempt to warm her up.

"There's a hot bath waiting for you upstairs," Charity said to Daisy. "I'll walk up with you."

Daisy shook her head. "It's OK, Charity. I'm not stupid enough to run away twice in a hurricane."

Ellen handed Dalton a towel.

Daisy sighed. "I shouldn't have left. It was a stupid thing to do. And dangerous. Thanks for not giving up on me."

Charity hugged her again and watched as the girl disappeared up the stairs.

Ellen shook the rain from her hands. "There's stew in the kitchen. Personally, I'm over all the excitement. I'm going to bed."

Before her mother could leave, Charity snagged her hand and squeezed it. "Thanks, Mom. I'm glad you were here."

Ellen blew out a breath. "I'm glad I was, too. But now I'd rather be home in New York." Charity grinned and watched her mother shake water from her arm as she grumbled and climbed the stairs, leaving her, Dalton, and Harold at the door.

It wasn't until after she'd wiped up the water puddled on the marble floor that they heard the cracking and falling sound that sent them running toward the back of the house. "What now?" Charity mumbled. Heart stopping as she gripped the kitchen window, Charity peered out to find that a large palm had just missed hitting the sleeping porch, her pottery studio now filled to the brim with plants and looking like something you'd see in a futuristic movie on a distant planet where all the nourishment was grown in tiny glass rooms.

She'd lost a palm. Not a big deal. They were all inside and safe. Plus, the weeping tree was fine.

CHAPTER 14

Aftermath

Charity had finally fallen asleep around three in the morning. Early the next day, the sounds of an island alive had interrupted her restless night. Hurricane cleanup was a common occurrence, and the island residents all joined the effort to restore the town to its prehurricane glory.

By noon, three neighbors had stopped by to see if everyone was all right and to share the bits of gossip floating around on after-storm winds. No casualties in town; the old boat shed had been destroyed—as they well knew—but damage to Founders Hall seemed the worst. Charity's only casualty had been the felled large palm tree. The weeping tree had weathered the storm like a champ, and though she still couldn't bring herself to step beneath the branches, she also couldn't explain the ones that had draped her shoulders as she'd cried.

In town, the buildings were fine, and the water was receding. Founders Hall had been vulnerable due to being in midrepair when the storm arrived. Now, more than ever before, they needed a new venue for the ball.

Charity found Harold sitting in the gazebo outside. Water had touched its edge but was already sneaking back out to the sea. Dalton had brought her plants from the sleeping porch and replaced them in the garden. Things were beginning to look like they had prestorm. She handed Harold a cup of coffee and sat down.

Charity's attention went to the sea, which was alive with movement, bits of debris, and the occasional coconut drifting onto the shoreline. The sun was as bright as she'd ever seen it, throwing sparks of light onto the vibrant water. "You've been quiet since last night. Everything OK?"

Harold rubbed a weathered hand over his knee. "I wasn't supposed to be here."

The air thickened with tension, enough to pull Charity's gaze from the exuberant water. Harold's wrinkles were deep, his soft, blue eyes filled with ghosts.

"I wasn't supposed to be here, and if I hadn't been, that girl would have died."

Charity reached over and placed her hand on his. "It was a blessing that you were here. Things are meant to be."

Pale blue eyes turned and studied her. In them, she saw years, life, regret. "I'm gonna leave. I think it's best."

What was he not saying? "Do you need to get back to the dance studio?"

He pursed his mouth and turned away. "Yes."

But the words didn't ring true. "Harold, what's going on?" He'd barely mentioned the studio since he'd been there.

"I, uh, don't exactly own the studio anymore." He stood and started to walk away, but Charity caught his hand and encouraged him to sit back down. Once he did, he told her the story of losing the studio by making a very bad judgment call.

Charity shook her head. "There has to be something we can do. We'll buy it back. I have money, Harold. Lots of money."

He patted her hand. "Nah, Lil' Bit. Sometimes you have to let things go. I'm OK with leaving it. I'd planned to sell."

She stood. "But not to lose it. Not like this. I have an attorney. I'll call her. See what she can come up with."

"You need to know what the girl and I talked about last night. I expect you know about the pictures of Marilyn and me?"

Charity nodded. But though she'd been tingling with curiosity, now it seemed unimportant—in the light of nearly lost lives and stolen businesses. "Whatever happened between you and Crum was obviously a long time ago."

"Daisy asked me if I was in love with Marilyn." He folded his hands in his lap and stared out at the water. "She was the most beautiful girl I'd ever seen. Honestly, I figured everyone who laid eyes on her was in love with her. But she picked me to be her friend and then to be her—"

"You don't have to talk about this if you don't want to." It seemed too painful for him. And Harold had been through enough.

"I want you to know." His gaze was tight on her, eyes glistening marbles of certainty.

Charity listened to his tale and fought back her own emotion.

"And maybe that's why I find it easy to lose the studio. Easier than it should be. It just seems like every good thing that comes into my life, leaves me. Every single one." Harold dropped his head.

Charity glanced up and saw Louise coming toward them. "Hello, Louise."

Harold came up off his seat quickly. She'd come from the side of the house that separated the mansion from the Barlows' home.

Louise smiled and stopped at the foot of the gazebo. Her eyes were on Harold, and there was a fresh electricity in the air that Charity recognized as chemistry, not the kind couples experience when they first meet, but a recognition born of years of mutual appreciation. This woman couldn't have been more different from the one she'd met yesterday who seemed terrified of Harold.

"Please, join us." Charity moved to make room for her.

Louise smiled. "I can't stay, but I wanted to make sure everyone was all right. I heard about what happened." Her eyes kept flittering to Harold as if she couldn't get enough of him and at the same time couldn't look him in the eye.

"We survived," he said, nodding, and as Charity zeroed in on his response to Mrs. Cready, she realized there was a schoolboy nervousness in his manner.

"I'm very glad." She turned to walk away.

Harold stopped her. "Louise?"

She turned, gripping the edges of her light jacket as if the material could anchor her. "Yes?"

Harold rubbed the back of his neck. "It'd sure be good to catch up with you."

She blinked several times. "I'm sorry for the way I reacted, seeing you. From the distance, you so resembled George, and he and I spent a lot of time together while he was ill."

Harold stepped down the gazebo steps to her.

For a long moment all was silent. Though Louise claimed she'd thought Harold was George, there seemed to be much more going on than a moment of mistaken identity.

Harold started to reach out to touch her hand but stopped himself. Charity watched as he captured the runaway hand with the other. He forced a bright smile. "Please, Louise. Could we just go for coffee? It'd mean the world to me."

It was only coffee, for heaven's sake. And yet, Charity knew the woman was about to say no.

Louise tilted her chin back. "Coffee would be nice."

The excitement Harold tried to hide crackled around them. He offered an arm to Louise. Smile in place, she brushed it off with a shake of her upturned palm. Harold sank his hands into his pockets, and the two headed around the side of the house.

Dalton met Charity on the gazebo after the elderly couple disappeared. "What was that about?"

She offered him the cup of coffee Harold hadn't drank. "Harold was in love with my Gram. Before she and my Gramps were together, of course, but it's strange to think of your grandparents that way."

"You told me once that Harold and your grandfather had a falling-out. Think it was connected?"

She'd wondered about it, but no. The pictures were from decades ago.

Dalton took a sip of the coffee. "It's cold."

"It was for Harold, but he's distracted this morning."

"By memories?"

She cocked her head. "By Louise Cready. I think there's a story there. She said the reason she freaked out yesterday was because George and Harold look so much alike, and she'd been with Gramps a lot before he passed."

"Do you think she and your gramps . . ."

Charity chewed her lip. "You know, I don't really think so. She seemed more distracted once she knew it was Harold."

"So, they knew each other way back when?" He took another drink and grunted.

"Yeah. I think they might have known each other pretty well. She seemed very apprehensive. But also relieved that he was OK after last night."

"How's Daisy?" Dalton set the cup on the railing.

"She's good. Came down for breakfast and then went back to bed. She said it was OK to call her mother, but I want her to be the one to do it," Charity said.

"Got any decent coffee in that house of yours?"

She bumped his shoulder. "I don't know. You going to get the rest of my garden in order today?"

He shrugged and headed for her door. "Not without caffeine."

"It's sure difficult to find good help these days."

They fell into step side by side. "Yeah. Almost as difficult as finding grateful neighbors."

❧

Charity hugged her mother good-bye—she'd decided that whether Ellen liked it or not, she was going to do it—and opened the car door for her. "It was a short visit, Mom."

Ellen fluffed the hair Charity had mussed with her physical affection. "Well, Leonard wants me home."

Something about the way she said it gnawed at Charity's gut. "Mom, he's not . . . mean to you, is he?"

Ellen flashed a dazzling smile, but it didn't match the look in her eyes. "No, Charity. He's just demanding. And the girls are demanding, especially now with the new baby. The three of them are hard to please."

So much sadness filled her mother's voice, Charity fought the urge to hug her again. "What happens there? The girls have moved out, right?"

"Yes, but that doesn't stop them from coming over and asking for my help on anything and everything that should be their responsibility."

"Can you say no?"

"Oh, I do. Then they call their father. And he *urges* me to help. *We're a family, Ellen. That's what we do.* Apparently that holds true for them, but not for me. I had a flat tire once and ended up sitting at the tire shop for five hours because Portia didn't feel like leaving her apartment to come get me." She waved a hand through the air. "It doesn't matter. I have a beautiful house and a perfect wardrobe and enough money that I'll never have to wonder where my next meal will come from."

Charity squeezed her mother's hands. "Mom, you don't need him for that. Gramps left me money. We'll be OK forever."

Ellen threw her head back and laughed. "Oh, Charity. You're so naïve. Money can go very quickly. It may seem like a lot."

"It *is* a lot." But something in Charity's gut told her not to pursue this part of the conversation further.

"I love him. He's everything I looked for in a man, and I will stay with him until the day he dies."

And then she'd have his money, Charity realized. She was in it for the long haul, and there was a pot of gold at the end of the rainbow.

Her mother crossed her arms over her ribs. "And I'll have earned every last dime."

Charity swallowed. "You sound bitter, Mom."

"Portia had been asking me to babysit every Friday night so she could go out with friends. After a few weeks I told her no, that I had other plans. Then her father decided Friday would be our date night. I was thrilled. We'd never had a date night. But the first one, he called from the office and canceled—said he had too much work to do. Then he told me that Portia needed a babysitter, and surely I wouldn't mind since our plans were off."

"I'm sorry. I didn't know things were like that."

"It's been worse since the baby. But Sonia, my housekeeper-slash-best-friend, has helped keep me sane."

"I'm glad you have a friend."

"Unlikely pair, we are. But even when I first met her, I was drawn to her. She had this air of worldliness about her. So confident. And she was happy. Can you imagine? Being a *maid* for people and being *happy* with it?"

Charity could easily imagine that.

"I mean, she'd lived this incredible life. Sometimes the princess and sometimes the servant. But content with all of it."

Charity remained quiet because this was the very thing she felt her mother had always lacked, a contentment with the present. She'd always strived for more, more, more. A wealthier man, more money, a better figure, more prestige.

"Anyway, she's European. It's different for them." With a dismissive shrug, Ellen slid into her rental car.

Charity sighed. Maybe her mom would never figure out what was really important in life. Or even worse, maybe her mom would figure it out too late to make changes.

∽

The coffee shop in town was open, and Harold and Louise walked the few blocks to get there. Harold found himself reminiscing in his mind about all the times he'd made this trip with Louise at his side and George and Marilyn a few paces behind them. The urge to reach down and take her hand was strong—just as he'd done a thousand times—but he slipped his hand into his pocket instead, squeezing arthritic fingers into a fist so they wouldn't reach out on their own. She'd been so skittish the day before, he didn't want to frighten her away now.

"Funny how it all changes, and yet it all stays the same, isn't it?" Louise cast a glance at his profile. He wanted to look back at her but opted for a slight nod of the head.

"I guess we've lived long enough to know how resilient things can be." Though there were branches down everywhere, the island was already in a belligerent state of recovery.

She chuckled and slipped her hands into the low pockets of a soft-yellow frock worn over her pale blue blouse. "Do you remember the day George borrowed that sailboat and the four of us got lost?"

Harold gave a good-natured grunt. "How could I forget? It was at night, and we were on the far side of that little island divvying up the last bits of water when we heard a car honk and realized how close we were to land."

Louise tipped her head back and laughed. "We were quite a foursome."

As they neared town, the sounds of island cleanup grew louder. Pickups hauled debris, while locals removed the sandbags that had protected their storefronts.

"Briella Bitner owns the coffee shop." Louise pointed. "You knew her dad. Brogan Bitner."

Harold scratched his head. "Oh yeah, mean as a snake and crazy as a loon."

"They had so many kids. Eight in all. Everyone on the island felt bad for those children and his wife. But she passed away, and suddenly he was the most gentle and kind man you could ever want to meet."

He stopped in his tracks and looked at her. "You don't say?"

With the wind at her back, Louise nodded, holding the strands of her strawberry hair off her face. "On my honor as an islander." A smile touched her lips.

Harold swallowed. "Death changes people." For a long time he looked into her eyes, the woman he'd shared many long nights with. Could Louise forgive him? He didn't know. He'd hurt her all those years ago. When her gaze flittered past him, to the sea beyond, he continued to look at her. She'd aged in the years since he'd seen her, but she was still lovely. Beautiful eyes, pretty smile. But then her shoulders stiffened, back straightened, and a defiant look lifted her chin.

"And some people will never change." Her gaze, cold and solid, landed on him for a moment, and then she continued walking toward the coffee shop.

If regret was water, he'd have a lifetime supply. Whatever he needed to do to repair the damage he'd caused Louise, he had to do it. She was the first bright light he'd seen in a long time. Maybe God was dealing him a second chance. Harold held the coffee shop door open. Though second chances weren't his strong suit—in fact, he'd pretty much flubbed all of them—he was determined not to mess this one up. Maybe even an old man could have a chance at happiness.

◌

Louise bid Harold good-bye and then closed the door to her house and leaned her weight against it as if doing so could keep out the flood of memories from so long ago. She anchored herself by looking around the contents and furnishings of her home. She'd always admired the bright-white Victorian home on the palm-shaded corner lot. Arched windows and black-and-white tile floors, a wide front porch where two rocking chairs used to hold her and Marvin. The chairs had been dragged inside for the storm, and now they sat like unhappy house cats at the window looking out toward the road and the seaside houses across the street. Already the crew had removed her storm shutters, and her house was cool and quiet. And lonely.

She'd known Marvin Cready most of her life but had always thought of him as a bit of a rube. Too quiet, too often walking past with an uncertain gait, his head down, once in a while muttering a "Good day, Miss" in her direction. It wasn't until she'd taken a summer job working alongside his mother that Louise learned Marvin was intelligent. Not normal intelligent, but genius kind of intelligent. He'd worked the fishing boats with his father until his dad could no longer do the work. The older Cready retired early, having made some brilliant investments, in the form of ten residential lots a friend needed to sell quickly. Cready had purchased the bunch—more to help his friend than anything else—and ten years later, they were worth a hundred times what he'd paid. Marvin didn't have to continue to run the fishing business. But he had. Because his father had poured his life into it, Marvin would do the same.

Louise had fallen for Marvin over that long summer when he'd taught her about the different types of clouds in the day and the celestial night sky in the evenings. She learned only later that Marvin had fallen for her the first time he'd seen her. He made her feel special, treated her like a princess. She never knew there could be so much love in the world.

Then he was gone. And she was alone again.

He knew she liked to dance, so he took lessons. He was heavy on his feet, but in a lovable way that only endeared him to her more. To him, she was the most important thing in the world.

That memory brought her thoughts to Harold. She'd been in love with him as well. But it had been years before her summer with Marvin. Harold was worldly and wild, and Louise had always felt like she was competing with the entire world for his attention. In reality, she knew she wasn't. She'd only been competing with one person. But she came in a distant second, no matter how hard she worked to win his favor.

In a bottom drawer of her armoire, she pulled out a small envelope of photographs. George and Marilyn, arms wrapped around each other, her and Harold, holding the same pose, but Harold's eyes looking right past her to Marilyn beside them. It was when she'd seen that photo that she knew her imagination wasn't the culprit in wondering about Harold's true feelings. Some flames never died. And some people never changed.

She was too old to suffer the pain of another broken heart. And who could ever compete with a ghost? No one. Certainly not her. There'd been a night, more than twenty years ago, when he'd left her standing on the pier waiting for him. She'd made herself a promise right then. Never again would she wait for Harold Baxter. Because never again would she allow him into her life. It was the summer just before Marilyn died.

Louise crossed the room to the rocking chairs and sat in one. It groaned in greeting, and she set it into motion. Whether she was old or not, the days were long and the house was quiet. And she was lonely. But lonely was better than heartbroken. She'd take lonely any day.

⁓

Charity had invited Emily over to discuss the business concerning Harold's dance studio. Emily and Jeanna McDouglas-Rudd arrived an hour after Harold and Louise left to go to town. Emily's power purse hung on her arm. "Mom came with. Hope that's OK. She's been checking on residents after the storm."

Charity ushered them inside and offered drinks. They settled on iced tea in the parlor. She marveled at how perfectly put together the pair were. And after a storm, no less. "I'm glad you came along, Jeanna. I actually need to talk to both of you."

"Intriguing," Jeanna said.

Charity explained Harold's situation—how he'd lost his dance studio—to Emily who took notes and promised to contact Harold's attorney in Birmingham. "It sounds pretty iron-clad, but I'll do whatever I can. Are you interested in buying the studio back from the man?"

Charity had discussed the idea with Harold, but he'd said no. "He doesn't want that snake, Ephraim Connor, to benefit even more from this. Harold said that if Ephraim has the studio, he also has to do the work to keep it running. If we sail in and buy it, the guy gets away with robbery and gets rewarded for it."

"Well, your uncle is right. We need better legislation to protect the elderly. It's a different day than when they were young, and a man's word was his bond." Emily placed her small notebook in her purse.

"Thanks for looking into it, Emily." Charity turned her attention to the mayor. "Now, Jeanna. I have a proposition for you."

"I'm all ears, Charity. What is it?"

"I heard that Founders Hall suffered some damage last night in the storm."

"I'm afraid we're looking at having to cancel the Founders' Day Ball." She leaned back into the settee and peaked a pencil-thin brow. "Unless . . ."

"In exchange for some information, I'll offer Baxter House for the Founders' Day Ball. It's still a couple of months away, so your committee will have time to arrange things." She could have asked Emily, but since Jeanna was the one who knew everyone and kept up with everything happening on her island, Charity figured she'd go straight to her. Today, she'd get answers because she had something she knew Jeanna wanted.

"And this information you seek?" Jeanna would make no promises until she heard the details. The perfect politician.

"Tell me what you know about the special orders I received and the weeping tree." The long pause had Charity's heart drumming, but she held Jeanna's gaze without flinching.

Jeanna leaned forward on the settee. "Why don't you tell me what you know and perhaps I can fill in the blanks."

Frustration caused her to grind her teeth for a moment. "That's the problem. I don't know anything. People show up and ask for the most ridiculous orders. A candy dish, a single plate. Did you know that three weeks ago a lady asked for a mirror? When I told her I couldn't fire a mirror in the kiln, she said that was fine, to just make a frame, and she'd have a mirror cut to fit it. I did the order and handed her an empty-looking glass with a handle, and she stared at it and then giggled and spun around like a little girl playing princess." Charity sat back and folded her arms. "That's what I know, Jeanna. And I'm getting sick of being the odd man out."

"How so?"

Charity threw her hands into the air. "Everyone in town seems to know more about my special orders than me. I need to know what I'm dealing with. Especially now."

Jeanna leaned forward, concern pinching her brows. "Why now?"

"I'm running out of the special ingredient. The bag is three-quarters empty."

Jeanna stood. "Oh dear. That really is a problem."

"Jeanna, please. Tell me." Charity wasn't typically one to beg, but desperate situations and all.

Jeanna's gaze landed for a moment on Emily, then went back to Charity. "There are a hundred different rumors about how the special ingredient works. But for the most part, people choose not to discuss it. It only comes up in hushed conversations, usually late at night. It's as if we all know that too much discussion could ruin the magic. What we know is that a piece of pottery made with it will help create whatever it is the person most desires."

Charity frowned. "A placebo. I mean, Jeanna, what you're suggesting is . . . impossible. But if people believe strongly enough in something, it can become a point of contact for their faith. They are their own magic."

Jeanna smiled. "Of course."

But Charity wasn't convinced. Jeanna might be a solid politician, but Charity had learned to read people, and the flicker in her eye before the smooth coolness suggested more. "You don't believe it's a placebo."

"What I believe isn't important, Charity." Now that was a politician's answer if she'd ever heard one.

"If it's unimportant, why don't you go ahead and share your thoughts with me? If you're truly interested in Baxter House for the ball."

Sharp eyes narrowed on Charity. "Have you ever thought of running for office?"

"No." Charity shook her head.

"You'd make a good politician." Jeanna drew a long breath and settled into the settee by stretching her arms across its velvet back. "To call this place magic . . . it's almost not enough. It's more than magic. The power of a place like this is beyond our comprehension. It's the essence of love and life and light. It holds power and wields it at will. But really, is it any more mystical than the sun rising? Than a newborn child's first cry? There is so much power around us. There is so much magic in the world, but some of it has simply become common."

Charity used to believe in magic. Back before her gram had died, and the world had gone from being a fairytale place to being a cold, unforgiving one. This was a philosophy she could have embraced back then. And a philosophy she'd like to embrace now. But . . .

"Was the looking glass for Annabelle Williamson?" Emily asked. She'd remained quiet through most of this discussion, but when Charity's eyes landed on her, she could plainly see Emily was as much of a believer as her mother.

Charity nodded. "Yes, it was for Annabelle Williamson."

Jeanna stood. "Let's take a drive, Charity."

They hopped into Jeanna's SUV and drove to the far end of the island. Jeanna parked beside a Tuscan-style two-story house with giant windows and a terra cotta roof. The hurricane shutters had already been removed, most likely by the landscaping company that helped place them for many of the older island residents. The long metal shutters lay beside the house and as the trio walked along the front sidewalk, Charity heard big-band music. A prickly sensation spread across her neck.

"Look," Jeanna said, pointing into the bay window on the front of the house.

There in the living room, Annabelle Williamson held the mirror at arm's length. Smiling, she spun around and around the living room, moving in rhythm to the big-band sounds that seeped from the home.

It was mesmerizing to watch. Her body swayed, and her feet floated along the hardwood floor. The woman seemed so entranced by the movement, it drew the spectators into her fantasy. Charity herself could almost picture the dance floor, the orchestra, lines of tables in a half circle around the space. She could practically hear laughter and the tinkling of glasses as people sipped champagne in the soft ambient lighting of an era past. "Wow," was all Charity could say.

When the music stopped, Annabelle went to the old phonograph. Just as she started the song again, she noticed the trio of ladies standing in her window. She waved, hugged the looking glass to her heart, and blew a kiss to Charity.

Charity lifted a hand to wave back, but emotions were so thick, all she could do was stand there, one hand up, heart beating at an unnatural rate.

Jeanna leaned closer. "Does it really matter how the magic works? The important thing is, it does."

Magic. Real or imagined, it didn't matter. Charity was looking through a window and seeing the kind of magic she used to believe in. The kind she'd always known existed on the island. And she was a part of it now. "You can have the ball at Baxter House. In fact, I'd be honored."

Jeanna nodded and laced her arm through Charity's. "Good. When we get back, we'll talk about the weeping tree."

⌒

"So the weeping tree takes on your deepest hurt and helps you . . . what? Deal with it?" It still wasn't clear to Charity, but she wasn't going to let Jeanna and Emily leave until she had a grasp, slippery as it might be.

"A tree that intercedes on our behalf."

Charity frowned.

"It carries our burdens. Lifts them, helps us see the light," Jeanna said.

Charity shook her head. "But Gramps never recovered after my Gram died. If all he had to do was sit beneath the tree—"

Emily cut her off. "He wouldn't sit beneath the tree, Charity." The words fell like bombs around her.

"Why? If it could erase his pain?" Charity asked.

Emily stood and came over to sit beside Charity. "Your grandfather felt responsible for your grandmother's death. He blamed himself, and he felt like he needed to live with that blame for the rest of his life."

"What? You must be making a mistake, Emily." Even as she spoke the words with certainty, a seed of apprehension took root in Charity's stomach.

"Charity, do you know the details of your grandmother's death?" Emily asked.

"It was an accident. She fell." That's what she'd been told as a child, and she'd never thought to question it. Now it seemed the very room around them was shrouded in mystery.

"Charity, a lot of people believe that your grandmother committed suicide." Emily's voice was soft, apologetic.

Her words ricocheted off Charity's heart as the room went dark around her. Charity's mind rejected the notion. Her grandmother was a sane, solid human being. Not even given to depression. There was no way she'd . . . and yet. Things had been different that last year when Charity arrived. Gram wasn't herself. Hadn't even come to meet Charity at the boat. Gramps had seemed worried about her but brushed it off whenever Charity asked why Gram was so quiet or why she'd slept so late. It was right after she'd gone home that summer that Gram fell and later died at the hospital. "Where was she?" Charity leaped up off the seat, suddenly needing to know details. "From where did she fall?"

Emily shot a look to her mother who gave an almost imperceptible nod. "The third-floor attic landing. She broke through the thin wooden railing. After she passed, your grandfather kept everything in there just as she'd left it. He told me it had been her hideaway, where she'd go to rest or to think. Charity, he never told me the details of that day. Just that she was gone, and it was his fault."

Now Charity wanted—needed—to know everything about it. Perhaps Harold could help her, but no. Harold and Gramps's falling-out had been before her grandmother's death. Harold wouldn't know what happened. A black ocean of emotions surged, swallowing her. "Gramps never forgave himself." The injustice of it clawed at her soul. She'd lost them both that day. Gramps was never the same. And now

Charity knew that he'd carried the burden of his wife's death all those years. "I think I need some time to process all this."

Emily and Jeanna made their way to the front door with Charity following them. The world was a tunnel, reduced to a pinpoint that only showed her what was just ahead, and everything else was a black wall surrounding her.

Emily threw her weight into tugging the door open. "I'm here, Charity. If you need to talk or just need a shoulder. I'm sorry."

Charity nodded, but her mind was floating somewhere far away. A place where everything you thought you knew about a person could be stripped away with one small revelation.

Jeanna reached out and took Charity's arm. "Charity, I don't mean to be insensitive, but does this change anything about the ball?"

"Mother!" Emily shot her a look.

"The ball?" It took a moment for Charity to understand.

The woman squeezed her arm. "I hate to bring it up, but I'll have to get the committee working on the arrangements ASAP unless you've changed your mind about offering Baxter House."

Really? Now she wanted to discuss this? Surely, it could wait. Charity thought about Gramps. Pointing a finger at her and closing one eye. "Let your word be a contract, Lil' Bit. You're only as good as your word." Charity rubbed her hands over her face. "No, Jeanna. I told you the ball could be held here. I gave you my word."

Jeanna reached out and hugged her, though Charity's hands were still folded protectively over her chest. "You won't be disappointed, Charity. I know this is a painful time, but you're doing the right thing."

Who cared about balls and festivities?

Emily hugged her next. "I'll see what I can do for Harold. I'll be in touch."

Charity watched them leave. Dalton was knocking on the back door, but it sounded so far away. When she didn't answer, he hollered, "Hey, you decent? I'm coming in."

She stared at the open doorway.

Dalton stepped behind her. "What's wrong, Charity?"

But she couldn't answer. Couldn't do anything but give a tiny shake of her head. Something deep within was driving her to climb the two sets of stairs and go to the attic. She headed for the steps and was aware of Dalton following her. Though he didn't say anything else, the electricity of his concern sparked across her back as she silently climbed the stairs.

Inside the small room, Charity sat down on the twin bed in the corner, seeing this space as if she'd never been there before. This was where her grandmother came? Was it a retreat or a prison? Dalton stayed in the doorway, his shoulders nearly stretching from one side of the narrow door frame to the other.

When she glanced over at him, he came in and sat beside her. With her hands folded neatly on her lap, she shared with him everything Jeanna and Emily had told her. Then she shared how different her grandmother had seemed on that last summer visit.

He listened, nodded occasionally, gave her a slight smile when she asked him questions no one could answer. When she was done, he said, "No one can understand what it's like to allow the unimaginable into your mind."

Charity angled to look at his face.

"When I got word that Melinda and Kissy had died, my mind just rejected the notion. I kept saying there had to be a mistake. I even tried to call her cell phone."

"Oh, Dalton."

"Our minds work to protect us from the thing that would hurt most. But when my brother showed up at the hotel I was staying in, and the cops left, I knew the nightmare was real."

"How did you survive?"

"Surviving is the easy part. It's actually living that is practically impossible. I walked around in a daze at first, then threw myself into work. When I realized I wasn't actually dealing with their deaths, I came here."

"Most people wouldn't be self-aware enough to know they weren't actually moving forward," Charity said.

He rubbed a hand over his face. "I'd still buy coloring books and washable markers at the store as if one day Kissy would just show up and use them."

"When did you start living? Or have you?" Charity asked.

"When I sat under the weeping tree. Something changed for me while the tree rained tears. It was as inexplicable as what I was going through. Sit under the tree, Charity. It'll help you with this."

She shook her head. "I just . . . can't." She didn't know why.

He reached for her hand. "Maybe one day."

She nodded. "This was the last place my gram was before she fell." The door to the landing outside loomed on the far wall. Charity stood and moved to it.

Dalton was at her side before she got the door open. There on the landing, she took in the great sea beyond, her hands spreading on the thin railing that must have been replaced after her gram's accident. What would cause a woman to choose to die? To leap to her death when she had so much to live for? "I don't want Daisy coming up here anymore."

"We can lock both doors on the way down." He gave the railing a little shake. "Tomorrow, I'll reinforce this railing."

"Thanks for being such a good friend, Dalton." The words came from the deepest part of her. How could she have gotten through this without him?

"We found each other. You've done as much for me." The sun glistened in his green eyes.

"In that case, I have a favor to ask."

"What?"

"There's going to be this ball. I'll need a date." It was a breathy admission.

He chuckled. "What about Red? I thought he was going to ask you out."

She stared up at the sun. "He called a few weeks ago to let me know he was seeing the woman who owns the coffee shop in town. Broom-Hilda or something."

"I think her name is Briella. Why didn't you tell me?" Dalton asked.

Her shoulder tipped up, and she angled away from him. "Embarrassed, I guess."

"Embarrassed about what?"

"About running off a man before ever even going out with him."

Dalton's laughter split the air. "He gets involved with someone, and that's your fault?"

"I have a pretty poor track record," Charity mumbled.

"I'll be your date. But I don't have to bring you flowers or anything like that, right?"

"You'd just steal them out of my own garden." She cast her eyes heavenward.

"Good point."

"You've got two months to brush up on your dancing. I'll let Harold know you're going to need some pointers." She turned and reentered the attic room.

"How do you know I need pointers?" He followed and locked the outside door behind them.

"I've caught you dancing to the radio while you were working in the garden. You have the rhythm of a rock." She grinned.

"Rock star, maybe," he said as they pulled the second attic door shut, locked it and headed down to the main house.

CHAPTER 15
The Call

This was dangerous, and Louise would do well to remember that. She sat on the pier, fishing pole in hand, with Harold at her side. He was as good-looking as ever. But he'd broken her heart twenty years ago, and though she was a different woman now, somewhere within her, she knew he held the power to break it again if she let him.

"When we walked to the coffee shop a few days ago, I noticed your limp was gone."

It had been for years. Only in the moment right after seeing Harold had it reappeared, and that was something she couldn't explain, but she knew it had to do with feeling self-conscious. "I worked hard to get rid of it. Years of exercise and therapy." Of course, to Marvin Cready, the man she'd married after Harold left for the last time, the limp had been part of her charm. At least, that's what he'd always told her. His broken bird, he used to call her.

She hadn't wanted to be broken. She'd wanted to be strong. So, she had become what doctors had told her she never would. Of course, Marvin still called her his bird, but his soaring one. She missed Marvin.

Life was lonely. But she *was* strong. She'd made the choice to be more than a survivor.

Lots of women lost their husbands. Louise figured most of them fell into two camps. The cold, stern ones with deep frowns and deeper wounds. Those women never left that place of torture, losing a spouse, knowing they might walk the earth alone for the rest of their days.

But there was another camp as well. A place where widows first grieved, then shook off the grave clothes of solitude. Those women donned purple hats. They laughed too loud at restaurants, they fawned over newborn babies and sang songs as they shopped the corridors of Walmart. Yes, Louise would much rather be counted as one of those women. She'd gladly choose camp life over camp regret.

"You married Marvin Cready, the commercial fisherman," Harold said, tugging on his fishing pole.

"Got a nibble?" She nodded to the water where his line disappeared into the surface and created an A-frame shape on the ripples.

"Nah. Probably just a crab stealing scraps from my line."

Louise tipped her face to the sun. "Marvin was a good husband. Practically retired when we started seeing each other."

"What about your folks?"

"I was seventy when I lost them. Both, the same year. Mama was ninety-one and Daddy was ninety-three."

Harold reached over and touched her hand. "I'm sorry. I know the three of you were always close."

"I rented out their house for a few years. But last year when Marvin passed, I decided to sell. Even as a child I loved Marvin's house. Of course, back then his whole family lived there. When his father retired, it became his. I always imagined living inside that pretty white picket fence." She gave her rod a good yank when she felt a nibble. The line went slack, and she knew something must have stolen her bait. But she didn't mind. She breathed in the ocean air, the tang of freshly cut bait, and Harold. His was a scent she'd known decades ago. A scent that would undoubtedly fill her mind as she'd drift off to sleep tonight.

Beyond the sea, the horizon was a straight line splitting the water and sky. Above, only blue. The bluest skies she'd ever seen often followed storms. This one was no different. So brilliant it hurt.

⁓

Charity watched as Daisy pointed out the plants and flowers Dalton was moving around in her backyard. The two women sat at the counter where one could just see the garden beyond. "How will I ever be able to keep up with the garden when Dalton goes home?"

Daisy's head jerked. "He's leaving?"

"One day. I don't think he's packing a bag or anything yet, but he has a life waiting for him back in Jacksonville." Charity tried to turn her attention to the carrot stick she'd planned to nibble on. She rolled it between her fingers, but at the mention of Dalton leaving, her appetite waned. She knew she had to get used to the idea. He had another life. It was not like he could just stay there forever *being her best friend.* And friends was all they were. That was enough for Dalton. So it had to be enough for Charity. Even though in the deepest part of her heart . . . She huffed. "His world is there."

Daisy dropped her gaze and mumbled, "He has a world here, too." Daisy had grown fond of Dalton in the time she'd been there, and for a teen who'd been wandering the streets for a year, connections with other people were everything. Charity would have to walk carefully here.

"I'd like to see him stay, too. But I'm not sure we get to make that call. Dalton's whole family is in Jacksonville," Charity said.

Daisy's bright-blue eyes settled on her. "Not his whole family."

Something caught in Charity's throat. She wasn't certain if Daisy was referring to the ones he'd lost or to the fact that they'd become an unconventional family.

Daisy tossed her long strands of hair over her shoulder. "I know how to take care of the garden." She shrugged. "You know, if I'm here."

"I love having you here, Daisy. But I also know you're ready to call your mom. I know you miss her." Several times Charity'd watched as Daisy picked up the wall phone only to take deep breaths while staring at the receiver. She'd then replace the phone on the wall and walk away.

"I've been trying . . ." The weight of uncertainty dropped Daisy's shoulders. "No time like the present, right?"

Charity knew how nervous Daisy was about making that call. It could so easily go wrong. But deep in Charity's heart, a flutter of hope had ignited. Daisy was going to be OK. Things were going to work out for her.

Daisy's young blue eyes filled with courage. "Let's go sit in the gazebo while I call. It's my favorite spot."

⁓

Dalton was up to his elbows in fertilizer. He watched Charity and Daisy walk out of the house and take a seat near where he was working. The wind carried their words to him, but he didn't have to hear anything to know what this was about. Daisy, back arrow straight, held Charity's cell phone in her hand. She must be readying to call her mother.

Since no one invited him over, he busied himself pulling weeds from under the edge of the weeping tree. A tiny shoot caught his eye just as he was about to pluck it from the ground. "You're not a weed," he mumbled to the miniature, ruler-tall shoot. "You'll never survive under here." Dalton grabbed an empty pot, casting long looks toward the gazebo as he worked. He wasn't eavesdropping, exactly. But Daisy had burrowed into his heart, and he knew how much bravery it must take to make that call. He packed the tiny willow into the pot by digging out a semicircle around it. After setting it beside his house, he kept a close eye on the body language coming from the gazebo. Dalton slowed his pace so he could watch the two women while he walked back to his task of spreading fertilizer.

His heart lifted when Daisy motioned for him to come over.

"Need all the moral support I can get." She smiled, but it was strained, her blonde hair flying in the coastal breeze. She caught it with one hand and hit the phone button with her index finger.

Dalton stood at the gazebo doorway. A nervous Charity sat at Daisy's side, her fingers rubbing together in an effort to short circuit her nerves.

Right away, he knew the call wasn't going as well as they'd all hoped.

"Yes, Mom. I know how long it's been. I'm sorry. I should have called sooner. I'm in Florida." Daisy chewed her bottom lip.

Dalton could hear a voice coming through the phone, but the words were lost in the wind. Charity's concern filled the gazebo, her face pinching into a frown.

"No. Mom, I understand what you must have gone through. I'm sorry. I want to—to make things right. Could you come down here? We can talk. I'm staying with—"

Charity cast a pain-filled glance toward Dalton.

Daisy went on. "No. I know you don't. But the lady I'm staying with said she'd fly you down here. If we can just talk—"

First sadness, then anger, spread through Dalton's system. He clenched his teeth and fists to keep himself from reaching out and snatching the phone to give this woman a piece of his mind. As far as he could tell, she hadn't even asked if her daughter was OK.

"I know you have work. But it would only take a couple of days. If . . . if you decide you want me to come home, we could fly back together."

Daisy closed her eyes. "I know I'm eighteen now." At that moment, something changed. Daisy's posture stiffened, her eyes going from pleading to cold. "No. We won't send a ticket for Bud, too. Mom, are you really still with that loser?"

Click. They all heard it. It was a mother slamming the door shut on the child she gave life to. Daisy slowly lowered the phone, her face frozen.

Movement at the sleeping porch caused Dalton to look up. There, Harold handed a fishing pole to Louise and made his way to the group gathered on the gazebo.

Daisy stared at the wooden floor. Charity slipped an arm around her shoulders as a single tear dropped onto Daisy's lap.

Dalton sent a long look to Harold, who nodded and spoke when no one else seemed able. "We caught dinner." He raised a hand to his forehead and looked out over the vast expanse of water beyond them. "I suppose there's no better place to be than an island in southern Florida. Sand, sunsets . . . in fact, I was telling Louise earlier just how blessed we all were to be here. To have one another. We might not be blood, but we're kin, just the same."

Charity gave him an appreciative smile. With great effort, Daisy looked up slowly and met his eyes.

He winked and pointed a crooked finger at her. "Family, girlie, is the people who stick by you. Thick or thin. And real family, well, nothing can keep them from you. Not even a hurricane." He tipped his fishing hat and started back toward the house, then paused. "We're having shark for dinner. It'll be on the grill in thirty minutes."

They watched him disappear into the house. Daisy threaded her fingers together on her lap. "She doesn't want me."

Dalton's gaze went to Charity, who seemed only barely able to hold back her emotions.

Charity grabbed Daisy's hand and squeezed. "We want you." She turned and held Daisy's hand to her heart. "You have a home right here for as long as you want it. I didn't want you to leave. In fact, I had to argue with myself even to encourage you to call. Daisy, I was so scared when you were lost in the storm. I've never felt anything like that.

Please. Please, will you stay here? At least for a while, until you decide what you want to do. We can get your high school records, and you can get your GED. Then we could look at colleges."

A tiny spark entered the deadness that had been Daisy's eyes. "I never thought I could go to college."

A sound, half relief, half laugh, escaped Charity's lips. "You can." Tears filled her eyes. "Whatever you want to be, Daisy. I'll make sure you get to."

Daisy smiled, but right on the heels of the freshly opened joy came the mistrust. That was something Dalton understood. A year ago, the universe had pulled the rug out from under him. He knelt in front of Daisy, his eyes intent on her. "I know people have let you down. And I know it's hard to trust. But I'm giving you my word that we'll make sure you go to college if that's what you want to do."

He could see the war. Her chin quivered, that hard outer shell cracking. She fought it. "You're going back to Jacksonville, and when you do, who's to say I'll ever hear from you again?"

He frowned and cast a quick glance at Charity, wondering why his home in Jacksonville had been a topic of discussion. "I'm not making any plans right now. I'm here for the next two months at least. And when I start thinking about returning home, you'll be the first to know. I swear it."

Daisy held his gaze for a long time. "Trust is scary."

He reached out and took the hand that was locked with Charity's. "It is. But living without it is far scarier."

He wanted to hug her. But maybe that would be too much. She was still skittish, and he didn't want to force her beyond her comfort zone. Instead, he squeezed her hand and let her go. "Come on, kiddo. I want to show you the new plants I got for the front of the house."

Charity stood. "The front of the house?"

He and Daisy had already started to walk away. "Yeah. You've got the whole island coming in two months. You really want a naked front yard?"

He heard the thump as Charity plopped back down on the gazebo seat. They both turned to look at her. She was ghost white.

Daisy tipped a shoulder. "She's not so good with social."

"Well, we've got two months to whip her into shape."

∽ා

Charity was practically bursting to tell Harold the news about the dance studio. She'd also considered pressing him for some details about the argument he and Gramps had all those years ago, but whenever she started to, something stopped her. Somewhere in the caverns of her heart, she knew the discussion would only cause him pain. Besides, what did it matter? Gramps was willing to forgive him. She should leave it alone. She'd learned a hard lesson with Daisy about minding one's own business. Daisy was doing great, though. She'd even taken a job at the coffee shop downtown.

Harold came down the stairs, looking dapper in a green shirt and jeans. Probably planning to spend the day with Louise. The two of them had been almost inseparable for the last two months. "New shirt?" she asked.

He nodded. "Louise picked it out. Said it makes my eyes sparkle."

"Personally, I think it's Louise that makes your eyes sparkle."

He blushed and waved a hand through the air.

"Guess what?" But she couldn't wait to tell him, so she didn't wait for an answer. "The dance studio is for sale."

He gripped the railing on the staircase, his hand covering the top of the dancing bear's head.

"And there's already been an offer made on it." Charity was practically giddy.

Harold looked pale. Maybe she should have had him sit down before telling him. "Lil' Bit, I told you I didn't want it back."

"We're not buying it. Your attorney is. Apparently, the situation somehow leaked to the local news, and they did an expose on Ephraim Conner. He's willing to sell for the sixty-six hundred dollars he'd given you as a down payment before tricking you into signing over the place." From what Charity had gathered, Ephraim Conner had convinced Harold to sell him the studio. Giving the money as a down payment—coupled with the hours he put in at the studio at Harold's side—had made him seem completely trustworthy. That was the tool crooks like him used. Get people's trust, and they'll let their guard down.

Harold placed a weathered hand to his heart. "Your attorney called the news station?"

Charity grinned. "No. That would be unethical. However, my attorney has a mother who is a politician. And they're sort of known for contacting news stations with juicy tidbits. Now, I'm not saying that's what happened. Just speculating."

Harold passed her and sat down at the dining table. "Phil's buying the place. That's good. He met his wife Mitzi there."

Charity sat across from him. "That's not all. He's going to keep you as a silent partner. Which means you get a paycheck each month but don't have to do anything to get it. Apparently, you're what people went to the dance studio for. It was the atmosphere you created, not the dance lessons that kept them coming back. Phil wants to honor that atmosphere and keep it going."

Harold pursed his lips, his watery blue eyes smiling.

"It's your legacy, Uncle Harold. I know you told me once that every good thing in your life leaves, but maybe it doesn't. Maybe you just don't see the lasting fruit of the seed you've sown."

He patted her hand. "You're a good girl."

She had to chuckle. "Thanks. You're a pretty decent old guy." But his smile quickly faded. "Harold, what is it?"

"I feel like there's things we need to talk about concerning the past. Marilyn and I—"

She'd watched him over the last two months being torn between the past and a newly rekindled relationship with Louise. She needed to put the questions about him and her grandmother to rest once and for all. "I don't care about any of that, Uncle Harold. What happened between you and Gram, it's ancient history. It's over. And she's gone. But Louise is right here, and she really cares for you. I'm scared that if you can't let go of the past, you're going to lose her."

"She's a special woman. Gave me a second chance when I didn't deserve it. She's better than I deserve." His voice was thick with emotion.

"Whatever happened between the two of you, it must have shaken her to the core, but you're worth it, worth a second chance. Everyone can see that about you except you," Charity said.

"Louise was my companion whenever I'd come to Gaslamp Island to visit George and Marilyn. The four of us had more fun together than should have been legal. Whenever I called, she was right here, ready to hop in the car and go dancing on the mainland or fishing in the boat or even just out to dinner here on the island. She didn't date other men much, always was self-conscious about her limp and her scars. I never noticed them."

"So, you two dated?" Charity asked.

He rubbed the back of his neck. "I was a stupid man. I didn't give her the kind of consideration one should give a girlfriend. I called her when I hit town."

"And when you weren't here? You never called?" Charity pressed.

"I just thought she was as happy with the situation as I was. She never let on like she wanted more. Then one night she called me and said she did. I was on my way to the island." Harold stared at the marble floor.

"What happened?"

His look of shame cut right to Charity's heart. "Once I knew how she felt, I told her I felt things for her, too. That we needed to try to make a go of it. I asked her to meet me at the pier."

"It didn't go well?"

He looked away, but not before Charity saw the ghosts swimming in his eyes. "There was a situation. I had to . . . I . . . should have gone to the pier. But I didn't. I left her waiting there just like she was always waiting on me. And she never forgave me. And I didn't deserve her forgiveness."

"She's forgiven you now." It was important for him to know that.

"She has. Speaking of forgiveness, I was wondering how things were going with your momma?"

Charity brushed a hand through her hair. She could feel the bits of clay snagging. She'd spent the morning at the potter's wheel—more out of nerves than need. For two months she'd been making pottery pieces to display around Baxter House during the Founders' Day Ball. With the inheritance from Gramps, she didn't need to work, but pottery was in her blood. The feel of the cool clay on her fingertips, the water from the sponge running over her hands, it was all therapeutic. And yet, it hadn't helped her deal with the feelings she'd been having about her mother.

"Lil' Bit?" A weathered hand waved before her.

"Sorry. Got lost in my own thoughts."

His brows were high, chin down as if readying for a battle. "I asked about your mother."

"Things were good when she was here." Better, in fact, than she'd ever remembered. Her mother had actually pitched in and helped to make the situation better, rather than throwing a dramatic hand to her forehead and claiming all the stress had given her a migraine.

Harold nodded. "They seemed to be."

"I thought maybe . . . maybe." All the anger started churning in her stomach. "Then, I listened to Daisy make that awful phone call to her mother."

Harold's smile was soft. "And it brought back all the times your mom—"

Her eyes were fire when they landed on him. "Rejected me. My mother rejected me over and over my whole life." Bitterness caused her muscles to tighten. "Maybe not as directly as Daisy's mom rejected her, but for a lifetime."

Harold put an arm around her shoulder.

Whenever Charity allowed her mind to drift down that path, the pain and anger surged as if it controlled her entire being. As if it controlled her life. "And then she comes here, and I see the tiniest bit of compassion, and I just act like all that rejection never happened. What happened to Daisy broke my heart."

"And for the first time, you saw it from the outside looking in," Harold said.

"I can't bring myself to forgive her, Harold. I've been trying. At least I think I have."

"You know, forgiveness isn't always a coat that you can just put on and take off. Sometimes forgiveness can only be accomplished layer by layer."

Was that her problem? Maybe she was trying to take too big a leap.

"What is it folks say about eating an elephant one bite at a time?"

She didn't know, but it made sense. There was only one problem. "I'm not sure I want to forgive her."

Harold squeezed her shoulders. "You will, Lil' Bit. I know you. You're not one to harbor hatred against another human being."

"I don't hate her."

"Maybe not. But isn't unforgiveness the seed of hatred? Unforgiveness breeds bitterness, and bitterness can only lead to hate. Maybe you could sit beneath the weeping tree and think about all this?"

Charity groaned. The weeping tree. The closest she'd come to sitting beneath it was when she'd stood at its edge and cried, and the tree had draped branches over her shoulders. "I can't." It was a hopeless sound, those two words slipping from her lips. "I've tried. But whenever I get close, something inside just stops me."

He turned her to face him. "Maybe Ellen Marie isn't the only one you need to forgive."

Each of his words dropped like bombs into the basement of her heart, depth charges absorbed by the solid concrete walls. "Maybe."

He angled her beneath his arm. "Time makes things clear."

"Thank you for being here, Uncle Harold."

He chucked her chin. "There's nowhere I'd rather be, Lil' Bit. Let's get some coffee."

Inside the kitchen, a grinning Daisy turned to greet them. "Fresh coffee's on. Mr. Hoggy-Pants over there"—she tossed a thumb in Dalton's direction—"drank the last of the pot I made earlier."

He shrugged. "Since she's been working at the coffee shop, I can't stay out of the brew."

Daisy crossed her arms over her chest. "Well, you're going to have to. Or I'm going to set out a tip jar."

Charity grinned at the two of them. In the early mornings, Daisy worked the rush hour for Briella. Afternoons, she worked on her GED test booklet, readying for the exam. In the early evenings, she went with Dalton, who'd promised to teach her about his work. They'd been doing jobs pro bono around the island so Daisy could get a feel for landscaping at a variety of levels. Charity couldn't be more proud of the young woman Daisy was growing into.

"Why don't you tell them your news, Daisy?" Dalton said.

Her eyes widened to the point they might pop out of her head, and then she cut a fire fight look to Dalton, who hid by taking a long drink of his coffee. Charity frowned. "What news?"

"Go on, Daisy. Tell them about Josh." His grin stretched from ear to ear.

She marched to him, grabbed the cup from his hands and hit him on the arm with a fist. "Maybe I'll just tell them about how the widow Malcolm undressed and left the shades open so you could spy on her."

Dalton coughed. Or maybe it was a gag.

Harold stepped deeper into the room and rubbed his chin. "Widow Malcolm is a fine-lookin' lady."

Three gasps echoed in the room. "Sure," Dalton said. "If you're ninety-five."

"You know, I heard that she fakes falls and calls 911 just to get some attention from the paramedics," Daisy added.

Poor lady.

Daisy pulled coffee cups from the cupboard and handed them to Charity and Harold. "Charity, maybe you could make a special order for her."

Charity filled her cup. "I'm not sure it works that way. Special orders have always been requested." Besides that, the special ingredient was practically gone. On the up side, there was a small piece of paper inside the bag, resting ominously beneath the last of the ingredient. It was the same onion skin as the note left on the top layer penned by her gramps's own hand. The problem was, whenever Charity started to pull this piece of paper from its place, something cold swept over her body and stopped her. Her hands shook, her stomach rolled. "Daisy, you changed the subject on us. I want to hear your news. Who's Josh?"

In true teen fashion, Daisy rolled her eyes.

"She has a date for the ball." Dalton grinned and ducked when Daisy went to strike him again.

"It's not a date," Daisy deadpanned.

Dalton took refuge behind Harold. "It's not? What would you call it?"

Harold leaned away from him. "Don't go hidin' behind me, hot-shot. You're on your own."

An elaborate and surrendering sigh escaped Daisy's mouth. "A new family moved in down the way. Their son is visiting. He just came back from boot camp. His name is Josh. We're just going to meet here." Her eyes narrowed to slits and turned on Dalton. "It's *not* a date."

"Don't young folks go on dates anymore?" Harold asked.

"Yes." Daisy huffed and poured herself a cup. "They just don't share all the gory details with their families."

Charity bit back a smile. Their families. Daisy hadn't even realized she'd made the reference, and that made Charity's heart nearly explode. Right now, in this very moment, everything was perfect. But somewhere deep inside, she knew that was all about to change.

CHAPTER 16

Founders' Day Ball

It was the day before the ball, and Daisy and Charity were trying on their new gowns one more time. Since Daisy was going on a *nondate* to the ball, Charity had decided the young woman needed the perfect dress. They shopped the Internet, the island, the mainland, and then returned to the island. While on their hunt, Charity had spied a slip of a dress in black velvet that hung from her shoulders like a second skin. She'd only put it on at Daisy's insistence and had no intention of purchasing the thing. Daisy, however, had other ideas. "If I'm wearing a nondate dress, then you are, too," had been her argument. Well, how does one argue with logic like that? After all, Dalton was Charity's nondate. To show her support of Daisy, she purchased the dress and tall, spiked heels studded with tiny rhinestones. They found a bright-blue sleeveless dress for Daisy that complemented her dark tan and blonde hair. Nude wedge sandals and a tiny clutch purse completed the outfit. They stood in Charity's room, staring into the full-length mirror at the two Cinderellas looking back at them. "Hair up or down?" Daisy gathered hers at the crown of her head and moved her chin from side to side.

Charity did the same. "I don't know. What do you think?"

Daisy shrugged and let her hair fall. "I don't know."

"We should wear makeup, though. At least a little bit," Charity added.

Daisy frowned and then nodded a reluctant agreement. "I guess."

One more thing on Charity's to-do list. Buy makeup. Learn how to use it before the ball tomorrow night or, better yet, maybe she could get them appointments for hair and makeup at Studio Gaslamp. "I can't believe the ball is so close."

Daisy locked eyes with her in the mirror. "We look really pretty."

"We do. Should we go over the schedule again?"

Daisy groaned and turned around so Charity could unzip her gown. "No. The extra tables and chairs arrive at nine a.m. The committee will be by at nine forty-five to set things up. The first batch of food arrives at noon, and we have to make sure the fridge is empty. Then the caterer gets here at twelve thirty to do the rest of the food prep. Pretty much everything is done for us by two, and the caterer takes over. We got this."

Charity nodded, trying to convince herself that everything would go smoothly. She'd finally begun to feel like she was part of the community and having the ball at Baxter House was risking everything she'd accomplished.

Daisy cocked her head. "What is it you think is going to go wrong?"

"Anything. Everything, maybe. I don't know." Charity sighed.

Daisy scrunched her face and gave her a mock frown. "We got this."

Charity laughed. "What is that look on your face?"

"My thug look. Mean-mugging. Gives you confidence. Try it."

Charity scrunched her face. "Like this?"

Daisy shook her head. "No. You just look constipated. Put some swagger in it." She forced Charity's head to the side and pushed on her hip until it was cocked. "It's all in the attitude. Yeah. Now you got it."

"And this helps me how, exactly?"

"Confidence. When I was on the street, I didn't get messed with because I had confidence. Everything is going to be fine. And if it's not, you just mean-mug your way through it."

Philosophy from a teenage runaway. She could do worse.

Everything is going to be fine. She repeated it like a mantra. The house was perfect, the caterer's driver had delivered all the ready-made foods, and the caterer would be there by twelve thirty to do the hors d'oeuvres that could only be completed at the last minute. Cases of white and red wine sat at the ready on her kitchen floor, the white would need to be chilled, but ice and coolers were coming with the caterer. The committee ladies had already done their morning inspection. Everything was perfect.

And that's what scared the daylights out of Charity. With a cup of tea, she sat down at one o'clock to recheck her list. The caterer was running late, but she'd been warned that that was his habit. Above her, sitting on a newly added wooden shelf, were three vases. Looking at them made her smile. She'd used a new technique with the glaze, and the finished product proved better than she'd imagined. Each vase had ocean colored swirls of deep-blues and greens. The luminescence of the glaze created depth and shimmer. They were likely the most beautiful pieces she'd ever made. Dalton had insisted on building a shelf to display them, and she'd gladly let him. They'd catch the eye of anyone who wandered into the parlor. Charity sipped her tea, letting the calming swirls slake the tension from her muscles. She set the to-do list aside.

At 1:05, the world began crashing around her.

~๑~

Charity tugged the front door open to find her mother, face smeared with mascara streaks, standing on her porch.

"It's over, Charity." Her hands were trembling when she raised them to her face. "I don't know what I'm going to do."

Charity was used to drama with her mother—in fact, the woman perfected it—but this was something more. This was honest despair. The haunted look in Ellen's eyes cut right to Charity's core. Instinctively, she reached out for her mother. But Ellen shook her head. She wouldn't be consoled.

Ellen brushed past her and went straight to the parlor. Though things on the main floor had been made party-ready, Ellen took no notice. She dropped onto the settee, and Charity realized this was a place her mother felt safe. There on the ancient crushed velvet, beneath the warm sunshine, where it pooled and heated one corner of the seat. Ellen, hugging herself, moved into the shower of sunshine, and that's when Charity saw the dark circles beneath her eyes.

"Mom, what happened?"

"Leonard wants me out of the house. I've been discarded, Charity. Just like yesterday's trash."

Charity knelt at her feet. "Mom, are you sure you're not overreacting?"

The wounded look on Ellen's face hinted at the depths of her despair. "I wouldn't have expected you to understand." Ellen stood and pushed past Charity.

Though the words rang with bitterness, Charity chose to ignore them. "Mom, did he tell you to leave?"

"Yes. Charity. He told me to leave. Must I spell it out? He doesn't want me. I raised his girls, horrible little monsters that they are, and now he's *done* with me."

Still, Charity was having a hard time finding where the reality of the situation ended, and the drama began. There would certainly be an *element* of drama in it. She just didn't know how much. "Did you two have a fight?"

She laughed without humor and faced the bookcase. "No. Actually, we didn't. I was going to go above and beyond and help him pack for his fishing trip and realized that all his gear was still in the garage. When

I asked him about it, he said he wasn't going fishing. He was taking a woman to Cabo."

Charity gasped. Pain and anger shot from her heart down. No matter how she'd been feeling about her mother, no one deserved treatment like that. "He's having an affair? Is he in love with this woman?" She didn't know why it mattered—it didn't, in fact—but her mind just wasn't firing enough to make sense of it.

"Barely knows her. Met her two months ago, and as a joke they discussed running away to Cabo together. Then, a few weeks ago, he decided it wasn't a joke. It was a trip he desperately wanted to take. He actually told me all this with a smile on his face. Like I'd be *happy* for him."

Charity's eyes closed. How could anyone be so callous? She stepped closer to her mother. "Mom, you're his wife. He can't just order you out of the house."

Ellen wrung a paper napkin in her hands. It was stained with makeup. "Actually, he can. We never married."

Wait a minute. What? "You told me the two of you married on a beach in Barbados."

"He told me he was scared to marry again so soon after his wife. So, we offered each other rings and performed a mock ceremony. I *believed* him."

Charity shook her head. "Mom, there are laws. You've been with him for years. What about common law marriage?"

"New York stopped honoring common law marriage back in 1938. I checked." Ellen tried to spread the napkin, but it had been reduced to shreds. She tossed it on the settee. "Look at me, Charity. I'm old and pudgier than I've ever been. My skin is starting to sag. How am I supposed to attract a man now?"

Charity bit down on her back teeth. Her mother was already planning to find another man. She went to Ellen and gripped her arms. "You don't need a man, Mom."

Fire filled Ellen's eyes, and she shoved away from Charity, her words spitting venom. "You don't know anything."

Caught off guard, Charity toppled backward, her arm connecting with a protruding corner of the bookshelf where she'd placed the three work-of-art vases she'd worked so hard to complete for the ball. Motion slowed to a crawl as the shelf absorbed the impact of her body. The vases tipped, then toppled to the floor, crashing around Charity's feet.

She held her arm where the pain shot like fire, intensified by her anger over her mother's words, the situation, all of it. Her gaze landed on her mother just as she was about to scream at her to get out.

Ellen blinked, face morphing from utter fury to complete anguish. She dropped to her knees and started picking up the pieces of the broken pottery. She paused only to sob. "Life's always come so easily for you, Charity. Sometimes I despised you for that."

Her mother had never used the word *despised* where she was concerned, but Charity would be lying if she said she hadn't felt it. "From the moment you were born, Mom and Dad adored you. In their eyes, you could do no wrong. And I could do no right."

Charity bit back the emotions. She'd never thought about how her close relationship with Gram and Gramps might have made her mother feel. At the same time, Ellen Marie, self-proclaimed Marilyn Monroe for a new generation, wasn't without blame. But Charity hated her own part in making her mother's life worse.

"Everything is so easy for you. For heaven's sake, you've got a hot piece of man-candy right next door, and you can't even figure out what to do with him. Why do you deserve to have such an easy life?" The lines of mascara made her mother's face look haunted. Swollen, blood-shot, she resembled a drunk who'd passed the point of recovery.

Charity's life wasn't easy. She'd lived in the shadow of Ellen Marie Baxter until she was old enough to move out. She'd lost the two people who'd loved her most, but kept on. She didn't shut people out. She didn't let hate rob her soul. But she wouldn't waste her words on a woman with no ears. "You can stay here, Mom. Until you decide what you want to do." Charity stood, leaving the pottery where it lay. "But I won't allow you to blame others for your own shortcomings. Including me." She held her wounded arm where it throbbed with each beat of her heart. Already, she could feel the bruise setting in. "You think my life is easy because you haven't walked in my shoes. Presume that of me again, and I will kick you out. There's a broom in the kitchen. Clean up your mess. We have a party here in a few hours."

Charity left the room feeling a new sensation spreading through her system. It was effervescent, like freedom after a long insurrection. Though parts of her heart were undoubtedly wounded from the skirmish with her mother, other parts were rising from the ashes of the fight. A wave of confidence shot through her. She glanced into the mirror on the far wall and gave her best mean-mug. For the first time in her life, Charity felt strong. As she passed the chandelier, on her way upstairs, she noticed something. No cobwebs. No cobs at all.

༄

At one forty-five, Charity was pacing the kitchen floor. The caterer was supposed to have been there over an hour ago.

Daisy stared at the list. "Should I call his phone again?"

Charity shook her head. "We've left multiple messages. Call the salon and cancel my appointment."

The disappointment registered on Daisy's face. When she dialed Studio Gaslamp and told them she wanted to cancel both their appointments, Charity tried to stop her. "There's no reason you can't go."

Daisy waved her off and focused on the phone call. "Yes, ma'am. I'm sure she'll understand. I'll have her call you tomorrow after the ball." She hung up. "They'll have to charge us half of the cost. Said it was policy."

"Daisy, why did you cancel yours?"

The teen shrugged. They were both in the sweat clothes they'd planned to wear to the salon. "You're going to need me."

Need her for what? Charity herself didn't even know what to do. "I guess I better call Jeanna Rudd. Explain about the caterer."

But just as she was lifting the phone to her ear, they heard the van pull in. Both women rushed to the door to greet him. "François, we are so glad to see you."

He rushed past them and into the kitchen, arms loaded and throwing a barrage of instructions in their direction—all in French. When they continued to stare at him, he barked, "There's more in the van." Fifteen minutes later, and with Charity and Daisy standing there, mouths agape and still holding the last few bags and containers of food, François rushed back out to his van and left.

Charity turned to find her mother on the bottom step of the staircase, one hand on the dancing bear's head, one hand on the lion's as if she were commanding the entire circus.

"What was he saying?" Daisy muttered, eyes landing on Charity.

Ellen spoke up. "A doomed and tragic love affair, sounds like. You know the French."

Daisy and Charity both stared at her waiting for more explanation. "In essence, he wants the two of you to cover for him for a few hours. He's off to the skyway bridge to stop his jilted lover from jumping."

"Oh my gosh! Should we call the police?" Daisy said.

"I don't think so." Ellen dropped onto the marble floor. "He said she's waiting for him to propose. If he doesn't, she's leaping."

Charity grabbed her head with both hands. "Why on God's green earth would he take the time to come here, first?"

"He was muttering about needing the job now that he'll have a fiancée. That's also why he wants you to do his work for him. He doesn't want the ladies league to know about this."

Charity huffed. "This is it. My worst nightmare come true."

Ellen grabbed the paper François had shoved into Charity's hands and studied it. "Oh, stop being so dramatic, Charity Monroe."

For all the anger Charity felt in this moment, she had to admit, her mom looked better than she had an hour ago. Dressed in a deep-red three-quarter sleeve sweater and designer jeans, her mom had washed the gunk from her face and pulled her hair into a ponytail at the back of her neck. Something about her looked more beautiful, more genuine, than Charity had seen her look in years. Memories took her back. Christmas morning had always been Charity's favorite because it was the one day Ellen would allow Charity to wake her early. She'd don a robe and wash her face, comb her hair, and tie it back with a ribbon or clasp and there, sitting beside the Christmas tree, they'd sip hot chocolate and open the presents Gram and Gramps had sent.

It was when her mother was most beautiful. And this moment mirrored all those.

"Nothing too difficult here," Ellen surmised. "Make a choice, Charity."

Her eyes cut into Charity's soul. "What?"

"Either call the women on the committee and rat this guy out or decide to pitch in. If we hit a roadblock on the cooking, I can call Sonia for advice. But most of this is typical cocktail food. Nothing we can't handle."

Now it was all starting to fall into place. Ellen had learned culinary skills from Sonia, her French housekeeper. She'd apparently learned more than a bit of the language as well, since she'd made sense of the half-English, half-French François had spoken.

"Daisy? You think we can do this?" It was an honest question, and she'd found Daisy to be a solid voice of reason in times of panic.

In answer, Daisy mean-mugged.

Charity laughed. "OK, what do we do first?"

Charity swiped the sweat from her brow as Harold and Louise entered the kitchen. It was four o'clock and Charity believed they were actually going to pull this off.

Louise already had her hair and makeup done but was wearing white pants and a button-up blouse, not yet in her ball gown. Her gaze flittered around the busy kitchen. "Oh dear. I thought you girls had salon appointments."

Ellen had been barking orders at them for the last two hours, and though they were both tired and sweaty, things were coming together. Ellen gave an abridged version of the story just as Dalton came in through the sleeping porch.

"What can we do to help?" Harold said.

Dalton took one look around and went straight to the sink to wash the pans that filled one side.

"Shall I put the white wine in the fridge?" Louise asked.

"Oh no. François didn't leave ice or coolers. The fridge is full." Charity stared at the case of wine.

"I'm on it." Harold grabbed the wall phone. He called a local fisherman and explained the situation. He requested use of two of his coolers and then he asked if the man could bring ice on his way over with them. "Thanks, Mack. Sure, I'll let her know."

When he'd hung up, he pointed to Charity. "You've made some friends here on the island, Lil' Bit."

She brushed the sticky hair from her brow. "What?"

"His momma is the widow Williamson. You made her a looking glass. She sees her husband in it, and Mack said she's happier than she's been in years. He'd do anything you requested."

Charity stopped for a moment. How many people had been touched by special orders? The result of being a vessel for the orders settled in. Because she made the pottery, she was bestowed with the credit. All she did was make what folks asked for. The almost empty bag of special ingredient niggled at the back of her mind.

"What is all this talk of special orders? It's only pottery," Ellen said, lifting a pot of boiling shrimp from the stove and dumping it into a colander in the open side of the sink. She thrust the colander into a large bowl half-filled with ice.

"Yes. And the weeping tree is just a tree," Daisy added, and a few snickers bounced around the room.

Ellen cut them with her eyes. Apparently, she wasn't fond of being the outsider to an inside joke.

The six of them worked for the next hour and a half. "OK," Ellen said, marking the last thing off the list. "Everything is done. The serving team will be here in about thirty minutes, and I think all of you who plan to attend this little soirée should go get ready."

Charity glanced around the kitchen at the rows of silver trays ready to be placed on the dining table. "We couldn't have done it without you, Mom."

"Of course you couldn't have. You used to burn even the simplest of recipes."

"Mom, I have an extra gown if you'd like to come to the party." Of course, it wouldn't fit her the same as Charity. Ellen was curvaceous everywhere Charity was thin and bony. But the gown was a stretchy cotton and spandex that would look divine on her mother.

"No, thanks." She held her hands up. "I'm going to have a long smoke on the front porch, then go to my room. I've had all the party I can take for one day."

She started to leave the kitchen but stopped in the doorway. "Knock on my door after you've showered, Charity. I'll do your makeup and hair."

Charity opened her mouth, but nothing came out. *Thank you, thank you, thank you* was floating around in her head, but the words wouldn't join together and leave her mind.

"You, too, Daisy."

"Really?" Daisy perked up. "Thanks!"

Louise, still looking lovely, sat down at the kitchen counter. "I'll wait for the service team. You two girls go on upstairs."

Harold sat beside her and took her hand. "When they get here, we'll fill them in, and I'll run Louise home to change."

Charity smiled at her family. "Thank you all."

⁓

In exchange for makeup and hair, Charity had promised her mother she would make an entrance. Not used to being in the limelight, she'd expected to step out to the banister that overlooked the entryway and dance floor beyond and say, "Welcome. Thank you all for coming." Then she'd float down the stairs like Scarlet O'Hara.

It was still early, and there were only a couple dozen people meandering the rooms below. Mostly the ladies league and their dates, middle-aged to elderly gentlemen who looked as if they'd put on a few pounds since last wearing their formal attire, by the way their shirts stretched over their bellies. What she hadn't expected was that Daisy would stop the music and point at Charity at the top of the stairs. Which of course stole all her words.

There was a pause, and Charity could feel the eyes on her. She'd pass out, but fear of tumbling headfirst down the staircase forced her to breathe.

And then there was applause. Widespread applause followed by a few cheers as Jeanna Rudd stepped from the group and said, "Ladies and gentlemen, our Founders' Day Ball savior, Charity Baxter."

Charity smiled at Daisy, who restarted the music. People went back to their mingling, but Charity still felt eyes on her. Intensely on her. Hair stood up on the back of her neck. She scanned the crowd. There, beside Harold and Louise near the front door, stood Dalton.

Her grip tightened on the banister. His eyes didn't leave hers as he mouthed one word. "Beautiful."

Charity reminded herself to breathe again when tiny spots appeared before her. She mouthed back, "Terrified." That made him chuckle. He was dressed in a black tux with a black velvet tie. She tried to swallow, but her throat was cotton as he made his way across the floor. She took her first step down the stairs. Her hand remained on the banister lest she fall off her stilettoes. But she couldn't tear her gaze from Dalton.

Feelings swirled inside her chest. Things she shouldn't feel for him. Couldn't feel for him. Those feelings frightened her. He was her best friend. Why did she always love people who were incapable of loving her back?

At the base of the stairs, he placed his hand over hers. "You look incredible."

"Daisy chose the dress. I had a more reserved one I bought first." His hand was warm over hers, and the touch chased away the emotions she'd had. Things would be OK. They loved each other as friends. That was all they could have, and it was enough for Charity.

"Come on, let's dance." He led her to the dance floor and turned her toward him.

For the moment, Charity would allow herself to let go and feel. She might hate herself for it tomorrow, but right now she just wanted to spin and turn on the dance floor with the man she knew she couldn't have.

＊

Harold twirled Louise in his arms. Years ago, he'd always been careful with her because of her injured leg. But tonight, he held her close, and with their thighs touching, they floated around the space as if the floor had been made only for them.

Two months of spending time with her, and Harold knew all he needed to know. Louise had been a tender part of his past. But now he wanted her to be his future.

She tilted back to look at him. "What are you grinning about, you fool?" she teased.

His eyes sparkled with a mix of expectation and joy. "Just how I may be the luckiest man in the room."

"And why is that?" She blinked several times.

He stopped and took her face in his hands. "Because I'm with the most beautiful woman in the room." With a gentle touch, he brushed his lips across hers. His heart floated right out of his chest when she laid her head against him.

This was what he wanted. Her. How could he have been so stupid all those years ago? They could have had a whole life together, but no. He'd been selfish and ignorant. "Louise, these last two months have been some of the happiest of my life."

He felt her stiffen—only slightly, but still—and he understood. But he'd be lying if he didn't admit it hurt whenever she seemed to pull away. "What can I do to show you I'm not the man I used to be? That I'd never again . . . take you for granted?"

"Harold, there's a lot about the past that we haven't discussed. What happened that night. Why you left me standing alone on a pier. Where you were when you were supposed to be with me."

Pain shot into his chest and rested there. That night. That night that ruined everything and everyone he loved. That night would haunt him forever, and there could never be healing from it, of that he was certain.

"Louise—"

She placed a finger over his lips. "Not now," she whispered. "I want to enjoy the ball and the dancing and spinning around in your arms. But Harold, there are things that will have to be talked about and brought out into the open." She cast a glance behind her. "Does Charity know?"

Shame crept up over his shoulders and scraped at his throat. "No."

He'd finally come home. He'd grieved for his brother even before George died because twenty years ago, Harold made a horrible, awful mistake that cost him everyone and everything he held dear. If he dredged it all up again, he ran the risk of losing it all again. He took Louise's hand and led her to the parlor where they gazed out the front window at the cars lining the street. But privacy was important. "Louise, what happened was twenty years ago. I'd like to move on, not go back to the past."

She turned to face him, and he could see that she understood. Still, there was a certainty in her stance. "The past always has the power to destroy you when you try to hide it. That's not fair to Charity."

She was probably right. But it put everything at risk. He slid a hand into his pocket to the small velvet box. "I'll tell her. I'll do it tomorrow. But tonight, I have something I want to ask you."

She reached up and pecked his cheek. "Then meet me at midnight on the pier."

He released his grip on the tiny box. "I'll be there at eleven thirty."

Louise gave him a tender smile. "Shall we return to the dance?"

"Be there in a minute. You go ahead." His heart was pounding like he'd run a marathon, not almost asked a woman to marry him. Once she was gone, he pulled the box from his pocket and opened it.

"Oh, that's nice." The voice came from behind him. Harold spun just as the shadowed shape took form. Paulette Grove stood on her ancient legs and came closer. Her sister, Agnes, stepped into the parlor with two glasses of wine in her hands. "Am I interrupting?" Agnes's eyes were alive with intrigue. Her bloodred smile made her resemble an evil clown.

Paulette yawned. "Not at all, sissy. I was just napping and opened my eyes to find a handsome man holding a—what is that?" She tilted her head to look into the box. "An engagement ring, I believe it is." Her silver eyes flashed.

Agnes gushed. "Oh, sissy, he's proposing to you? I didn't even know you two were an item."

It was a jest, but even joking, the words made Harold silently plead for escape.

"You always got all the suitors," Agnes said.

The sisters were at least five to ten years older than Harold's seventy-five years and reminded Harold of twin snakes. He'd never cared much for them. Years ago, they'd found it humorous to make fun of Louise's limp.

When he saw Daisy waving furiously at him from the edge of the parlor, Harold excused himself. Daisy was chewing her index fingernail. "What's wrong, Daisy?"

She glanced beyond him to the front door, eyes like saucers. "My date's here. I mean, my nondate, and he's with his *parents*." Nervous energy flew off her in sparks. "What do I do?"

He placed a firm hand on her shoulder. "First, calm down. You're going to explode, or all your joints are gonna come loose and go flying in all directions."

Her chin tilted down. "Wouldn't that be the same as exploding?"

Harold cast a glance behind him. "They look like nice enough folks. Good-looking young man, too. Your age?"

"A couple of years older."

Josh and his parents were already being greeted by Jeanna and Emily Rudd. While the parents chatted with Jeanna, Harold waved to Josh.

"What are you doing?" Daisy said through gritted teeth.

"When you need to rip off a Band-Aid, you just do it." He moved her to stand in front of him. "Won't it be easier to meet his parents once you and he have had a few minutes to chat?"

"Good thought." She pulled in a breath and forced it out quickly.

Harold watched Paulette and Agnes slink from the shadows where he felt snakes belonged and rejoin the party. The two sisters made their way toward Jeanna—always the type to hitch a post to the closest politician or whoever they thought had the most power in the room.

As Josh neared, Harold held out a hand. "Hello, young man. I'm Harold, Daisy's uncle."

But the boy could only see the beautiful girl in front of him, not the crusty old man beside her. He mumbled a greeting and told Daisy she looked great.

She blushed beneath that deep tan of hers, and the two young people headed for the table where trays of food waited.

~⑨~

"And this is the weeping tree." Daisy traced the outline of one of the leaves. She and Josh had stepped outside for fresh air and because young people could only handle so much grown up conversation.

He sat down on the short rock wall beside the tree. "You said there are legends about it. Are they true?"

When he dusted a spot for her, she sat beside him, the glistening sea at their backs and the tree before them. "I think so."

"You never put it to the test?" His arm brushed against hers when the breeze kicked up. Rather than moving away, he kept his skin against hers.

"I guess I've been saving it. You know, if something really bad happens—"

He reached over and slid a finger down her arm. "Well, you have my word nothing bad is going to happen tonight." Josh pivoted so he could look at her. Gently, he dipped down and brushed a kiss across her mouth.

Daisy's eyes drifted open slowly, and without a thought, she pressed her mouth to his again. He tasted like the peach and lime punch they'd been drinking, and there was a bit of salt on his upper lip from the peanuts he'd had before she'd brought him outside. When the kiss deepened, Josh's shoulders tilted so he could gain more access to her body. One hand pressed against the small of her back, the other twined into her long hair, and she was happy she'd followed Ellen's advice and worn it down.

She broke the kiss to find him more than a little out of breath. His sparkling eyes scanned her face, then used a fingertip to touch her cheek. "I think boot camp would have been a breeze if I'd had an image of you to keep me going."

Daisy smiled and allowed him to cradle her against his chest. It was good there, warm and perfect. Now she understood what Cinderella felt like.

"So, this is the garden you take care of?" His words were deep vibrations against her ear.

"Not alone. Dalton, the next-door neighbor, is teaching me about it. I'm applying for college in a few months."

"That's great, Daisy." He ran a hand over her long hair, letting his fingers play in the strands as if he'd never felt anything like it before tonight.

"But I've already learned so much. I'm even growing some orchids. You want to see them?"

He grinned. "Sure."

"Wait here." Daisy navigated the darkened path to the spot just inside the sleeping porch where two potted orchids waited for her gentle touch. She scooped them up carefully, slowly stepping over discarded hedge trimmers and other tools. She reached the door when Josh's mother came around the far side of the house. She stared to holler a greeting, but the look on the woman's face stopped her. Daisy swallowed and moved to a spot just behind the edge of the weeping tree where she could hear their conversation.

"What are you talking about, Mom? I'm not ready to leave yet. You guys go on."

The woman stepped closer and lowered her voice. "That girl. The girl you're with. She's a transient."

Daisy sucked in a breath. In all the months she'd been on the street, all the times people had made fun of her, picked on her, or simply ignored her, none of them hurt as much as the words she'd just heard.

Josh brushed a hand through his hair.

Defend me. Defend me, Josh.

"Mom, what are you talking about?"

Daisy's heart sunk a little deeper into her chest.

"She was homeless. Living on the street for months, I don't know, maybe for years. We're going home, you're going with us." She grabbed his arm, but he jerked away.

"I'm not a ten-year-old anymore, Mom. You can't just order me around like one."

Her hands went to her hips. "Are you telling me it doesn't matter that she's a transient who's been doing God knows what to stay alive?"

Josh rubbed his face. "Of course it matters. But I'm not a child. And it's not your call to decide when I'm leaving. Go home, Mom. I'll handle this."

The battle of wills only lasted a few moments. "This girl is nothing but trouble. Get away from her quickly, Josh."

Daisy bit into her lip to keep from crying. She placed the orchids at her feet and started to walk away. A twig snapped, alerting Josh that she was there. He found her on the opposite side of the weeping tree. "How much did you hear?"

She crossed her arms over her chest. "All of it."

"She doesn't know anything." He shrugged.

But the damage was done. No return, no going back at all. "She knew more than you."

His gaze narrowed. "Yeah, you could have warned me."

Daisy clamped her teeth together. "Sorry I didn't *warn you* about me. I didn't realize that was my duty."

"That's not what I mean, Daisy." His wide stance and posture would be intimidating if she were easily intimidated. She wasn't.

"What she said, is it true?" Josh said.

The fact that it mattered enough to him to keep asking her told her everything she needed to know. "Yep."

He stared out over the water, his hands on his hips like he'd just ran a race and was cooling down. "All of it?"

Because her heart was in the process of shattering into a thousand tiny pieces, she lied. "Every last word." Her look was defiant. She'd practiced it in a broken mirror before ever coming to the island.

When his eyes found hers, there was pain in the depths, but she couldn't stop herself. "Doing *God knows what to stay alive* isn't so bad, really. I mean, it's better than going hungry or sleeping on the ground."

He turned away from her, seeking the water again, where a crescent moon threw slashes of silver on the darkened gulf.

She'd never allowed anyone to touch her while she'd been on the street. But Josh hadn't earned the right to know that. He believed what his mother told him, and that's all he'd ever see in Daisy, so what did it matter if it was true or not? Clean cuts were better than jagged ones.

It was a long time before he spoke. "I think I better go home."

"Yeah," she agreed. She watched him walk away. He didn't bother to go through the house but went around the side of the building instead. Away from her, away from the weeping tree. He paused at the corner of the house, and she knew he was going to look back, so she turned away from him and faced the water, stiff as a marble statue, the kind that stood guard over ship ports and towns, ever searching ahead, never looking back. When the sting of his eyes on her was gone, Daisy cried.

Behind her, the wind worked into the branches of the weeping tree causing them to moan. She turned, and though something in her was inexplicably drawn to the tree, she stilled herself. "Who's to say you don't cause horrible things to happen to people just so you can help them feel better?"

The rustling of the leaves stopped. The tree was silent.

Daisy laughed without humor and leaned closer to the tree. She whispered, "I don't trust you."

CHAPTER 17

Snakes in the Parlor

A party was hard for Ellen to resist, so against her better judgment and with a fresh glass of wine in her hand, she joined the festivities clothed in Charity's spare ball gown. It would have been unattractive on her daughter—shapeless and dull—but Ellen made it shine. It was her gift, to shine. She'd first flirted with a young man around Charity's age, an attorney, if she was to guess by the look of his expensive suit and plastered shiny hair. Then she'd walked away as if there were others she needed to converse with. It was all part of the game. Didn't want to appear desperate.

She'd readied to step up behind him and begin another conversation when she heard him talking with another man of the same age. Ellen stepped closer. She was hidden behind the edge of the kitchen door, and they were a few feet away at the dining table. Ah, they were discussing her. The shark-eyed attorney was saying he might take her home with him. Ellen's heart jumped in her chest. She hadn't flirted in so long—too long, really—and knowing that her skills were intact made her feel like the powerhouse she was. She imagined a great stage. Applause. Stepping forward and bowing deeply for her adoring fans. But the scenario that ran in her head came to an abrupt halt. A screeching, fatal, abrupt halt when she heard the words, "You mean the old one?"

"Yeah, the old one."

She couldn't breathe. Air came into her mouth but lacked the ability to infiltrate her lungs. They'd shrunk to tiny, deflated balloons inside her chest. *The old one.* Her. She used to be the *pretty* one. The worst nightmare she could realize was unfurling before her aging face. She'd fought her entire life for the freedom the right man could give her. Now, now it was too late. Leonard and her real enemy, time, had taken the very best of her and left her in ruins. On every level. Complete ruin. For all the clawing and climbing she'd done, here she was. *The old one.*

She started to leave the party by going upstairs but opted out of that decision. She'd only stare into the wall mirror and see the haggard old woman she was. No, she'd not do that. Down here at the party, people had been kind. Telling her she looked beautiful and that they were honored finally to meet George's daughter and Charity's mother. The older men were gracious, with their long looks of approval. But they were old men. They also looked that way at antique cars, fishing poles, and rocking chairs. Still, she couldn't leave on the low she'd experienced, or she'd be fighting a heinous depression, and she had no meds to combat it.

After an hour of monotone dribble, she got into her first good conversation since the fiasco earlier. It was with two women—sisters, by the look of them—just as the party was ending.

First, she'd been bored, as they'd started talking about Harold and that woman, Louise, but Ellen had yawned her lack of interest and was just getting ready to make her escape when they brought up Charity and the massive inheritance left to her. Ellen's skin heated first, then cooled with gooseflesh crawling over her like ants at a picnic. The amount of money they spoke of was obscene. Beautifully, deliciously obscene. Of course, she'd known her dad was worth something, but millions?

Practically everyone was gone when Ellen found Charity and dragged her into the parlor.

Charity didn't seem to notice the death grip Ellen had on her. Charity spoke before Ellen had the chance. "Mom, have you seen Daisy?"

"No, Charity. I haven't." She was spitting venom. It tasted bitter in her mouth. She liked it. "Is the inheritance Dad left you in the millions?"

Charity blinked. Her mouth opened, but no words came out. Ellen grabbed her arm but loosened her grip when Charity yelped. Oh, she'd run into that ill-placed shelf corner before the party. "It's a simple question, Charity. Yes or no."

Charity held her arm. "Yes."

Fury shot down Ellen's flesh. All these years, all this time working to protect a future when more than enough money was right here. Being a trophy wife. Sitting home long hours. Caring for two brats who lacked the ability to appreciate all she'd done for them. A man who tossed her to the curb as soon as he found someone younger, firmer, prettier. "I want half of it." She deserved more. She deserved it all.

Charity swallowed. "Mom, this isn't the time to discuss this."

Ellen's rage exploded. "No, the time for discussion is far past. You're going to go to your attorney tomorrow, and you're going to sign over half of the inheritance to me."

Ellen was shocked at the defiance that entered Charity's gaze. "No. I'm not." Charity dropped her hands and fisted them at her sides.

Ellen reached out and seized Charity's arms. When Charity refused to flinch, she squeezed.

The battle was on. Ellen's eyes flashed down to the injured arm, but Charity wouldn't even blink. *Who are you?* Ellen wanted to ask. When had her daughter grown a backbone? She'd need to change her tactic if she hoped to get through. "Charity, I need the money. You know that."

"And where does it end, Mom? You always need, need, need. There's never enough for you. You're never satisfied. You think money will make you happy, but when it doesn't, you'll have nothing left because in having money, you push away everything and everyone who actually matter. Money is your hope. But it doesn't equal worth. I think Gramps kept the money from you because he knew it would destroy you."

Ellen's grip loosened, but only marginally. The words stung. There was a thread of truth there; she knew there had to be from the way each phrase cut jagged slashes in her heart.

"You have to find happiness in who you are, Mom. Not in what money can provide you."

Blackness crept over her, a cloak destined to swallow her. Was it true? Her mind rushed to defend. No. She shook her head. "No, Charity. Everything I did, I did for us. I was so young when I got pregnant with you, and all I ever wanted was to have a good life for you."

Charity's hands shot up. "Stop it. Just stop it, Mother. It's always been about what was best for Ellen Marie Baxter. For heaven's sake, I care more about what happens to Daisy than you ever cared about me. And she's not even my daughter. Not even my family at all."

"You don't think of me as family?" Daisy's voice drifted into the parlor from where she stood at the doorway.

❦

Oh no. Charity turned to go to Daisy, whose face was streaked like she'd been crying, but Ellen stepped in front of her.

"You're *not* family," Ellen said. "However, you seem to be quite important to her. In all her life, Charity never could resist strays."

Charity shoved her mother out of the way. "Daisy, that's not true. What I said—"

Behind them, Ellen spoke. "What she said was that she cares more about you than she does me, and I'm her own mother."

Charity angled for a moment to face Ellen. "Do you ever stop?"

Ellen's shoulder tipped.

Charity gripped Daisy's arms. They were cold to the touch, she must have been outside. "Daisy, I do care. What you heard me say . . . it's not what I meant."

Daisy jerked a nod.

Charity scanned her eyes. There was a detached deadness in them. Something she hadn't seen for so many weeks.

"I'm tired." Daisy gently tugged from Charity's grasp. "I'm going to bed."

"Honey, have you been crying?" Charity reached up, but Daisy recoiled.

"I'm fine," Daisy said. "We can talk about it tomorrow."

She was walking away and had made it to the foyer when Charity marched over to her and grabbed her in a bear hug. Daisy remained stiff. Charity dropped a kiss on the side of Daisy's head. "You promise we will?"

"Sure. I swear." She disappeared up the stairs, and Charity noticed there was still a handful of party-goers working their way to the front door.

Charity returned to the parlor and turned her anger on her mother. "How could you? You know what that child's been through."

Ellen inspected her fingernails. "She's tough."

Charity shook her head. "I'm not giving you a dime, Mother. I know Gramps left you a trust that is enough for a single woman to live on, plus the family home in Atlanta. You have a place to live and money. If you want more, you'll have to sue me for it."

Charity left her mother in the parlor and went out to see the last of the party-goers home. She should have known this would happen. Life was messy and not confronting issues only made them fester. But the money hadn't been an issue until her mother's rich doctor threw her out.

Dalton came out of the kitchen just as the two sisters, Paulette and Agnes—if Charity had their names right—were slipping on fur shawls. The shawls made the two overdressed, even for the ball.

"You OK?" Dalton's hand landed on the small of her back. His touch was warming, and it brought the first stream of peace.

She closed her eyes and drank him in. "Yes. Problem with Mom and with Daisy." She leaned closer to him. "Can anything else go wrong tonight?"

He offered a half smile that said more than words, and it melted a piece of her heart. It was a wink to an inside joke. It was a secret kept safe and locked away between two people who shared more than common space. For some reason, she found it inexplicably difficult not to reach up with her fingertips and capture that smile. To touch his cheek. To allow him to continue touching her soul where his thumb made tiny circles at the base of her spine.

Without warning, Dalton leaned closer, and closer still, until his lips brushed over hers. Lightning zinged into her stomach, and heat rushed to her cheeks. She tried to draw a breath, but there was nothing there, no oxygen, no air. Just Dalton. Green eyes, soft lips, warm skin. His chest rose and fell, hers caved. A scent like maple filled the space between them. Calming, sweet. Home.

When he moved a few millimeters away from her, the world spun back into view. There were the remnants of party sounds around them, hushed tones, the tinkling of the last few glasses as the cleanup crew worked its way around the room, Dalton breathing.

Dalton swallowed and raked a hand through his hair. "I'm sorry. I shouldn't have done that."

Was he really apologizing? For what? Shoving her down a roller coaster hill without warning? For branding her mouth with his own, something she'd surely think about long after the last guest left, and the last wine glass was emptied. "I'm glad you did it." There. It was out in the open, no backpedaling now. Her face creaked into a smile.

But his expression saddened, the green in his eyes liquefying. "I shouldn't have. It won't happen again."

And just like that, her Cinderella moment faded away. Near the front door, the two sisters—bathed in fur—peered at them with great interest. Charity cleared her throat and stiffened, though Dalton continued to stand beside her.

With him at her side, Charity said good-bye to Jeanna and Emily Rudd and then watched as they stepped out into the cool evening, where the breeze off the bay grabbed the hems of their gowns. Next in line were the two sisters. They were the last. Charity thanked them for coming and prayed that saying good-bye to Dalton next wouldn't be laden with awkwardness.

Agnes took her hand and shook it. Her crepe skin moved beneath Charity's touch. "And where is your uncle Harold? I'd love to say good-bye to him." The woman looked past Charity as if searching, but the room was empty.

"I guess he's gone up to bed." Charity hadn't seen him since the last song, when he'd spun a laughing Louise around the room. Her heart warmed, thinking of the happiness her uncle had found with Louise.

"Eleven forty-five. Past our bedtime as well," Paulette added. "By the way, dear. We just wanted to let you know it's marvelously big of you to allow Harold to be here."

Charity cast a glance at Dalton. He lifted and dropped his shoulders in an *I don't know* gesture.

"After what happened and all—"

The first threads of panic entered Charity's system by way of her ears. Sometimes, poison came in tiny bottles with skull-and-crossbones markings; sometimes it came in uncontrolled tongues. She didn't know what the sisters had to say, but already, she knew they were champing at the bit to get it out. "What *happened?*"

"The affair, dear." Agnes didn't bother to lower her voice.

Charity tried to draw a breath. "Affair?"

"Harold and your grandmother. Goodness, it must have been twenty years ago." Agnes turned to Paulette. "How long ago did Marilyn die?"

Dalton's hand stiffened against her back. His free one reached to open the front door; obviously he thought it best to get rid of these women before more damage was done, but Charity stopped him. "Do you mean when Gram and Harold were young? Kids?" She knew they didn't. The words *twenty years ago* and *when did Marilyn die* had been used. Fear raced through her, numbness infusing her joints.

Agnes leaned forward, hands resting on the fox carcass she wore as if perhaps she'd hunted the thing herself and then ripped its throat out with her teeth. "Kids? Heavens no. It was quite the island scandal, I must say. Everyone here loved George. How she could have done that was beyond all of us." Her brows rose. "But I guess in the end, she couldn't live with it, either."

Charity's heart pounded in her chest, but it was a cavern, and her blood pumped through it only with great effort.

Paulette placed a thin hand to her breastbone. "Poor dear. George was never the same after."

Agnes turned to her sister. "Well, you wouldn't be. Watching your spouse leap off a balcony to her death."

Charity gasped. Gramps was there? He saw her? How had that bit of information been kept from her? Surely Emily Rudd knew. Charity's mind returned to that summer so long ago when she'd come to visit. She knew something, something awful, had happened that summer when she was eleven. Gram hadn't been herself, though whenever Charity asked her, she'd don a smile and tell her everything was just fine. She'd been distant with Gramps, too. All the summers before, Charity would fall asleep hearing the murmurs of her grandparents in the kitchen below. But not that year. Often, Gram would go up to bed even before Charity. And Charity fell asleep each night with only the silence of the house and the sound of the Gulf slipping through her open window.

"Anyway, dear." Agnes blinked, a smile as wide as an animal trap on her face. "We think you're a very big person to allow Harold to be here at all after what he's cost you. Oh dear, look at the time. Almost midnight."

The sisters left. Dalton faced Charity.

Harold. Harold was here, and she'd let him permeate her life and her world. She'd known he was harboring a secret, but this? This? All these years she'd blamed herself and the weeping tree for her gram's death. And all these years he'd known who was really to blame. "It's his fault." The words were breathy. It was all she could get out with the emotions swirling through her system.

"Charity," Dalton said, placing a hand on her arm. "We don't know what really happened."

She huffed. "Don't we? My grandfather hadn't spoken to his brother for twenty years. Then when he dies, suddenly Harold shows up?" Her stomach soured. The hors d'oeuvres she'd eaten over the course of the night roiled in her gut. She was going to vomit. "I've been so stupid."

Dalton led her toward the parlor just as Harold appeared at the base of the stairs.

Harold smiled and hooked a thumb behind him. "I'm headed out and running late. Been talking to Daisy. I have to go meet Louise, but will ya'll keep an eye on the girl? She doesn't seem OK."

Charity clamped her teeth together to keep from screaming at him. She tried to concentrate on her breathing lest she pass out, but things around her were going dark. "You had an affair with my grandmother."

The blood drained from his face, eyes opening like a frightened child's. If she wasn't so angry, she'd almost feel bad. Charity took a murderous step toward him. "You cost me everything."

Dalton tried to grab her arm, but she jerked away. "You came here and moved in, knowing, knowing that you caused her death."

His body started to tremble. Eyes, scared and filled with ghosts, closed. "I'm—I'm sorry."

"Because of you, she cheated on my grandfather and killed herself."

The old man straightened his spine and took two steps toward her. "She didn't. Don't you say that. She'd never do that!" Harold was practically yelling by the time the last word left his mouth. When he stumbled forward, balance lost in the pain, Dalton reached out and gripped him by the shoulder. Harold's weight fell against him as if there were no power left to stay erect. He whimpered, "She'd never do that. She fell. She fell off the balcony landing."

"Or she jumped, Harold." Charity didn't want to think that. In her heart, she knew it just couldn't be. Yet, right now, she wanted to hurt him. She wanted to take everything away from him because he'd taken everything away from her. Why did she always love the wrong people? Anguish flickered over her flesh, creating its own cocoon, its own armor, the kind of shield she'd fought her entire life to avoid. With it came emotional barricades that kept one from truly feeling, truly loving. With it came the ability to see the true harshness of life for what it was. A weapon set to destroy you.

Harold shook his head. "It's not like you think. We didn't plan—"

Charity held a hand up. "Don't. I want you gone. I want you out of my home and away from me." She'd once looked at him and seen her gramps. But not now. Her gramps was gone, and she needed to be strong enough to realize that, strong enough to say good-bye.

Harold's lip quivered, and he pressed his mouth into a straight line to keep from breaking down again. She didn't care.

Dalton shored him up, and wasn't it just like a man to take another's side! Of course, if he hadn't, Harold might have ended up a heap on her marble floor. Dalton's eyes pleaded. "Charity, let's sort things out tomorrow. It's late."

She hugged herself, staving off the cold. "No. I want him gone tonight."

Dalton turned to face Harold. "You can stay with me tonight. Let's go upstairs and grab a few things." He kept his hands firmly on Harold, who seemed almost incapable of putting one foot before the other.

Charity turned around to find her mother leaned against the parlor doorjamb, her arms crossed over her chest, her hip cocked. A hint of a smile on her face. "And I'm the one who has always hurt you? You need to pay more attention to the company you keep, Charity Monroe. You're not the best judge of character."

Her mother was a master at taking potshots. Charity had long ago learned to ignore them. As a kid, she'd watched a nature special on TV about a type of animal that will pick on the weakest in the pack, sometimes actually taking bites out of their flesh. If that's how some animals were, then that's how some people were. At a young age, she'd decided her mom was like those animals. It wasn't her fault, really. It was just how she was made, and she couldn't help it. Charity knew she'd just once again made excuses for bad mothering. But right now the fight was gone from Charity. She wouldn't spar with her mother anymore. She was just opening her mouth to say so, when she heard the commotion upstairs.

CHAPTER 18

The Railing

Dalton came running to the railing. "She's gone. Daisy's gone."

Charity rushed up the steps and entered the room where Daisy was staying. The space looked mostly the same, except the backpack that hung by the door—always filled with a few of Daisy's clothes—was missing. Charity threw the closet door open to find hangers on the floor, some hanging empty and at strange angles, as if the things hanging on them had been grabbed in a hurry.

Charity slung the top drawer open and scrounged around until she found the recipe box. "She kept her money in here."

Dalton paced the floor. "Where would she go?"

"She's a runaway. She could go anywhere." It was Ellen, standing at the door of Daisy's room.

"We'd have seen her leave." Then Charity realized. Her heart lurched into her throat as she ran across the hall and into her own room. There on the wall where she kept the attic door key, the nail was empty. "She must have left through the attic."

Just like she knew she would, Charity found the attic door unlocked, the key still resting in its keyhole. She was the first onto the attic stairs, her mind filled with a barrage of emotions too great to manage. She couldn't explain why—in this of all moments—her thoughts went to her gram. The fear, the pain. The shame. Charity looked down at her own feet, but saw her gram's, covered as they always were in white lace-up shoes instead of the stilettos Charity wore at the party. Her legs clad in Gram's seersucker capris—her staple.

She could hear Dalton behind her, and Harold behind him, both yelling at her to slow down as she ran full force up the narrow attic stairs. But she realized it wasn't Harold's voice. It was her gramps, and he was pleading, begging her to stop! *Slow down!*

Both attic doors were open, the one leading into the room and the one leading out to the small landing. Charity pushed away the thought that she'd look over the landing down down down three stories below and see Daisy's lifeless body lying there, broken and bleeding.

Or worse. She'd see her gram, the life forced out of her by the sudden stop at the end of her . . . of her . . .

Charity flew through the room and crossed the final threshold. It's said that just before people die, they may sense the strangest things. Charity felt the sudden moonlight on her skin, the smell of freshly churned ocean, and the taste of its salt landing on her mouth. She heard the whispers of water fairies as they danced on waves and the calming rustle of the leaves on the weeping tree.

She was aware of someone lashing out, nails dragging down the exposed flesh of her spine above her velvet gown. She was aware that just before the hand grazed her, she was plummeting forward, her foot having caught on the weather stripping of the attic's exterior door. Her ankle twisted. All the air left her lungs in a great oomph. Something slammed into her ribs, causing her to fold forward. The hand behind her dug into the side of her flesh, the meaty part of her skin between her ribs and hip. Below, there was only ground. She was hanging, suspended. Caught between heaven and earth. Life and death.

The grip tightened and suddenly, she was flung backward, hitting a brick wall and then the floor. Another oomph. This one, from Dalton who cradled her against him. *He* was the brick wall. As she looked up to the railing above her, she knew what had happened. Both this night and all those many moons ago. Her gram really had fallen. Her grandfather had chased her up the stairs, and she'd wanted to escape, but not escape life. Escape him. She'd tripped on the doorjamb. And fallen through the railing. Just as Charity would have tonight if Dalton hadn't reinforced it months ago and hadn't grabbed her in a death grip moments ago.

They were puddled on the floor, and he was trembling. Of course he would be. He'd lost a wife and child, and though his feelings for Charity didn't run that deep, this was a close call.

Her ribs ached, there were inflamed streaks on her back, and a crushing bruise would likely materialize tomorrow on her waist. But she was OK. "I'm sorry, Dalton."

His feet scraped the wood flooring as he rose from behind her. "We have to find Daisy," was all he said, but Charity couldn't help but hear the sharpness in his tone. It was a sound she was used to, but not from him. From her mother. He practically shoved her off him.

"She couldn't have gone far." Charity's body ached, but she ignored it. Her eyes fell on Harold. She'd ignore him, too, for now. His face was pale and washed with worry for Daisy. Right now she wouldn't order Harold away. They'd all lost enough tonight.

Dalton went into the attic and looked around as if there might be some clue. "What time is the last ferry to the mainland?"

"Just after midnight. I heard folks talking about it at the party. The ferry is running for those who came over." Harold's words were tentative, as if he might be screamed at again.

"If she gets on the ferry and makes it to the mainland, we'll never find her." Dalton rushed out of the attic.

They raced down the stairs and piled into the car. Ellen followed them out but remained standing in the driveway. Charity paused. "You're not going?"

She tilted a shoulder. "Why should I?"

Charity shook her head. "I don't know why it took me so long to give up on you." With that, she slammed the door shut and prayed they made it to the ferry before it left.

⌒୭

Ellen hated drama. At least, she hated the kind of drama she'd just witnessed. If Dalton hadn't lashed out and grabbed Charity, maybe she would have gone right through that railing. Maybe Ellen would be planning her daughter's funeral right now instead of trying to figure out how to manage life with this new sensation running rampant inside her. When Charity had fallen forward, Ellen felt like her guts were being ripped from her stomach. It was worse than childbirth because the pain had leached into her soul and was ripping that away, too. *You almost lost her,* her mind hissed.

Ellen forced the feeling away. It was just the moment—heightened tensions and intense circumstances. She went straight into the kitchen and found the unopened bottles of wine. She poured a glass and watched the rich red liquid dance as she lifted it to her mouth, surprised to find the drink quaking, a miniversion of the hurricane waves she'd seen two months back. Her hands were trembling, causing the crimson tempest. She drained the glass and poured another, willing herself to calm. Three more and suddenly, the warm and blurry sensation stole her focus from what she'd felt earlier. She poured the last of the bottle into an oversize glass and popped the cork on another, filling the thing nearly to the rim. She tested the steadiness of her hand by holding it out a few inches below eye level. Muuuuch better.

Ellen found her cigarette stash in the drawer and carried her companions outside. She'd tripped once, in the sleeping porch, and sloshed wine onto the floor. *No matter,* she sang in her head. No one would know she was the culprit.

Outside the air was cool and rich, all her senses alive and floating on a red wine yacht. She stared up at the moon. It was bright and crescent-shaped and made her think of gondolas in Italy. She'd never go to Italy now, and even if she did, what did it matter? No one would notice her. She might as well trade her designer clothes for white sneakers and pastel capris. She could wear no makeup and a hideous hat on her head. She'd keep her ChapStick in a fanny pack and squint at the sun without regard to the wrinkles such action would ultimately cause. She'd eat pasta until she puked and not bother to wipe her mouth until her plate was empty. And she'd be just like everyone else.

She lit up while balancing the wine glass. Just like everyone else—her biggest fear—just like . . . just like her mother. A rustling at her side fought for her attention, but Ellen opted to ignore it. Maybe it was the young man from earlier, returned to tell her what a mistake they'd made in considering her old. Maybe it was Leonard, hoping to draw her home with promises of trips and time and, most important, his fidelity.

The rustling sound grew, but she refused to look. Who would she find standing there? Whoever it was, she didn't care. But knowing she had an audience for her moment caused her to stand a little straighter. She took a long drag from the cigarette—something she'd learned by watching the silver screen greats Bette Davis and Lauren Bacall. She tilted her head just enough to catch the moonlight so it cast her in a perfect pool. Whoever stood nearby would be awestruck. Her head was hot now, thoughts fuzzy little creatures drifting in and out of her brain. If she spun around, they'd all collide. But if she spun, she might spill her drink, or worse, the several glasses she'd consumed so quickly would revolt on her. There was no beautiful way to regurgitate. Not even Vivien Leigh as Scarlett could pull that one off.

The wind picked up and as it did, the sound increased. She finally cast a glance, readying for a conversation. But there was no one there. It was the willow tree making the sound. She'd had no audience. She'd been performing for an oversize bush.

The wind died, and Ellen found herself studying the tree. Long, slender branches, a leafy waterfall, spewing from the top and gently brushing the ground below. She stepped closer, draining half her glass in one long swig. The breeze kicked up again, this time pressing her closer to the tree. She moved easily, as if on a cloud, floating toward an answer. Her chest tightened. *Step beneath the tree,* something whispered, but the words were as vague as her thoughts and instead, she stopped dead just outside the branches. "So, you're what all the fuss is about?" she asked and waited for the tree to comment.

She placed her hand to her ear, careful to keep the lit butt away from her hair, another trick she'd learned watching Bacall. "You don't have anything to say? Not a word?"

In answer, the leaves rustled.

"You seem to be quite a big deal. Quite the celebrity." A bigger celebrity than her, but she wouldn't voice it. It sounded far too petty and desperate.

She started to turn and go back into the house but stopped. "I'm glad Charity hated you all those years. I'm glad she was scared of you. You don't deserve the attention given to you." With that, Ellen drew the last of her cigarette and tasted the vile, burned end. Before going back to the house, she flicked the butt into the high branches of the tree.

CHAPTER 19

Fault or Forgiveness

They found Daisy sitting alone on the dock as the last ferry made its way to the mainland. The air was chilly off the water, and Charity moved to her slowly.

Daisy glanced up at her, a sheepish look on her face. There was no *run* left in the girl; she simply looked small, worn out, and hopeless. Charity dropped onto the salty wooden bench beside her. Daisy drew her knees to her chest.

"You didn't leave," Charity whispered.

The girl turned to face her, the blue in her eyes intense. "I wanted a family. But . . . I wanted it perfect."

Charity nodded.

She sniffed. "But family comes with problems."

Charity reached over and tucked some strands of blonde hair behind Daisy's ear. "Yes, it does."

"I guess you have to make a choice. Run away or stick it out. But it's never going to be perfect."

Charity slipped an arm around Daisy's shoulders. "You have to decide if it's worth it." Charity's gaze went to the dark water where the last of the light from the ferry disappeared. "I'm hoping you've decided it is. That *we're* worth it."

Harold and Dalton made their way to the end of the pier where Daisy and Charity sat.

Dalton dropped to his knees in front of Daisy. "When you were trapped after the hurricane, do you remember what you said to me to get you out?"

Daisy nodded. "I said use your brute strength and love. Even if it's not love for me."

Dalton swallowed, his eyes misty, his mouth a straight line. "It was love for you, Daisy. I didn't want to admit it, but I was terrified we'd lost you. I didn't want to go through that a—" His voice broke, and he pulled a few deep breaths. "I didn't want to go through that again."

Harold stepped behind Daisy and placed his hands on her arms. "Come on, girlie. It's time we go home. *All* of us."

Charity stood and faced Harold. "She's right. Family is never going to be perfect. Sometimes, the things that happened in the past need to stay there."

The blue in his eyes dimmed. "But—"

Charity came around the bench and approached him. "It's in the past, Harold. Seems like you've spent most of your life paying for your mistakes. Maybe it's time to start fresh."

A weathered hand covered his mouth, but he couldn't quite contain his emotions. Charity took a firm grip on his shoulders. "Fresh start. For *both* of us."

"It's more than I deserve." His craggy voice choked on the words.

Charity shook her head. "No. It isn't. It's exactly what you deserve."

They gathered Daisy's things and headed home. The first part of the drive was quiet, a peaceful hush in the car echoing throughout the night-dark island. But when they made the last turn onto Charity's street, they saw it, the orange glow illuminating the sky.

First, she'd thought her mind must be playing tricks on her, but as they neared, and as the cloud of smoke she'd mistaken for low clouds became clear, her blood stopped pumping.

Daisy grabbed her hand. "It's the garden."

It is said that nothing lights up a landscape like a blazing fire. Golden yellow and heat that permeates land and sea, clawing from the flame and reaching its fingers in all directions. It was both beautiful and horrible. Terrifying and tender, the blaze was like uncontrolled passion, and yet the tiny droplets of gold embers fell like tears on the surrounding ground.

⌒∽

Charity felt herself sinking as she stared at the scene before her. Dalton slammed the car into park, and they got out and ran around the side of the house, where the weeping tree stood engulfed in flames. Ellen held a water hose in her hands, and spray from the end arched onto the blazing branches. It was instantly absorbed in giant puffs of steam.

"Mother!"

Ellen turned, her face and dress smeared with soot. Her feet were bare, and blackened toes peeked from beneath the tattered garment. "I don't know what happened!"

Dalton grabbed her and dragged her from the tree just as a branch broke and came crashing toward her.

The golden branch landed, tossing sparks up and toward them. A wave of heat—an oven door opening—warmed Charity's face. Gold sparks flew at her. As soon as the branch was down, her mother ran straight over it, once again grabbing the hose and spraying it onto the tree, which was virtually overwhelmed by flames that shot up, puncturing the night's sky. One or two branches remained, but none would survive unscathed. The remaining branches throbbed, great billows of smoke rising off them, ready to burst into full flame like the rest of their siblings. Smoke also rose from the trunk and poured from the cracks in the bark.

"It's gone," Charity whispered. The incredible tree that interceded for people. The amazing tree that took others' burdens and knitted their hearts. The tree she'd never sat beneath because she couldn't. And now it was gone. In front of her, Ellen stepped closer and closer to the smoldering heap. She continued to spray the hose up at the remaining flames, but the tree would never survive the damage. Charity's gaze dropped to her mother's feet. She was standing on a burning limb. Charity yelled at her. But Ellen only answered by changing the arch of the water and spraying the lower section of the trunk. A spark ignited at the base of Ellen's dress and what was one tiny glowing spark became a flame.

"Mother!" Charity dove for her, knocking her to the ground and landing atop her. She felt the fire beneath her hands and though her mind screamed to get away from it, Charity smacked the edge of her mom's gown until the flame died. The molten material landed on her mother's leg, and Charity tried to swipe at it but heard the searing of flesh. Beneath her, Ellen remained still, even with the melted garment fusing to her skin.

Charity rolled off her, concerned now for the sanity of a woman who could have burning material land on her leg but not react to it. Ellen's eyes were wide, circled in soot and streaked with clear streams of sweat. "It's my fault." She whispered the words over and over as if confessing could somehow bring back the tree. "I did this."

Thus far, there'd been no explanation of the tree's sudden eruption. Ellen's hands were trembling when Charity reached out to capture one. It seemed her mother would combust. With each breath, she grew more frantic. "I did this, Charity."

"Mom." She grabbed her mother's hands, her shoulder digging into the ground around them. "You're in shock. You have to calm down."

Her mother had run over flaming branches in her bare feet; she'd stood on one until her gown ignited at her ankles. The woman had to be in shock.

"I did this, Charity." Ellen's eyes were dark, bottomless pools of shame.

"Mom, listen to me. You didn't do this. It was an accident."

Ellen laughed without humor, a beaten-down wisp of the person she'd been before the fire. Charity saw madness in her eyes. She'd never known an insane person but thought this was the frightened look such a person would have.

Charity cast a glance to the tree that had, for generations, helped the people of the island. Those same people had kept its secret for all these years. Harold's words echoed in her head. He'd once told her that he ruined everything he cared about. Maybe it was their family curse. Before she came to the island in hopes of starting anew, of being part of a real community, the tree had flourished. Now it was gone. Forever. She hated every evil word she'd spoken about the tree. When she'd arrived, she'd wanted to rip it out by the roots. Now she felt as though she was losing yet another family member. She'd not allow this night to take another. Still lying on the ground, she clamped her hands on her mother's face. "Listen to me."

But Ellen wouldn't raise her head, her eyes squeezed shut.

"Mom." Calming now, soothing, Charity would have to coax her.

Ellen's eyes flew open. "I lit the fire, Charity. I tossed a cigarette butt into the tree."

All the air left Charity's lungs in a great whoosh. Her muscles froze in place. On purpose? Her mother had intentionally burned the tree?

Ellen's head shook quickly from side to side, eyes scanning left, then right. Again, Charity was hit with the very real possibility that this just might be her mother's undoing. Ellen's sanity seemed to be hanging by one thin, precarious thread.

"It's. Just. A. Tree." Charity tossed a look to the trunk in apology. Its smoldering branches watched the scene unfold. "Mom. Intentional or not, I forgive you." It was perhaps the hardest thing she'd ever said. And in choosing to stand by her mother, she knew the town would ostracize both of them. If Charity had presented herself as a victim, maybe, just maybe, they could forgive the incident. But if she aligned with her mother, there would be no forgiving, of that she was certain, because their magical tree was gone. And whether Charity's involvement was intentional or not, she was the keeper of the tree. It was her job to protect it. But right now it was her mother, not the town and not the tree, who needed her loyalty.

Ellen's mouth opened, her cheeks lengthening. "You can't forgive me. I don't deserve it."

Charity forced a smile, the tiniest shred of hope opening the gate to her heart. "Forgiveness is rarely deserved. That's what makes it such a gift."

Ellen's eyes filled with tears. She tucked her head into Charity's shoulder, and she lay on the ground and cried.

❦

Harold made his way to Louise's house as soon as the fire was out. He'd left half a dozen messages on her phone, but she'd never picked up and never called back. He'd left her again. Standing on the pier just like he'd done all those years ago when he arrived at George and Marilyn's house to find George gone for the night and Marilyn crying because she thought George was having an affair. As Harold had cradled her in his arms, she'd told him of the many months since they'd been intimate, how she'd tried to make him interested in her, and how he'd recoiled from her again and again. Always coming up with some excuse not to touch her, always giving a reason why he didn't feel like being close.

He'd even started pulling away when she'd brush against him. He'd placed a pillow on the bed, keeping her away.

For months the silent sorrow went unanswered. She'd changed her hair, purchased new clothes, donned makeup. Still, though he'd tell her she looked nice, the emotion didn't reach his eyes. She worked to get her aging body into better shape, joined a gym, all the while hoping something would turn his eye back to her.

And then Harold arrived. On that fateful night when he'd told Louise to meet him on the pier. But he'd gone to drop off his things at George's house to find Marilyn alone and in ruins. He was so angry at his brother he'd have beaten him to a pulp if he had been there. Instead, Harold had turned his anger into the unrequited lust he'd carried for Marilyn all those years. That night, they lay in each other's arms, saying all the things that had gone unspoken for so long.

In the morning, she'd told him that whether or not George was being unfaithful, she refused to walk that road. They'd had one night together, and it was the culmination of the passion they'd shared as teens.

George returned home, and before they could admit what had happened, he told Marilyn he'd been seeing a doctor for a male condition. He'd been embarrassed, ashamed, hadn't wanted her to know because she was the most wonderful and beautiful thing that had ever happened to him. The surgery was a simple procedure. He should have been honest with her from the beginning. Could she ever forgive him?

She admitted what had happened between her and Harold. With more hurt than anger, George told his brother to leave. Never to come back.

Harold had gone to Louise's house. He had to explain. But there were no words, so he'd stood at her front door for half an hour, his hand raised to knock, but he hadn't the will to do it.

He ruined every beautiful thing in his life.

And now here he was. Going yet again to the woman who deserved so much more, so much better. But this time, he'd knock. This time, he'd take the abuse she would surely offer because yet again, he'd left her standing on a pier waiting for him. He pooled his strength as he made his way to her front door. The gate of the white picket fence squeaking, then slamming shut behind him as if a premonition of the reception he'd receive.

Louise opened the door. Her body was stiff but her eyes kind. "Is everyone all right?"

He'd not expected that and had to rearrange his thoughts so he could answer.

When he didn't, she opened the door a bit more. "I heard about the tree. Daisy running away, Ellen's burns. One of the neighbor's stopped by. Is everyone OK?"

She shouldn't be asking that; she should be yelling at him. His eyes misted. "I left you standing at the pier."

She nodded. Behind him, a crow squawked, and the wind rose, lifting the leaves on the nearby palms and making them sing. "You did."

"I tried to call."

Her mouth was an untelling straight line.

"May I come in?" He looked past her into the house.

"No, Harold." Her grip tightened on the doorknob.

And his heart shattered. "Please let me explain."

She pulled a long, slow breath and let it slip from her mouth. "You don't need to. I know what happened."

His hand started to reach out, but Louise leaned back, withdrawing from his touch. He bit down hard and folded his hand and placed it safely in his pocket. "You know I didn't leave you there purposely."

She nodded, the lines of her face deepening slightly. "It wasn't your fault. It was out of your control."

He nodded, hope unfurling in his heart. "Exactly. It was out of my control." Maybe she was going to give him one more chance. So much more than he deserved, but people were capable of more love and more forgiveness than he'd ever imagined. Maybe part of the reason every beautiful thing he'd been given left him was because he hadn't fought for them. He should have fought for George. He shouldn't have stayed away so long. There was always hope for amends. He believed that. He believed that in his heart and knew it to be as true as the rising of the sun in the day and the moon at night. Even for an old man, there could still be hope. He believed. Until Louise opened her mouth and stripped away every shred of hope he'd just mustered.

"It wasn't your fault. But it doesn't matter. I was still left standing there waiting. I waited for you for so long. You never came all those years ago. And then I found Marvin, and life was good, but one day he left me waiting. He was gone. And sometimes I still feel like I'm waiting on him to come home from fishing. I just can't do it again. I'd rather know no one is coming than to know one day I'll be left waiting. Sorry, Harold. You deserve better."

Emotions were horrible little things, staying quiet one moment, then exploding the next. There was a sound deep his throat, a choked cry; then the tears came in a flood, flowing from his eyes and landing on his shirt. "I don't deserve anything. I destroyed my brother's family."

"It was one night. You made a mistake."

He wiped a weathered hand to his cheek. "How do you know that?" He'd never discussed the details of that night with anyone.

"George and I were close at the end. He told me you slept with Marilyn. He told me why it happened."

"He hadn't been able to . . . she thought he was having an affair . . . but, but really, he was going to a specialist on the mainland to see what was wrong with him."

She smiled, her own tears—careful, cautious tears—making the apples of her cheeks shine. "I know all of it, Harold. You needn't go over it again. It must be painful."

He wiped his eyes with the back of his hand, wishing he still carried a handkerchief, but he'd given his up years ago. "Why was George so open with you? He seemed so ashamed."

"Because I was the one who was supposed to send his letter."

Harold remembered walking to his mailbox at the dance studio and finding the letter postmarked less than a week before. The letter that arrived weeks after his brother's death. "The letter? It came after he died. Why did you wait? He and I could have reconciled."

She nodded. "Yes, he knew that. Even wanted that. But Charity was more important. He knew Charity would need you. He wanted you to be here for her. She's all that matters now. Harold, I know you want to run. But she needs you. It's time you tell her exactly what happened. The whole truth. You can't carry all the blame."

He shook his head, rejecting the thought. "I need to carry the blame. I don't want her thinking her grandfather did anything wrong."

"Blame is seldom on one man's shoulders. If he'd been honest with Marilyn . . . Harold, truth is better than sacrifice. Trust Charity to be big enough, to have enough Baxter blood running through her veins to understand. You're not blaming George. That would be ridiculous. But he has a fault. As does Marilyn. Be honest with her and stop trying to protect ghosts."

He was still processing the chain of events. "But, you couldn't have sent the letter. You were shocked, nearly terrified when you saw me."

She nodded. "I'll admit, I didn't think you would come. You've always carried so much burden for all the things around you. I figured it was too late, that you'd shut that door and thrown away the key. But I *tried* to prepare myself to see you—just in case—but I have to be honest, all those feelings and emotions from so long ago took me by surprise."

Even her limp had returned with the memories. She'd limped to the front door. But by the next time he saw her, the limp was gone.

"Louise." It was one word. One man's desperate plea to hang on to the last splinter of a boat that had long since sank. "Is there anything I can do?"

"Go to Charity. She still needs you." Louise offered a tiny smile and closed the door.

Instead, he sat down on the lone rocking chair on her porch. Charity needed him, yes. But for once, he was going to be the one waiting. He set the chair into motion. He'd sit there for hours if need be; all night, if necessary. He'd sit there and rock and wait for Louise. He'd wait as long as it took. Hours. Days. Weeks. Because for the first time in his life, he was going to fight for what he wanted.

೧৯

It was late in the night when Ellen Marie drifted down the steps. Her feet were wrapped in bandages, and she felt the squishing salve between her toes, though she barely noticed. Still the sensation reminded her of something, something far away as if it had happened to someone else and she'd mysteriously felt the ghost sensations of it. Or maybe it was from her past, so far back she couldn't access it. It had something to do with wet sand and retreating shorelines.

Ellen placed a cold hand on the banister, partly to steady her shaky legs, partly to anchor her. Her heart ached like a foreign thing deep in her chest. In her gut, an emptiness clawed, deeper than anything she'd ever felt. Not when she'd lost her mother. Not when she'd lost her father. Those were situations she merely knew she must stiffen her jaw and deal with. She hadn't allowed the pain to permeate past the plan. Too young, she'd been left to fend for herself. But she'd been doing that since she was twenty, so life for her hadn't really changed. After her mother died, she'd tried to reach out to her father, but he'd been as stubborn as she. Unfortunately it all came off wrong and cost her everything because once the words, "Either cooperate, or I'm moving Charity to New York," were out of her mouth, there was no going back.

No, she hadn't grieved for her parents at the time because she'd been too busy trying to figure out how to compensate for being left without a mother and then without a father. Money. She'd been so certain money would help her heal from the loss. It all seemed twisted now when she thought of it. Perhaps she hadn't grieved for them at all, and that fact alone made her grieve now.

The last step was the worst. Ellen winced and touched first her toes, then her heel, to the marble floor. The house was quiet but held the acrid scent of something recently burned.

The stinging at the bridge of her nose surprised her, but Ellen sniffed and bit back the tears that could so easily fall. It was madness to feel such loss over a tree. Charity's face filled her mind. Driving up, flying out of the car, and then stopping as if struck while emotions ran rampant across her face. Ellen squeezed her eyes shut to drown out the memory. She shuffled across the kitchen floor and carefully made her way through the sleeping porch. She constantly ran into things in the overcrowded, makeshift pottery studio and with her feet burned and bandaged, the last thing she needed was to stub a toe. Small as that could be, she instinctively knew it would break her.

Outside the air was cool and carried the scent of burned wood. A blackened, irregular circle marred the ground around the stub of the weeping tree. It stood like a ghost in an enchanted forest. Alone, one narrow branch that had escaped the flame was still hanging on. When the wind swirled, the few remaining leaves rustled. It was a siren's song. Moonlight lit a path to the tree, and Ellen found herself moving closer. The sandy ground was soft against her feet, as if cradling each step. It was cool from the night air and moist against her bandages.

She stopped just shy of the remaining branch and slid a hand over the leaves. Some were charred and brittle, like the leaves at the end of fall when the last one gives up its hold and floats to the ground, finally settled to be a carpet for the coming snow. But some of them were still pliable, and hope entered a desperate place in her heart as she thought perhaps the tree would mend.

But no. It was beyond all recovery, and it was because of her. Still, she chose to believe that since one branch remained, there was hope. The wind shifted, and Ellen loosened her hold on the branch so it could move freely. Its rustling song—so lonely in its tone—cut to her heart. "I'm . . ."

Sorry, was what she wanted to say, but the word lodged in her throat. She was sorry, so sorry. Whether there was anything mystical or magical about the tree, she couldn't say. All she knew was the deeply rooted sense of loss she now felt, lifetimes of grief unleashed on her soul.

It was everything she should have felt when she'd lost her mother. But she'd lost both her parents long before that. In a way, she'd lost them to Charity. Everything had changed when Charity arrived. And Ellen had blamed the squalling, pudgy, constantly needy infant girl. As if the baby had made a choice to be born, to be her grandparents' joy, to steal the spotlight. Every year she half expected them to try to get custody of Charity, pushing Ellen away completely. More than once, she'd considered giving her to them, but she knew that even though they would rejoice in having Charity full time, it was a bridge that if Ellen ever crossed, she'd never, ever be in her parents' good graces again. And somewhere inside, she'd wanted to be in their good graces. Wanted them to be proud of her.

The tree rustled again, and Ellen wondered if it was in pain. Had it felt the burning, the flame? Were the charred ends of each leaf stinging like the tender flesh of her feet? With a great quaking sob, Ellen stepped beneath the tree in an effort to comfort it. Her hands found their way to the trunk, and soot covered her palms as she stroked the tree and cried. "I'm so sorry." Each breath was a giant, gulping sob coming from so deep within her soul, it went beyond pain to release.

She pressed her cheek to the trunk and let the bark leave its imprint on her skin. "I'm so sorry," she cried again, the words insignificant compared to the loss. For a moment, she pushed off the tree, taking in its body from top to roots. "I did this. I did this," she repeated as if confessing her sin might somehow repair things. She choked back one more sob, but the floodgates opened, and pressure from deep within caused her to moan—the pain of her life, a life she could have lived so much better, permeated from the lowest corridor of her heart. The moan became a growl, something guttural, primal, and filled with disgust for herself. For the first time, Ellen Marie saw herself for what she'd chosen to be. And it was an ugly, horrible creature.

The growl became a scream, long and loud, breaking the night air into fractured pieces. Ellen dropped to her knees. Her left one landed on a root, causing pain to shoot from her leg up. It would bruise, but she didn't care. Nor did she care about the scars she'd carry on her leg from the melted spandex of the ball gown. The burns on her feet held no disgust for her. She'd once looked at scars on women as imperfections, horrible little blemishes. Not these. These would be her trophies. They would forever remind her of the night when everything changed. And as she drew a deep breath and raised her head from its dropped position, she knew beyond any doubt that tonight everything was about to change.

She blinked rapidly when the first raindrops landed on her face. She didn't see clouds above, hadn't heard the thunderclap that so often preceded rain, but there, floating above her head, giant drops landed on her. She found herself crying tears that mingled with the drops, her soul emptying of the refuse it had held for so long. The cleansing came from the outside in, but also from the inside out—each breath, each cry eroding more and more of the iron core that anchored her heart.

The rain continued, a thick curtain causing her to be both warm and cold at the same time. She'd cried all she could and surprised herself by standing in the downpour and spreading her arms wide. There, she began to laugh. She laughed like she never had before, bubbles of joy rising from deep within, so full, so great, they seemed like they might combust inside if she didn't allow them to escape.

Her nightgown was drenched. Her bandages ruined. Her hair clung to her scalp and cheeks while streams of water ran the length of her spine. When the rain finally stopped, Ellen pulled deep breaths of fresh salt air. She pushed the hair off her face and didn't bother to swipe the mascara streams she knew must be present. She laughed again. It gurgled from her. She couldn't contain it if she'd had to. And that made her laugh even more.

A hand stretched forward and caressed the trunk of the weeping tree. "Thank you," she said. "I understand now."

A small, shuddering sound drew her attention, and Ellen looked overhead and to the right where the last branch's fingers released their hold. In slow motion, it floated to the ground at her feet. She sucked a breath, and though her mind screamed at her to feel remorse for this, the final branch, she somehow knew this was meant to be.

This tree. This moment. This change. Her father had known. Somehow he'd known that this day would come, where everything in life became clear to her. That's why he'd left the home and money to Charity. That's why he'd left little to her. These things he'd done as much for her as for her daughter. Somehow, he knew she'd be the last changed life for the weeping tree.

And that realization rooted her soul. There were no tears left to cry because all was as it was supposed to be. "I love you, Dad."

She picked up the branch lovingly and carried it to the sleeping porch. It wouldn't lie on the wet ground, no. It would lie on a high shelf, a place of honor, inside the sleeping porch, where it could forever look out onto the shore and garden where it had changed so many lives.

Ellen Marie slipped through the kitchen and into the downstairs bathroom, where she could dry off before going back to bed.

She scrubbed the towel against her face and hair and flipped on the light. There in the mirror—amid the mascara smears and the lines of a middle-aged woman—she saw it. Beauty. Ellen's breath caught in her throat. She leaned forward to look more closely. Beauty that emanated from every pore on her face. Beauty that glowed from a well so deep, it was everlasting. Trembling fingers touched her cheeks.

She was beautiful. And it had nothing to do with how she looked.

It was 11:00 a.m. the morning after the fire when the first of the townspeople arrived at Baxter House. Every muscle in Charity's body ached, and she pulled the door open, expecting to find an angry neighbor on the other side. She'd rehearsed over and over what she'd say. Her mother had been angry; in her anger, she'd flipped a cigarette into the tree, not knowing it could potentially burn it to the ground. It was a desperate act, and unforgivable; still it was her mother, and she would stand beside her. But when Charity swung the door open, Mrs. Gorben from across the street held out a candy dish capped with white peaks.

"It's a pudding pie, dear. I'm so sorry for your loss." Mrs. Gorben pushed her way past Charity and into the house. "I'll just set it here on the table."

Maybe she was still dreaming. She'd dreamed through the night. Horrible, painful dreams. In one, she searched and searched for a glass of water but finally fell to the ground, lips splitting and bleeding from lack of moisture.

Another knock at the door caused her to glance over, but Mrs. Gorben kept chattering. "I would have made something more grand, but I wanted to get right over here. You shouldn't be alone at a time like this." She patted Charity's hand and went to the door.

On the other side, two more neighbors greeted Mrs. Gorben as Charity stood in the center of the room wondering what was happening. She heard murmured voices discussing her at the front door.

"I just got here myself."

"Poor dear."

"She seems to be holding up."

Charity shuffled her feet until she stood closer, but the shock of what was happening stole her ability to form words. Then she heard the words, "her mother," and everything about last night came rushing back to her.

"Charity, Charity, honey." Mrs. Gorben came and placed a hand on her arms, which were crossed carefully over her chest. "We were wondering if your mother was OK? We heard there were burns."

Scattered thoughts floated in her mind as if each were a puzzle piece, and someone had placed them in a giant fish bowl to shake them up. Charity's brow furrowed. "She burned the weeping tree." Obviously these people didn't know what had happened.

"Yes, dear, we spoke to Al last night."

"Al?"

"One of the firemen."

She'd heard the fire truck arrive. An ambulance followed, and while Dalton spoke with the firemen, and they sprayed the tree until it neither blazed nor smoldered, she'd stood alongside her mother while Ellen was treated for burns on her feet and on her leg. "She didn't go to the hospital."

Mrs. Gorben smiled. "Well, that's a good sign."

The trio talked on as they settled into the house. For the next thirty minutes, people continued to show up, all expressing their sorrow and hugging Charity, telling her they were sorry for her loss. Her loss. She'd only been guardian of the tree for a few short months. It was their loss. Their loss and her fault. How could they have it so backward?

It was an hour later when Emily and Jeanna arrived toting a pot pie and a casserole. "Keep the dishes," Jeanna told her as she handed the casserole to Charity, who'd started opening the door at Mrs. Gorben's suggestion. Her house was practically as full today as it had been the night before. People meandering around, helping themselves to plates of food and cups of coffee from a pot that was emptied as quickly as it was made. Someone had brought paper plates and cups; someone had brought plastic utensils and napkins. Some of the men chose to use real plates from her cupboard, and Mrs. Gorben encouraged them to rinse them and place them in the dishwasher.

Emily eyed her at the door. "Have you eaten?"

Charity jerked her head, no. She leaned forward. "Emily, what in the world is going on here?"

Emily smiled, bright-red lips curving. She handed her plate to someone standing nearby. Charity didn't glance up to see the person's face, but sandy boat shoes covered his feet. Emily dragged her out onto the front porch. "Have a seat."

Charity sat down but glanced behind her at her own front door. "Why is everyone saying, 'Sorry for your loss'?" At first they had been sweet words to hear, a healing balm as they entered her system. But as more and more people arrived, Charity began to wonder if she'd blocked some horrible thing that had happened last night. Had she lost someone? Faces filled her mind. And had she blocked it? She was suddenly terrified. She hadn't seen Dalton this morning. Or Daisy. Or her mother. She hadn't seen Harold. Her hands flew out, fingers gripping Emily. "What happened last night? What am I missing?"

Emily blinked, ever cool, but her eyes betrayed her. "Your mother burned down the weeping tree."

Charity nodded for Emily to continue.

Emily pulled a deep breath, and Charity's panic escalated. It was that thing people do when they're trying to deliver horrible news. "And?"

Emily scanned her face, then tilted a shoulder. "And the fire department came and put the flame out." When Charity waited for more, Emily said, "And your mother experienced some burns but didn't want to go to the hospital, so they treated her here."

If that was supposed to help things fall into place for Charity, it didn't. "Everyone is here. Why aren't they mad at me?"

"Mad at you?"

She knew Emily couldn't be a shrewd attorney and be this dense. "And why are they saying, 'Sorry for your loss'?"

"Because the weeping tree is dead." Emily gave her a moment to process. "Charity, what did you think would happen? They'd chase you from the island with pitchforks? The tree was yours. The house is yours. The special ingredient that changes people's lives . . . all yours. You freely shared all that with us. It was a gift."

The poem she'd heard a thousand times as a child rushed into her head.

> *Will you come, sit with me*
> *We'll tell our troubles 'neath the tree*
> *The tears we shed will surely be*
> *Water for the weeping tree.*
> *And in its shade our woes will fall*
> *Pain and suffering, sorrow and all*
> *They'll fall like glistening diamond drops*
> *You see, the tree, our pain, it stops.*

"It's still working, isn't it?" Charity said.

Emily cast a long glance down the road. "The magic of the tree? Seems so."

Charity placed a hand over her heart. "I've never felt forgiveness like this." It was warm sunshine after a cold winter; it was a waterfall in a desert. It gurgled and rose, springing up and chasing away the doubt.

Emily smiled. "That's the thing about forgiveness. It's contagious."

CHAPTER 20

Moving Forward

It was almost a month later when Dalton packed the last of his clothes into the last of his duffel bags. He'd always traveled with duffel bags, never going the suitcase route. He'd already talked to Daisy about leaving because once, long ago, before the party and before the tree burned, he'd told her she would be the first to know his plans.

He hadn't talked to Charity and didn't plan to until the last minute. It was going to be rough on him, and he knew it.

After watching her run up the stairs and nearly fall over the banister, something in him had changed. Charity had effectively burrowed under his skin, and it was something he'd started hating. An itch that felt great while being scratched only to irritate the skin again and again.

He himself could only take partial blame for the situation. He'd argued with himself many a night while lying in the cottage and staring up at the ceiling, where the moonlight slashed the wall and split the room into two distinct sections. He imagined himself in one of the sections—a place where a man stood alone, a man who'd lived long enough to bury a wife and child. That changed a human. Yes, one could move on, whatever that meant, but one could never escape the memories. He felt old. Used up. Like he'd lived one lifetime, and it was inappropriate to ask for another.

In the other dark section of the room stood Charity. Young. Beautiful. Still filled with the hope of an ever after that included a man of her dreams with the same zest and energy she carried, the way he carried his sorrow. Sure, she'd been through things, but those things hadn't defined her. Charity—in her ageless wisdom—had forgiven Harold. She'd opened her home to her mother, a woman who was only now at age fifty-something learning who she really was outside of the pretense of what she should be.

He'd watch the shadow split and slowly creep across his room, adding space to her area. Leeching space from his. By morning, he was little more than a narrow strip, a ghost of what he had been. In the last weeks, he'd watched as Charity had opened all but a small part of her heart to everyone. But it was that small part that concerned him. Because in it was the power to wreck her world. Of this, he was sure.

He'd asked time and again if she'd sat beneath the remaining trunk of the weeping tree. Again and again, she'd shaken off the question. Everyone knew there were no more branches to fall. "It's done its work on me," she'd say, face smiling, eyes filled with light and hope.

If he could only believe that.

But then she'd blink, and the smile would morph into a sort of grimace, as if pain had zapped her from some unknown place. And each time, he knew his leaving the island was more imminent than the last time he'd asked. He wasn't certain how these things worked together; he just knew they did. She was half the problem. He was the other half.

The tree did not grow back. Its ghostly trunk stood silent in the garden. Its song no longer whispered on the wind. Still, no one had the desire to uproot the corpse. So there it stayed while rains fell, and winds rushed. While sun hammered the island, and sand crowded its base.

It was all intermingled—him, Charity, the tree. But he didn't understand how. Like a dream that's forgotten at daybreak. No matter how much he tried to put the pieces together, he always returned to the same conclusion. It was simple. Charity was a woman who'd finally made peace with the ghosts of her past.

And even though the tree had taken his despair, there were things he might never be able to offer a woman, even a woman he loved. Even Charity. And she deserved so much more. She was fresh earth.

He was used-up soil, nothing but filling—no nourishment, no minerals. They'd all been stripped from him. Perhaps one day he'd find a woman who sparked the dead places inside him the way Charity had. But he figured that was years and years down the road. A widow, perhaps. Someone who understood the loss of a soul mate. Or a divorcée whose suffering matched his own. They could help each other, all the while knowing that, for both, their best years, their best efforts at a perfect life, were sitting on a distant shore that they'd drifted far, far away from on an island that had been swallowed by the sea.

He'd have a hard time getting over Charity. This, he knew. There was sunshine in her eyes and starlight on her skin. Before meeting her, he thought he'd never again feel this way about a woman. At least not for years. Now he was reduced to a man with a lot of duffel bags. He loaded his things into his car and went back inside to give the cottage a last look. That's when he spotted the runaway coffee cup. He stepped to the sink and rinsed the cup there. The sun glinted off the sea, casting brilliant light on the yard. To his left, the single trunk of the weeping tree, lonely and grayed, still stood. But it was not the tree that drew his attention. It was her, hunched beneath the trunk, a bag and a small silver scoop beside her and a spade in her hand. She reared back and thrust the spade into the ground again and again, pausing only to wipe the sweat from her face. He leaned closer to the window until his breaths made puffs of steam on the pane. It wasn't sweat she was wiping. It was undoubtedly tears.

Dalton watched, and something in him snapped. He found himself fighting his own tears as if he could feel every emotion as she stabbed and scarred the ground. He had to look away. But he couldn't; emotions swelled inside him, twisting and swirling through his system like a sudden onset of the flu.

He swiped his face with the back of his hand. But his gaze quickly returned to her. The woman with sunshine in her hair and starlight on her skin.

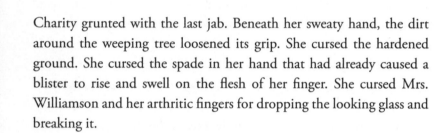

Charity grunted with the last jab. Beneath her sweaty hand, the dirt around the weeping tree loosened its grip. She cursed the hardened ground. She cursed the spade in her hand that had already caused a blister to rise and swell on the flesh of her finger. She cursed Mrs. Williamson and her arthritic fingers for dropping the looking glass and breaking it.

She cursed the woman for showing up at her house thirty minutes earlier and pleading for Charity to make her another. In her haste, Williamson had frantically tried to glue the pieces, but to no avail.

"I can't. There's no more special ingredient left," Charity had told her. She'd escaped special requests for weeks while the town mourned the loss of the weeping tree. Mrs. Williamson had left defeated and after Charity watched the lost woman shuffle down her driveway—as if stunned—she'd gone straight to the potter's wheel and looked up at the bag she'd placed on the high shelf, almost out of reach, the perfect place for it.

Charity had stretched and reached, telling herself that maybe, just maybe, she could scrape enough out of it to make one last piece, a small piece. A looking glass. She'd avoid the paper in the bottom as she'd always done.

But the shelf tipped, the bag listed, and she lost her balance, grabbing at air as the contents—the last shreds of special ingredient—were lost on the wind she created by falling. The bag landed silently beside her. The paper floated to the ground, landing faceup rather than facedown. The words were plain. Clear. And for her.

Good girl, Lil' Bit.

Now, go and fill the bag again. Use the scoop. The special ingredient waits for you under the weeping tree.

Gramps

She'd avoided the tree so far. Never stepping beneath it. Never allowing it to take her deepest hurt and turn it into something new. Because her deepest hurt couldn't, wouldn't—no, she wouldn't *allow* it to be removed from her shoulders. She'd worked so hard her whole life to forgive the people who'd hurt her. Who'd used her. But there was one. One she knew she couldn't forgive.

Charity swiped the tears from her eyes as she sat sprawled beneath what was left of the tree. There were no branches to fall, so maybe her secret was safe, but as memories began to flood her mind, she knew there was nowhere safe in the shadow of the weeping tree.

She stared up at it, letting the tears finally fall unhindered. Her nose ran, and when she swiped it, she felt the slick moisture it left on her cheek. Charity gritted her teeth. "I can't . . ."

She stabbed the scoop into the softened earth and placed a heap into the bag.

The tree was silent.

She scooped another and another, feeling the burning sun on her back and the sting of salt air on her exposed places, every nerve of her body frazzled and raw. "I won't."

She threw the silver scoop aside and dug her hands into the soft dirt. Not quite sand, not soil, and not dust. Cool, soothing. "I won't forgive"—but when she pulled a breath, she knew something within her was being stripped of its power—"myself."

It was the one person with whom she couldn't reconcile. Though she'd spent a lifetime forgiving those who didn't deserve it, she had harbored unforgiveness against herself.

Her head tipped back, her eyes filled, and the deepest, most mournful sound she'd ever heard ripped from her own belly and clawed its way out of her, stripping her anger and shame with every inch it took.

She drew a breath, but when she exhaled, it was a moan, a desperate sound that scorched her ears and crushed the secret places of her being where she'd kept it all locked away. Not enough to please her mother. Not enough to protect her gram. Not strong enough to be there when Gramps needed her. She'd spent a lifetime picking up pieces like a good little daughter should. Like a perfect grandchild should. But she'd harbored an anger and a hatred for herself, all the while resenting her inability to foresee and salvage. That's why she'd had few friends. That's why her business had gone under. She was only good at repairing what was broken and never creating something beautiful herself.

The island had given her hope. But it was a hope she couldn't afford because if she allowed it in, it could also destroy her. She was Charity Monroe Baxter. Unwanted child. Daughter to a woman who half hated her. She was a good girl and knew how to please.

Charity wiped the dirt and tears and snot from her face. Her hands were caked with the lifeblood of the weeping tree. The soil. She was surprised when a humorless laugh escaped her mouth. Then another. The bag sat between her legs, now filled to the rim with special ingredient. In the center there was a divot, a darkened place where her tears had fallen.

The poem skated through her mind.

The tears we shed will surely be water for the weeping tree.

There'd been no rain; she'd felt only the moisture of her own tears and the sweat she'd accumulated while wrestling with her torment. When she stood, she felt spent, dizzy, but somehow lighter. Her throat was raw, and her neck and shoulders ached. Her fingertips stung, and she figured one or two were bloody from her rant. But inside, a sensation like pixies dancing on waves swirled in her stomach. Something was missing from inside her soul. Something she'd carried so long, it had become a part of her. But it had been reduced to dust.

The voice from just behind her was such a shock, such an interruption to her moment, she spun around quickly, nearly knocking herself off balance.

It had been her name, spoken softly, yet such a disruption, she almost screamed.

It was Dalton. He looked foreign standing there, his hands grasping a plant—the sort she didn't recognize—and slowly lifting it for her to take from him. His eyes were unsure, brows high on a forehead marked with worry lines. Maybe he was questioning her sanity. She certainly was. This new and unusual stream sloshing around on her insides made her want to question everything.

His eyes dropped to the pot. She was supposed to take it. Obviously. Her hands came around the bottom of the plant that stood about two and a half feet tall, but Dalton didn't let go. When her fingers closed, thumbs gently grazing his pinkies, a whoosh of air left her lungs. "Myself," she whispered. "I forgive myself." She said it straight into his eyes and watched the dawn in them arrive.

That's when the rain began. It fell around both of them, watering the ground, the bag, the unusual tree held between them. It drifted over her flesh and warmed her in spite of its cooling touch.

They stayed there, she and Dalton, the plant between them, her every fear being eroded like acid on iron. When the rain finally stopped, she closed her eyes and breathed deeply. Freedom, resurrection, joy. It was inexplicable and yet as common as her next breath.

He looked over at the ashen trunk of the weeping tree. "You finally had your weeping tree experience."

She nodded and couldn't seem to keep the smile from her face. "I guess I did."

It was then that she noticed one of the many thin, narrow branches on the small tree between them. It gave up its hold and fell to the ground.

EPILOGUE

One year later

Dalton had explained to Charity that he'd found the sprout beneath the weeping tree the day Daisy had called her mother. He still didn't understand how he could have forgotten about it—sitting in the pot he'd placed it in, at the side of his house where the sun gave it warmth, and the rainwater gave it nourishment. He'd explained that he'd passed it dozens of times, not giving it a thought for all the weeks leading up to the ball. Then for a month knowing the weeping tree had died. Quietly, in its pot filled with dirt from its mother tree, it had continued to grow. He hadn't remembered it until he was leaving. He'd planned to return to Jacksonville, and there it had been, sitting at the corner of his cottage, practically calling to him. Confused about how he could have forgotten, he'd reentered the cottage and noticed a coffee cup he'd missed. He placed it in the sink and looked outside where he'd seen Charity finally beneath the weeping tree.

That day had been a new beginning for all of them. Louise and Harold had married in the spring. Louise had once feared being alone, being kept waiting for someone who might never return home. She'd decided waiting for someone who might not come was better than having no one on the way.

They all ate dinners together several nights a week. Ellen had gone to work for François, who needed all his spare time to care for his new and needy bride. Ellen remained single. Daisy came home on breaks from college, and sometimes a friend or two would join her and they'd stay out too late at the Ice House or the Dive or at a local party, but Charity knew the girl had a good head on her shoulders and wouldn't make bad choices for long, if at all.

Dalton had presented Charity with an engagement ring on Christmas morning before anyone else was awake. His family had been there to visit twice and seemed to like her, though such words were never spoken, only felt. She liked them as well.

Charity took her coffee outside and sat at the bench that had been made from the trunk of the last weeping tree. No one could explain the unnatural growth of the new tree. Only a year ago, it had been a sprout, a couple of feet tall and spindly. Now its waterfall branches reached as high as the roof of her sleeping porch, twelve feet in the air. It was tall enough to sit beneath, if one needed to. But she figured it would continue to grow just as its mother had done, stretching far beyond the thirty or so years these types of trees usually lived. It was, of course, no ordinary tree. It had grown ten feet in a year. Still, no one could explain the magic of the tree at all. They simply accepted it, respected it, and allowed it access into their lives. It was a garden song that would continue to serenade. It was a sanctuary for some, a second chance for others. But for all, it was promise. And it was hope. And hope was the light of the world, where no darkness could penetrate.

A NOTE FROM THE AUTHOR

Thank you so much for taking the time to visit Gaslamp Island with me. This was such an enjoyable story to tell because I really do believe in the kind of magic that hovers around Gaslamp Island—like the pixies in the rising tide and the hope in the weeping tree branches. That same magic resides in each of our hearts. Is yours open to the possibilities that dance like fireflies on summer nights? I hope so.

I'd love to hear your thoughts about Charity and her weeping tree experience. Do you think Harold and Louise will have many wonderful years together? Do you think Daisy will return to the island after college and settle there? What about Ellen Marie? Was her weeping tree experience one that will stand the test of time, or do you see her returning to her old ways when life gets complicated?

It's always been my heartbeat to tell unforgettable stories—the kind that linger in our hearts long after the story is finished. I'm often asked by readers what they can do to spread the word about my books. If you enjoyed the story of the weeping tree, I'd be honored if you'd take a minute to leave a short review on Amazon or your other favorite e-book retailer. If you'd like to stay in touch with me, there are two easy ways to do that. Follow me on Amazon— www.amazon.com/author/heath-erburch (just click the yellow "Follow" button below my picture)—or visit my website at www.heatherburchbooks.com, where you can sign up for my biannual newsletter, Heather's Happenings, filled with information about my books, fun facts, and freebies.

All my best,
Heather Burch

ABOUT THE AUTHOR

Photo © 2016 Melinda Hanks

Heather Burch is the bestselling author of the novels *One Lavender Ribbon*, *Along the Broken Road*, and *Down the Hidden Path*, as well as several acclaimed young adult novels. *One Lavender Ribbon* was in the top 100 bestselling books of 2014 on Amazon. Her books have garnered praise from *USA Today*, *Booklist*, *Romantic Times*, and *Publishers Weekly*. Heather's deeply emotional novels explore family, love, hope, and the challenges of life. She tells unforgettable stories of love and loss—stories that make your heart sigh. Heather lives in southern Florida with her husband and has two grown sons who are the light of her life.